Praise for Sarah Cla[...]

'Suspenseful, claustrophobic with more twists and turns than a black run. I loved it.'
Katy Brent, author of *How to Kill Men and Get Away With It*

'A fast-paced tale of revenge where no one can be trusted, all set against a glamorous snowy backdrop and with some brilliant twists. Loved it.'
Catherine Cooper, bestselling author of *The Chalet*

'A tense and twisty thriller that keeps you guessing.'
Nikki Smith, author of *The Beach Party*

'A clever, slick and chilling read, I found myself glued to the pages and suspicious of everyone right up to the heart-racing denouement. Clarke is at the top of her game!'
A.A. Chaudhuri, author of *The Final Party*

'An explosive revenge thriller packed with enough twists and turns to leave you breathless – I love it!'
Mira Shah, author of *Her*

'A pacy, chilling, claustrophobic thriller . . . revenge, suspense, tension and some completely unexpected twists thrown in for *après ski* . . . I devoured it!'
Diane Jeffrey, author of *The Other Couple*

'With its brilliantly atmospheric setting and cast of duplicitous characters, *The Ski Trip* keeps you in its icy grip until the very last page.'
Sarah J Naughton, bestselling author of *The Mothers*

SARAH CLARKE is a writer living in South West London with her husband, children and stubbornly cheerful cockapoo. Over twenty years, Sarah has built a successful career as a marketing copywriter, but her dream has always been to become a published author. Sarah graduated from the Faber Academy Writing A Novel course in 2019 and her debut novel *A Mother Never Lies* published in 2021. Sarah has continued to write bestselling psychological thrillers and *The Night She Dies* is her fifth novel.

Also by Sarah Clarke

A Mother Never Lies
Every Little Secret
My Perfect Friend
The Ski Trip

The Night She Dies

SARAH CLARKE

ONE PLACE. MANY STORIES

HQ
An imprint of HarperCollins*Publishers* Ltd
1 London Bridge Street
London SE1 9GF

www.harpercollins.co.uk

HarperCollins*Publishers*
Macken House, 39/40 Mayor Street Upper,
Dublin 1 D01 C9W8

This paperback edition 2024

1

First published in Great Britain by
HQ, an imprint of HarperCollins*Publishers* Ltd 2024

ISBN: 9780008608484

This book contains FSC™ certified paper and other controlled sources to ensure responsible forest management.

For more information visit: www.harpercollins.co.uk/green

Printed and bound in the UK using 100% renewable electricity at CPI Group (UK) Ltd

For Scarlett, Lily & Millie
And all teenage girls

Prologue

I killed someone.

I say the words soundlessly into the mirror. It's dark – I haven't switched the light on – but I watch my mouth move in greyscale.

I killed her.

Worse than someone, a girl. A young person with most of her life still unlived.

Was dying young her fate? Written in the stars alongside other people's love stories or long, dull existences?

Or did I rock the universe when I lost my temper and didn't think through the consequences?

I turn away from the mirror, but I refuse to feel ashamed. I can't say whether she deserved to die, but no one could argue that I wasn't provoked, that I didn't have good reason.

They say that revenge can make people to do crazy things, and I guess tonight I proved that was true.

I look back at the mirror.

Do I regret the killing?

Would I do it again if I could choose?

Will my life be forever changed from this point on?

So many questions swirl around my head, but one is by far the loudest.

Will I get caught?

BEFORE

Monday 15th April

Jess

Jess looks down at her phone. Smiles.

'What's so funny?' Amber asks, leaning over to check Jess's screen.

'Nothing.' Jess clicks out of Snapchat, then drops her phone into the pocket of her blazer. 'Just a TikTok.'

Amber nods, then shifts her gaze down the aisle of the school coach, her mind already elsewhere. 'Look at her,' she murmurs under her breath, nudging Jess and nodding towards a girl sitting a few seats further up. 'Can you imagine being that ugly?'

'Her skin is so pale she looks dead,' Jess agrees, her confidence boosted by the message she's just read. 'Do you reckon if we killed her, no one would notice?'

Amber snorts a giggle. The noise leads to a few heads turning in their direction, but not for long. In the nine months they've lived in Chinnor, people have learned not to hold eye contact with Amber. 'Yeah, maybe,' she says with approval.

Jess feels a warmth in her cheeks; pride for making her sister laugh. She knows it's stupid. Amber is nineteen months younger than her for a start, so really it should be her looking up to Jess. But it's never been that way around. For as long as she can remember, Amber has been the boss, and Jess is the one who's needed looking after.

Like when she moved up to that massive, faceless, secondary school, Amber stuck in primary for another year. There were days when she thought she wouldn't survive it, the story of her tragic past coming up again as kids traded gossip to look cool. There were other days when she coped by not showing up at all. Then Amber finally arrived. And under her watchful glare, the snide whispers dried up.

That was a few years ago now though, and a different school. Luckily no one around here knows their story, so when she started at Lord Frederick's in September, she didn't have to suffer the shame for a third time.

'Let's get off at her stop,' Amber suggests. 'Do it now.' Amber doesn't laugh this time, and its absence sends a chill down Jess's spine. Of course she knows that Amber would never actually kill Lucy Rose, but she might take things too far. Because Amber hates Lucy. For who she is, and what she's got. And while Amber is a head shorter than the older girl, Jess knows who'd come out on top in a fight.

But Jess also knows she shouldn't care about Lucy Rose. That the girl doesn't deserve her sympathy.

Ten minutes later the coach swings left and then right onto Chinnor high street. It always drops at the posh end of the village first, Jess and Amber's ever-growing housing estate its last stop. Clearly even the coach company thinks poorer kids need to wait their turn. But today they're getting off early. Amber taps Jess on the hand, and they both slide out of the seat. A couple of seconds later, they catch up with Lucy in the aisle.

As soon as Lucy sees them – just a quick glance before looking down at the floor – tears well up in her eyes. She's so pathetic.

4

How can a 15-year-old girl cry over something like this? They've never even hurt her. Not properly. And anyway, what damage does Lucy think they can inflict between the bus stop and her twee little cottage a few hundred metres up the street? Jess finds her weakness embarrassing, awkward even. But Amber seems to feed off Lucy's fear. The more the girl cowers, the harder Amber pushes.

'Hello, Lucy,' Amber says, her voice low and menacing. 'Me and Jess thought we'd walk you home.' She falls in step beside the mute girl, close enough for a shoulder barge that makes her stumble. Jess wants to walk on the other side, to hem Lucy in for maximum effect. But there's not enough space on the pavement, so she drops in just behind. In Amber's shadow, like normal. Lucy doesn't respond, at least not verbally. She closes her arms over her chest, squeezes the straps of her rucksack between coiled fingers and keeps walking.

'We looked for you at lunch today,' Amber goes on. 'Couldn't find you. Were you crying in the loos again, like last week? Shame that photo of you there got shared around Year 10. People can be so cruel, can't they?' A few seconds of silence. Another shoulder barge. 'I don't know why you're so desperate to avoid us anyway. Do you think you're too good for us? Because we're scummy foster kids?'

'Leave me alone, please,' Lucy whispers.

'That's not very kind, Lucy,' Amber warns. 'Did you hear that, Jess? Lucy doesn't want to be friends with us. And after we've made this effort to walk her home.'

Jess senses Lucy's pace increase. She's not running, but her steps are getting faster, as though she thinks she can escape without them realising. How stupid does she think they are? Amber must notice too because she suddenly grabs Lucy's spindly forearm and yanks it backwards, keeping her fingers locked on, the pressure turning Lucy's flesh white. It forces her to stop, and Jess shifts her position to shield her sister's aggression from view. Which also means she's looking away, which is secretly a relief.

'Why the hurry?' Amber hisses, the tease gone from her voice. 'If you're not careful, I might take it personally.'

'Why me?' Lucy whimpers. 'Why do you pick on me?'

Amber slips her free hand into her bag for something. Jess twists to look. It's a triangular blade, meant for a craft knife. Jess holds her breath. Amber got her to swipe it from the Art department, but now she can see it, so close to Lucy's bare arm, she wonders if she should have refused.

'Why did you give Jess the silent treatment last term?' Amber asks, taking a step towards Lucy, dipping the point of the blade against her skin. 'She was the new girl in your tutor group.'

'I didn't …'

'She tried to make friends with you, and you gave her the brush-off. Because she's a dumb-arse social care kid.'

'No, I …'

'She's wearing your sister's old blazer. Did you know that? Bought at the second-hand sale. Still got the label in it. Milla Rose. I guess it'll come to me one day. If I ever get as lanky as her.'

Jess looks away again, her face burning. A car rumbles past, but the driver is oblivious to the three of them. She turns back.

'I'm sorry,' Lucy whispers. 'Please. Don't hurt me.'

'Invite us back to yours then,' Amber hisses. 'Prove that we're not too scummy for you.'

Lucy doesn't respond, but Jess can see fat tears bubble in front of her pale-blue eyes. God, why does she do that? How is she so spineless? 'Fucking crybaby,' Jess murmurs.

'Lucy?' A voice suddenly rings out from across the street, followed by the dull thud of a car door closing. 'Is everything okay?'

Amber pockets the blade; releases her grip on Lucy's arm. 'Come on,' she says to Jess, giving the woman a sideways glance. 'Let's go.' She starts striding up the road, away from an unwanted confrontation with an adult, and Jess has to scurry to catch up. Following Amber's lead, they pass a small parade of shops, then veer off the road and onto a country path. Jess knows where they're going without needing to ask. They cross the old railway line and continue up towards the woods.

Half an hour later, they arrive at Chinnor Hill nature reserve. It's not much more than a small opening in the trees, but it feels like a secret hideaway. They discovered it last summer, soon after they moved to their new foster home. The mud mostly kept them away during the winter, so it's good to be back. Jess sinks down onto the blanket of tiny wildflowers and long grass, lies back and stares at the grey-blue sky.

'Was that her mum?' she asks, as her sister drops down next to her.

'Yeah,' Amber says, nodding. 'I've seen them out running together.' Amber's voice is monotone now, mechanical, and Jess knows from experience what that means. That there's some emotion threatening to spill out, a door that needs to be slammed shut.

Amber is good at putting on a show. Hard bitch at school. Suck-up foster kid at home. Sexy minx whenever Sean gives her a second of attention. Only Jess has glimpsed the real Amber, the one who still misses her mum, and hates the world for taking her away. It doesn't help that most of her memories of Jacqui are bad ones. Like the smell of her after a day on the booze. All fumes and vomit. Or how Jacqui would curl up and cry when Tyler stormed out after an argument, her face a mix of blood and blue skin where he'd hit her. And then that final time.

Jess was a bit luckier than Amber. Being a year and half older means she still remembers Jacqui before she met Tyler. They were never a family like the Roses. Single mum on benefits, two young girls from different fathers, vodka in Jacqui's coffee mug most breakfasts. But they laughed a lot back then. Jess was too young to notice how their life differed from other families, and her mum always seemed happy. Even after everything Jess's dad had put her through, and then having another baby all by herself. They'd been through tough times and survived them.

7

But then Tyler came along. And despite everything he did to her, Jacqui couldn't stop loving him. Until he killed her. On 14th August 2016, when Team GB won five gold medals at the Rio Olympics, Tyler celebrated with six bottles of Desperado and then beat their mother to death.

Ever since then, Jess and Amber have only had each other.

Jess shuffles closer to her sister. 'Well, you can see where Lucy gets her rank looks from then,' she says.

Amber smiles. Reaches into her bag and pulls out a joint. Lights it up and takes a long toke. 'Yeah, two pale-faced bitches,' she says, passing the joint to Jess. 'I wonder who'd miss them.'

THE NIGHT SHE DIES

Friday 3rd May

Rachel

'The first session is always the hardest,' I say softly. It's not necessarily true – the real issues can sometimes take a while to emerge – but I feel an urge to reassure Mrs Gray. The meeting went on for over an hour, two social workers and an assortment of other professionals crowded around her small living room, and she didn't move from the arm of the sofa. Perched on her sit bones, knees glued together, hands interlinked in her lap. And Mr Gray didn't hide his resentment as he watched the proceedings from the armchair.

'I wish this was the *last* session,' she murmurs as she leads me towards her front door. 'In fact, I wish it hadn't come to this at all. It was such a stupid thing to do, but it won't happen again. I scared myself more than I scared Dylan, I'm sure of it.'

'I'm sure too,' I say. And I mean it. I know that a momentary loss of control might not even register with a 3-year-old, yet it could haunt a mother forever. But it shouldn't be ignored either. Especially when her outburst happened in the playground of her older children's school. I want to reach for her hand, to show her that I'm on her side, and I would have done once upon a time. But we're too professional for physical contact these days.

'I'm sure it must feel overwhelming,' I say. 'All these strangers in your house. But we really do just want to help you and Shane get through this. A diagnosis of autism is a lot to take in, for any family. And especially with other children to think about. Use us, our expertise,' I urge. 'The community support team is all about prevention, and I promise we're here to make things easier for you, not harder.'

'Thank you,' she whispers, blinking away a tear.

My colleagues have already left, so I use the opportunity to break with protocol. I rest my hand on her arm, and she gives me a grateful smile.

'Maybe we could do with some help,' she admits quietly.

It's at moments like this that I wish I was still a regular social worker. Working directly with families. But at least my promotion within LCSS means I get to train other social workers to do this job – and support them at initial meetings like this from time to time. I push my lips together to stop myself from giving Mrs Gray my phone number, and return her smile instead. 'And that, right there, shows how strong you are,' I say. 'Dylan's lucky to have you.'

I can feel my phone vibrating in my pocket, so I quickly say goodbye and slip outside. It's a withheld number, but that's not unusual – all our office phones are – so I click to accept the call.

'Is that Mrs Rose? Um, sorry, I mean Ms Salter, Lucy Rose's mum? I'm calling from Lord Frederick's.'

My daughters' school. I feel a prickly sensation on my skin. 'What's happened?'

'Lucy is fine. Well, sort of. She's not injured,' she clarifies, her voice sounding more rattled with each word. 'There's been an incident,' she finally settles on. 'Ms Munroe wondered if you could come in?'

I screw my eyes closed and focus on breathing until the urge to cry recedes. 'What incident?'

'I think it's better if Ms Munroe explains in person,' the voice says. 'Could you make it here for four o'clock?'

I look at my watch: 3.30 p.m. The Grays' house is in Cowley to the south of Oxford. It's a forty-minute drive home, but the school is closer. 'Yes, fine,' I say. Then I race to my car and head for the dual carriageway.

'Thank you for coming in today, Ms Salter.' The head teacher gestures to the chair opposite her desk.

'The woman I spoke to said something's happened to Lucy,' I start, lowering down until I feel the thin cushion. 'Is it to do with the bullying?' I want her to say no. I'd even prefer her to tell me that Lucy has been misbehaving. But I know that's just wishful thinking.

Ms Munroe sighs. 'Possibly, yes.'

'Possibly?'

'Lucy had netball practice during lunchbreak. When she got back to the changing room, her sports bag wasn't there.' She pauses, swallows. 'Someone had emptied its contents over the lawn, and um, hung her school clothes on the surrounding trees.'

'What?' My heart rate ticks up. 'All her things?'

'Yes.' She sighs heavily. Ms Munroe is the archetypal smart headmistress – cropped hair, fitted suit, sensible shoes – but she looks uncomfortable now. 'And I'm afraid that includes underwear. Lucy had changed into a sports bra for netball, and apparently there was also a spare pair of knickers in her bag. You know, just in case.'

I look away. Imagine the shame of collecting up those items with all her peers watching on, laughing, filming no doubt. The room starts to sway. I take a deep breath.

'Most of the students were very kind apparently,' Ms Munroe continues, reading her mind. 'Helped Lucy gather up her things. Of course there were a few who found it funny, but they have been dealt with.'

A burst of rage rattles through me and I push hard on my knees to control it. Those stupid little bitches.

'Her shirt had a small tear, from a branch I presume,' the head teacher goes on. 'But I appreciate this won't be your main concern.' Her voice drifts away.

'And what are you doing about it?' My tone is clipped, acidic. So unlike my normal voice that I hardly recognise it. 'I assume those girls, Amber Walsh and Jess Scott, were behind it?'

Ms Munroe leans back in her chair and moves a pencil a few centimetres to the right. 'Lucy believes so. But no one saw them do it.'

I want to shout that of course they wouldn't, that those girls have already proven themselves too clever for that. Like the photo that went round the school, Lucy crying in the loos, taken over the door of the cubicle. Everyone saw it, but no one had a clue where it came from. Supposedly.

'And both Jessica Scott and Amber Walsh have denied involvement.'

'And you believe them?' My voice is squeaky now.

'No,' she says carefully. 'But I don't not believe them either. Without any proof, I can't apportion blame.'

Breathe. 'But there have been plenty of incidents before this one. I've been telling the school for two months that those girls are bullying Lucy. And that Lucy is so petrified of them, she struggles to go to school some days.'

'I know.' Ms Munroe nods her head. 'But when I speak to Jessica and Amber about it, they promise it's just a misunderstanding, that they're trying to make friends with Lucy. And Lucy herself blows hot and cold. Sometimes she says there's nothing to it.'

'Only when they've scared her half to death, for fuck's sake!'

Ms Munroe releases a gasp of disapproval. I ram my lips together. 'I'm sorry,' I stutter. 'That was inappropriate. But you have to understand how tough it's been for my family over the last few months. Watching our once happy child withdraw into herself. And now this, her underwear on display. Do you realise how upsetting that is for a 15-year-old girl?' My eyes feel hot. But I mustn't cry, lose focus. I owe Lucy this, and so much more. 'You know what, we've had enough of your inaction. If you don't punish those girls, I'm going to take this issue to the governors.'

Ms Munroe's expression hardens. 'I can't punish them without proof.'

'Of course it was them! Unless you have other toxic children in your school?!' I know I'm going too far, but I can't stop myself. How can she be so blind? How can she sit on the fence when the chasm between the abusers and the victim is so vast?

'I'm not sure how much you know about Jessica and Amber,' she starts.

And there it is. Their constant get-out-of-jail-free card. The same context that put my relationship with Lucy into freefall for a while. 'I understand they live with foster carers,' I say.

'That's right. And this is their second long-term foster family. And a new, very different part of the county for them. I can't share any details, but they've suffered significant loss. And now they're having to rebuild their lives for a second time. New family, new school.'

'I agree that's very sad, but it doesn't give them carte blanche to …'

'I understand that Lucy is your priority, Ms Salter,' she cuts in. 'But I thought you'd have a bit more sympathy for their circumstances.'

'Because I'm a social worker?' I spit out.

'I suppose I imagined that you'd be more aware of how scarred children like Jessica and Amber can be. And that disruptive behaviour is really a cry for help.'

I wish I could scream the truth.

Of course I'm aware, you cold-hearted jobsworth. And yes, it's true that I feel like I'm betraying my profession every time this rage builds up. But understanding why those girls are bullying Lucy doesn't make their actions any less vile. Any less damaging to my child.

'They terrorise Lucy,' I say, breaking eye contact. 'And now this, today. Utter humiliation. Whatever has happened to them, this is not acceptable.'

'Of course it's not,' Ms Munroe snaps. Then she sighs. 'And whether they're responsible for today's incident or not, I agree that we need to address the issue, for everyone's sake. So I'm going to contact their social worker, talk to her about the bullying. That will be a strong message to the girls that they need to leave Lucy alone.'

I sit back in my chair and wonder who their social worker is. The foster team are part of Children's Services too, and based in the same building as me, two floors above. But we rarely interact, and I'm not sure I know any of their names. It's strange, I suppose, that we keep such distance from each other. But perhaps not. If we need to involve their team, it means we've failed at keeping a family together.

'And do you really think that will stop them?' I ask.

'The girls are happy at Lord Frederick's – they both told me that – so they won't want to risk things not working out. I'm sure escalating this to their social worker will bring an end to it for good.'

'I hope so,' I murmur. 'Because this really needs to stop.'

THE NIGHT SHE DIES

Friday 3rd May

Rachel

The only person who uses the front door of our house is the postman, so I walk down the narrow driveway to the side door. As I step through the small flagstone porch into the open-plan living area, there's a sense of stillness. I'm pretty sure both girls are here, but they'll be holed up in their rooms, and I feel a momentary pang for the chaos that used to engulf me when I got home from work – tight hugs from Lucy, Milla talking me through her day at breakneck speed, our au pair Anya interjecting whenever Milla's account veered too far into fantasy. That period came with its problems too – exhaustion, compromise, moving seamlessly from professional social worker to domestic slave – but I did feel in control of my daughters' lives back then. Able to make a tangible difference.

Unlike now. Now I just get to sit on the side-lines and hope my pep talks and silent prayers are enough.

Although I can't use that as an excuse for my delay in helping Lucy. That was entirely down to my own distorted beliefs.

It was the last night of the Christmas holidays when Lucy first confided in us about the bullying. We were all in a grump – Milla facing her A-level mock exams, Matt militant in his mission to remove every last fragment of tinsel – so I didn't think much about Lucy seeming even quieter than usual. But when I suggested she get an early night before school, she burst into tears, and pleaded for us not to make her go back. It was so out of character – the outpouring of emotion as much as the request itself – that it was a shock. When the tears dried up, she told Matt and me what had been going on. That from a few weeks into the autumn term, the new girl in her year – Jess Scott – and her younger sister Amber had been picking on Lucy.

We should have told the school straight away, but Lucy mentioned that the girls were in foster care, and my social worker instincts took over. I told her to remember they were new to the school and that they deserved some time to settle in. To my shame, I even asked Lucy to remember how lucky she was compared to them, having a family to confide in. She listened too, went back after Christmas with an instinct to forgive, but it didn't work. The bullying continued. When Lucy started claiming sickness to avoid going to school, I realised how much I'd let her down.

So I contacted her form tutor. Then her head of year. They said all the right things – that they would deal with it, investigate, punish the girls, stop the bullying. But nothing changed. And now this. Lucy having to disentangle her knickers and bra from a tree in front of half the school. I can't bear to think how traumatising that must have been for her.

I open the fridge door and reach for a can of Coke. I'm due out tonight with some girlfriends but I half think I should cancel, hang out with Lucy instead. Milla has her best friend's eighteenth birthday party tonight, so she won't be around. Matt is due back in the next couple of hours, and normally that would work perfectly – while we love the girls equally, our natural fault line has always been Matt and Lucy, Milla and me. But after a long flight back from Thailand – international travel being one of the perks of his new job – Matt will probably need to crash. And I hate the thought of Lucy being alone tonight.

I take a long sip and head up the stairs. I knock on Lucy's bedroom door, wait a few seconds, then push it open. She's lying on her bed, headphones on, staring at the ceiling.

'I don't want to talk about it.' There are two pink spots shining on Lucy's pale cheeks, and I hope it's not shame.

I hesitate for a moment, then drop down at the end of her bed. I'm careful not to touch her – the days when Lucy demanded tight hugs are long gone – but I'm not giving up that easily. 'Why didn't you call me?' I ask gently, trying not to think about my hour at the Grays', and how I would have ignored my phone until the meeting had finished.

'I can fight my own battles.' Silence hangs in the air; both of us trying to push aside the mounting evidence that she can't.

'How are you feeling now?' I say instead.

Her eyes dart towards me. 'How do you think? My knickers were hanging off a fucking tree.'

I'm not prudish about swearing – living with Milla would make that difficult – but it's rare to hear it coming from Lucy, and the harsh word jolts me. 'It might help to talk about it,' I say tentatively. The line between supportive and prying is always thin with teenagers but right now it feels like gossamer.

She stares at me for a moment, as though weighing up whether to let go of her emotions, and I silently plead for her to remember who I am – her strongest advocate. But it doesn't work.

'No.' Her mouth strains with the effort of not crying. I reach for her hand, but she yanks it away from my outstretched fingers and whips her body over to face the wall. As I stare at her back, her shoulders hunched with tension, a wave of fury towards those two girls washes over me again. I want to tell Lucy how much I hate them. How I dream of ripping every layer of skin off their smug faces. But of course I can't do that.

17

'Munroe said your shirt ripped on a branch,' I choose. 'Shall I see if I can fix it?'

'I threw it away.'

I frown. Not because I care about the shirt, but it feels out of character. 'Why did you do that? It would be easy to sew up.'

'Just drop it, okay, Mum?'

My heart kicks up a gear. 'Is there a reason you didn't want me to see it? Did it definitely rip on a tree? You know, if one of them has a knife, you need to tell Munroe.'

'What, for her to not believe me again? To take their side, like always?'

'She didn't today, at least not totally,' I say. 'I think she's starting to get it. She told me that she's going to speak to their social worker, and that's actually a big deal.' Lucy rolls onto her back and a look of mild interest appears on her face. It spurs me on. 'With children in foster care, the social worker takes on a lot of the traditional parents' responsibilities. Including discipline.'

Lucy's interest vanishes. 'Discipline? Like being grounded for a few days?' She shakes her head in disgust. 'The only way I'll be free of them is if they're expelled, and Munroe's too under their spell for that.'

I bite my lip. I've been a social worker for twenty-five years and a belief in rehabilitation, in second and third and fourth chances, is inbuilt. But vulnerable children have never been my enemy before. 'I could ask around at work. Find out who their social worker is, explain how bad it is.'

Fear sprouts on Lucy's face. 'No, you can't do that. If Amber found out, she'd tell everyone that I was using my mum to get her in trouble. Then she'd get you fired. Like that boy did with Dad.'

'What? This is completely different. Why would you say that?' It's been over two years since that hand grenade was launched at our family, a male student at the school Matt used to teach at accusing him of assault. Things are back on an even keel now, but it was a difficult time, and I don't need reminding of it today.

Lucy turns to look at me, her expression darkening. 'Dad's life was almost destroyed because some boy decided he didn't like him, and then caused him shitloads of trouble. That sound familiar?'

Guilt flares inside me. Because she's got a point. But when Matt faced the accusation, followed by suspension from the job he loved, I was only outraged. I didn't ask him to show compassion for the boy, even though there were probably challenges in his life too. Is it because Amber and Jess are in the social care system so their disadvantage is more obvious? Or because I expect more empathy from Lucy than her father?

'I know it must feel like things can't get any worse at the moment,' I say, trying to lift my mood as much as hers. 'But we've got a bank holiday weekend ahead of us, all together, and things might not seem so bad by Tuesday.'

'I'm not 6 anymore, Mum. You can't make everything better with an ice-cream.'

'Hey, guys. Is this a private argument, or can anyone join in?'

I twist my head towards the door. 'Hey, Milla.' While Lucy looks like me – pale-skinned, blue-eyed, ash-blonde hair – Milla is all Matt. Taller, broader, with hazel eyes and thick auburn hair. And with her stronger colouring comes a fiercer temperament too. Milla turned 18 in March, and one of the first things she did was get a tattoo on her wrist. An infinity symbol to represent the number of barriers she's going to break down in her lifetime.

'I heard what went down at school today,' Milla says. 'Honestly, Luce, you just say the word, and I will hunt those bitches down.'

Milla and Lucy's relationship is hard to define. They're not close – they're too different for that – and they live quite separate lives. But there's something unspoken between them. An underlying bond that transcends the day-to-day. And I can hear that emotion in Milla's voice now.

'Thanks, but I've got this,' Lucy murmurs with a new steeliness. I wonder what she means by that, but Milla seems to accept it.

'Good,' she says approvingly. Then she turns to me. 'When's Dad back?'

'Around eight,' I say. 'Will you have left by then?' Milla's best friend, Ava, turned 18 three days ago, and she's going big with the celebrations. Marquee in the garden, most of their year invited to the party, Ava's older brother Charlie on the decks.

'Yeah, I'm going out at seven, helping Ava with last-minute stuff.'

'Okay, well, don't get too drunk.'

'It's my best mate's eighteenth. Of course I'm going to get drunk.'

'Don't you have exams in a few weeks?' I ask, more meekly than I planned.

'Yeah, so?' She releases a dramatic sigh. 'And anyway, Felix will be there, so I'll need a drink.'

'You two still haven't made up?' I ask. Milla and Felix started dating in Year 11 and have been a surprisingly solid couple over the last two years. But all that changed a few weeks ago when Milla announced that he was a *fucking dick*, and their relationship was over. Felix has been the archetypal lovelorn teenager ever since, begging for her to reconsider, but so far Milla isn't budging. And the rest of us have no idea what caused the rift.

Her eyes blaze with indignation. 'Not now, not ever.'

I sigh. It's probably for the best with them going off to different universities in September. 'Well, I hope you manage to have fun despite him.' I turn back to Lucy. 'I was supposed to be going out too, but I'm very happy to stay—'

'No,' she cuts in. 'I meant it when I said I've got this. And that starts with you not changing your plans.'

I hesitate, then nod – both grateful and crushed – and head towards my room.

THE NIGHT SHE DIES

Friday 3rd May

Rachel

I push my finger into the centre of the poppadom and listen to the crack as it fragments. Then I pan out and take in the other noises around the restaurant. The clinking of cutlery against dishes. The buzz of conversation – made louder and more enthusiastic by the pints of Cobra beer most people seem to be drinking.

I'm here with Annie, Lou, Charlotte and Kate. The five of us became friends at the St Andrew's Primary School gates, close to fourteen years ago. And while the kids becoming more independent has meant we've drifted apart, we still make an effort to meet for a curry every couple of months. Usually I love these nights out – especially as we always go to the Indian restaurant at the bottom of the high street, ten minutes from my house – but I can't relax this evening. They say a mum is only as happy as their least happy child, so perhaps it's no wonder I'm struggling to enjoy myself.

It doesn't help that Annie is Felix's mum, and he's her golden boy.

'It's such a shame that our two split up, isn't it?' she says mournfully. 'You know, I'm sure Felix would love to get back together with Milla. Do you think he has a chance?'

I hesitate. *Not now, not ever.* I don't want to lie to Annie, but I don't want to offend her either. And I know how sensitive we can all be about our children. 'Milla's very much a closed book with me,' I say carefully. 'But I think they respect each other well enough to work things out amicably.'

'Yes, I think so too,' Annie says, although I detect some disappointment in her voice.

'How's Lucy?' Charlotte pipes up as she reaches across me to dunk her poppadom in the mango chutney. 'Last time we met up, you said she was being bullied? A couple of mean girls from the estate?'

I take a gulp of my pint. I feel disloyal discussing Lucy's problems with my friends, but I can't pretend everything is fine. 'She's not great,' I admit as I place the glass back down. 'And the two girls are sisters, in Lucy's year and the one below. But Munroe called me in today about it, and I'm hoping this is the beginning of the end.'

'What's Munroe going to do?' Charlotte asks.

'Talk to their social worker. Hopefully he or she will read them the riot act.'

'They've got a social worker?' Annie cuts in. 'So they've been in trouble before?'

I shake my head. 'No, not trouble. At least, not that I know of. They've got a social worker because they're in foster care.'

'Not those two girls staying with Molly and Bill Wainwright?' Charlotte asks, dropping her voice and taking a quick glance over each shoulder to check no one's eavesdropping. 'I know the Wainwrights from church – they're an amazing couple. Well into their sixties, and still fostering kids. One girl's tall with ginger hair, and the other's small and dark.'

'I'm not sure where they live, but yes, that sounds right.'

'I didn't realise they were sisters,' Charlotte muses, wrinkling her brow in confusion. 'They don't look anything like each other.'

'Probably different fathers,' Annie surmises. 'It's not exactly unheard of with, you know …' She tails off, but I know what she was thinking. *With people like them.* I shift in my chair. Annie is a good friend in many ways, always generous with favours, but our values are miles apart.

'So where's their mother?' Lou asks.

'I don't know the details, but from something Munroe said, I think she might have died,' I say softly.

'Gosh,' Lou stutters. 'No father around, then your mother dies. Those poor children.'

'Who are making Lucy's life a misery,' I remind everyone.

'Yes, of course,' Annie says, squeezing my hand across the table and nodding. 'And I hate to say it, but children from troubled backgrounds are often the worst offenders. I can see how your gorgeous, gentle Lucy is no match for them.'

I feel a sting of irritation at that, but I don't know why. In our family we talk, we listen, we walk away from conflict. So why does some primeval part of me wish Lucy would just whack the pair of them?

'But why have they singled Lucy out?' Kate asks. 'She's hardly the antagonistic type.'

I sigh. 'Apparently Amber – that's the younger one, and the ringleader – says that Lucy rejected her sister when she tried to befriend her at the start of the year, but Lucy doesn't even remember Jess trying to talk to her. And she's not the type to behave that way.'

'Lucy is quiet though, shy. Could that be mistaken as stand-offishness?' Lou asks gently.

'And didn't Lucy's best friend move to Wales over the summer?' Annie adds. 'I imagine she was quite glum at the start of the school year. Maybe she brushed this girl off without realising it.'

It's true that Lucy was devastated when Bronwen and her

family moved to Cardiff, to be near David's ageing parents after living in Chinnor for most of Bronwen's life. The girls sat next to each other in Reception class at St Andrew's, and that sparked a friendship that aged and strengthened over the following decade – until Bronwen left. But I still can't see Lucy taking her own issues out on a new girl.

'Maybe,' I say with a shrug. Suddenly I'm desperate to change the subject. Either that or throw down my napkin and race back home to my daughter. But I know that would be a mistake. Matt will be home by now, and he's always been more on her wavelength than me. 'Anyway, enough about my problems,' I say, plastering on a smile. 'How's A-level revision going?' And it has the required effect because a collective groan echoes around the table.

As I look at Matt's car butted up against mine in the driveway, I wonder whether he'll be awake. And if he is, what kind of mood he'll be in.

Being accused of assault by a student can be career suicide for a teacher, and that's the way things were going for Matt initially. He was suspended by his school, and later had his licence to teach revoked. So we were both hugely relieved when he was offered a job at Lionheart Education – a group of private British day schools overseas – by an old university acquaintance. The money was better, and as the role, Director of English Studies, involved minimal contact with students, he didn't need a teaching licence.

The job also involves visiting their schools around the world, which, secretly, was an additional relief for me. Some breathing space. Matt is a good man, and we have a strong marriage. But people deal with adversity in different ways, and I bore the brunt of his frustration. Matt has always liked a tidy house, but his obsession rocketed during those long months in limbo – waiting for the court case that never even materialised, because, just four weeks before the trial date, the only witness admitted they'd lied. Matt isn't the type to shout, but he'd sulk for days over the smallest thing, and it was exhausting.

But things are much better now. And we've got a three-day weekend ahead of us, including the village fun day on Monday. I'm really looking forward to some quality family time.

'Hello?' I call out as I push open the back door. In the silence, I can hear a slight slur in my voice, and it makes me wish I hadn't agreed to the third pint. Especially as I want to do my usual Saturday morning trail run tomorrow, a ten-kilometre route along the Ridgeway. As I reach for a water glass, I notice that the drainer is clear of pans, and today's post that I dropped on the side has disappeared. It's more proof that my husband is back, but there's no response to my greeting, so I walk into the living area. And there he is. Sparko on the sofa.

I kneel down by his side. 'Hey,' I whisper, nudging him gently. 'Time for bed.'

He groans in his sleep, then shifts onto his side. It's a long sofa, easy for him to lie out straight without the threat of a cricked neck. And he looks so comfortable. Maybe it's pointless trying to move him. I pull the throw off the back of the sofa and lay it over him. Then I kiss him lightly on his cheek, and head upstairs.

It's only 10.45, so Milla won't be back for a while, but Lucy will be asleep, and I need to see her before I can relax. Maybe even sneak in a clandestine hug without her conscious enough to reject me. I push on her bedroom door and stumble forwards in the darkness, slowly, waiting for my eyes to adjust.

But there's something wrong. I can sense it.

I run my hand over her duvet, feel its smooth uniformity.

I flick on Lucy's bedside light. My chest swells.

The room is empty.

THE NIGHT SHE DIES

Friday 3rd May

Rachel

'Matt, Matt, wake up!' I shake my husband. His eyelids flicker open. A millisecond of confusion and then he rubs his eyes.

'What is it?' he asks. 'What's wrong?'

'Where's Lucy? Did she go out? Did she tell you where she was going?'

'Hey, slow down,' he says, pushing up to sitting. 'Lucy's upstairs. She went to bed ages ago; said she wanted an early night.'

'No, she didn't!' I screech. Then I pause, take a breath. I need to calm down, to think straight. 'Or maybe she did, but she's not there now. Where would she go? Did she mention anything? Meeting a friend?'

I can almost see the news sinking into Matt's consciousness, slipping in via his pores. Matt's looks have never suited his person-ality. He's dark and brawny. Long hours cycling through the Chiltern Hills have honed his muscles but haven't tapered his wide frame. And his square jaw, shaven head and thick eyebrows make him look thuggish. But his appearance disguises who he really is. A clever, thoughtful, disciplined man. Despite his jet lag, he will be assessing the situation, considering the multitude of possible explanations for Lucy's absence – the innocent and the worrying – at breakneck speed.

'No, not a word,' he answers, running his hand along his smooth head, a familiar coping mechanism. 'She was quiet when I first got home, distracted. But not hostile. I'd got your message, about not pushing her about what happened at school, so I talked about Thailand instead. Then about nine, she said she was tired and went upstairs. I must have fallen asleep soon after that, but I would have heard her, woken up, if she'd left the house.' He sets his jaw in self-belief, but it's disingenuous. She's not here.

'You were comatose when I came in! I even tried to wake you and you just rolled over!' I can hear the accusation in my voice. *Lucy disappeared on your watch; our bullied, traumatised daughter is alone, outside, because of you.* I know I'm inflaming the situation, but I can't stop myself.

'Have you tried calling her?' There's accusation in his voice now.

And he's right. Why didn't I do that when I first realised she was missing? 'Fuck, shit,' I mutter as I wrestle through my bag for my phone. I prod at her name and listen to it ring. And ring. 'She's not answering,' I splutter in frustration as it clicks into voicemail. I leave a message, then tap straight into Find My iPhone. Now I have my phone to hand, I remember what a lifeline it is, how it's helped me track down Milla dozens of times over the last few years. I click into Lucy's details and wait impatiently for the blue circle over Chinnor to zoom in to the phone's exact location. I moan when the address finally comes up. I take the stairs two at a time, burst into Lucy's bedroom, and there it is. Her phone, on her desk, glowing bright in the darkness. It's good, in a way, because surely it means she hasn't gone far. But what state of mind was she in to leave the house without it?

I hear Matt arrive just behind me, his shadow looming in

the doorway. 'We need to go and look for her,' he says, his voice gravelly now.

'But where do we start?' I wail. 'And what about Milla?'

'Milla won't be back for ages; we'll have found Lucy by then.' I know he's trying to convince himself as much as me. 'Can you drive?' he adds.

'I've drunk too much,' I admit, shame smarting my cheeks. 'But I can go on foot, check the recreation ground, call her friends maybe.' Neither of us voices our thoughts, but we share a look. Which friends am I referring to? Bronwen was Lucy's friend. But she's in Wales now. And I haven't seen Lucy hang out with anyone else since she left.

We're pulling on our shoes when I hear the back door swing open. 'Thank God,' I exhale. But the respite is short-lived when I realise it's not Lucy. 'Milla?'

'Party came to an abrupt end,' she explains without waiting for the question. 'Some boys tried to gate-crash, which caused a bit of a drama early on. And then Ava's dad realised that Adam and Caitlin had taken pills, fucking idiots, and went apeshit. Shut the whole thing down. Felix didn't turn up at all. Apparently he'd heard that I was bringing a new guy, which is complete crap, but still, what a total dick.' Then she dips her head to one side and assesses us. Her expression turns to one of concern. 'What's wrong?'

'Lucy's gone missing,' Matt says matter-of-factly, hiding his terror. 'So Mum and I are going to look for her.'

'Fuck.' Milla breathes out, furrowing her brow. 'She's definitely gone?'

'She went to bed, but she's not in bed,' I explain, exasperated. 'So she must be out there.' I fling my hand towards the window. 'Somewhere.'

'Those fucking bitches,' Milla murmurs.

'Why did you say that?' I push. 'Do you know something?'

'No, nothing,' Milla backtracks. 'She was just upset earlier, wasn't she? About what those two girls did at school.'

'Can you stay up?' I ask. 'And call us if she comes home? The instant she walks through the door?'

'No way,' Milla counters, shaking her head. 'I'm not sitting around here, doing nothing. I'm going to look too.'

'No, Milla,' Matt starts.

'Lucy is my sister,' she throws back. 'And I know where kids hang out in this village much better than either of you. I'm not staying at home, Dad.'

Matt lets out a sigh of surrender. 'Okay. But you must keep in touch, do you understand? Via the family WhatsApp group.' He turns to me. 'As you're on foot, can you check back here regularly? In case she comes home on her own?'

I nod. 'Of course.'

'Right. I'll drive up to the Ridgeway, then across to the Kiln Lakes.'

Fear fizzes along my spine. 'You don't think she's gone up to the old quarries, do you?' Chinnor Cement Works was once a big deal in this village, but it closed twenty years ago, and the area was left derelict for a while. It's been redeveloped now, the quarries transformed into azure blue lakes and sunken fields, but while it's lovely in daylight, I imagine it's terrifying at this time of night.

'I don't, but we need to check everywhere until we find her. Milla, where will you go?'

'Don't worry about me. There are a few different places I want to check. Can you drop me by the railway station?'

'Yes, fine,' Matt says impatiently. 'Shall we go?'

'Actually, wait.' Milla pauses. 'I might get a torch. Can you hold on a second?'

'Can't you use the torch function on your phone?' I ask, impatient to leave.

'I haven't got much battery left. I want to save it for making sure I can keep in touch with you, like you asked.'

'Good thinking,' I mutter, slightly surprised that Milla would show such foresight.

'There's one in the shed,' Matt tells her. 'On charge. Grab it quickly.' Milla disappears into the kitchen, and then I hear the flick of the lock on the patio doors, and her rushing into the garden. A minute later, she reappears, this time with a torch in her hand. She stuffs it into her small rucksack, and we tumble out of the house together.

But I pause for a moment as I'm about to lock the door. Is this a good idea? Leaving the house empty? What if Lucy comes back, desperate for some comfort? Indecision anchors me to the spot. God, why does parenting have to be so difficult?

'Come on, Rachel,' Matt says. 'We need to find her.'

His urgent tone launches me into action. I turn the key, give him and Milla a quick glance, and then head off down the driveway and towards the recreation ground, praying that, wherever she is, she's safe.

BEFORE

Friday 19th April

Jess

'Tea's ready!' Molly's voice hollers up the stairs.

Jess rolls over on the top bunk and drops her head over the edge. 'Shall we go?' As fake parents go, the Wainwrights are okay, despite being ancient, but Molly does get arsy if they ignore her when she calls them. Usually Jess doesn't care too much, but she's meeting someone tonight (can she call him her boyfriend yet?) and she doesn't want Molly to suddenly decide they're grounded. Or more accurately, she can't be bothered with the hassle of lying to her foster carers and sneaking out the back door when they're watching TV.

'Yeah, in a minute,' Amber says, but she doesn't show any sign of moving. 'Just got a text from Sean.'

'Oh?' Jess sits up in bed, her mess of red wavy hair skimming the ceiling. 'What does it say?' She twists her body and climbs down the ladder. When they first moved in with the Wainwrights, they were offered a bedroom each. But when Amber said she wanted to share, Jess jumped at the chance, even though it meant bunk

31

beds. It had been a horrible few weeks for her in the run-up to them leaving their last foster carers – Lou and Justin – and Jess wasn't sure she'd be able to sleep in her new home without her sister close by.

'He wants me to call him,' Amber says, her expression folding into a frown. She taps the crappy Nokia against her leg in thought. The dumb phone, they call it. Just phone calls, and texts, nothing smart about it. But Sean gave it to Amber soon after they moved to Chinnor and told her to only ever use that one to contact him. He's changed the SIM card a couple of times too. The guy's proper paranoid.

They met Sean soon after Amber started at secondary school. Jess was always a bit wary of him, but Amber loved his bad-boy style. It was all yes Sean, no Sean, eyelashes fluttering. He was 16 at the time while Amber was only 11, so he can't have fancied her. But he acted like he did sometimes. Just enough to keep her hanging on, Jess always thought. A lot happened to Sean during that year, none of it good, and he went from bad boy to actual criminal. Jess was starting to worry that even Amber was in over her head, but then everything went to shit anyway.

Jess thought them moving to Chinnor would mean cutting ties with Sean, but he had other ideas. Now he comes to Thame, the nearest town to them and where their school is located, about once a month. Amber meets him – never the same place, but always away from any CCTV cameras – and he gives her a bag of skunk and sometimes some pills. On his say-so, she's made it known at school that she can get drugs if anyone needs them, and someone usually does. So the next time Amber and Sean meet up, she gives him the cash she's made, and he gives her a fresh supply – plus fifty quid or so in payment.

'You don't think he's found out about the extra cash, do you?' Jess asks. While Amber still idolises Sean, there are signs the spell is breaking. Like how she's started skimming an extra fiver off every gram of weed she sells.

32

'Nah,' Amber says. She sounds confident, but her bottom lip gives her away. 'I give him ten quid a gram, same as always. He doesn't know anyone at our school, so there's no way he could find out I've upped the price.' She puts the phone in a sunglasses case, beside two long-finished lip balm tins, and drops it in her top drawer among her knickers and socks. It's not exactly a secure hiding place, but they know that Molly and Bill would never rifle through their stuff. The right to privacy got at least half an hour on the foster carers' refresher course. 'I don't reckon he'd care even if he did know anyway,' Amber goes on. 'Doesn't change what he makes out of our deal, does it?'

Jess isn't sure she agrees, because she doesn't think that selling drugs is just about making money. It's about control. Being more powerful than the other guy. Jess reckons that Sean would go batshit crazy if he found out that Amber had been cheating him. But she's not going to risk antagonising her sister by saying that. 'Suppose not.'

'He probably wants to tell me when he's next coming to Thame. We can go to the rec after tea, and I'll call him from there.'

'Uh, yeah, okay.' Jess drags her front teeth along her bottom lip. She hasn't told her sister that she's already got plans for tonight. She and Amber do everything together, and she knows she'll get an onslaught of questions if she leaves without explaining where she's going. But she's not ready to tell Amber yet. She doesn't know why – or maybe she does, but she doesn't want to think about it, her fear that Amber might try to ruin this one good thing that's happening to her.

Her vague plan is to show her face at youth club with Amber like normal – it's cringe dull, but it gets them a free pass from Bill and Molly every Friday evening – then claim a headache and pretend to go home rather than to the rec like usual. Then she can double back and head to the disused train carriages where she's arranged to meet him. Amber isn't the type to walk her home, or cut her own evening short, so all being well, that will give Jess at least an hour without Amber having to know a thing.

She will tell her soon – that goes without saying – but not just yet.

Amber crawls out of her bed cave and they head downstairs together.

'You took your time,' Molly complains, but with a fondness that means they're not in trouble. As a foster kid, it takes quite a lot to get into any real trouble at home. Jess has never worked out whether that's because their tragic start in life cuts them extra slack, or because not having any shared DNA means foster carers aren't so bothered about the kids in their care doing well. But neither Lou and Justin, nor Molly and Bill, have ever moaned about disappointing grades, non-existent table manners, or the state of their bedroom. One of the reasons they moved to Chinnor was because Amber said she wanted to study Arabic at GCSE, but when she changed to Dance a day after she started at Lord Fred's, no one even mentioned it.

Not that Jess's actual parents would give a shit about those things either. Before she died, Jacqui might snuggle up in bed with them every now and again, but other than that, she limited her mothering to making sure they got the basics – food, clothes, to school on time most days. Beyond that, it was all about the vodka bottle and trying to make Tyler happy enough not to smash her face in.

Her dad has got an excuse for his crapness, Jess supposes. He joined the Army when he was 16, just a year older than she is now, and met her mum when he was based in a barracks north of Oxford. Jess was conceived just before he went on a tour of Afghanistan, which she's always found quite romantic, even though that's where the nightmare started. He was hit by shrapnel from some roadside bomb. Two other soldiers died, so he was lucky in comparison, but he still had to have a load of operations. He wasn't the same after that. Jacqui threw him out on Jess's first birthday – some over-the-top reaction to the party poppers apparently – and a couple of weeks later he tried to top himself. That's when the Army stepped in, got him counselling and stuff. He's more stable now, but he doesn't have a job, and no one's ever suggested he might want to take responsibility for his daughter.

Jess isn't sure which is worse. Having a dad who doesn't want to look after you, or not having a clue who your father even is, like Amber.

'Great tea, Molly,' Amber mumbles as she scoops up a forkful of cottage pie and shovels it into her mouth. For all her backchat, Amber must be a joy to feed because she eats anything. 'You not eating?'

'I'm going to wait for Bill – he's at a church meeting – but I'm glad you like it. Give you some energy for whatever you kids get up to at youth club these days.' Molly gives them a smile, then disappears into the kitchen. Jess can hear her running the tap.

'I wish Lucy Rose would hang out at the rec on a Friday sometimes,' Amber muses, now that Molly is out of earshot. 'You can only cause so much grief at school.'

'She never leaves that house though, does she?' Jess slides a thin slice of mashed potato off the meat and drops it onto her tongue. She hates the texture of mince. Maybe she should become a vegetarian. 'She's too scared to leave the protection of Mummy and Daddy.'

Amber pushes air through her nose. 'She's pathetic. Do you reckon her parents are embarrassed that she's such a baby?'

Amber is trying to disguise it, but Jess can hear the hope in her voice. Like she needs to believe that parental love isn't all that special. But Jess knows that's bullshit. Most parents, *normal* parents, love their children so much that they're blind to their faults.

'We should trick her, shouldn't we?' Amber says when Jess stays silent. 'Get her to leave her cosy little house one night. Then we could be waiting for her.'

'An ambush,' Jess whispers, thinking of her dad, and that roadside bomb.

'Oh my God, she'd crap herself, wouldn't she?'

Then they both dissolve into giggles until Molly tells them to shut up and finish their tea.

'We'll need her phone number,' Amber says thoughtfully. 'Find a way to get hold of it at school next week, yeah?'

THE NIGHT SHE DIES

Friday 3rd May

Rachel

I've lived in this village for seventeen years – since we outgrew our little flat in north Oxford after Milla was born – and I've never felt scared here. Not on those solo walks back from The Crown after a class mums' night out. Not even when I'm out on a trail run in winter before sunrise. But tonight, the dark streets feel ominous.

Where is she?

She'll be in the recreation ground. Both Milla and Lucy have spent hundreds of hours there over the years, first with me, and then on their own as they got older. Lucy and Bronwen too. They would lie on the giant disc swing, heads together, discussing their futures. Lucy as a writer or architect, Bronwen, a detective or podcaster. I can imagine Lucy finding solace there this evening, staring at the stars.

I pick up my pace, and I'm almost running by the time I reach the entrance to the recreation ground. I don't know if it's exertion or fear, but my heart is racing, and I pause for a moment to take a few deep breaths. The sports pavilion on the left is just a black mass, no lights on, and the pitches in front of it appear empty too. But I can see people in the playground in the far right-hand corner, eerie silhouettes against the dim glow of streetlamps from Station Road. From this distance it's impossible to tell if one of them is Lucy, so I up my pace again and jog across the field.

But when I push open the gate to the playground, I realise, with crushing disappointment, that she's not there. There are about eight people in total, all teenagers, a mix of boys and girls, but none that I recognise. They stare at me with a mix of surprise and horror.

'Sorry,' I say instinctively, as though I need to apologise for trespassing on their domain. 'I'm looking for my daughter.'

The crack in my voice gives me away instantly. Desperation. And with it, any authority my adulthood might have evoked disintegrates. Most of them back away, uncomfortable with the drama I'm bringing to their evening. But three girls don't move, curious expressions settling on their faces. The one who's sitting on the swing sucks on a vape, then blows out a huge cloud of fake smoke. A sickly sweet smell permeates the air.

'Who is she?' she finally asks. Even in those three words I can tell that she's drunk. I dip my eyeline and notice the empty wine bottles and crushed cider cans on the asphalt. Not that I'm going to judge them. I've held Milla's hair back too many times for that.

'She's called Lucy Rose,' I say. 'You might know her, she's in Year 10 at Lord Fred's.'

The girl squints for a moment, in thought, then relaxes her features. 'Oh yeah, Lucy Rose,' she slurs. 'Milla's little sister.'

'You've seen her? Tonight? Do you know where she is now?' I shoot out the questions like bullets.

'Huh? Nah, I just mean that I know who she is. Never spoken to her. We're older,' she adds, as though that explains it. The regimental nature of school. Friendships across age groups firmly banned.

'And she hasn't been here tonight?' I press. 'You're sure?'

The girl shrugs, sucks again on her vape. 'There was a Year 10 girl here when we first arrived,' she says, as though just remembering.

'That wasn't her daughter,' one of the other girls says. A hiccup escapes from her throat and she stifles a giggle. 'Sorry. That was the druggie girl. And I think she's in Year Nine.'

'Shit, really?' the girl on the swing murmurs. 'The foster kid? She looks older.'

She must be talking about Amber. Panic scratches at my skin. Has Lucy seen her? Have they done something to her? 'What time was this?' I push.

'We got here about eight fifteen, didn't we?' Swing girl looks to the others, and they nod in response. Another hiccup slips out. 'And she left maybe fifteen minutes after that.'

So 8.30 p.m. Lucy was with Matt then. I feel a wave of relief.

The girl's eyes are glazed, unfocused. I should tell them to go home. They think they're grown up, these kids. Because they're 16 or 17, old enough to have sex, to fight for their country or whatever. But they're just babies really. Vulnerable.

But I have other priorities tonight.

I mumble my thanks and turn back towards the gate. The easiest way out of the recreation ground from here is via Station Road, but it's been fifteen minutes since I left home, and I need to go back. Check if Lucy's there. The more I imagine it – Lucy letting herself in, calling our names, wondering where we are – the more it feels real, so when I push open our front door and the house is empty, I feel her loss all over again.

I have no idea where to try next. I think about messaging Matt and Milla, but what would be the point? If either of them find her, they'll let me know. So I look at the contacts in my phone instead. I've collected various parents' phone numbers over the years, but none of their children feature in Lucy's life anymore. There's always the chance she's rekindled old friendships without me knowing, but it's nearly half eleven. Is it really worth waking these people up when I know deep down that they won't have a clue where Lucy is?

I can't wait here though. I scribble a quick note – *Lucy, we're out looking for you. CALL ME* – then lock up again and head back onto the high street. It's been getting warmer – spring finally arriving – but it rained when I was in the restaurant and it's cold now. As I zip my parka up to my chin, I pray that Lucy took a coat, and scold myself for not checking that at home.

Just to go somewhere different, I head up the road instead of down, towards the parade of shops. As I round the corner, I can see The Crown in the distance. Muffled noises spill out as people make their way home from the pub. I don't think Lucy is in there – she doesn't look 18 for a start, plus the owners Steve and Jade know exactly how old she is – but maybe someone has seen her?

I start walking towards it but pause halfway there, outside St Andrew's Church. I look at the sign. *All welcome.* We rarely go to church, but both girls were christened here. And it's a place associated with salvation. I push open the gate and take a few tentative steps down the path. The church entrance is around the back, which means walking through the graveyard. There are no lights, and as I walk further away from the road, it feels eerie, the gravestones casting sinister shadows either side of me. I turn my phone torch on and direct it towards the path. It has the dual effect of lighting up my route and plunging the wider landscape into darkness. It's frightening, but I shake the feeling away and keep walking.

The church has a deep porch with an ornate iron gate, flagstone tiles on the floor and hard stone benches running along each side.

And in the corner, perched on a bench, is Lucy.

No coat, but a thick, oversized jumper at least. And she's safe. I burst into tears. She whips her head around at the noise.

'Mum?' she calls out, her voice shaky. 'Is that you?'

'Oh Lucy,' I exhale. 'Thank God I've found you.' I drop down next to her and reach out, but she shuffles away, beyond my grasp. I want her to cry too, to fold into my open arms with relief. But she seems almost scared of me. Like an animal caught in a trap. My eyes pull away in disappointment, and it's only then I notice the blood on her hands and the cuffs of her jumper. 'You're hurt,' I say. 'What happened?'

'It's nothing,' she says, pulling her arms away and curling them into her lap. I hesitate, not sure whether to ask again or let it go for now – the important thing is that I've found her – when the light from my phone catches the glass bottle next to her. It's a bottle of Smirnoff vodka, empty. The red screwcap is missing, and the neck is broken, shards of glass still hanging from it.

'Did you cut them on this?' I demand. Then my voice rises with alarm. 'Did you drink from the bottle after it smashed?'

She lifts her hands reluctantly, and then inspects them as though it's only just occurred to her that she might have injured them that way. 'I didn't drink any,' she says softly. Even at low volume, each word is enunciated perfectly, and I breathe a sigh of relief. 'I dropped it on the pavement,' she goes on. 'But I didn't want to leave it there. Sorry for stealing it,' she adds dully. She must have taken it from our drinks cabinet.

I lean against the cold stone of the church, and despite everything, a smile of relief forms on my face. Lucy is upset enough to steal alcohol late at the night, then hide in a dark churchyard all by herself. But she's also sensible enough not to drink from a broken bottle. She hasn't been lured outside by those bullies, or injured by them, physically or mentally.

Things aren't good, but they could have been so much worse.

I pull out my phone and tap into WhatsApp.

I've got her.

41

THE NIGHT SHE DIES

Friday 3rd May

Rachel

I warm milk on the hob. I could use the microwave, but it feels more wholesome this way, the method my mum used when I was little. I watch for the tell-tale bubbling at the edge of the pan, then pour it into two mugs – my hands still shaking even though the danger has gone – and stir until the hot chocolate powder turns the milk a purply brown.

I hear Lucy pad down the stairs, and a moment later, she appears in the kitchen doorway dressed in her pyjamas, the blood gone, and her hands now littered with plasters. On the walk back from the churchyard, I'd offered to clean and dress her wounds myself, like I did when she was small, but she turned down my offer, and disappeared upstairs as soon as we got home. The bloodstained jumper hasn't made it downstairs. I consider asking if she's put it in to soak or left it on her bedroom floor, then decide it doesn't matter. Unlike Milla, Lucy has inherited her father's neatness genes, so I'm not going to start hassling her now.

'Thank you,' she whispers, reaching for the mug. Her arms

are shaking too, I notice, but that could be down to the cold temperature as much as the after-effects of adrenalin. She walks over to our kitchen table, a solid structure made from reclaimed pine that carries the scars of seventeen years of family meals, and drops onto the bench that runs along one side. I sink into the chair opposite her and nurse my own drink. Silence reigns for a while as I try to figure out what to say. There are a dozen questions circulating my head, but I can't work out which one to ask first. Or whether I should be asking anything at all. Maybe getting her home in one piece is enough.

'I'm sorry to run out like that,' she says eventually.

I sigh. 'We're not cross with you. We know what a difficult day it's been for you. But you did scare us. Dad said you'd gone to bed, so it was a shock, seeing your room empty.'

She takes a sip of her drink, then drops her chin into cupped hands, and raises her eyes to mine. 'Where is Dad anyway?' she asks.

I look at my watch and feel my forehead crinkle. Because it is strange that Matt isn't home yet. It's been nearly half an hour since I messaged the family WhatsApp group, and neither Matt nor Milla has shown up yet. Milla is on foot, so she might take a while longer, but surely Matt should be home by now? A lurch of fear makes my chest tighten for a moment, but I breathe it out. Nothing has happened to him – this instinct is just a hangover from the terror I've already felt tonight.

I pick up my phone, but I don't even get chance to click on his name before I hear the low rumble of a car arriving in the drive. A moment later, the side door swings open and Matt walks into the kitchen.

'Lucy,' he breathes. 'Where the—' The words catch in his throat and he stops abruptly. 'Never mind,' he says. 'But please don't do that again.'

'I'm sorry,' she says meekly. 'I won't, I promise.'

'Do you want a hot chocolate?' I ask, gesturing towards my mug.

'No, I'm fine.' He scratches his neck, looks at Lucy, then back at me. He seems anxious, as though, even with her sitting in front of him, he can't believe she's safe. 'Actually, maybe I will,' he continues, nodding his head. 'I'm feeling pretty wired to be honest; it might help me sleep.'

'I suppose it's morning in Thailand,' I say. 'Your body clock must be all over the place. Sit down and I'll make it for you.'

'Thanks, yes.' He keeps nodding but doesn't move towards the table. 'You know, I'll just use the toilet,' he spurts out. 'I'll be back in a minute.' He disappears out of the kitchen, and as I grab the milk from the fridge, I hear him walking upstairs. We have a toilet off the kitchen, and I wonder why he doesn't use that.

I check my watch again. Maybe I should warm enough milk for Milla; she'll be back any moment and is bound to be freezing cold. I can't actually remember what she was wearing when we headed out – I was too panicked to notice details like that – but I doubt it's anything sensible. As I wait for the milk to bubble for the second time, I become aware of a new sound against the window and realise that it's started to rain again.

'Come on, Milla,' I mumble to myself, tapping my foot against the flagstone flooring. Milla comes across so capable that I don't worry much about her being out late anymore. She's an adult after all, and our village is hardly crime central. But after everything that's happened tonight, I want all of my family under one roof.

Lucy yawns behind me and I turn to face her. 'Do you mind if I go to bed?' she asks. 'I'm so tired.'

I fight the urge to remind her that we're all tired, and if she'd gone to bed when she claimed tiredness the first time, we'd all be fast asleep by now. Including Milla. 'Of course you can,' I say instead. 'And try to have a lie-in tomorrow.' I know I'll be up – I'm already looking forward to my early morning trail run after the stresses of tonight – but Lucy needs the rest. She shrugs, gives me a half-nod, and pushes away from the table.

I feel a sense of loss when she's gone – not for her leaving, but for the goodnight hug that never comes anymore – but then the milk starts to froth dangerously high, and my focus returns to the task at hand. Matt walks back into the room just as I drop the pan into the sink. He's changed too, I notice. Fleece pyjama bottoms and his favourite Rapha hoodie.

'Thanks,' he says, taking the mug from my hand. Matt hates being out of control of things, and he must be exhausted after his long day, but he's been a rock tonight, and I feel a swell of love for him. Our marriage has been through some difficult patches – when the allegation of assault was made against him, and also around the time Milla was born – but our commitment to each other has never broken. I can see him eyeing the pan in the sink and I instinctively turn around to wash it up. 'Is Milla here?' he asks my back.

'Not yet. But she can't be long. It's been ages since I messaged you both.'

'Yeah,' Matt says. It's quiet for a moment and I imagine him stroking his smooth head. 'Maybe we should call her,' he adds.

I flip the pan onto the drainer and turn to face him. As our eyes connect, my heartbeat quickens. Not at his question, but for the things he doesn't say.

Where is she?

Why did we let her search for Lucy alone?

Have we swapped one missing daughter for another?

I grab my phone, click on Milla's contact, and wait for the dialling tone, but it clicks straight into voicemail. Milla never switches her phone off, not even at night, not even after us punishing her for it for years. I strum my fingers impatiently as I wait for the robotic voice to finish the familiar instructions, then I leave a quick message – *Milla, where are you? Call me back* – and click into Find My iPhone. The icon whirs for too long, then settles on: No location found.

'Why can't I get through to her?' I say, my voice rising, warbling. I tap into WhatsApp and scroll. 'She didn't read my last message.'

'Shit,' Matt mutters. But he seems more frustrated than panicked. 'She said her battery was low, didn't she?' he reminds me. 'It looks like her phone's run out of juice.'

His explanation makes sense and my panic subsides for a moment. But not for long. It's the middle of the night. Our daughter is out there, alone, in the rain. And unaware that we've found her sister. I look at the full mug of hot chocolate, not hot anymore, and feel my face slip.

'Don't cry,' Matt says, reaching out, then pulling me into him. I rest my head against his broad chest, smell the fresh scent of our shower gel. He must also have had a shower when he went upstairs.

'You know what Milla's like,' he reminds me. 'She's probably gone to Felix's, decided on a whim to take him back. Or she might even have been dragged into The County Arms for a lock-in – you know what that pub's like on a Friday night. We'll find her, then we'll ground her, just like always. Trust me, she's fine.'

'I hope so,' I whisper, the sound muffled against his soft hoodie. Then I draw back and add, 'Yeah, you're right,' with a new sense of resolve. 'Okay, so I'll call Felix; you go back out there.' He turns to go, but when I lay my hand on his arm, he pauses. 'And if you find her first,' I say, 'tell her I am really going to kill her this time.'

BEFORE

Sunday 28th April

Jess

'Maybe we should hitch a ride,' Amber murmurs, scuffing the heel of her Air Force Ones against the edge of the pavement. 'Don't want to be late for Sean.'

'Bus will be here in a minute,' Jess responds. 'May as well wait.' Jess doesn't want to be late for Sean either, but she hates hitching. Not because she thinks it's dangerous, but because it forces her to talk to a stranger in the confines of their car. Answer their dumb questions. And it would be extra bad today because her nerves are already shot.

She doesn't usually go with Amber to meet Sean. After what happened a year ago. Amber says that Sean doesn't care about that anymore, and Jess semi believes her, but it's been easier to stay away. Amber gets Sean all to herself (not that he's ever given Jess any attention) and she gets a few hours to practise not being attached to Amber's side. But this morning Amber asked her to go too, and she's never been good at saying no to her sister.

'Where are we meeting him?' Jess asks, trying to distract Amber from the still-missing bus.

'Up at the war memorial,' Amber answers, then looks up the road at the sound of heavy tyres coming over the brow of the hill. 'About bloody time.' She reaches inside her cropped Puffa jacket for her pass as the bus swings in next to them. Sometimes Amber dresses in whatever clothes she dumped on the floor the night before (and still manages to look good). Other times she goes to a huge effort – make-up, curling wand, fake eyelashes – and today is one of those days. It usually is when Sean's involved in her plans.

'Isn't that a bit out in the open?' Jess asks, falling in step behind Amber and then dropping her pass against the reader. The memorial has a garden area with benches and trees, but it's still adjacent to the main road coming in from Chinnor.

Amber shrugs. 'It's just mates catching up. Why does it matter if people see? No one's going to notice us swapping bags when we leave.'

'I suppose,' Jess says, narrowing her eyes in thought as she winds up the stairs after her sister. Sean is verging on psycho about secrecy, so the war memorial must have been Amber's idea. Did she choose somewhere public for insurance, in case Sean has found out about them skimming a bit extra?

Is that why she wants Jess with her too? Safety in numbers?

Or one of those human shields?

The dot-to-dot of realisation must show on her face because Amber reaches for her hand as they drop onto the seat. 'You don't have to come, you know,' she says. 'If you're too scared. I can meet Sean by myself.' There are always two sides to Amber, Jess thinks. The sister who talks about it being them against the world. And the resentful orphan who gets her biggest kick out of putting Jess down.

'It's fine,' Jess says, sounding as flippant as her shallow lungs will allow. 'It's not like he's still pissed off with me, is it?'

'Yeah, exactly,' Amber agrees. Jess searches her face for any signs that she's lying, but she knows it's pointless. Amber is too good a liar to leak clues. She leans back against the cushioned seat and stares out of the window. When the bus slows at a mini-roundabout, her pulse starts to quicken, because it means their stop is next.

'I got Lucy's phone number by the way,' she spurts out.

'Awesome.' Amber smiles. 'One night soon, we'll get her out. You know, maybe I should take a knife, wet her,' she adds in a low, teasing voice. 'Sean would think I'm fucking cool if I did that, wouldn't he?'

An image suddenly appears in Jess's head. Blood pooling on the carpet. Stillness. Fear and indecision. It's a bad memory that she's supposed to have blocked out. She shakes it away. 'I don't think,' she stutters. 'It's not a good …'

'All right, chill out.' Amber clicks her tongue. 'I was only messing with you. Come on, this is our stop.' Amber stands up, and Jess follows suit.

When they arrive at the memorial garden, Sean is already there, taking up a whole bench with his arms spread across the back. He looks like a drug dealer – black Puffa jacket zipped up to his chin, fat joggers, white trainers, and a black cap pulled low over his eyes – but so do most teenage boys around here. And anyway, he looked like that when she and Amber first met him, when his mum was still healthy, and he didn't sell drugs for a living.

'Hey, Sean,' Amber calls out. She's trying to sound chill, but she's not fooling anyone.

'Hey.' Sean's voice is deep and lazy, but Amber still beams at him. She drops her bag on the ground – a cheap mini backpack from Decathlon, identical to Sean's – and sits onto the bench sideways, curling her knees up under her chin. Jess hovers a few metres away, Sean ignoring her like he always has.

'How's business?' Sean asks Amber, pushing his cap up a notch so that his face is on show. Brown eyes, taut jawline, neat scar above his eyebrow. No denying he's good-looking.

'Same as usual,' Amber says. She's still smiling, but there's a tremor in her lips now. And a slightly higher pitch to her giggle. 'The pills all went. Got a few tens of skunk left, but I've written it all down. In code,' she adds quickly. 'Like you said.'

Sean nods. 'Sounds like trade's good to me. Maybe we should increase the price now you're mixing with all these posh countryside kids. What do you reckon?'

Amber looks away, but Jess forces herself to observe Sean's face, to try and read his expression. Is he making a point? Does he know what they've been doing? Or what Amber decided to do without telling Jess, she silently corrects – although of course they'll both suffer the consequences if he ever finds out.

But Sean doesn't know anyone in Thame, she reminds herself silently. So there's no way he could have found out.

'Yeah, maybe,' Amber murmurs.

She's still looking at the memorial, and Jess decides to follow her gaze. It's a big stone structure with a cross on the top and a bronze plaque with loads of names engraved into it. She's not close enough to read them, but she supposes they're dead soldiers. It makes her think about her own dad, and how there's no memorial for him because he's still alive, but also lifeless. She wonders which is worse.

'But they're not all that posh really, or rich,' Amber goes on, her voice getting a bit stronger. 'And there's a big party in the village next weekend. A girl's eighteenth. I've already had a couple of orders placed, and I'm going to wait outside the girl's house to see if I can sell some more. It might be a problem if we change the price now.'

Sean removes his arms from the bench and rests his elbows on his knees. His head drops low between his shoulder blades, hiding his face. 'A party,' he murmurs into his jacket collar. 'In Chinnor?'

'Yeah,' Amber says. 'A massive house off Lower Road. There's going to be one of those big tents in the garden.'

Finally Sean looks up. 'Okay, if you want to stick at ten, we'll stick at ten. I guess I'm going to have to trust you on this.'

'Of course you can trust me,' Amber whispers.

'Really?' Sean's voice hardens, and his eyes narrow, drilling into Amber's.

He still hasn't acknowledged Jess. She wonders if she should make a run for it. And if she did, whether Amber would follow.

'So why did you choose this place to meet then? It's hardly discreet, is it?' Sean's voice is lazy again. Jess releases a sigh as quietly as she can.

'Just a couple of mates hanging out,' Amber says, repeating her logic from earlier. Then she shakes her head, and suddenly the sassy Amber is back. 'And there was another reason I chose here. I've got a surprise for you.'

'Oh yeah?' Sean starts looking around him, suddenly furtive. It must be exhausting being him, Jess thinks. Always checking over your shoulder, expecting the feds to turn up at any moment.

'It's nothing bad,' Amber says, lifting her palms. 'I just want you to meet someone. A friend of mine, and he works near here. He's due to finish around now.'

Jess shifts on her feet. She's got no idea who Amber's talking about. Sean is surprised too because he pushes up off his knees, slides along the bench until he reaches Amber's shins and glares at her. 'What friend? Who the fuck have you told about me?'

'Calm down,' Amber says, giggling at Sean's reaction. She must feel on stronger ground now. 'He doesn't know about our arrangement. He just thinks you're a mate from my old life, which you are, remember, so it's not exactly a lie. The thing is …' she looks triumphant, or defiant maybe '… he's my new boyfriend.'

Jess draws in a silent gasp. She's not sure whether the shock is more down to Amber having a boyfriend she didn't know about, or her flaunting him in front of Sean. Amber has kept quiet about

51

whether she's ever done stuff with Sean, which probably means she hasn't, but it's always been obvious that she wants to. Is this about making him jealous?

'So what's that got to do with me?' Sean asks, not showing much sign of jealousy.

Amber shrugs. 'I thought you might want to check out who's fucking me.'

Jess flinches. She knows it's old-fashioned, being squeamish about sex, but it was fucking the wrong guy that got their mum killed. Amber is only 14. If she's already doing it, what are her chances of getting into the same trouble as their mum?

Sean raises his eyebrows. 'Not really, but I suppose it's better to have eyes on the bloke most likely to nick my gear.'

'I'm not that stup … Hey, there he is.' Amber points towards the entranceway, then morphs the gesture into a wave. Jess quickly turns, stares. The boy walks towards them, gives Jess an embarrassed nod, then hangs one arm over Amber's shoulder. He's tall, but not as muscular as Amber usually goes for. Blonde-haired, blue-eyed. Nothing like Sean. So not her type at all really.

'Hey man, I'm Caden,' he says to Sean. 'It's good to meet you; Amber talks about you a lot.'

THE NIGHT SHE DIES

Saturday 4th May

Rachel

I rest my forehead on the kitchen table and clench my fists in my lap. I'm both exhausted and agitated. My body hangs heavy, but my limbs are twitching. I rear back up, eye my phone for the millionth time. But there are no new messages from Matt. There was a flurry at first – *Not at Ava's, party def over; No sign of life at pub; Rec and churchyard empty.* But there's been nothing since the message *Will keep looking.* And that was an hour ago.

I've done my part too. Woken Felix up, opened his wound of rejection by telling him his ex-girlfriend hasn't come home. In return he told me – stonily – that he hadn't seen her all night. After almost begging him, he did check the map function on Snapchat for me, but it put Milla at home, and the timings tallied with when she came back. She hasn't used the app since, which is why no new location has been uploaded.

I consider phoning her friends, but who would I call? Ava is Milla's best friend, and I already know she isn't there. Otherwise, she has a wide social group, but no one that stands out. And it's nearly 2 a.m. I can't wake up a dozen girls – or even worse, their parents – on the off chance.

I push up to standing, then immediately fold over the wooden worktop. Was it really just a few hours ago that I was dipping a poppadom into mango chutney and worrying about Lucy's underwear being scattered on the school lawn? And a few hours before that, reassuring Mrs Gray that lashing out at her autistic toddler doesn't have to define her?

Bile forms in my mouth as I imagine something violent happening to Milla. A drunk man attacking her on his way home from the pub. Or a rejected husband cruising past in his car. Or maybe just a sick mind taking advantage of a young woman, alone, vulnerable in the darkness.

I can't do this anymore.

I pick up my phone, prod Matt's number. He picks up after half a ring. 'Is she home?' he asks desperately.

'We need to call the police, Matt.'

He sighs. His millisecond of hope extinguished. 'No, not yet. I'm still looking. I'm sure I'll find her.'

'We haven't heard from her for nearly three hours. We need people out there, Matt, police officers, searching for her.'

He doesn't speak for a moment, and I listen to his heavy breathing as he tries to control his emotions. I know how much he hates the police. It hasn't always been the case – a hardworking grammar school student from the outskirts of Manchester didn't have much cause to – but that changed when he was arrested for assault, in front of his colleagues, at the school he'd spent most of his teaching career.

'They'll twist things,' he moans. 'Say it's our fault, that we're bad parents for letting her go out by herself in the dead of night. Christ, Rachel, we are bad parents!'

'I know!' I wail back. 'But we can't let that stop us. This is about Milla, not us.'

Matt goes silent and I imagine him alone in the car, both hands gripping the steering wheel, his face tightening as he interprets my plea as a reprimand.

'You're right,' he says abruptly. 'I'll come home. We can call them together.'

We hang up and I feel both relieved and petrified. Contacting the police will hopefully draw an army of specialist help, but it will also make Milla's disappearance feel more real. Transform her from a teenager behaving badly into a potential victim. Suddenly the house feels too empty. I think about Lucy upstairs, fast asleep, oblivious to the trauma of her missing sister. I won't wake her, but I feel a compulsion to look at her.

I walk up the stairs slowly, then pause outside her room. The door is closed, like usual, and I take my time pushing down the handle so that I don't make a noise. I expect there to be total darkness, but there's a light glowing as I edge the door open. And when I can see more, I realise that Lucy isn't in bed after all. She's sitting at her desk with her back to me – her laptop screen the source of the light. She's flicking between websites, and there's a sense of frustration in the way she taps at her keyboard. I hesitate, unsure whether to announce my presence or retreat. But before I get a chance to decide, she whirls around, then flips down her screen.

'Mum? What's going on?'

'I thought you'd be asleep,' I say. I don't want to tell her that Milla is missing, that her own brief disappearance might have led – however indirectly – to something much worse.

She drums her nails on the closed laptop lid. 'I tried, but I couldn't switch off.'

'Being on a screen won't help,' I say. 'The blue light keeps you awake.' It's the automatic response of every parent, but Lucy has always preferred sketchbooks and journals to electronic devices, so it's something I'm much more used to saying to Milla. My eyes grow hot as memories flash up in my mind. What I would give to find Milla scrolling through TikTok under her duvet right now.

'Yeah, you're right,' Lucy says with an apologetic half-smile. 'I'll give it another try.' She unfurls her legs from her desk chair and makes the few steps over to her bed. As she falls against her pillow and pulls the covers over her head, I'm surprised that she hasn't grilled me on why I'm still awake. A slow wave of sadness rolls over me as I realise how much this bullying must be affecting her. As though her mind is so full of it that there's no room to notice life happening around her. I feel a stab of self-loathing for taking so long to figure it out, which morphs into a fireball of regret as I close her bedroom door.

Why did I allow Milla to search for Lucy by herself?

How can I love my kids so much and still make so many mistakes?

I suddenly feel exhausted and wonder if I'm going to collapse, right outside Lucy's bedroom door. But then I hear a rustling coming from the porch, and the door swing open. Matt is home. I take a breath and walk back downstairs.

My eyes widen. I waver. I reach for the back of the sofa. 'Milla?'

'Shit,' she says. 'Have you been worried? Have you been looking for me?'

She's standing just inside the house. Her hair and clothes are wet, no jacket, but otherwise she looks the same as she did a few hours ago. Alive. Unhurt. Indestructible.

'Jesus, Milla!' I screech. It's loud. The realisation that I'm going to wake the neighbours registers somewhere, but I can't hold back. All the pent-up fear is escaping through my open mouth. 'It's two in the morning, of course we've been looking for you! Where on earth have you been?!'

She leans back against the porch door and pushes her lips together. Even as adrenalin courses through my body, I can see that she's conflicted. Her instinct is to shout back, to deny wrongdoing. But she's also smart enough to know how her disappearance will have affected us.

She lets out a deep sigh. 'I'm sorry, okay?' she says begrudgingly.

'But it wasn't my fault. My phone died, then it started raining. And my foot was hurting; I think I've got a blister. So I sat on a bench by Kiln Lakes, just to rest for five minutes. But then I started thinking about Felix, and what the fuck happened to us. I probably drank a bit too much at the party, I guess. And the next thing I knew, I was waking up, and a couple of hours had passed. I ran home as soon as I realised. It was just one of those things. And now my foot's killing me.'

I look up at the ceiling. The light wobbles under my teary gaze. No angry drunk or resentful ex-husband attacking my daughter. No psychopath hunting for prey. No crime at all. Just Milla doing what she so often does. Exactly what she bloody well wants.

I slink down into the sofa and close my eyes.

AFTER

Saturday 4th May

Rachel

The house is silent again, but this time I soak it up. I've only had four hours' sleep – Matt carrying me upstairs like he did on our wedding night, minus the flutter of anticipation – but I don't feel tired. I imagine it will hit me later, after my run, but I almost look forward to it. No doubt Matt will be tired too, and we can drift through a lazy Saturday together. I know our problems aren't over. I still have the rough waters of Amber Walsh and Jess Scott to navigate next week. But after the terror of last night, I feel invigorated this morning. And for the next three days, the long weekend, I want to enjoy it.

I pull on my trail-running shoes and yank the laces. I need them to feel like an extension of my feet when I run over the slick mud and hard lumps of chalk along the Ridgeway. The trail is an ancient route sometimes called Britain's oldest road, or the chalk spine of England. It starts fifty miles away in Wiltshire and finishes just north of London. Sometimes I take the path west, past the Kiln Lakes, but today I'll run in the opposite direction, through Chinnor Hill nature reserve and along the Icknield Way.

I zip my house key into the small pouch at the back of my Lycra leggings and head outside. Some runners like to carry a backpack, but for me, any practical gains are far outweighed by the sheer joy of running unimpeded. Even though my dad ran when I was growing up, I didn't get into the sport until I became a parent. When the girls were young, every minute away from them felt precious – both a sacrifice and a treat – and I wasn't going to waste it driving to the gym or relying on other people for an organised sport. Running meant I could just put my trainers on and go. It's the same for Matt, I think, with his cycling. He only took it up after we moved here, but he's hooked now. Heading up into the Chiltern Hills whenever his work schedule allows.

The Ridgeway skirts along the top of the village, so I set off up the high street and take the narrow lane towards the fields. Last night's rain has made the mud sticky again and I have to concentrate on placing my feet to keep from slipping over.

I cross over the single railway track – a heritage railway that's only used on commemorative occasions – and head up towards the treeline. It's a steady incline and I can feel my heart pump faster, my breaths become shallower, as my body adjusts. But the sun is peeking over the fields to my right, and the weak blue sky is decorated with white vapour trails above me, and my good mood grows as I reach the chalk white pathway.

The Ridgeway played its part in us moving to Chinnor. Matt and I met at Oxford University – seemingly the only two state school kids with provincial accents at Magdalen College – and moved to Jericho, in north Oxford, when we finished our degrees. We rented for the first few years, and then after we got married, we bought the flat we were living in. It was good for a while – me advancing my career as a social worker in the city, Matt publishing English textbooks at Oxford University Press – but then I got pregnant with Milla, and Matt's dad was diagnosed with an aggressive stage-four lung cancer.

Over the next nine months, Matt became a different person. Or perhaps a dormant part of him awakened. The flat seemed to shrink in his eyes, and he became obsessed with keeping it tidy. I'd watch him throw away things that I'd grown to love. Listen to him swearing under his breath as he lined up our shoes, or found crumbs that had escaped into the corners of the kitchen floor. After Milla was born, it got worse, but it was also harder to bite my tongue as he shouted at me to put away her tiny things, or be a bit more fucking house proud.

Matt's mum, Judy, was his saviour – and probably the saviour of our marriage. I didn't know her well before Matt's dad got sick. We'd meet up at regular intervals – Christmas, Easter, Mother's Day – but conversation wouldn't go much deeper than pleasantries.

It was only when Judy became a widow that I discovered how amazing she was. While she must have been weighed down by grief herself, she was the first to see that Matt's obsessive tidying was a sign of him breaking, and then dedicated herself to fixing him. She would come down most weekends and take him off for a few hours, give me some time away from him, and Matt the space to work through his difficult mix of grief and joy. After listening to him carefully, it was Judy who persuaded Matt to give up his job and train as a teacher – the vocation he'd always wanted but had never pursued.

It was also Judy who – after selling the family home to move somewhere smaller – gave us a financial gift that enabled us to buy a house. And she'd offered Matt the money during one of their walks, a route that Judy had found, along a prehistoric trail near a village called Chinnor.

I reach the ridge and turn left, the terrain instantly flattening out. Sometimes I see a dog walker, or another runner, out on the trail – it feels like I'm deep in the forest, but there's actually a small car park only a fifteen-minute walk away – but today I'm on my own, and I breathe in the solitude. It's not quiet though. The birds are making a racket from deep inside the trees, and there's rustling at ground level too. Squirrels or maybe a rabbit. After about a kilometre, I pause to push open a gate and jog into Chinnor Hill nature reserve. There's a pocket of green space here – a secret garden – but the surrounding woodland is more dense, and a sense of unease prickles on my skin. If I were dragged into the trees, no one would have a clue I'd been taken. But I shake the feeling away, frustrated with myself. This is my home. I won't allow myself to be scared of it.

It's harder to run here because the path has disappeared and the grass is long and wet, but I've got plenty of experience, so my pace hardly slows as I traverse the steep hill, drinking in the sight of new bluebells sprinkled along the ground. I can see the gate that will take me back onto Icknield Way ahead of me, but something lower down the hill, half-hidden by a hawthorn bush, catches my eye and makes me pause. I slow to a stop and concentrate on my breathing as I consider my options.

In the autumn I came across a dead deer on one of my runs. I've seen plenty of lifeless animals before – squirrels, mice, pheasants, foxes – but the sheer size of the deer was intimidating. There was no logic to it – it couldn't do me any harm – but I still felt the physical signals of panic as I tried to slow my thoughts enough to decide what to do. In the end, I memorised the phone number on the nature reserve welcome sign and ran home to call them. When Matt and I walked the route the next day, the carcass had gone.

Is that what I should do now?

With my heart rate increasing, I take a few slow steps towards the dark mass. Now that I'm closer, I decide it looks more like a large rucksack than a dead animal. But something – some sixth sense perhaps – stops me from investigating further. My heart pounds in my chest. There's a noise behind me, a rustling, and I whip my head around. But there's no one there.

This is stupid. What am I scared of? I take a deep breath, then walk purposefully towards the bush. I push the branches to one side.

And scream.

Stumble backwards. Lose my footing and fall. Scramble away on my heels and hands.

Spew watery vomit on the grass.

Not a backpack, not a deer.

The dark mass is a human body.

AFTER

Saturday 4th May

Rachel

What do I do?

I don't have a phone so I can't call anyone.

I'm at least a kilometre away from the main path, so I can't scream for help.

Oh Jesus – a thought barrels into my brain with so much force it makes me dizzy – what if it isn't a body at all, but a person, still alive?

My legs are too weak to stand, but I need to check, however repellent the thought. So I crawl on my hands and knees, towards the bush, closer to the body. It's completely still. I can't see the face, but long hair, mussed and tangled, is hanging down their back.

Her back, I think. Long hair, small frame, a dip at the waist. Female.

I take a deep breath and reach out towards her shoulder. But my hand is shaking so much that I can't really control it, and I grab more roughly than I intended. She drops onto her back with a thud, and I scream again. Except this time, I can't stop.

Because her face is bruised and disfigured. Her hair matted with blood and eyes glassy. She's definitely dead.

And Christ, I don't really know her.

But still, I recognise her.

'Hello? Are you okay?' A muffled voice from far below me, from the path at the bottom of the hill, makes me physically jump. But this is exactly what I need. Reinforcements.

'HELP!' I scream. 'I need help!'

Low but rapid murmuring. Footsteps rustling in the long grass.

'Rachel? Oh my God, what's happened?' I look up. It's Annie. With her husband Robert and their spaniel, Coco, held firmly on the lead. Then Annie shifts her gaze to my side and her face contorts. 'Oh fuck!' she cries out, then her eyes widen. 'Not Milla, please not Milla!'

I flick my head around, as though I need to check it's not my daughter, but of course it isn't. Why the hell would Annie say that? Then realisation hits. Felix must have told her about me calling him in the middle of the night, frantic about Milla's whereabouts. 'No, it's not Milla!' I say quickly. 'That was a false alarm. She fell asleep on a bench. This is … someone else.' I can't bear to say the name. Because it's a name I have sworn over, wished ill on for months.

The girl who has caused my daughter, my family, so much distress.

The dead girl is Amber Walsh.

Half an hour later I'm sitting on the muddy path at the edge of the nature reserve. I was guided here by the first police officer to arrive after Robert called 999. He asked me a few questions – the red light from his bodycam making me feel nervous, even though his voice was calm and professional – then told me that a detective would arrive soon, and he needed me to wait. I have a blanket wrapped around my shoulders, given to me by one of the paramedics, and Annie is sitting by my side. But I'm still shaking like an overfilled washing machine. I want to go home and pretend none of this has happened. Eat breakfast with my family and binge-watch Ted Lasso, wrapped in a duvet. That's why I turned down Robert's offer to call Matt. I might not be able to leave, but at least I can keep my family in blissful ignorance for a while longer.

If I could force myself to look down towards the village, the horrors of my discovery would be out of view. But I can't seem to drag my eyes away from the scene. It's busy now. A tent has been erected around the body, its edges crinkling over foliage, the bluebells long since trampled by heavy boots. The paramedics have left, but I can count six police or forensic officers combing the scene, the rustle of their protective clothing perceptible even from this distance.

'Poor girl,' Annie says in a low voice. 'I wonder who it is. She was tiny, wasn't she? A child even. God, when I thought it was Milla, how Felix would take that news, it doesn't bear thinking about.'

I want Annie to stop talking about my daughter. The detective will be along soon to talk to me, and I don't want Annie mentioning how Milla was missing for hours, on the same night that Amber was killed.

Not that the two incidents are connected, of course.

'It doesn't bear thinking about, whoever the victim is,' I whisper, then hope my comment doesn't sound judgmental. The last thing I want is to offend Annie, especially now.

'Excuse me,' a voice filters through. I look up at a man about my age with a large forehead and penetrating blue eyes. He's wearing protective overalls and has a scrunched-up facemask in his hand. 'Ms Salter? I'm DI Finnemore, from the Thames Valley Major Crime Unit. My colleague told me that you were the unfortunate person who found the victim. How are you doing?'

I was expecting questions, not kindness, and my resolve instantly starts to slip. But I want to get this over with as quickly as possible, and that means staying strong. So I push up onto my feet, ride the weakness in my legs, and face the detective. 'Looking forward to going home.'

He nods. 'Of course,' he says. 'It must have been a terrible shock.' Then he looks at me expectantly. I know this is a ploy to get me talking, but I've got nothing to hide, so I repeat what I told the uniformed officer. Through it all, Annie stands next to me, her hand resting on my back.

'Thank you,' he says when I fall silent. 'And do you know the victim, by any chance?'

It's the question I've been dreading. I stare at the detective, but his face blurs. Do I know Amber? We've never met. All the conversations I've had with her – the tolerance at first, then the pleas, and finally the furious threats – have been in my head, not in person. I only recognised her at all because Lucy took a clandestine photo of her once. I take a breath, swallow. 'No,' I say, shaking my head. 'Sorry, I don't know who she is.'

The look in his ice-cold eyes sends a shiver down my spine. But is that wrong? Is it my own lie that has caused this sense of foreboding? He's turning to Annie, asking her the same question, but his voice sounds muffled now, like I've created a new distance between us. My role within Children's Services is around early intervention, so direct contact with the police is rare. But I attend monthly Multi Agency Safeguarding Hub meetings alongside specialist police officers, and I have always felt that we're part of the same team. Even when Matt was charged with a crime he didn't commit, I blamed the boy, and the fake witness, not the detectives involved.

But what about now? By denying I know who the victim is, have I broken that trust? Crossed a line?

'I didn't recognise her either, I'm afraid,' Annie says. 'Not that I looked. Well, once I realised it wasn't Milla.'

I jerk my head towards Annie, then back to the detective. A new level of panic hits me.

'Milla?' he asks. He says it nonchalantly, but his nose lifts a few millimetres, like a gun dog picking up a scent.

'Just a misunderstanding,' I blurt out. But I need to rein it in, for Milla's sake. I force a smile. 'Milla's my daughter,' I explain in a more measured voice. 'But she's at home, in bed. She's 18 so, you know.'

'Sleeps until lunchtime,' he offers. 'Yes, I've got a couple of those myself.' He rolls his eyes in solidarity, and I hope it's enough to distract him. But the scent is clearly too strong. 'And sorry if I'm missing something,' he continues, turning back to Annie. 'But why would you initially think the victim was Ms Salter's daughter?'

My friend hesitates before answering, and I can sense her connecting the same dots that I'd linked much earlier, and even without knowing who the victim is. I'm grateful for it – Annie's instinct to protect Milla – but also horrified that she feels the need. 'I don't know really,' she finally says. 'Panic, seeing Rachel, making some illogical association. But it was only for a moment.'

'Okay, I see, that can happen,' the detective says nodding. I hope he can't read the relief on my face as he turns back to me. 'Thank you for explaining everything,' he continues. 'We will need to formalise that into a statement for you to sign. Is that okay?'

'Yes, of course.' I've read plenty of police statements over the years, but having my own stored on their database makes me feel nervous.

'And we also need your fingerprints and a DNA swab, plus your clothes, all for elimination purposes. We're based out of Aylesbury, and I don't want to have to drag you over there. Perhaps I could drop you back home and we can do all the necessaries there?'

I imagine walking through the door with a policeman. The shock and fear that would emanate from Matt. But I don't feel like I've got a choice, and I am desperate to get home. 'Okay, but could I just call my husband? Warn him that you're coming?' I wonder if that makes us sound guilty, like Matt needs prior notice because we have something to hide. But DI Finnemore just nods.

'Of course, absolutely you should.'

'Use my phone,' Annie says, thrusting it towards me. I take it out of her hand, tap in Matt's number, and wait for him to pick up.

AFTER

Saturday 4th May

Rachel

I close my bedroom door and lean against it. I feel bad leaving Matt alone with DI Finnemore – for both their sakes – but I needed a moment to breathe without police scrutiny. I only earned this reprieve because the detective asked me to bag up my clothes, so I force myself to push away from the door, then peel off my leggings and running top. I fold them into a square pile – perhaps my way of apologising to Matt – and slide them into the evidence bag. I add my socks and hairband and fasten it closed.

My trail runners are already sealed away – DI Finnemore taking them off me as soon as we got to his car – and the detective has also taken my fingerprints and a DNA sample, as well as getting me to e-sign my statement. Going through the different tasks with Matt silently watching on was excruciating, his expression never veering from wary. But I couldn't risk engaging with him, giving him more than a few bare words, in case the whole truth of my discovery spilled out. I'm only grateful that the girls haven't surfaced yet.

I pull on some fleece joggers and grab a hoodie from the top shelf of my wardrobe. I'm desperate for a shower, to wash off the horror of finding the body, but that will have to wait. I steel myself for a few more minutes of tension and head back downstairs. Both men are wearing relieved expressions when I reappear, and I try not to wonder how they've been passing the time. I proffer the bag.

'Thank you,' DI Finnemore says. 'These will go to the lab, but you should get them back eventually, might be a few weeks.'

'No problem.' I know I'll never wear those clothes again, that they'll go in the bin, too contaminated even for the charity shop. But I don't need to explain that to him.

'Well, that's everything for now, so I'll leave you in peace. But remember you're a victim of this crime too. I'll get a family liaison officer to email you, and you can contact them if you ever need any support.' He hesitates for a moment, as though wondering if he should end our conversation with something more heartfelt, but then gives me a small nod and turns towards the door.

Matt and I stand at the window and watch the detective's car reverse out of the drive. I'm free to talk now, but my mouth is too dry for words to form. Images of bruised skin and tangled hair keep flashing in my mind. Matt must sense my discomfort – I suppose thirty years together can do that – because he brushes the small of my back and then takes a step away. 'Why don't you go for a shower,' he says. 'And I'll make us breakfast, banana pancakes maybe, something sweet for the shock. And we can talk then,' he adds more gently.

'Thank you,' I whisper. As I watch him retreat into the kitchen, adjusting the doormat with his foot as he walks past, I think again that it was a good decision to work at our marriage when it became difficult. Because look where we are now. Solid.

I push away from the window and head for the stairs.

*

'Amber Walsh?' Matt asks incredulously, dropping his cutlery with a clatter. 'Are you sure? How did you even recognise her?'

I sigh, push my plate away. I managed to eat the first pancake, but my second is untouched, and I stare at the syrup-slavered banana glistening in the weak sunshine filtering through the window. Ever since I found the body, I've been questioning whether I might have made a mistake about her identity. I've only ever seen Amber from a distance, or on that photo Lucy showed me. And the victim's face was smeared with blood. But I was certain in that moment, so it's hard to believe I got it wrong.

'I've seen her around,' I say quietly. 'I didn't tell the police anything, because, you know, I could be wrong.' I look up at him, seeking redemption maybe, but he's still processing the bombshell. 'But I think we should assume it's her,' I finish.

'Oh Jesus, Rachel.' Matt pushes his empty plate into the middle of the table and leans on his folded forearms, head hung low. 'A teenage girl killed in our village is crazy enough, but for it to be one of the girls who was bullying Lucy …' He lifts his chin, shakes his head. 'Not that it's got anything to do with that, of course,' he adds quickly.

'No, of course not,' I mumble in agreement. I take a few breaths, try to calm my thoughts. 'But there is something we need to consider.'

'What do you mean?'

'Milla went missing last night, didn't she? For hours.' I automatically turn towards the doorway, as though saying her name might make her appear.

'Yeah, so? She came back safe and sound.' Seconds tick past and I watch comprehension spread across Matt's dark features. 'Hang on, you can't think?' He shakes his head. 'That's ridiculous. She fell asleep on a bench. She drank too much at Ava's party. My God, Rachel, what are you suggesting?' With my words fully embedded, he gives me a look of disgust and pushes up out of his chair. As I listen to the sharp clang of him dropping dishes

70

in the sink, shame engulfs me. Because he's right – what was I thinking? Milla is amazing – a regular teenager in some ways, a formidable tour de force in others. But not a killer.

I will hunt those bitches down.

Just words. Nothing more.

But it's not about what I'm thinking – which is why I don't need to admit to myself that I'm almost sure Milla *was* wearing a jacket when she left, but not when she got home – it's about other people. Felix. Annie. Our neighbours might have heard me shouting at Milla when she finally came home in the early hours. Yes, Annie kept it to herself when DI Finnemore asked, but will she be so discreet when the gossip starts?

'I'm not saying that Milla did anything,' I plead. 'Of course not. I just mean that she was out, wasn't she? Alone. And there's motive, I suppose, with all the bullying Amber and her sister have been putting Lucy through. I'm scared that the police will find all this out and then think Milla's involved.'

'From what Lucy's told me, Amber was trouble, hanging out with older boys, selling drugs maybe. A teenager in social care. People won't make a connection with Milla.'

I ride the sting of his words, the prejudice that I'm sure he never used to feel. 'This is a sleepy village, Matt. Amber's murder will ricochet through this place like a force-five cyclone. Everyone will be talking about it, sharing multiple theories over a pint at The Crown. We've got to assume that Milla going AWOL will feature at some point.'

Matt curls his hands into fists and pulls his face tight. 'So what do we do? Warn her?'

'Oh, I don't know.' I sigh. 'It feels cruel, telling her she might be a suspect in a murder when there's not even been a formal identification. But on the other hand, maybe it would give her a chance to get her head around it before anyone says anything.' I stare out of the window, but when my phone buzzes on the table beside me, I automatically look over at it. It's a message from Charlotte to our mums' group. For a moment, I assume the news of my discovery has filtered through, but her message has a different angle.

Saw Bill Wainwright this morning. His foster child Amber didn't come home last night. Wants people to keep an eye out. Xx PS @RachelMilla is that Lucy's bully?

Tears form over my tired eyes. 'It's definitely her,' I whisper. 'It's started.'

'It's who?' A sleepy voice curls around the doorway. 'What's started?'

I turn to look at my daughter. Lucy is more patient than her sister, so I know I have a few seconds before I need to answer. A moment to consider how my youngest will take this news. However much she's got the right to be pleased that Amber is no longer around to bully her, I hope that she isn't. That the death of a teenager is more devastating to her than the joy of discovering her personal battle is over. 'We're all fine, but something terrible happened this morning,' I say. 'Come, sit down.'

A shadow passes across her face and she sinks into the chair furthest away from me. 'What is it?' she asks nervously. 'What's happened?'

'On my run this morning, well,' I stutter to a stop. Lucy is only 15. Am I really going to fill her head with the realities of a violent death?

'Someone has died,' Matt says gently, sitting down next to her and taking her hand – an intimacy I doubt she'd sanction from me. 'Mum saw the body, but from a distance. Annie and Robert happened to be passing and they called the police. Mum's fine.'

'A body?' Lucy asks, her voice quivering. 'You said her, when I first came in. And that something has started. Whose body did you find, Mum?'

'I'm not sure,' I say quietly. 'But Amber Walsh is missing.'

Subject: Saturday 4th May update

Sir,

As you're travelling to Copenhagen tomorrow, I'm planning on running silver briefings on a daily basis, and keeping you updated via email until you're back from the conference.

Body of a young female (IC1 or IC2 – unable to determine at scene) found at Chinnor Hill nature reserve at 8.10 a.m. by a local woman while out running – Ms Rachel Salter. Victim transferred to the morgue. Post-mortem will take place on Monday (by Dr Julian Hill – I will attend alongside DC Bzowski) but initial observations show significant head injuries, which is why it was given to us straight away. CSI still working scene. Expected to finish tomorrow. A second team in place at victim's home.

Victim has been identified as Amber Walsh – initially via a bus pass found in her pocket. Amber was 14 years old and under the care of Oxfordshire Children's Services (mother deceased; father unknown) alongside her half-sister Jessica Scott (father alive but not deemed a competent caregiver). Their assigned social worker Colleen Byrne did the formal identification. She also mentioned a possible lead. Seems tenuous to me, but I'll get one of the team to follow it up – and update if anything comes of it.

Foster carers – Bill and Molly Wainwright – are being supported by the FLO (PC Anoushka Tahta). Both are in their sixties, and I understand medical treatment was required for Mrs Wainwright. Jessica has been moved to crisis foster care for forty-eight hours. She is understandably distressed and not currently talking – as in mute – but I'm hoping she'll break her silence tomorrow – am liaising with the social worker about speaking with her then. Bill Wainwright told us that Amber went to the youth club in the church hall like normal (uniforms following that up) and texted at around 22.00 to say she was home. Wainwrights were already in bed and didn't check. Turns out she wasn't. They called 999 at 08.15 this morning when it was clear Amber's bed hadn't been slept in.

Closest CCTV coverage is in village of Chinnor – approx. 1.5 km from scene. Mainly shop cameras, plus the railway station car park. I have tasked DC Williams with securing all relevant footage. Will update further tomorrow. Victim's phone recovered at scene. No fingerprint ID unfortunately. Security code not known by Wainwrights so hoping sister will be able to provide. Only other tech found so far is family PC at victim's home but apparently Amber has never used it.

Amber was a pupil at Lord Frederick's in Thame. Have spoken to her head teacher and asked if we can interview Amber's friends at the school to save time/resources. She gave her consent but needs agreement from school governors. There was an allegation of bullying against Amber – a student called Lucy Rose – so possible lead there, but she's the straight-A, well-behaved, middle-class type so I doubt it will come to anything.

Initial door-to-door inquiries carried out by uniformed officers among Chinnor residents suggest that Amber might have been involved in low-level drug dealing – nothing concrete at this stage, but this will be our primary line of inquiry for now.

Will update again after post-mortem on Monday. Safe travels.

Simon

AFTER

Monday 6th May

Rachel

By an unspoken consensus, we've hardly left the house since Saturday morning – just Matt escaping for an early morning bike ride on Sunday – and Lucy has hardly emerged from her room the whole time. But the Family Fun Day is a village tradition, every May Day weekend, and in all the time our family has lived here, we've never missed it. In a brief fit of optimism this morning, I said that the tragic death of a teenager shouldn't keep us locked away forever. And when both girls responded with a flat no, I made it compulsory.

But now that we're here, I wish I'd listened to them. Milla found a few of her friends soon after we arrived and skulked off, and Matt has disappeared to the bar, so it's just Lucy and me, huddled together as though we need to protect each other from some unknown enemy. Everything looks the same as normal – the tombola and face painting, the steel band at one end and beat the goalie nets at the other – but there's a charged atmosphere, as though the low buzz of gossip is creating a menacing new energy.

And I can't help wondering how much of that gossip is aimed at us.

'Mum,' Lucy murmurs, pulling on my sleeve like she did as a child. 'I don't want to be here.' Even though it's warm today, she's wearing a big baggy hoodie.

'Just give it half an hour,' I coax. 'We can get some hotdogs, and the raffle draw is soon. I bought us a strip of tickets each, so we might win something.'

'But everyone's staring at me,' she continues, looking down at the ground. 'They know Amber's dead. They probably think I killed her.'

'Don't be ridiculous,' I snap, masking my distress with hostility. I exhale, soften my voice. 'I'm sorry, that came out wrong. I just mean that no one would ever think that. If anyone is looking in our direction, it's because I found her body.' The images fly back – shoulder, blood, matted hair – and I swallow down a rush of nausea. 'Just ignore them,' I add weakly.

A few minutes after I read the message from Charlotte on Saturday morning, Annie responded. There were lots of *omfgs* and sad-face emojis, but the main part of her message was a detailed explanation of what the two of us had been through at the nature reserve. She'd ended with the inevitable finale – *could the body be this Amber girl?* – which caused a frenzy of new messages, and they haven't slowed down much since. I might not have left the house all weekend, but I still feel up to date with the police investigation. At least, how it's rumoured to be progressing based on village gossip.

The victim has been confirmed as Amber Walsh. Apparently Molly Wainwright was so distraught, she had to be admitted to hospital after hearing the news. At first, the messages said that she'd suffered a heart attack, causing another wave of alarm, but a few hours later that was downgraded to a flare-up of her angina. The victim's sister – Jess – was reputed to have shut down completely and had been moved to stay with a trained crisis foster carer in another village for a couple of nights. Someone even reckoned she'd been put on suicide watch.

The cause of Amber's death was said to be blunt-force trauma to the head – although I don't know whether that had come from anywhere official. It could just have easily been someone who watches a lot of crime programmes making assumptions based on Annie's account of what she saw. Would they even do a post-mortem this quickly? Theories about who could have killed Amber were rife too, with suspects ranging from her biological father to a wandering serial killer. But when gossip about Amber dealing drugs filtered through, the belief that it must be someone gang-related became the mainstream view.

And I think it was that development which gave me the confidence to suggest attending the fun day. I can't know for sure that people haven't been gossiping about Milla's late-night roaming, or Lucy's connection with Amber, on WhatsApp groups I'm not part of. But a drug-dealing gangster is a much more likely killer than my daughter, and I'm sure it's not just me who thinks that. As a social worker, I'm trained to help everyone irrespective of what they've done, but it also means I know the statistics. Stereotyping can be dangerous, so we always try to avoid it at work, but it's true that its origins are based on fact.

'What if someone asks you about finding her though?' Lucy presses, bringing me back to the fair. 'And what if the stress of the conversation makes me look guilty?'

I turn to look at her. It's true that she looks miserable. As though all the world's problems are her fault. I love how much empathy she has, but sometimes I wish she wasn't so sensitive. Bronwen has a similar awareness of people's feelings, but her personality is tougher, so it doesn't upset her in the same way. I'd often tell Lucy to watch and learn, but of course that's not possible anymore. I'm sure they're keeping in touch on Snapchat, but a friendship limited to messaging is so much narrower in scope.

Perhaps I need to be a bit more understanding.

'Listen, why don't you go home. Dad and I will stay for one drink, show our faces, then bring Milla back with us in a bit. I know she'll hate that, but with everything that's happened this weekend, I don't want her roaming the streets.' I wonder if my words will frighten Lucy – the possibility of a killer on the loose – but she seems unmoved.

'Thanks, Mum,' she murmurs. 'I'll see you later.' She slides her headphones over her ears and flips the hood of her jumper up. As she does so, her face flinches, as though she's in pain, but then her expression clears. She bows her head and walks slowly towards the exit. I watch a few people's stares linger on her for a moment longer than feels natural, then they look away.

'She didn't last long,' Matt observes, handing me a can of Chiltern Lager and putting the unclaimed Coke in his pocket. I listen to the dull fizz as I pull back the ring, then take a long gulp.

'Well, you know Lucy,' I say. 'She's never been great in crowds.'

Matt nods, a grave expression on his face. 'And all this stuff with Amber must be tough for her,' he says. 'Going from probably wishing her dead to her actually being so.'

'I don't think she wished for that,' I say spikily, my shoulders tightening. 'Expelled yes, but not dead.' *I will hunt those bitches down.* I blink Milla's image away.

'You're right,' Matt says quickly. 'Bad choice of words. Lucy is much too kind-natured to think along those lines.' He takes a swig of lager. 'Unlike me.'

I shoot him a warning look, but he doesn't back down.

'What? Are you saying you haven't thought it too? That Amber not being around anymore is good news for us?'

'I saw her dead body, Matt,' I murmur, taking another gulp myself. 'How could I ever associate that with good news?'

Matt looks instantly contrite. 'Of course, sorry. I must sound like a heartless shit. I suppose because I never met her – she was always just Lucy's bully – it's easy to think of her death

78

as an absence rather than a loss. Does that make sense? Am I redeeming myself at all?'

I don't speak, but I reach for his hand as a sign that it does, and we both turn our attention to the fair, scanning the crowd. Matt's grip tightens. 'Oh shit,' he mutters under his breath.

'What is it?'

He gestures to the right side of the stage. 'Milla looks like she's about to lamp that girl.'

My eyes widen at the sight. Milla is clearly arguing with another girl and Matt's right, her hands are clenched into fists, and her face is scowling. We half shuffle, half run, past the stalls in Milla's direction.

'Milla, what's going on?' Matt says calmly when we get close, finding his teacher's de-escalation voice.

'Stupid bitch was saying stuff about Lucy.'

'What stuff?' I can't help asking. I turn to look and realise it's the drunk girl from Friday night, the one sitting on the swing and vaping. My stomach lurches as I remember our conversation, me asking if she and her friends had seen Lucy, telling them that she was missing. All weekend I've been worrying about people jumping to the wrong conclusions about Milla. Do I need to worry about Lucy now too?

'Leave it, Rachel,' Matt says. 'It will be bullshit whatever it is. Come on, Milla. She's not worth your energy.'

'Sounds like the whole family's got anger issues,' the girl says, snorting air in a semi-laugh. 'Not just Lucy.'

'Shut your fucking mouth, you stupid bitch.'

'Milla!'

'You're right, Dad. She's not worth it,' Milla says, ignoring my rebuke. Then she throws the girl a look of intense disdain and marches away. After a moment of hesitation, Matt and I follow.

But I daren't look back, in case the girl can see the doubt on my face.

BEFORE

Wednesday 1st May

Jess

There's a Co-op linked to the petrol station in the village, and as Jess pushes on the door, a man comes out; suited and booted, car keys and a packet of mints in one hand, a phone in the other, clamped against his ear. Their shoulders catch for a moment and Jess comes off worse, getting knocked a few centimetres to the side. She waits for the apology, but the bloke just sails past, oblivious.

'Fucking dick,' she murmurs. What is it about her? She's tall, her hair is bright ginger, and her face is covered in freckles. And yet people still act like she's not there. Like being in foster care is an invisibility disease.

She pulls her shoulders back and strides into the store. But her swagger wilts instantly. Because she doesn't really know why she's there. She's 15 years old. She shouldn't be running to the sweet shop just because someone's given her a bit of cash. But she's got time on her hands, and what else is there to do in this village?

Amber had wanted to see Caden, and that meant Jess covering for her to Molly and Bill. They convinced the older couple to let them go to the park (they're not usually allowed out on a Wednesday night) and then Caden turned up in his beat-up car – he bought it on loan from the garage he works at apparently – and took Amber off. But before she left, she gave Jess a tenner. She called it a thank-you for keeping her secret, but to Jess it felt humiliating. Like Amber was patting her on the head and telling her to fuck off at the same time.

Although Jess supposes some time on her own might give her a chance to get her head around Amber being with Caden. It's weird that she hadn't talked about him before Sunday, because since then, she hasn't stopped. How he's nearly 18, not much younger than Sean. And that he called her the most beautiful girl he's ever dated. (Jess wasn't surprised about that; Amber *is* beautiful.) How he was at Lord Fred's for a while, but left after Year 9 because his mum's Catholic or something. And now he works for a car mechanic in Thame. The only time Amber became tight-lipped was when Jess asked where they'd met, just saying 'around'. That made Jess suspicious, but it doesn't really matter. Amber and Caden are together, and she's got two hours to kill with nowhere to go.

She picks up a bag of Skittles and joins the queue for the cashier. There are some self-checkouts in the store now, but she doesn't have a bank card and the machine always spits the cash back out whatever angle you slide it in at. That's another reason to get a bank account, but Colleen says they need to earn it, whatever that means. She's turning out to be just as bad as their last social worker. As much as Molly and Bill cut them slack, Colleen does the opposite, expecting them to rise above their challenging circumstances and make something of themselves. Heartless bitch.

Eventually she gets to the front of the queue, and a minute later she's back outside, walking down Oakley Road and ripping open the Skittles. Mollie cooked pork chops and boiled potatoes for tea. Amber shovelled it down – clearly desperate to get out – but the smell was enough to put Jess off, so she slid her plateful into the bin when Molly wasn't looking. She doesn't diet like some girls do, but she's not really a fan of meals. That's why she's lean. Flat-chested. Not that she likes her figure. She wishes she was shorter, smaller in general. She might not have any fat on her, but she inherited her dad's broad Scottish frame instead of her mum's petite one (Amber got that).

Sweets do give her spots though, so she has been trying to avoid them lately. But there's no point in even doing that anymore. Not now she doesn't have anyone to impress. It's ironic really. Just as Amber's love life takes off, her own comes crashing down. She shouldn't be surprised. It was early days, and it's not like anything ever goes right for her. *I made a mistake. Sorry.* She's just glad she hadn't got around to telling Amber about him, so at least she's saved one humiliation.

She takes a right down Station Road, walks past the primary school, and pushes open the gate to the playground. Even though the weather is decent, the place is empty, so she drops onto a swing and stares aimlessly at the playing fields where a personal trainer is barking orders at a group of misfits in Lycra in the distance.

God she's bored.

She wonders whether Amber really is shagging Caden, or if that comment was just to make Sean jealous. Amber might only be 14 and small, but she looks older, all curvy and pouty, and has done other things with boys that Jess hasn't got the stomach for yet. Sometimes Jess wonders if there's more to it than Amber having a good body to show off. That her sister says yes to boys because she thinks it's the way to make them want her, just like their mum did. Jess wonders if that's why she resists. A fear of falling in love with someone like Tyler.

Not that her caution has done her any favours so far. She's the one who's single after all.

She pulls her phone out of her pocket, opens Snapchat, and clicks into her saved message history with the boy she thought was her boyfriend. Should she have read the situation earlier?

He didn't give any hint that he was going to dump her before that final, devastating message, but of course the circumstances themselves were a clue. A glaring red flag that she'd ignored. She feels her eyes start to burn, so she quickly shuts the app down and stares at her home screen instead.

And that's when an idea starts to form. A way to lessen the boredom.

It was easy enough to get Lucy Rose's phone number – Jess cornered a girl in Lucy's tutor group in an empty classroom – but she and Amber haven't done anything with it yet. Amber has been too wrapped up in her new boyfriend to think about anything else. But Jess doesn't need her little sister's approval, she can think for herself. With a flutter of excitement in her belly, she opens a new text message, finds Lucy's contact, and starts to type.

Hey, guess who?

The three blinking dots shows that she's replying. Jess is suddenly transfixed by her phone. She's not sure why anticipating a message from a stuck-up crybaby is so thrilling.

Leave me alone

Jess giggles. The dumb cow has bitten.

Aw don't be like that. Just wanna be friends. Wanna meet me in rec?

Jess stares at the phone, willing Lucy to keep the chat going. For a moment, she wishes that they were friends, that Lucy would say yes, and they could hang out in the rec together. Forget that one of them has been brought up by a normal family while the other one's dad tried to top himself, and mum got beaten to death.

I'm blocking you. Stop messaging me.

Jess flicks her head back, away from the screen. She feels an urge to hurl her phone into the air, but of course she can't. It's not like she could go running to mummy or daddy and ask for a new one. She grips it tighter, then shoves it into her pocket, out of harm's way. She pushes off the swing. What is she even doing in a playground? She stomps to the exit, swings open the gate, and walks back onto the road. She's still got over an hour to kill before meeting up with Amber and she hates being by herself in public.

That's when she spots the bottle of wine. This road is part of the original village before the estate was built and Jess imagines it's the sort of street where everyone knows everyone's business. Where a noisy party is complained about for weeks, but a hospital stay conjures up an assortment of cottage pies and home-baked cakes. There's a card with the bottle, and Jess wonders if it's someone's birthday or just a thank-you present for some wholesome favour like mowing the lawn or feeding a cat.

She slips through the gate, swipes the wine, and is back on the pavement in seconds. It's even a screw top. She smiles in triumph and turns back towards the park – the swing much more inviting now she's got something age-appropriate to do on it.

'You little toerag, I saw you pinch that bottle!'

Jess sighs, louder on the inside. Of course someone would see her. She's the unluckiest person alive. She turns around, faces the bearded man in an army-green fleece gilet with his finger pointed at her. Wonders fleetingly if she should crack the bottle over his wrinkly head. 'No, I didn't.' Because denial is always the best option. 'You're seeing things, Grandad. This is my bottle.'

'You stop with Bill and Molly, don't you?' he says, narrowing his eyes and ignoring her claims of innocence. 'I thought I recognised you. They are the salt of the earth, those two, and this is how you thank them?'

Suddenly she's tired. Exhausted. 'Oh, take your fucking wine,' she says, thrusting the bottle into the old man's hand. 'Sounds like you're more in need of getting loose than I am.' Then she stalks off, towards Mill Lane, and another dead end.

AFTER

Tuesday 7th May

Rachel

'Rachel?'

At the sound of my name, I snap back into focus. But I didn't hear what came before it, so I have no idea what my manager – Hugh – is asking me. I was hoping a change of scene would take my mind off Amber Walsh, but even in this magnolia-walled open-plan office, her image is everywhere. Alive, and dead. Luckily Hugh scratches his greying beard and tries again. 'I was just asking if you're sure you're going to be okay this week?' His voice is deep, but gentle. 'After the incident on Saturday?'

If I'd had a choice, I wouldn't have told Hugh about finding Amber. I just want to put it behind me and get back to normal life. But with the job I do – making decisions that will affect society's most vulnerable children – it would be unprofessional not to make my team aware. 'Thank you, but I'm fine,' I say. 'It was a shock, and very sad, but it's not like I've lost someone I know. The victim went to my daughters' school, but she wasn't in either of their years.' I haven't told anyone at work about Lucy being bullied – it's always felt a bit too close to home – and I'm grateful for that now.

'Such a tragedy,' Elaine murmurs, shaking her head. 'And so awful for you.' Her sympathy makes me want to cry. Elaine is my job double – we divvy up cases based entirely on workload – but she's so much wiser than me, and I'm always discussing my more nuanced cases with her. She gives inspired advice, and I wish I could confide in her now. Tell her everything – and ask why I feel guilty when no one in my family has done anything wrong. But that feels disloyal somehow, to my girls, so I just smile my gratitude and mouth *thank you*.

'Is it right that she's one of ours?' Victoria asks, the newest member of the team, and only recently out of university. She's impossibly glamorous, and I wonder why she makes so much effort for a team meeting when the rest of us are dressed in cheap suits from Next.

'Yes and no,' I say. 'Amber Walsh was a looked-after child, so she was with the foster team upstairs.'

'Who's her assigned social worker?' Elaine asks gently. 'Do you want to introduce yourself? I'm happy to come with you for moral support?'

I shake my head, push my lips together. I don't trust myself to speak.

'Of course,' Elaine murmurs, clocking my distress in an instant. 'There's no need for you to do that. I'm sure he or she will have their hands full with the police today anyway.'

'And I've got a no-names consultation this morning,' I add, still feeling like I need to explain my reluctance to Elaine. 'A teacher who's got some concerns about a child in her class. She's phoning at eleven, so I need to be on hand for that.'

Hugh looks at his watch. 'It sounds like we should wrap this up, and I think we've covered everything,' he says. 'Thanks, everyone, my door is always open, et cetera, et cetera.' He pushes out of his chair, picks up his pad of paper and a lever arch file, and leaves the meeting room. I watch him walk across to his office – the only one of us to have one – and pull the door closed behind him. I smile at the image, the first I've managed in days, then head over to my desk.

My office phone rings almost straight away. It's only ten to eleven, but I don't get many calls these days – replaced by fifty times as many emails – so I assume it's the teacher, Miss Sampson. We had a short conversation last week, but I could tell she was struggling to open up. Teachers know their responsibility is always to the child, but that doesn't mean they enjoy exposing parents' shortcomings, stirring up a possible hornets' nest. That's why a no-names consultation is a good starting place – a chance for teachers to air their concerns without any repercussions – but they know that anonymity can't be protected forever.

'Good morning. This is Rachel Salter.'

'Good morning, Ms Salter, this is DI Finnemore.'

My heart switches from a standing start to a gallop. I cover the mouthpiece and take a breath. But why am I reacting like this? Because I didn't name the victim, when I wasn't even sure who it was anyway? It's not exactly a crime. At least I hope it isn't.

'I wanted to check how you are,' he continues. 'And see whether a family liaison officer has been in touch?'

'Yes,' I whisper. 'Someone called PC Yates.' I deleted the email as soon as I saw it. I knew Matt wouldn't like me getting support from the police.

'That's good.' A short pause, then he continues. 'You might have heard, on the news, that we've got an identification for the victim.'

'I did, yes.'

'You said you didn't know her.'

There's a mix of accusation and disappointment in his voice, but that's not fair. I didn't know Amber Walsh. 'That's right, I didn't,' I say, trying to inject some authority into my words. 'But I knew her name when the news came out.'

'Because of your daughter Lucy?'

I close my eyes. But Lucy's bullying complaint was common knowledge among the senior leadership team at school; of course this connection was going to surface. It doesn't mean she's guilty of anything. 'Yes, that's right. Amber was bullying Lucy. The school was aware and the head teacher was dealing with it.'

'I've just come off the phone with Ms Munroe. She said that you last spoke to her about the issue on Friday. Because there'd been an incident earlier in the day.'

I pause, starkly aware of the timing. 'And in that meeting, Ms Munroe confirmed that she was going to speak to the girls' social worker,' I explain. 'She thought that would do the job of stopping them.'

'And how was Lucy?' he asks. 'After Friday's incident? Ms Munroe gave me the details. I imagine she was very upset, angry too no doubt.'

I choose my words carefully. 'It was distressing. But she was grateful that Ms Munroe was escalating things.'

He doesn't respond immediately, and the silence is excruciating. 'We're talking to a few students from the school who knew Amber,' he finally says. 'And it would be helpful if we could have a chat with Lucy.'

'Do you really need to?' I blurt out before I can stop myself. If Lucy couldn't make eye contact with people at the fair yesterday, I can't see her coping with a police interview. 'It's just that Lucy is quite shy. The idea of talking to a police officer will petrify her. And it's not like she knows anything about Amber's life – in fact, she avoided her as much as was humanly possible.'

'I understand,' DI Finnemore starts carefully. 'But this is a murder investigation, Ms Salter, which means we need to cast our net very broadly. I'm not suggesting Lucy is a suspect, but if we can talk to her, we might be able to get a better picture of who Amber was. See if she knows anything that might help. If you bring her to the station for nine tomorrow morning, you can stay with her throughout the interview, and we'll have her back in school by ten.'

I close my eyes again. I wonder for a mad moment if I should get a lawyer. Would Drew Torrance come if I called him? Throughout it all – the anonymous witness, the CPS deciding they had enough evidence to charge – he always believed in Matt's innocence. At least he said he did.

'Of course it is entirely voluntary,' DI Finnemore adds.

I flick open my eyelids. Lucy doesn't need a lawyer. She's done nothing wrong. 'That's fine,' I whisper. 'We'll be there.'

AFTER

Tuesday 7th May

Rachel

'I'm not going, Mum.' Lucy shakes her head. 'No way. You can't make me.' She drops onto the sofa, starts to pull her knees into her chest – a familiar position for her – then changes her mind and slides them away. 'Please,' she begs. 'Tell them I'm sick or something.'

I drop into the opposite sofa. 'I can see how talking to the police seems scary, but lots of kids from school are being asked. It'll be a ten-minute chat, max. There's nothing to worry about, I promise.'

'But what if they think I killed her?'

'Oh, Lucy!' I lean back against the sofa cushion. 'You keep saying that, but why on earth would people suspect you? Yes, Amber bullied you. But you were doing something about it via the proper channels. Lucy, you are the kindest, most gentle girl I know. Totally incapable of any type of violence, let alone murder. And the police will realise that as soon as they talk to you.'

'Do you really think so?' There's hope in her voice and I latch on to it.

'I know so,' I say in my most confident tone. 'Just tell them the truth and it will be fine.'

'Even about being out by myself on Friday night?'

I fall silent. I can't believe I'm not reacting instantly, saying yes, of course, you've got nothing to hide. Is this because of what happened to Matt? Knowing that innocent people can be labelled guilty if the circumstances stack up against them? 'I don't think you need to mention it,' I mumble, not managing to hold her gaze. Then I remember the girl who goaded Milla at the fair yesterday, what she knows. 'And if they ask directly, just say that you went out for some fresh air at about quarter to eleven, then I found you about half an hour later, and we walked back home together. Just so that DI Finnemore knows for certain that you couldn't have been on the Ridgeway.'

Her face drops. 'But I was in the churchyard the whole time, I promise!'

'Oh, I know.' I reach for her hand, to reassure her, and realise that she's shaking. The cuts on her fingers are still healing, and they feel ragged against my skin. 'You must know that there isn't one cell in my entire body that thinks you could have killed Amber Walsh,' I say. But the words ignite a flame of guilt. Because I didn't feel quite so certain about Milla at the weekend, before news of Amber's drug dealing filtered through.

'Will you come with me to talk to the detective?' Lucy asks.

'Of course.'

'And step in if he asks any difficult questions?'

I want to ask what she means by that, what questions she'd consider difficult. But I don't want to risk losing any ground I've made, so I just nod and smile instead. 'Listen, dinner's almost ready. I've made a green Thai curry.' The Asian dish is Lucy's favourite, and I've cooked it on purpose because she's hardly eaten since the incident at school on Friday. Or since I found Amber's body, it's hard to tell what sparked her lack of appetite.

'Amazing, thank you.' She smiles but it doesn't reach her eyes, and I ride a wave of sadness. Then I smile too – perhaps if we all pretend everything's fine, it will become so – and I head back into the kitchen.

'Nearly as good as it tasted in Bangkok,' Matt decrees, taking another mouthful.

'Ignore him,' Milla cuts in. 'It's delish.' She swirls her fork through the dish, mixing the curry sauce with the rice, then takes a large mouthful. Both of my children have a healthy relationship with food, and I've always been grateful for that. Except it doesn't look that way anymore.

'Are you not hungry, Lucy?'

Lucy looks up, startled, as though her mind was elsewhere. 'What? Sorry. I guess I'm just a bit nervous about tomorrow.'

'What's tomorrow?' Milla asks, shovelling another mouthful in.

'Oh, DI Finnemore – that's the detective who's leading the investigation into Amber Walsh's death – has asked me to take Lucy into the police station for a quick chat,' I say, trying to sound nonchalant. 'Just because she knew Amber, and they're trying to get a fuller picture of who she was.'

Milla puts down her fork. Her face suddenly drains of colour. 'But Lucy hardly knew Amber – she stayed as far away from her as possible.'

'I know, I did mention that.'

'So what can she add to the investigation? I think you should tell him she can't do it. Say she's sick or something.'

I narrow my eyes, shift my gaze between my daughters, who seem to be purposely not looking at each other. Have they already talked about this? They can't have discussed it face to face – Milla was upstairs until I called her down for supper – but Snapchat is their preferred form of communication these days. 'I've already been over this with Lucy,' I explain. 'It's just a chat. Lucy can explain that she never really knew Amber, and that will be it.'

'But Amber was bullying Lucy. The police might think that

gives Lucy motive to kill her. And you know what they're like – once they decide someone's guilty, they twist the evidence to prove it.' Milla turns to Matt. 'Don't they, Dad?'

Matt's smooth head has a new shine, a glean of sweat. 'Milla, you can't apply what happened to me to every police investigation.' He sounds guarded, like he's hiding whatever emotions are bubbling underneath. 'I know you're just looking out for your sister, but Lucy would appear more guilty if she didn't go.'

'But you were innocent,' Milla throws back.

'True. But for some unknown reason, there was a witness claiming I wasn't. No one is going to say they saw Lucy killing Amber Walsh, are they?'

Milla stares at Matt but doesn't answer straight away. She drags her bottom lip between her teeth. 'No, of course not,' she finally mutters. 'I just don't like that the evil little bitch is still causing her grief, even when she's dead.'

'Milla!' I snap. Lucy is sitting opposite me. Her head is down, but I can hear her breathing become more ragged.

'Let's talk about something else,' Matt suggests, lining his cutlery up on his empty plate. 'How was school today, Milla?'

'It was fine.'

'Care to expand on that?'

Milla lets out a loud sigh. 'We had a talk about dealing with exam stress. It's all about breathing apparently.'

'And good preparation,' Matt reminds her, still a teacher at heart.

'Can I leave the table?' Lucy asks, pushing to standing. 'I'm not hungry and I've got loads of homework to do.'

I sigh, nod, and watch my daughter disappear through the doorway. When I've finished my meal, I push my plate towards the centre of the table.

'Why don't you go and sit down,' Matt says. 'I'll clear up.'

'We could both go, leave the dishes until later?' I know Matt doesn't like walking away from a messy kitchen, but I'm impatient to talk to him about tomorrow, get his advice on how to handle the police. But he gives me one of his disparaging looks, then reaches for my plate.

I shake my head in defeat and walk through to the living room. I had planned to stop there, switch the TV on. But Matt's inflexibility has annoyed me, and the industrious banging and clattering from the kitchen is hurting my ears. So I climb the stairs and push on Lucy's bedroom door. She's not in there, but the sound of a toilet flushing from behind the bathroom door explains her absence. I'm about to step back, to wait for her to appear, when some words on her laptop screen catch my eye. After a split second of indecision, I walk into her bedroom.

The website is familiar – Google's search engine is endemic across the world – but the search request sends a shiver through my whole body. Poor Lucy. The words she's typed don't incriminate her in Amber's murder, of course they don't, but they do explain why she's scared about talking to the police. Why she's worried they're going to ask some difficult questions.

I feel a shadow behind me. Lucy, standing in the doorway. I turn, and our eyes connect for a moment, before we both shift our gaze to the computer screen, and the question Lucy has typed.

How do you hide a blog from the police?

AFTER

Wednesday 8th May

Rachel

I cut the engine and lean back against the headrest. 'Are you ready?' I ask gently.

'I'm scared, Mum. What if they've found the blog? All the stuff I've been writing about Amber and Jess?'

'It will be fine, I promise.' When Lucy realised that I'd seen her search criteria last night, she'd wavered for a moment, angry with me for invading her private space, but relieved that she could finally open up about what's been eating away at her since Saturday morning. And relief won out because she'd sunk onto her bed and told me everything. How she'd set up the blog a couple of months ago, in an anonymous name, but using her regular email address which is linked to our IP address at home. That she'd taken it down as soon as she heard about Amber's death but is paranoid that the police will still be able to find evidence of it.

Lucy loves to write, and while she's always got physical notebooks to hand, I know that blogging is the modern-day equivalent of journaling, so I wasn't exactly surprised. But I dreaded what private thoughts she might have shared online, and the impact they could have on the murder investigation. She refused to let me read her posts at first. But when I explained how I needed to know what we might be dealing with, that if the police ever found it, it was better for me to be forewarned, she'd eventually relented and opened up her WordPress account. Her blogger name is @ForBron and seeing it had brought Lucy's loss into focus once again. And how gutting it is, that at the point when Lucy most needs a best friend, Bronwen isn't here.

The blog – hidden from public view rather than deleted – made for uncomfortable reading. There are no names, but it's easy to work out who Lucy's referencing. The evil ringleader and her flame-haired sidekick. She describes her gnawing fear, but that she doesn't know what's scarier: the physical threat of a blade or the relentless humiliation. The blogposts hold plenty of self-criticism too. How she feels weak, cowardly, pathetic for not being able to stand up for herself. But it's the final piece that turned my discomfort into nausea. Posted on Friday afternoon. Describing how Amber had gone too far this time, that Lucy wouldn't stand for it anymore.

And from the safety of her bedroom, what she craved.

I wish she was dead.

The only wisp of good fortune is that none of Lucy's blogposts have hashtags, and she only has one follower – @cariad15, a profile without a photo. She explained to me that the purpose of the blog wasn't to find a community, but just to expel her frustrations. And that of course she didn't really want Amber dead.

I wrote a journal all the way through my teenage years, so I understand the need, but I wish she'd just put pen to paper like I did rather than upload it to the web. Because then we could have destroyed her writing, burned it on the fire or something. It sounds dramatic, but it's the opposite. It would keep life simple, and make sure the police could concentrate on finding out who actually killed Amber.

'I know how bad it reads,' she murmurs. 'But I never thought that something like this would happen.'

'Of course you didn't,' I say, too quickly. I take a breath. 'But I really don't think the police will have come across it, so you have nothing to worry about.' I think I believe it too. After all, it was just a silent cry for help into a virtual black hole. 'Remember, you're not a suspect.'

She nods, then gives me a half-smile. I squeeze her hand, then we both climb out of the car.

'Thanks for coming in, Lucy, sorry to keep you waiting. I'm DC Bzowski.' The detective drops into the chair opposite and places a thin cardboard file on the laminate table between us. She looks to be in her mid-twenties. Her dark hair is tied back, and her lips are glistening under a fresh layer of plum-coloured lipstick. She smiles at Lucy but doesn't offer her hand, and I'm grateful for the lack of formality. I was expecting DI Finnemore to appear, but this is better; someone more junior. It makes the whole thing feel less important.

'That's okay,' Lucy says. Her voice is singsong, and it highlights how young she is.

'I won't keep you long,' the detective promises. 'I just wanted to ask you a couple of questions and give you a chance to tell me anything you know that might help with the investigation.' She pauses. I wonder if Lucy might ask for clarification, a fuller explanation of what might help uncover a killer, but she just nods.

As my mind wanders to the crime dramas I watch on TV, I realise something is different. 'Don't you normally record interviews?' I ask.

'It depends on the type of interview,' the detective explains. 'Lucy isn't being interviewed under caution; this is just a chat, which is why we're in here.' She opens her palms and I glance around the room. Grubby white walls, thin carpet squares, and no recording equipment. 'We're actually hoping to set up an informal interview room at the school to talk to other students who knew Amber,' she goes on. 'But there's some reluctance from the governors, and we were keen to get started while memories are still fresh.'

I smile, but it's tight. It's a relief to know Lucy's words won't be stored anywhere, but she must be high on their priority list if they're not waiting to talk to her at school with the others.

'Okay,' DC Bzowski says, turning her attention back to Lucy. 'Lucy, we spoke to Ms Munroe, and she explained that you'd told your teachers that you were being bullied by Amber and her half-sister Jessica Scott.'

'Yes,' Lucy whispers. 'But …' Her voice trails off. Thank goodness. I don't want her blurting out another denial about murdering Amber.

'And did things improve at all with Amber at any point before her death?'

'No,' Lucy murmurs, her shoulders hunching up.

'Okay.' DC Bzowski nods, moves on. 'I understand there was a specific incident last Friday at school. Could you tell me what happened?'

'They stole my sports bag,' Lucy explains softly. 'And then emptied it.'

'That must have been upsetting.'

Lucy nods, pulls at her bottom lip.

'And did you manage to recover all of your items?'

Lucy looks ashen for a moment, the trauma of remembering, then her expression clears. 'Yes, eventually.'

'I explained to DI Finnemore that Ms Munroe was dealing with the bullying,' I say. 'She asked me to go in after school on Friday, and when I left that meeting, I was confident that it was the beginning of the end. We both were, weren't we, Lucy?' I look at my daughter, willing her to agree with me, but she just stares back blankly.

'Lucy, do you have a phone?' DC Bzowski asks. Lucy gives her a small nod. 'Would you mind telling me your number?'

I lean forward in my chair. Why is she asking this? Is she allowed to? Lucy looks at me but I'm no help. I stare back mutely, then give her a small nod. *It's fine; you've done nothing wrong.* That now familiar trope.

I listen to Lucy whisper the eleven-digit number and watch as the detective checks it against a printout. I can see that she's trying to keep her expression neutral, but a slight softening of her features gives her away. 'Thank you, Lucy,' she says, looking up at her. She waits a moment, then opens the file in front of her. 'I have Amber's phone records for Friday night here,' she says. 'They show that Amber sent you a text message at—' she checks the printout '—7.22 p.m. And that you responded a couple of minutes later.'

Lucy blinks. My ribcage expands as I hold my breath. A text conversation? With the girl who was making her life a misery?

'We are hoping that Amber's sister will be able to give us the code to unlock Amber's phone when she's ready to talk to us, so that we can check the content of those messages, but in the interests of time, could you tell me what they said?'

Lucy catches my eye, silently begs for my help. But I don't know what to say. I was primed to defend a threatening blog, not an exchange of text messages. I want to believe that Lucy just told Amber to leave her alone, but this is the second time she's kept something from me, and I'm starting to question my grip on the situation. Eventually Lucy turns back to the detective.

'She asked to meet me,' she admits in a whisper.

'Okay. And what did you say?'

'Um.' Lucy looks at me, the overhead light flickering against her blue irises. 'I said no.'

The detective nods, like she believes Lucy. I hope she does, but I'm not sure I do anymore. 'According to the records,' she continues gently, 'there are a further three text messages between

100

you in quick succession, followed by an incoming phone call from your number. What else did you and Amber talk about?'

'I don't remember.'

The detective crinkles her brow, an exaggerated gesture, clearly for effect. 'Really?' she asks. 'It wasn't that long ago.'

'Um …' Lucy's eyes skitter as she tries to find a coherent response. 'I just told her to stop texting me,' she finally offers.

'Wouldn't it have been easier to block her instead?'

'I didn't think …'

DC Bzowski suddenly flashes another one of her lipstick-framed smiles. 'Okay. So to clarify, you didn't go out to meet Amber on Friday night?'

I try to make eye contact with my daughter, but Lucy's avoiding my gaze altogether now. I'm not sure whether that's because she's angry with me for not shielding her from DC Bzowski's questions, or because she's about to lie. Again. 'No, I didn't meet her,' she says. 'I called to say I was blocking her,' she clarifies. 'And to leave me alone.'

The detective leans back in her chair. She's quiet for a moment, as though deciding what to say next. 'Did you go out at all on Friday night?' she finally asks. 'I understand there was a big party in the village.'

Lucy's eyes flit towards me again. I wish she didn't look so guilty. 'I didn't go to the party,' she says. 'It was my sister's best friend's eighteenth, so it was mainly the Year Thirteens.'

'So you stayed at home?' the detective prompts. Her eyes have narrowed with focus and a burst of realisation explodes inside me. She knows Lucy went out. There must be CCTV or something, proof that she was roaming the streets – the village shops might have cameras, and some people have those video doorbells that pick up passers-by.

'I went out for a bit,' Lucy mumbles. 'I couldn't sleep so I went for a walk around the village.'

'What time was this?' the detective asks. I try to blink at Lucy, as though she might be able to decipher the acronym CCTV from my frantic eyelids.

'Around quarter to eleven.' My chest shrivels. The lie is out, and I have no idea whether DC Bzowski can prove it or not.

'On your own?'

'At first, yes. Then Mum came and we walked home together. About half an hour later.'

'And you definitely didn't see Amber?'

'No, sorry.'

Lucy's voice is wobbling. I need to do something. 'DC Bzowski, Lucy's already told you she didn't see Amber,' I say. 'Can we move on?'

The detective looks at me, her expression hard to read. 'We've been checking CCTV from the post office, and a girl who looks a lot like Lucy passes by, but it was earlier than ten forty-five, before ten in fact.'

Lucy throws me a petrified look. 'That's strange,' I ad-lib while my mind clatters through what to say next. The post office is on Keens Lane, around the corner from the parade of shops. Lucy wouldn't come into view on the route to the church unless the camera has a very wide-angled perspective. 'How clear are the images?'

'Not hugely,' the detective admits. 'But we're keen to work out who the girl is.'

'Why her specifically?' I ask. 'I guess there were plenty of people walking past during the evening?'

'There were, you're right,' DC Bzowski says. 'But there are reasons why this person is of particular interest.' She smiles again. I fight an urge to launch myself across the table, grab her shirt collar and demand a fuller explanation.

'Lucy, have you ever smoked marijuana?' the detective asks.

'What? No.'

'Taken ecstasy?'

Lucy shakes her head. 'I've never done any drugs, ever.'

'Do you drink alcohol then?'

'Not really,' Lucy murmurs, her confidence waning again. 'I've tried wine a few times.'

'Have you ever drunk vodka?'

I tense. Remember the bottle Lucy stole, the shards of glass hanging from its broken neck in the churchyard. 'Why are you asking that?' I say, wishing I didn't sound so defensive.

DC Bzowski hesitates for a moment then apparently decides she wants us to know. 'Preliminary reports on Amber's clothing suggest that there were significant traces of vodka on both her top and jeans. The girl in the CCTV image was carrying a plastic bag with something heavy inside. We wondered if it might be a bottle of vodka.'

Email from DI Finnemore (SIO) to Det Supt Bishop

Subject: Wednesday 8th May update

Sir,

Hope conference is going well. Investigation is in a good place, I think. We have a suspect – but evidence is circumstantial at the moment and I'm conscious we need to strengthen the forensic case against them. Will update you as and when I have more concrete info.

Have received initial post-mortem results for victim (excludes toxicology, DNA, etc.). Cause of death was subdural haematoma. There was bruising and lacerations to the victim's face and a fracture on the frontal bone of the skull, but the fracture that caused the fatal bleed was to the occipital bone at the back. Initial theory is that the victim was hit face-on with a weapon, causing her to fall backwards onto a rock which ultimately killed her. Blood spatter supports that. No weapon retrieved from scene, but based on size and shape of the front impact wound, plus evidence of tramline bruising, it's likely to be a blunt cylindrical instrument. Possibly a baseball bat. Forensic team are looking at potential matches. But too narrow for a vodka bottle apparently – see later.

There were also cuts to the victim's hand. Specks of glass were removed and sent for analysis. No evidence of sexual assault. Saliva detected on skin around mouth. Skin cells found underneath victim's fingernails signifying some evidence of fighting back. Both sent off for DNA analysis. A couple of hairs found on victim's top. No follicle on either so can't retrieve DNA but don't belong to victim. Long and light in colour – so could be cross-contamination from woman who found the body (Ms Salter). Will get a sample from her for the forensic team. All clothing swabbed. Awaiting results of blood analysis but clear smell of alcohol on victim's top and jeans – best guess is vodka but waiting for confirmation.

Time of death between 10 p.m. and 4 a.m. so not overly helpful based on what we know already. Confirmed that murder took place at scene. No footprints found yet, but CSI are checking route back to the village. It rained quite heavily overnight so not optimistic. Perpetrator could also have driven – there is a car park a fifteen-minute walk south of the crime scene, away from the village. Tyre tracks from two cars visible despite the rain, but these may well be unrelated.

Victim's sister has moved back in with foster carers but was difficult to interview. Very wary of me. Her mother was beaten to death by her partner – when Jessica was 8 years old, and in bed in the next room – so maybe not surprising. Decided not to ask for DNA sample (for elimination purposes) just yet – will wait for forensics before deciding if it's necessary. Jess didn't know the code to Amber's phone unfortunately, so we only have phone records – and masts are over a kilometre apart, so triangulation results are too broad to be helpful. Jess did admit to knowing her sister wasn't home at 23.00 – she texted her to ask where she was – but then she clammed up again. My guess is she fell back to sleep, and now feels guilty for it. And we have contacted Meta and Snapchat for access to those accounts but I'm not holding my breath.

CCTV from three shops in the village plus the post office and railway station car park has been collected for the ten hours between 20.00 Friday and 06.00 Saturday and we have started to look through it. Amber picked up three times between 20.12 and 21.47. Always alone. Nothing after that, but the uniforms confirmed she didn't attend youth club at all. We have started interviewing students at Lord Frederick's and there is a consistent narrative that the victim was dealing marijuana and ecstasy. Nothing found at the foster home, but toxicology and forensic reports might reveal more on that.

Both reports due tomorrow.

Simon

THE NIGHT SHE DIES

Friday 3rd May

Jess

Jess scrabbles around for her phone. She knows it's on the duvet somewhere, but she's too tired to sit up and look for it. Pulling that stunt with Lucy Rose's sports bag, then getting bawled out by Munroe, has left her exhausted. Eventually her fingers graze over the cool glass screen. 'She'll just block you like she did me,' she warns her sister as she scrolls through for Lucy's contact details.

'Just read out her number,' Amber orders from the bottom bunk. She's not even trying to pretend they're equals this evening, and Jess feels a mix of anger and anxiousness. Amber was her usual sassy self when they went back to class after lunch, but she was different when they met up after school. Quieter. Which is never a good sign with Amber.

'Lucy Rose will meet us tonight, trust me,' Amber adds.

Jess rises up from her pillow and curls over the bed frame until she can see her sister. But her expression gives nothing away. 'Why are you so sure?'

Amber tilts her head to meet Jess's eye. 'Because I found

something in her school bag. Something important. At first I thought it could be bad for us, but then I realised it's an opportunity. A chance to show Sean what I'm capable of.'

Jess curls back onto her mattress and stares at the ceiling. Her and Amber's lives have never been good, or stable, or secure. There was time with their mum and Tyler, then a blur of temporary foster homes, followed by Lou and Justin's, and now this place. But throughout it all, there have been moments when they've been able to forget about all that. Amber dressing up in Lou's high heels and model-walking down a pretend catwalk. Jess feeding her entire meal to the neighbour's visiting cat without Justin noticing, until the cat gave her away by throwing up on the carpet.

Maybe they've got too old, but that kind of fun doesn't feel possible anymore.

With a sense of defeat, she reads out Lucy's phone number and listens to Amber tapping on her phone. 'What are you saying?'

'Telling her what I've got. And to meet us at ten if she wants it back. We'll be busy before then – I don't even reckon we'll have chance to show our faces at youth club tonight, because I promised two Year Thirteens that I'd sort them out in the rec before that big party, and I want to hang around the birthday girl's house for a bit too, try to make a little extra cash. I'll message Bill saying we're back home – they'll be in bed by then and won't check – and then we'll meet Lucy. It'll be fully dark by ten too.'

'She's already petrified of you. I can't see anything being important enough for her to risk coming out for.'

'She'll come,' Amber says, staring at her phone. 'And she'll have the bottle of vodka I've told her to bring. And that's all you need to know for now.'

Jess bites her lip. But it's always been this way, she reminds herself: Amber putting herself in charge. Treating Jess like a toy she can play with. It's too late to kick up a fuss now. 'What about Caden?' she asks. When she met her sister at the bus stop on Wednesday night to walk back home, Amber couldn't stop talking about him.

'I don't know. I'm kind of getting the ick.'

Jess feels a sudden spasm in her chest. She rolls back over her bed frame, looks down. 'I thought you were totally into him?'

'He's too needy. Keeps going on about how beautiful I am and stuff. He reckons he's going to try and gate-crash that party with some mates. If I see him, I might finish it. I don't think Sean liked him either.'

Jess stares at Amber. Why does someone so heartless get Charli D'Amelio looks? It's obvious now that her thing with Caden was just about making Sean jealous. Jess wonders again what Sean's power is, why Amber is so enthralled by him. She wishes it was something romantic like chemistry, but deep down she knows it's more depressing than that. That it's because he's dangerous.

A buzzing noise interrupts her thoughts. Then the sound of Amber typing.

'What are you saying?' Jess asks. 'Is she going to meet you?'

'Shit, she's calling me,' Amber says. 'She must be crapping herself.'

Jess wonders again what Amber has of Lucy's, but she doesn't ask. She's done with being patronised by her sister. Instead, she listens to Amber's one-word answers. 'So?' she asks when Amber finishes the call.

'We're meeting her at ten,' Amber says. 'On the track that goes up to the Ridgeway. By the double gates next to the railway line.' She unfolds from the bottom bunk and walks over to the mirror. 'Better put some make-up on. This is stacking up to be an interesting night.'

'What do you mean I can't go out?!' Jess squeals. 'It's Friday. We've got youth club!'

'Yes, I know,' Molly says, trying to pretend she feels bad about it. 'But you're grounded, remember? For trying to steal that bottle of wine from Mr and Mrs Gilbey.'

'Oh for fuck's sake.' Anger flares in Jess's belly. Amber might get to treat her like shit, but Molly doesn't. 'I didn't steal the fucking wine!'

'Right, that's enough,' Bill says, taking a step forward, protecting his wife like he thinks he'd stand a chance. 'You don't speak to Molly like that. I want you to go to your room until you've calmed down.'

'No,' Jess spits out. 'I'm going out.' She folds her arms, glares at him. If he touches her now, she will swing for him, show Amber that she can be tough too. But it's her sister's hand that rests on her forearm.

'She's really sorry,' Amber says, taking a micro step forward, the honey voice back. 'But Jess was never going to steal that bottle. I dared her to grab it, just to see if she could. We were always going to put it back. But then the old man from your church saw her, and got the wrong impression, and, well, you know the rest.'

Jess looks at her sister. How can she be like this? Horrible one minute, then having Jess's back the next? Indecision hovers on Molly's face. Jess wills the old lady to relent.

'It's good of you to stand up for your sister, Amber,' Bill says, stepping in again. 'And I can see how that situation might have occurred. But there's no excuse for swearing at Molly. And you girls need to learn that if we dish out a punishment, we follow through with it. It's just one Friday night, Jess. You can watch TV with Molly and me or hang out in your room.'

Jess and Amber share a look. But for the first time, Jess can't decipher her sister's silent message. Does she want Jess to sneak out? She's done it before. Or is this the night that Amber stops needing Jess's help with her plans? Has Jess blindly become such dead weight that Amber doesn't want to be dragged down anymore?

Either way, she needs to lower the temperature in the room.

'Okay, fine,' she manages. 'And, um, sorry for swearing at you, Molly.'

'That's okay, love.' Molly gives her a relieved smile.

'Will you stay in with your sister, Amber?'

'I would, but I promised Ellen that I'd braid her hair at youth club,' Amber lies. 'And we're making up sweet bags for the fun day on Monday, I think.'

'Of course, love. That will be fun.' Molly looks at her watch. 'My goodness, it's coming up eight o'clock. You better be going.'

'Thanks, Molly. I'll text you when I'm back, but I've got my keys, so don't wait up. See ya, Jess.' Amber winks at Jess – somewhere between conspiratorial and triumphant – then waltzes out of the back door.

'Want to watch *Gardener's World* with us, Jess?'

'No. Thanks,' she adds. 'I'm really tired actually, I might get an early night.' Jess manages a half-smile, then walks up the stairs. She drops onto Amber's bunk. Should she stay at home? Let Amber do to Lucy whatever it is that's going to impress Sean?

Or should she shove pillows under the duvet and sneak out?

And would it be to help Amber, or to stop her doing something stupid?

AFTER

Wednesday 8th May

Rachel

Shit, shit, shit, shit. Lucy must have met Amber on Friday night. It's too much of a coincidence otherwise – her sneaking out without telling anyone, swiping the bottle of vodka from our drinks cabinet, two things she's never done before. And possibly being caught on camera on Keens Lane. But she can't have killed Amber. Lucy is a sweet, kind, well-adjusted 15-year-old girl, for fuck's sake. Statistically speaking, there must be more chance of her winning the lottery than committing murder.

Jeez, where did the lottery analogy come from?

I shake my head, grip the steering wheel more tightly. The muscles in my hands ache with the effort, but I don't ease off.

'Are you okay, Mum?' Lucy asks meekly.

'What do you think?!' I can't help raising my voice, even though she's the one who's been through the stress of DC Bzowski's questioning. I do stop myself from making eye contact though. I've never been good at hiding my feelings, and one quick check in the rear-view mirror reveals how much I'm seething. 'You met

Amber on Friday night,' I say, staring at the grey asphalt flying towards me through the windscreen, not willing to pose it as a question. 'Did you not think to tell me that part before we walked into the police station?'

'Mum, please.' Her voice cracks and I can tell without looking that she's crying. And with that realisation, my anger evaporates. Motherhood has always been like this for me. Swerving emotions, moments of fury that vanish in an instant. The heavy weight of love.

'I'm sorry,' I whisper, and allow myself a glance in Lucy's direction. It will take me about half an hour to drive to school, and I'm grateful for the time. Lucy's eyes are red-rimmed, and her chest is convulsing with swallowed sobs, but I can't give her the space to recover yet. Not until I've found out exactly what happened on Friday night. 'But can you please just tell me the truth?'

Lucy sniffs. 'I did agree to meet Amber,' she admits. 'And I stole your vodka because she demanded a bottle.'

'But why would you do that?' I ask.

'She took something out of my schoolbag,' Lucy whispers. 'I didn't realise at first – I was too stressed about my sports bag. But when she texted, I checked, and it was gone. I needed it back.'

'What was it?'

'I don't want to tell you,' Lucy says dully.

'A girl is dead, Lucy! The same girl who stole whatever it was you were so desperate to get back.'

'It was a letter, okay?' Lucy cuts in, suddenly exasperated. 'From Bronwen. It was …' She trails off, and we sit in silence for a few seconds until she finds the words. 'It was for my eyes only.'

I want to ask exactly what Bronwen had written, but that would make me as bad as Amber, so I let it go. Silence settles between us for a while, but as we pass the signpost for Notley Abbey – a medieval building once owned by Laurence Olivier – I realise that time is running out. I think about the bottle of vodka, how it was broken, but still in Lucy's possession when I found her.

'And did you get the letter back?' I ask.

'No,' she says mournfully. 'I was supposed to meet Amber on the old railway line, by the gates we go through when we're running. But I fell over on my way up there, I was so nervous, and I dropped the bag. The bottle of vodka smashed on the pavement. I figured Amber would never give me the letter without anything to exchange, so I didn't go and meet her. I went to the church instead.' She scoffs. 'I decided praying was all I had left.'

I think back to finding Lucy folded up in the church porch. I want to believe her, but the detective's final words repeat in my head. 'If you didn't meet her,' I ask, 'how come Amber had vodka on her clothes?'

I sense Lucy chewing the inside of her cheek. 'I don't know, Mum. Honestly. But I guess she got it from someone else. Teenagers drink vodka like your friends neck Prosecco.'

She's right. It's crazy that kids cut their teeth on forty per cent proof alcohol, but I know vodka has always been Milla's staple drink. Then another thought hits me. If Lucy didn't get the letter back, does that mean Amber had it in her possession when she died? And if so, why didn't DC Bzowski mention it? Is she waiting for Lucy to incriminate herself? Unless Amber didn't have it on her. She could have been lying about giving the letter back just to entice Lucy out. Does that mean it's in her bedroom? Will the police search there?

My head is so full that I almost miss the turn-off for Lord Frederick's, but luckily my muscle memory kicks in, and I swing into the car park just in time. 'Will you be okay?' I ask when Lucy doesn't move. But then she dabs her lower eyelids, and picks up her bag with a small grimace.

'I'll be fine,' she says, pushing open the car door. 'At least I don't have to hide from anyone anymore.'

I nod, force a smile, then watch her walk towards the school reception. But her newfound freedom isn't something I can celebrate.

Matt is hovering in the kitchen when I get home. He's flying to Geneva this afternoon, a short trip to the Lionheart school there, and I was secretly hoping he'd have already left. I couldn't bring myself to tell him about Lucy's blog last night, and now there are even more revelations. But I know I would have waited for him if our roles were reversed, so I suppose I can't blame him.

'Well?' he asks.

I flip down the kettle switch and listen to it groan into life. Then I take a long breath and tell Matt everything. Lucy's blog, her text exchange with Amber, Bronwen's letter, and the aborted rendezvous.

'Wow,' he mumbles. He picks the dishcloth out of the sink and runs it along the oak countertop. His expression is so vacant that I wonder if he even realises he's doing it. 'But DC Bzowski seemed satisfied with Lucy's answers?' he finally asks. 'If Lucy didn't meet up with Amber, and the police believe that she didn't, then things are okay, yes?' He folds the cloth and places it back in the bowl.

'But what if they decide that it is Lucy on the CCTV?'

'Then she says she got confused about the timing because she'd left her phone at home. None of the kids wear watches these days, so it's perfectly plausible.'

'And if they've found Bronwen's letter on Amber and haven't mentioned it yet? I think Bronwen might be Lucy's one follower on that blog,' I continue. 'The name looks like a Welsh word, and Lucy's username is @ForBron. Which means she'll know what Amber and Jess have been doing to Lucy. What if she refers to it in her letter? Or even encourages Lucy to fight back?'

'Come on, Rachel. You're not thinking straight. Bronwen is as unlikely to suggest anything violent as Lucy is to carry it out. If the detective didn't mention the letter, it probably means they haven't found it.'

'So where is it?'

Matt runs his palm from his forehead to the back of his neck. 'Maybe Amber threw it away. Or perhaps she never had it. And sorry to say it, but there's always the chance an animal took it from her corpse overnight. What's most important is that we don't worry about something that isn't yet a problem.'

I know he's right, and it's good to hear him say it. I manage a half-smile. 'Why do you think Lucy didn't tell us?'

'About her text conversation with Amber?'

'Yes. And going out to meet her. And the blog. It's almost like she feels guilty about something.'

Matt's eyes narrow. 'Something like murder you mean?'

'No, of course not.'

But Matt doesn't let me off the hook. 'On Saturday morning you as good as accused Milla of killing Amber, and what, now it's Lucy's turn? Just think about what you're saying. That our wonderful daughter followed Amber onto the Ridgeway in the dead of night, then smashed her skull in with some makeshift weapon she happened to have on her person. Do you really think she's capable of that?'

I look away. My legs buckle and I slide down the cupboards onto the floor. Matt stands over me with a rueful expression.

'I'm sorry, I shouldn't have been so graphic. I just wanted to make you see how crazy the idea is. Maybe Lucy had a motive, and yes, I suppose Milla had the opportunity. But that doesn't mean anything without the means – which includes the mental capacity to take a life. And you know neither of our children have that.'

I look deep into his eyes. They're so different to mine, dark and impenetrable, like Milla's. I haven't got the energy to speak, but I mouth 'thank you' and reach my arms out. He folds his own around me and pulls me up to standing. We stay like that for a while, me trying to infuse his unwavering belief in the innocence of our daughters, until he slowly disentangles himself.

'I'm sorry I have to leave you with all this going on,' he says, checking his watch and stepping away. He snaps up the long handle on his cabin bag.

'It's fine,' I say. 'We'll be fine.'

He smiles. 'I'll be back on Friday, okay? Late morning. Tell the girls I love them.' He gives me a quick kiss – perfunctory now he's back in work mode – then heads outside. I follow him into the porch so that I can wave him off, and then watch his car disappear down our narrow drive.

As I turn to go back inside, I notice a plastic bag wedged up against the porch door frame. And when I look inside, I find four huge cooking apples. A gift from Mrs Jones next door – she must have dropped them off when Matt and I were talking. A rush of fear runs through me as I think back to our conversation, what she could have overheard. But I'm being paranoid. The walls of this old cottage are too thick for level voices to travel.

Our porch is the one place in the house – other than the girls' bedrooms since the agreement was reached a couple of years ago – that Matt isn't neurotic about keeping tidy. As a result, it's a mess, with mud-caked wellies, tennis rackets, old flip-flops and other odds and sods cast around. I wonder if I should tidy it up as a gesture of goodwill. But as I pause to consider the task, I spot the torch on top of a box of old newspapers. Milla must have dumped it there when she got home in the early hours of Saturday morning. I roll my eyes, pick it up, and slide it under my arm carrying the apples. I walk through to the kitchen, and it's only when I drop the bag on the worktop that I notice the stains on my jumper.

'Great,' I mutter under my breath. The torch handle is filthy. Milla must have dropped it in some mud when she fell asleep. With a sigh, I run it under the hot tap, and leave it on the drainer to dry.

AFTER

Wednesday 8th May

Rachel

I'm supposed to be working from home this afternoon, and I've got half a dozen reports to review, but I can't concentrate. With a sigh, I lean back in my chair and flip down the laptop screen.

Maybe I need some fresh air.

Decision made, I pull on my trainers and head outside. The temperature is fresh, but the sun's shining and there's a sense of spring in the air. I suck it in. Amber's death is a profound tragedy, and my heart goes out to her sister, who's already suffered so much loss. But I have no reason to feel guilty. Because her death has nothing to do with my family.

By the time I reach The Crown, I'm warm and thirsty. We've been coming to this pub, off and on, for seventeen years, so I know most of the bar staff, and especially Steve and Jade who've been running the place for even longer than we've lived here. I push open the door and head to the bar. It's relatively quiet – just a couple of tables filled with people I don't recognise – and Steve comes straight over. 'Hey, Rachel, don't normally see you in here at lunchtime?'

I climb onto a bar stool. 'Working from home today, fancied a change of scenery.' I was planning to order a Coke, but now I'm sitting opposite the gleaming draught pumps, I hear myself order half a Moretti instead. I watch Steve pour the drink, then raise the glass to him when I take my first sip.

'Terrible business, isn't it,' he says, nodding his head in the vague direction of the Ridgeway. 'A murder in Chinnor. Hard to believe.'

'Mmm,' I murmur, taking another sip. I left home to get away from thinking about Amber Walsh, but I should have known better.

'They're journalists over there,' Steve continues when I don't bite, gesturing towards one of the tables where two men and a woman are hunched over empty coffee cups and oversized iPhones. 'The *Bucks Herald*, the *Oxford Mail* and the *Bucks Free Press*,' Steve lists, counting them off on his fingers. 'Apparently a couple of the nationals were sniffing around at the weekend, but as soon as they heard that the victim was a foster kid dealing drugs, they lost interest. Like it's not really news if someone like her gets killed.'

'God, that's shit, isn't it?' While the last thing I want is for this case to get any more publicity, I hate the idea that lives have different values. If Amber was middle-class and played the violin, her picture would be on the front page of every newspaper. My eyes grow hot as that thought develops. If it had been Lucy up there on the Ridgeway, or Milla, they would be household names by now. Talked about in coffee shops and around family dinner tables up and down the country. But not so with Amber. She's destined to be a statistic, an anonymised example of how the state is still failing our most vulnerable.

As a social worker, it's my job to rail against this reality, to show the world that looked-after children deserve the same love and respect as their peers with stable homes, and that every backward step on that journey is a tragedy. But that's not how I feel today.

Right now, those statistics are my reassurance. A framework to hang my own children's innocence on.

'Have you heard anything?' I ask. 'About the police investigation?'

'Well,' Steve starts, pretending to sound reluctant, then leaning in. 'Between you and me, I did hear that the police fancy someone for it.' He shrugs. 'If the girl was selling drugs, maybe he was her dealer.'

'Really?' It comes out as a squeak, so I take a sip of beer. 'Who told you that?'

'Do you know Julie and Keith?' he asks, lowering his voice.

I shake my head, shrug my shoulders.

'Yeah, you do. He's a Formula One nut, always banging on about that TV show *Drive to Survive*. Anyway, he works at the tyre place in Thame. Which is next door to McCormick's garage. Do you know where I mean?'

An image of a small, tired-looking unit on the industrial estate comes to me. Cracked alarm box and forest green hoarding. 'I think so.'

'Keith was on his lunch break yesterday when two detectives turned up and hauled off some young bloke from the garage. He asked around, and apparently it was in connection with the murder.'

'Wow,' I say, taking a bigger gulp of beer. A male mechanic. Strong enough to smash a girl's face in. Of course it would be someone like that. 'Did Keith say anything else?'

'Only that the lad's been in trouble before. McCormick was giving him a second chance. Oh, and that the police took some bits away with them, in those evidence bags.'

'What bits?'

'I dunno. Christ, I hope she wasn't whacked with one of McCormick's tools,' he adds, grimacing. 'Can you imagine how much damage a wrench or a hammer would do in the wrong hands?'

I force a murmur of assent, which turns into a cough, my eyes watering with the effort. Steve's face drops. 'Shit, sorry, Rachel. I forgot you found her. How are you? God, here's me going on about the murder weapon when you saw it all with your own eyes.'

'It wasn't the best,' I manage.

He nods, but his expression morphs into awkwardness. As though he's worried that I'm going to start crying on him. 'Another half?' he says hopefully. 'On the house?' But I need to get back outside, find the sunshine again.

'No. Thanks though. I'll see you soon, Steve.' I drain my drink, give him a quick wave, then slide off the bar stool. I focus my gaze on the polished wooden floor in case any of the journalists try to make eye contact, but they seem more bored than curious.

Clouds have come over while I've been inside, and the wind's picked up, but I still feel better than I did before I left home. If Steve's right, someone is going to be charged with the murder soon, and we can all start to move on. I need a few things for supper, and I'm in no hurry to go back to my empty house, so I turn left instead of right out of the pub, and head towards the Co-op, inside Chinnor's only petrol station.

I push open the door and bump straight into Annie holding a basket. I expect her to launch into conversation, but she doesn't say a word. I worry for a moment that it's awkwardness, the secret I've forced her to keep about Milla without saying a word. But then she angles her head towards the next aisle along and gives me a hard stare. A stare that says, DON'T LOOK OVER THERE. I automatically shift my gaze to where I'm not supposed to. Then wish I hadn't.

Jess Scott stares back at me, her face ashen. I think it's grief at first, but then realise it's white-hot rage.

I want to turn away, pretend I don't recognise her, leave the shop. But I can tell she knows who I am, Lucy Rose's mother, and the woman who found her sister. I need to be braver. 'Hello,' I say. 'It's Jess, isn't it?'

She nods but doesn't speak. Her red hair is loose on her

shoulders and looks like it hasn't been brushed in days. She's tall, angular, and with a wildness about her that makes the shelves appear like the iron bars of a cage. She's holding a bag of Skittles, but her grip is so strong, I worry that it's going to burst.

'I'm so sorry,' I start. 'About your sister. I can't imagine what you must be going through right now …' I trail off, and silence reigns once again, but Jess is staring so intently, that I don't feel like I can break eye contact. I sense Annie backing away, and I'm both sad to lose her support, and grateful that she's not witnessing this exchange.

'Bill said you found her,' Jess says suddenly, making me jump.

'Um, yes, that's right,' I answer, nodding. 'I go running up there.'

'I know,' she cuts in. 'Amber used to watch you. With Lucy.'

I pull my bottom lip with my teeth. The thought of Amber watching us run causes a rush of nausea, even though she can't hurt us now. But I shouldn't take it out on her bereaved sister. Lucy always said that Amber was the real bully, Jess just her sidekick. 'That's right. We run together sometimes, but I was on my own on Saturday.'

'So did Lucy tell you where to find her?'

My pulse rate ticks up. 'Sorry?'

'Where she left Amber's body after she killed her?'

My heart is booming now. My skin fizzing. I'm aware this means my fight-or-flight mode has kicked in, but I don't seem capable of either. 'That's, that's not true,' I stutter.

She takes a step towards me. She's taller than me, but her face is still childlike. 'Are you sure?' she presses. Her eyes are blue, impossibly bright, and her face is covered in freckles. She's beautiful, I realise. I hadn't noticed at first.

'Of course I'm sure,' I whisper. I want to take a step back, but I'm already close to the shelves and I don't want to knock anything off, give the other shoppers a reason to look over.

'We'll see about that,' she says, then twists away from me and walks out of the shop.

AFTER

Wednesday 8th May

Rachel

I pull the door closed behind me and let out a sigh of relief. I was desperate to get out of the house earlier, but now it feels like my sanctuary. Shelter from Jess Scott's wild stare. I wander over to the sofa, fold into the worn cushions, and close my eyes. Did Jess accuse Lucy of Amber's murder to upset me? Lashing out because she's in pain? Or does she really think Lucy killed her sister?

I think about what I've discovered over the last twenty-four hours. It makes sense that Jess knew about Amber trying to meet up with Lucy – the sisters were clearly close – so perhaps she assumed they did, and then decided Lucy must be guilty because she was the last person Amber saw.

But they didn't meet up. That's what Lucy said.

I drop my head back, open my eyes, and stare at the white ceiling. I heard via one of the WhatsApp groups that Jess was grounded on Friday night, so she won't have seen anything herself. But she was Amber's sister, and I remember DC Bzowski mentioning that they'd talked to her about Amber's phone. Did she tell them that she thinks Lucy's the murderer? And if she did, would they have taken any notice? The police know about the bullying, and how Jess and Amber didn't like Lucy, so surely they wouldn't take any accusations she might have made seriously?

But if that's true, why did DI Finnemore insist on Lucy coming to the station, rather than waiting to talk to her at school? They didn't know who Amber's text conversation was with until they asked for Lucy's phone number. And the CCTV of the blonde girl outside the post office could have been a couple of dozen different girls who live in the village. Was it something Jess said that singled Lucy out as a person of interest?

And while I can hardly bear to think about it, is there a chance they've also found Lucy's blog? *I wish she was dead.*

I push off the sofa. I feel on edge now, like I need to expel some tension, so I start pacing, up and down the carpet. The mechanic that Steve told me about killed Amber, I remind myself. He was probably her drug dealer, like Steve said. Forensics will prove he did it and this will all be over.

I freeze. An image from Friday night blows up, high definition, in my mind.

The cuffs of Lucy's jumper covered in blood.

Her blood. From the cuts on her hands. Wasn't it?

I blink, then grab the banister and rattle up the stairs. I don't hesitate before pushing open Lucy's bedroom door – she's lost all her privacy privileges. When we got back on Friday night, Lucy went straight upstairs to dress the cuts. And when she came back down for hot chocolate, she'd changed into her pyjamas. I haven't seen the clothes she was wearing since then, not in the laundry, or hanging out to dry, so they must still be in her room.

For years, both girls' bedrooms were always immaculate, because their pocket money was conditional upon it, and Matt has high standards. But two years ago, Milla negotiated a new normal. It was soon after Matt was charged with assault, but it wasn't about Milla sensing vulnerability and taking her chance. She was old enough by then to recognise how Matt's obsessive nature grew more and more extreme as his stress levels rose, and this was a way of protecting them both. She promised to stick to his strict rules in the rest of the house, if he gave her free rein over her own bedroom.

Lucy was given the same privileges, but she's never taken advantage of them. I'm not sure whether that's because she likes her things to be tidy too, or because she wants to please her dad, but either way, it doesn't take me long to find the only item of clothing not folded away. A scrunched-up pair of jeans shoved under her bed.

Tentatively I straighten them out, then inspect them like I imagine a police officer would. There are muddy patches on the knee and shin areas, but that fits with Lucy's explanation that she fell over on her way to meet Amber. There are a few darker stains higher up, and I ride a wave of nausea as I realise that it's dried blood. Could Lucy really have bled this much from a few finger cuts? But I saw Amber's wounds too, and these marks aren't big enough to be from her injuries. With only the slightest stab of guilt, I drop the jeans by the door – they need washing after all – and carry on with my search.

I look through every drawer and along each hanger, but the jumper Lucy was wearing isn't here. Has she taken it to school? Has she worn it even though the cuffs were filthy?

Does she have a reason to hide it somewhere?

My phone buzzes in my pocket, and when I fish it out, I see that it's a message from Matt. He's arrived safely and is in a cab on the way to the Lionheart school in Geneva, excited to see it for the first time. He sounds so normal. So unburdened. Why can't I be like that? With a deep breath, I pick up Lucy's jeans and head back downstairs and into the kitchen. I put them on the hottest possible wash, with added stain remover, and watch as they curl around the drum for a few seconds before being engulfed by froth and bubbles. Washing the problem away. It feels like good advice.

A quick glance at the kitchen wall clock shows me that it's almost 3 p.m., and I haven't eaten lunch, or done any work yet. I push off my haunches and lift the lid off the bread bin. As I drop two slices into the toaster – Marmite on toast always my go-to comfort food – I notice the torch on the drainer. I may as well put that back in the shed while I wait for my toast to pop up. But when I reach for it, I realise I haven't done a great cleaning job, because there's a residue mark left on the white enamel. It's a rusty colour – a mix of brown and red – and I inspect the torch for signs of erosion. But the black aluminium is as good as new. And it's rechargeable so batteries can't be the culprit. I frown. Maybe the mud is redder up by Kiln Lakes. It is an old industrial site so that probably makes sense.

With my confusion settling a notch, I carry the torch out to the garden. It's heavy – a couple of kilos maybe – and I'm surprised that Milla agreed to take it with her. She's never liked being weighed down by anything. But it's lucky that she did, because her phone would have offered no help against the darkness once it ran out of power.

The shed sits against our back fence and it's immaculate inside. There are shelves and cubbyholes, plus equally spaced hooks with different tools hanging down. The Maglite's charging cradle sits just inside the door, so I drop the torch in and listen to the satisfying click as it connects. But the memory of Steve's words, the forensic bags removed from that garage, makes me pause. Will the police come here one day? Stretch on latex gloves and pick through the items, searching for … what? A wrench? A hammer?

My stomach drops.

I will hunt those bitches down.

I close my eyes, but it doesn't help. Because all I can see is the faint rusty stain on my kitchen drainer. Rivulets of tarnished water drying before they have chance to escape.

Please make this stop. It was mud. Not blood.

Neither of my daughters are killers.

Without looking back at the torch – its heavy-duty handle now a possible murder weapon in my head – I walk out of the shed and close the door.

Back in the house, I drink in all the family photos on the garden room wall. A cycling holiday in the Pyrenees that Milla moaned about relentlessly, until she won the prize for fastest teenage cyclist in the group. Christmas at my parents' house, their front room barely recognisable under all the decorations and presents. The girls in their school uniforms from year to year, stepping stones through their childhood. The view settles me. Reminds me that we're just an ordinary family. Honest, responsible, and of course law-abiding.

My toast is cold, and I've lost my appetite anyway, so I slide both slices into the food waste bin. But I still can't face working. I drum my nails against the work surface, until my eyes rest on Mrs Jones's apples. I'll make a pie for supper, I decide; something wholesome. Serve it with vanilla ice-cream from the freezer.

Fifteen minutes later, the pastry is a satisfyingly smooth solid ball. I cover it in clingfilm and put it in the fridge. The stirring and kneading has done its job, and I feel calm enough to fire up my laptop while I wait for the pastry to chill. I've got about fifty unread emails, so I spend the next forty-five minutes browsing through them, and thankfully dragging most of them to my 'no action required' folder. When the timer goes off, I get the pastry out of the fridge, scatter some flour on the work surface, and reach into the utensils drawer for the rolling pin.

I frown. Burrow my fingers beneath spatulas and wooden spoons. Start pulling out things I didn't know we owned – bamboo chopsticks, an ornate cocktail stirrer, an old-fashioned carrot peeler – but no rolling pin. It's not there. I close the drawer, lean against the curved edge of the worktop, and drop my forearms onto the thin layer of flour. I don't want to question where it is. I don't have any energy left to justify its disappearance. Instead, I let the images slip back in. The broken bluebells. Amber's damaged face and bloodstained hair; her glassy, blank stare. How small and innocent she looked in death.

Then I pick up the ball of pastry and drop it into the bin.

AFTER

Wednesday 8th May

Rachel

'Hi, Mum, loads of homework, going to my room.' Milla pulls down the heel of her trainer with her toe, then kicks it into the porch. Lucy has photography club after school today, and won't be back for an hour, so this is my best chance to talk to Milla alone. To remind myself that she's not capable of murder, and nor is her sister. There will be an innocent explanation for the missing rolling pin – I haven't used it since Christmas after all – and I'm almost sure the mud by Kiln Lakes is a reddish colour now I've had the chance to think about it.

I just need her to make eye contact.

Milla's second trainer somersaults into the porch and she hoists her rucksack back onto her shoulder. She starts walking towards the stairs, still not looking at me. I exhale a breath of frustration. 'Aren't you going to ask how it went?' I call out. 'At the police station?'

She turns, assesses me. 'I assume they asked Lucy some dumb-arse questions and then let her go?'

I replay the conversation with DC Bzowski in my mind. 'I guess you could describe it like that.'

She nods wisely, as though she never doubted it. 'Good. Can I go now?'

I bite my lip. I want to keep her downstairs with me. What I really want is to dunk sponge fingers into cups of tea with her, and have to get a spoon for the sugary dregs. But life moves on. 'Why did you not want Lucy to go to the police station?' I ask. 'Last night, at dinner, you suggested she pretend to be sick. Why did you say that?'

Her eyes flit away from me, towards the stairs, and I wonder for a moment if she's going to leg it. But she doesn't move. 'Lucy's scared of stuff like that, isn't she? I didn't think she should have to go through it when she's a victim too.'

I may be imagining it – my heightened anxiety makes that a distinct possibility – but Milla's answer sounds forced, as though she's acting. 'Did you know that Amber texted Lucy earlier in the evening?'

Milla doesn't answer immediately and in the quiet, I listen to her breathing. It's regular but pronounced. 'Yeah, Luce told me,' she eventually mutters. 'Messaged me when I was at Ava's party, asking whether I thought she should go and meet Amber.'

'What did you say?'

'I told her no fucking way of course! I couldn't believe she was even considering it. For what? A stupid letter?'

'She didn't take your advice though. Did she tell you that too?'

Milla looks down at her socked feet. 'Not at the time. I was pretty firm in my message, so I assumed she'd gone along with it. Then I put it out of my mind. It was my best mate's party, after all. But when I got home, and you said she was missing, well, it didn't take a genius to work out where she'd gone.'

'And did you go to the meeting place to find her?'

'Yeah. I got Dad to drop me at the railway station, then I doubled back along the track. But she wasn't there of course. No one was,' she adds.

I hesitate for a moment, then plough on. 'And were there any signs that she had been there? Any broken glass for example?'

She looks up at me and her hard expression takes my breath away. Milla is 18, so a woman, not a girl anymore. It doesn't feel like that a lot of the time – the *have you washed my jeans?* and *what's for tea?* questions – but right now I see an equal, an adversary even. 'Why are you asking that?' she says, her tone accusing. 'Lucy didn't meet her. That's what she told me, and I'm sure that's what she told you too. So how could there be evidence they met when it didn't happen?'

She stares at me, an icy glare, and I don't know how to answer her. She's calling me out for not trusting my own daughter, and she's right. I'm not sure I do trust Lucy anymore. But why not? Yes, she's kept things from me – the blog, her text exchange with Amber – but only because she's scared. And who wouldn't be under the circumstances?

'It's such a mess,' I finally say, dropping onto the sofa. 'I feel like we're up to our necks in a murder investigation, and I can't fathom how that's come about. Especially after what happened to your dad. We know we're good people, so why does this keep happening to us?'

Milla sighs, and I see the tension release from her shoulders. She sits down next to me. 'We're not involved in this murder, Mum. None of us. That's what you need to focus on right now.'

'I know, but—'

'I saw this TikTok,' she interrupts. 'Did you know that only seven per cent of murders are carried out by women? And I don't know how many of them are under 16, but it must be close to zero per cent.'

'I'm not suggesting …'

'And there was all that stuff about girls in care, wasn't there? How they're groomed by dodgy gangs. Isn't it right that they're way more likely to be victims of a crime compared to kids who live with their parents?'

'Yes, that's true.'

'Well think about it then. Yeah, it's awful that Amber's dead, even if she was a bitch to Lucy, but it's not completely shocking. She was only 14 and already selling drugs. It wasn't her fault, more her shitty circumstances, but she did put herself in harm's way, didn't she?'

I envy Milla at moments like these. 'You're right, I'm sorry.' I give her a sheepish, grateful smile and she repays me with a bright one of her own.

'And anyway,' she adds, curling her arm around my shoulder. 'Can you really imagine my weedy little sister going full Mortal Kombat?'

I start to smile, then remember a child has died, and pull out of it. But Milla does have a point. I feel my shoulders relaxing. 'By the way, I found the torch you left in the porch. It was filthy.'

'Is that where I left it?' she asks, removing her arm and shifting forwards on the sofa until I can only see her in profile. 'I meant to put it back,' she mumbles. 'It must have got dirty when I fell asleep; it slipped out of my hands.'

'I cleaned it, put it in the shed.' I want to see her face, check whether her expression registers anything incriminating, but it's hidden by her hair. And then my attention is drawn away as the door pushes open. I watch Lucy walk inside. 'I thought you had photography club?' I ask.

She sighs. 'I couldn't face it.' Her skin looks even more pale than usual and there are dark circles under her eyes. I imagine I look the same. It's hard to believe it was only this morning that Lucy was being quizzed in Aylesbury police station.

'Why don't you go for a bath,' I suggest. 'I'll sort dinner. We've got stewed apple and ice-cream for dessert, then we can all have an early night.' I see Milla turn around, open her mouth to protest. I lift my hand to ward it off. 'No arguments.'

*

There's a snuffling sound. Sniffing. I've always been a light sleeper, and I whip my eyes open, instantly alert. My watch is charging on its stand, and I check the time: 02.38. I don't bother turning my bedside light on – the dim glow of streetlamps slipping under my curtains is enough to see by – just swing my legs out of bed and pad over to the door. When I step onto the landing, my eyes blinking as they adjust to the night-light we still turn on, I accept that the noise is crying. And it's coming from Lucy's room.

But before I get the chance to knock on her door, Milla appears on the landing too. 'I'll sort this,' she says. 'You go back to bed.'

I hesitate. Milla doesn't normally show such concern for her sister, or even function at this time. 'Really?' I say, still hovering. I'm not sure if this is me not wanting to devolve my parenting role to anyone, or suspicion about Milla's motives. 'She might prefer me if she's upset?'

'You'll be too dramatic. Go back to bed,' Milla instructs.

I waver. When did Milla take over the reins? And how did I not notice it happening? I watch her push open Lucy's door without knocking, then pull it closed behind her. It's the natural progression of motherhood – slipping from omnipotent to impotent over a couple of decades – but it still hurts.

I know I won't sleep so I perch on the bottom of my bed instead, staring at the closed door, listening intently in case I can pick up either of their voices. There's only silence for the first ten minutes, but then a low buzz starts. Still a whispered conversation, but loud enough for me to realise they're disagreeing about something. I'm about to investigate when my bedroom door flings open. My eyes connect with Lucy's, and she bursts into tears.

Milla appears in the doorway behind her, a look of defeat on her face. She didn't want to tell me, I think. Whatever this is, I'm only finding out because Milla lost the argument.

'What's going on?' I ask.

'Something bad has happened,' Milla admits, looking down at the carpet. 'Something you may not approve of.'

THE NIGHT SHE DIES

Friday 3rd May

Jess

Jess levers down the back door handle and pulls it towards her until it clicks into place. Maybe she doesn't need to be this quiet – Bill and Molly have already gone to bed and they're both half deaf – but why take the risk? She breathes in the cool night air and feels the fist of tension in her neck ease a bit. It's not raining anymore, but she can still smell the dampness, and feel it on her skin.

There's a sliver of space between Molly and Bill's house and their neighbours', so she sidesteps down it and then veers onto the neighbours' tiny patch of front garden to avoid her shadow passing Molly and Bill's bedroom window. Five minutes later she's off the housing estate, and the only danger now is Molly checking on her. Discovering pillows shoved under the duvet instead of a human. But Jess doubts that will happen. They'll go to sleep as soon as Amber texts them, and only a grade-A emergency would persuade them to get up.

She pulls out her phone and taps open Snapchat to message

Amber, then freezes. There's a new message from him. A warmth collects in the pit of her stomach, and her fingers start to tremble. Why is he contacting her now? She bites her lip. They only met just over a month ago, in the rec one Sunday when Amber was in Thame meeting up with Sean. But things moved quickly. She kissed him in the woods that afternoon. Then they started meeting by the disused train carriages whenever Jess could get away. They saw each other five times in total.

And then he lost interest.

But if he's messaging Jess now, does that mean he's having second thoughts about breaking up with her?

She opens the message.

Was supposed to be at that party tonight but can't face it. Ex-girlfriend there. Want to meet up?

No apology for dropping her. Not even an acknowledgement that he had. She should tell him to go fuck himself.

Especially as she sneaked out to be with Amber. To help her deal with Lucy Rose. If she meets up with him instead, she'll be leaving Amber to fend for herself. And of course she owes her sister much more than she owes him. Amber doesn't call her a mistake and drop her in one stingy message.

But Amber isn't exactly nice to Jess either. She wouldn't tell her what she'd nicked from Lucy's bag. And she didn't seem at all bothered when Jess was banned from going out tonight. Or guilty, even though the only reason Jess was bored enough to nick that bottle of wine was because Amber wanted to see Caden. The guy she's apparently getting bored of now. Jess looks back at the message, biting the inside of her cheek as she considers how to respond.

She couldn't believe it when he first told her he liked her, and she never stopped half-expecting to appear in some joke meme on TikTok. But that didn't happen. Yes, he finished with her. But he didn't shame her. And when they spent time together, he treated her like an equal. It wasn't true – he was better-looking, older, funnier – but she still loved him for pretending.

Fuck Amber. *Where?* she types back. She hopes that he reads her message quickly – which is a bit hypocritical because she's realised that his own message came through thirty minutes ago, when she was too busy faking going to bed to check her phone. A second later, the description turns from 'delivered' to 'opened', but he doesn't respond. She waits a couple of minutes, then types. *Hello?*

Still nothing. Jess shakes her head, exasperated. She's hovering on the pavement near the petrol station, her plans for the evening now on hold until he responds. He made the first move, but now it's her hanging around, waiting for another scrap of attention. She looks at the time on her phone. It's 21.57. She'll give him three more minutes and if he hasn't messaged her by then, she'll ignore him. Amber is meeting Lucy at ten by the double gates on the railway track, so she'll only be five minutes late.

A message alert: 21.59. Her heart hammers. She clicks it open.

Soz. Ignore my last msg.
Headfuck moment.

Hot tears scald Jess's eyes. She screws them closed. Of course he was going to say something like that. He's already proven that he's a heartless prick. Why was she even considering meeting up with him after what he's done? God, she's so pathetic. Her heart is still pounding, and she feels an urge to drop her phone on the pavement and stamp on it until it shatters. But that would mean him winning, taking even more from her, so instead – as calmly as she can with shaking fingers – she presses both side buttons, then slides the device into her pocket, and sets off towards the railway track.

Jess hears their voices before she can see them. Amber sounds like she always does around Lucy. A mix of teasing and threatening. But Lucy sounds different. Her usual teary whispers have gone, replaced by full-scale anger. She's shouting about how she's done with being bullied. And that Amber stealing her letter – is that what Amber took from Lucy's bag? A letter? – isn't going to work. She's still going to tell everyone the truth.

What does she mean by that?

Jess can see the two girls now, further up the lane, in between the gates that protect the old railway line. In the darkness they're just shadows, although Jess can see a plastic bag swinging from Lucy's right arm. Jess should go up there, make sure Lucy knows it's two against one, but something holds her back. It's not fear. Jess knows that between her and Amber, they'd win that fight easily. It's more that she feels like she'd be third-wheeling if she got involved. That this argument is personal between them.

She steps to one side of the pathway, close to the thick hedgerow, and tries to decide what to do. Their voices have lowered, and Jess can't make out specific words anymore. Just a buzz of hostility. She watches Amber make a sudden lunge for the plastic bag – maybe that's got the vodka inside – but Lucy is too quick for her, yanking it away, shouting, 'NO!' It must be slippery up there though, because Lucy foot-slides away from her and she drops onto one knee before staggering back up again.

It's exciting viewing, Jess realises. And with that thought, she pulls her phone out, taps on her (shit) camera icon, and slides it to video mode. Then she starts to record. Amber is up in Lucy's face now and the flash on Jess's camera is just enough to make out their expressions. Both of them twisted with anger. It's a shame the microphone can't pick up their conversation, but Jess keeps recording. Amber reaches for the bag again and makes contact this time. They start wrestling with it, fighting for possession, and suddenly there's a low thud and a higher-pitched crash – it must have fallen and hit the metal train tracks. Lucy drops onto her knee again, except this time on purpose, to protect the contents of the bag. When she stands back up, she's holding a bottle of vodka out in front of her, like a weapon.

'You broke the fucking bottle!' Amber shouts out, loud enough for the microphone now. 'You're not going to get your precious letter back now!'

'No, you broke it!' Lucy screams back, fury spiralling out of her, the bottle swaying in her grasp. 'And you're too stupid to give me the letter anyway! You think I won't use what I know; that I'm too scared to tell everyone who you really are? Well, you're wrong!'

'You know nothing,' Amber spits out. 'That fucking dyke is a liar.'

'Don't call Bronwen that!'

Jess's heart starts to race. Who's Bronwen? What does Lucy know?

Are she and Amber going to get in trouble? Just because her sister is so desperate to impress Sean?

'Why not?' her sister counters harshly. 'That's what she is, what you both are! Eating each other's faces. *Oooh, it felt totally right,*' she mimics in a high-pitched voice.

Jess gasps as Lucy charges at Amber. With the change in their positions, she can see that the neck of the bottle is broken. The cap is missing and there's jagged glass at the top. It catches Amber on the hand. She yelps, and stumbles backwards, but flails her arms forward. Lucy lunges again, into Amber, and they both fall, out of sight.

There's a noise in the hedgerow. Further up, where the bushes are thicker. Was it a cry? Is someone else watching Amber and Lucy's fight? Jess narrows her eyes, peers forward, her heart thudding. But she can't see anything; it's too dark.

Her phone buzzes in her hand. The shock of it loosens her grip and the device falls to the ground. 'Fuck,' she murmurs, crouching down, fumbling for it in the darkness. A fox bounds past her, too fast even for a scream to rise up. Her breaths come fast and shallow. When her phone landed, she heard the clink of glass against stones, and she prays the screen isn't cracked. A few seconds later, her fingers find its smooth surface and it lights up in response. Her breathing calms a notch. She takes a few deep breaths, then reads the message.

It's from Sean. Her fingers shake as she reads it for a second time. She looks back at the bushes. But the cry came from a fox, she reminds herself. Sean's not there.

She reads it again. So what does he mean?

And is there any way that it might not be really bad?

She flicks the message off her screen, out of view. Pushes back up to standing. The video is still recording – even though it's only picked up Chiltern mud and stone for the last minute or so – and she angles it back at the railway line and the girls.

But there's no one there. Both Amber and Lucy have disappeared.

She shivers in the dark silence.

AFTER

Thursday 9th May

Rachel

'How many more lies Lucy?' I shout, my decibel level reflecting the fury surging through me. My youngest daughter is sitting cross-legged on my bedroom floor, sobbing, her face hidden in her palms. Her phone is lying on the carpet between us, where I dropped it after watching the video that Jess Scott emailed her in the middle of the night. I know shouting won't achieve anything, but I can't help it. I'm done with her hiding behind her sweet nature. And with me always believing her because she's supposed to be the good one.

Because she did lie. Brazenly. Lucy did meet Amber on Friday night. I've just watched timestamped footage of them together, up on the railway track by the path to the Ridgeway. But it was more than just a meeting. Lucy lashed out at Amber with the broken vodka bottle. Did she cut her?

Was it Amber's blood on the cuffs of Lucy's missing jumper?

No wonder Jess accused Lucy of killing Amber in the Co-op, with this video in her possession.

'This is the last lie, I, I, promise,' Lucy stutters, the muffled words leaking out between her fingers. But I want to see her eyes, to drill into them until I can excavate every last morsel of truth. Because the stakes are higher now. Lucy showed a level of violence I didn't know she was capable of. *I wish she was dead.*

'Look at me!' I screech.

'Mum, chill,' Milla instructs, taking a step towards me, her voice annoyingly authoritative. 'You want the neighbours to hear?' She clicks her tongue, disappointed by my overreaction, but the sound ignites a new flare of rage inside me.

'Don't you dare speak to me like that!'

'Stop, please,' Lucy begs, her voice still like honey. She lifts her face to me. 'I wanted to tell you the truth,' she continues. 'But I was scared that you'd make me tell the detective. And then they'd definitely think I killed Amber, wouldn't they? If I was up there, fighting with her? And they'd be right, in a way.'

I gasp. 'What do you mean?'

'Don't talk crazy, Lucy,' Milla warns. 'You didn't kill her.'

'But I was jabbing a broken bottle at her face!' She looks away. 'And I said some nasty things. I was so angry. And soon after that, she ran up towards the Ridgeway, where she died. Which means I sent her to her death.'

'You can't think like that,' Milla hisses, a toxic mix of fear and frustration emanating from her. 'Amber was trouble. A drug dealer. It's not your fault that someone who she's pissed off, for whatever reason, caught up with her.'

In the subdued lighting, just my bedside light on, the images start to return. Amber's lifeless torso in the bluebells. Her tangled hair. The bruises. All that blood.

I squeeze my eyes closed, breathe to loosen the grip of panic, then open them again. Lucy didn't cause that.

'So have you done what she asked?' I ask, wanting to move the conversation on. Jess sent the video to Lucy via her school email address – I can't bear to think what server that is sitting on – with the demand that Lucy unblock her as a contact on her phone. I know that messaging apps like WhatsApp or Snapchat are encrypted so I assume she wants to move the chat to one of those.

'Yeah,' Lucy whispers. 'Milla said I should.'

Milla shrugs, the capable adult performance weakening a notch. 'I get that it's not ideal. But Jess holds all the cards at the moment, doesn't she? She threatened to post the video online if Lucy didn't unblock her.'

'She still might,' Lucy whispers, her face creasing again. 'I didn't know she filmed us; I didn't even know she was there. And she'll have that forever, that hold over me.'

'Not when the police find the real killer,' I say, trying to reassure her. 'Then it will just be an argument between a couple of teenage girls, something that happens all the time.' I know that's not true. All those armchair detectives and conspiracy theorists, diving on any so-called new evidence and declaring Lucy the real killer, no trial, no chance to defend herself. But at least she wouldn't be in jail. And keyboard warriors often have short attention spans.

Lucy looks away. 'But it's not just that,' she mumbles.

'You heard what Amber shouted,' Milla explains in a low voice. 'About Bronwen.'

I replay the words in my mind. *Fucking dyke. You both are.* Realisation hits. Is that why Lucy was so desperate to get Bronwen's letter back? Because something more than friendship happened between the girls before Bronwen left? Hopefully Lucy knows that we wouldn't care, but it's true that Bronwen's family – including her grandparents who still live in the village – are much more conservative. They might not approve. But it's more than that, anyway. Working out your sexuality is a scary, often bumpy road for every teenager. It should never be used as entertainment.

I'm about to say something to that effect when a light flashes from the carpet. Lucy's phone glowing with a new message. We all stare at it for a few moments, then Lucy picks it up, her arms shaking wildly. The crying restarts almost instantly.

'Can I read it?' I ask. 'Whatever she's said, we can deal with it together; you're innocent, remember.'

Lucy looks up at me, a mix of fear and gratitude on her face. This Lucy is so much more familiar than the aggressive stranger I watched on Jess's video. As she gives me the phone, I squeeze her fingers. Then I look at the screen.

I saw you. You killed my sister.
Give me 10 gee and I won't go to the feds.

'What does it say?' Milla asks, reaching for the phone. I hand it to her in silence then watch her read it. 'Fuck,' she exhales, elongating the word. 'Well, I guess it's good that it's only ten grand. We can afford that, right?'

'What?' I spurt out. 'We're not paying her!'

'Please, Mum,' Lucy whimpers.

'Not you as well!' I push off the bed and start pacing the room. 'Look, this is blackmail. Illegal. When you've done nothing wrong.' But as I pause for breath, the message replays in my mind. 'She said she saw you,' I mumble.

'Sorry?'

'On the message. Jess said she saw you kill Amber.'

'Well, she didn't,' Milla blurts out. 'How could she? And you saw the video – Amber was completely fine except for a few cuts.'

I pause. I can't believe I'm asking this. 'Could there be another video?'

'What? No, of course not! You can't think I actually killed her, Mum?'

'What happened to your jacket?' I ask.

She sucks in air. 'What?'

'You were wearing your denim jacket in that video, but you only had a jumper on when I found you.' I want to add that I can't find that either, but that would mean admitting I'd searched her room, and this isn't the time to be losing my moral advantage.

She's quiet for a while, an imploring look on her face, then she drops her gaze to the carpet. 'I'm not sure,' she whispers. 'I felt all hot and bothered after our fight, so I took it off. I must have put it down somewhere, maybe in the churchyard. I only realised I'd lost it when you forced us to go to the fun day and I wanted to wear it.'

'That's convenient,' I can't help muttering.

'Oh my God, you're unbelievable!' Milla calls out, jumping to her sister's defence again. 'This is Lucy, remember? The most sweet-natured girl in the world? The one you're supposed to love unconditionally? Her explanation makes perfect sense!'

'I do love her unconditionally,' I whisper, not adding what the term means, that I'd still love her even if she had killed someone. 'And I do want to believe her; there's just so much to take in.'

'Well, try harder. Lucy didn't kill Amber, okay?'

I bite my lip. I wish Matt was here. For all Milla's swagger, I know she's scared of him. But he's not back until Friday. 'Fine,' I say. 'Lucy's done nothing wrong. But that's even more reason to not pay this ransom demand. Because Jess *is* committing a crime. And this message,' I continue, pointing at the phone in Milla's hand, 'is our evidence.'

'But if we don't pay her, she'll put that video online, and then millions of people will think I killed her sister. I'll be trolled by the whole world!'

'And everyone knows the police are lazy bastards,' Milla says. 'Unless there's masses of DNA incriminating someone else, they'll see the footage and pin the murder on Lucy. They won't care that it's not what happened. Think about what Dad went through.'

'Milla, you can't let one unjust incident affect your opinion of the police for the rest of your life.'

'It's not one incident though, is it? The news is full of stories about the police fucking up. We need to deal with this, Mum. By ourselves. Dad's earning way more than he did as a teacher, so I bet you've got at least ten grand in the bank. It's not that much

143

to you, but it's a fortune to a 15-year-old foster kid. Maybe she wants it so that she can get out of Chinnor. And then we'd be free of her.'

'And if that's not her plan? If she wants to get our money and then post the video online anyway? Or take it to the police? Amber was her sister. Do you really think ten thousand pounds will be enough payback for her?'

Milla gives me a dark stare. She doesn't like it, but she knows I'm right. 'We'll scare the shit out of her then.'

'Sorry?'

'There's only one of her, but there's four of us. If Jess thinks Lucy killed Amber, what do you reckon she'll think Dad is capable of? Lucy's always said that Jess was the weaker one of the two. The follower. Doing this must be way outside her comfort zone. So we give her the money, but say if she ever posts the video, Dad will hunt her down.'

'You want us to threaten violence against a grieving 15-year-old vulnerable child? Dad, a teacher. Me, a social worker?'

'For Lucy,' Milla reminds me.

Then Lucy's phone lights up in her hand. She passes it to her sister. Lucy blinks as she reads the message, then looks up.

'She wants us to drop it in a bin by Kiln Lakes. At midnight on Friday night. Please, Mum, can we give it to her?'

AFTER

Thursday 9th May

Rachel

'You could have worked from home again, you know,' Elaine says, her forehead creasing with concern as she leans over my desk and assesses me. I must look dreadful. I sent the girls back to bed after Jess's second message, but I couldn't sleep myself. I tossed and turned for a while, and when I couldn't bear the oppressive silence of my bedroom anymore, I tiptoed downstairs, made a mug of tea, and put the TV on low. I found a nature programme on Netflix and tried to lose myself in the tropical rainforest. It worked for a minute or two, but the questions kept snaking their way back in.

Are we really going to pay Jess Scott blackmail money when Lucy's innocent?

And threaten a vulnerable child with violence?

Is there any chance that Lucy could have killed Amber?

The video kept replaying in my head too. Bronwen's letter. Lucy's angry threats. *You think I won't use what I know.* What did Lucy mean by that?

And then I remembered the sound of the plastic bag hitting the railway track when it dropped. There was the high-pitched crash of a bottle breaking, but I'm sure I heard a second noise too. The thud of something more solid than a bottle. I thought about the missing rolling pin, Amber's injuries, and I couldn't sit still anymore.

At seven o'clock I went for a shower, and then tried to cover my dark circles with some make-up – which, judging by Elaine's expression, I failed to do. When I poked my head around Lucy's door, she announced she was too sick to go to school, and I didn't try to change her mind, secretly grateful to have her contained in the house for the day. Milla was already dressed when I knocked on her door, and breezed past me as though our conversation in the middle of the night had never happened.

'I'm fine,' I say, smiling at Elaine as brightly as I can. 'I'm not sleeping brilliantly, but I prefer to be in the office – with you – than at home on my own.'

'I get that,' she says, smoothing out her forehead and returning the smile. 'By the way, the girl you found on Saturday, her social worker popped down yesterday looking for you. Her name is Colleen Byrne.'

'She did? Why?' I sound defensive, and Elaine's eyes squint in confusion. I soften my voice. 'Sorry. Did she say anything specific?'

'Not really. Just that she'd heard that Amber's body had been found by a fellow social worker in Children's Services. And it felt like too much of a coincidence to not introduce herself. I think she wanted to check you were okay mainly.'

I nod slowly, giving myself time to process this news. I don't want to see her. For one, I want to distance myself from this murder inquiry as much I can. And there's also the chance that Munroe has told her about the bullying, and my connection to it. But if Colleen Byrne was Amber's social worker, then she will be Jess's too, and do I really want to give up an opportunity to find out as much as I can about our blackmailer?

146

'Is she in the office today, do you know?' I ask.

'She said she would be,' Elaine says, nodding her head. 'I can hold the fort here if you want to go upstairs?'

It turns out the second floor is a carbon copy of our office on the ground floor. Grey, industrial-looking carpet. A sparsely furnished meeting room at the far end, and a tiny kitchenette in the corner. More than half the desks are unmanned – a mix of people working from home and out on visits – but a woman with long dark hair and piercing green eyes stands up.

'Are you Rachel Salter?' she asks in a soft Irish accent, her face opening up into a smile. She looks like one of life's good people, and my stomach churns with shame for only being here to wring information out of her. But it's for my family, so I smile back, and drop into the chair opposite her desk when she gestures towards it.

'I couldn't believe it when the police said one of my colleagues had discovered Amber's body,' she says. 'I think I wanted to say thank you – I don't know why. It's not like it made any difference to Amber, but I suppose I felt a bit better, knowing the respect you would have shown her.'

I think about Saturday morning. How I scrabbled backwards, screaming, disgusted by what I'd found. 'I'm so sorry,' I manage.

'It's very sad,' she agrees. 'But an occupational hazard, I suppose, in our line of work. Have you been a social worker long?'

'Twenty-five years, if you can believe that. All Children's Services, but I've only been based here in Community Support for the last three. How about you?'

'Similar. Lifelong profession, but I only moved to Oxfordshire in 2022.'

'Oh.' My shoulders drop an inch. 'Does that mean you didn't know Amber very well?'

'I was getting to know her,' she explains. 'Doing my best anyway. Amber had a difficult start in life. There was a lot of violence in the home where she lived with her mum, and both girls were

147

there when Jacqui was murdered by her partner. They were in their bedroom, but the police report said their door was partially open. We don't know what they saw – neither girl has ever been willing to talk about it – so we can only hope they didn't see their mum's injuries. And then with no father named on her birth certificate, Amber became a 6-year-old orphan with no one in the world except her almost 8-year-old half-sister.'

'You know, when I first became a social worker, I thought I'd be able to stop domestic violence,' I admit quietly. 'Not for everyone of course, but for the mothers I met, with children who were at risk of abuse too. I thought I'd be able to convince them to leave. I rarely succeeded.'

She nods. 'There are so many layers to it. It's hard for us to get our head around.'

I don't need to ask who she means by us. Do-gooders with worthy aims. Strangers from a different world who are happy to ignore sinks filled with dirty dishes or sticky milk bottles stuffed between sofa cushions, as long as we can go back to our comfortable houses, our neat families, at the end of the working day. I feel a wave of self-contempt.

'You know, I thought Amber would have a better life than her mum,' Colleen continues. 'The team managed to find foster carers who'd take both sisters. A lovely couple in Littlemore. And the girls stayed with them a long time, nearly five years, before they had to move. Amber had her problems of course, and an attitude so sassy I swear you could light a match off her.' Colleen smiles at the memory. 'But she was a survivor. I thought she was going to be one of my success stories.' She gives me a sad smile. 'All I can hope now is that the police find her killer and bring them to justice.'

I look away so she can't see the tears forming in my eyes, then blink them away. She doesn't mean Lucy, I remind myself, I'm just tired. 'Have the police kept you updated on how the investigation is going?'

'Not really. I spoke to them initially, gave them Amber's file, talked to them about her background and so on. But they seem more interested in the here and now. Apparently Amber had a boyfriend; I didn't even know. And between you and me, I get the impression they think he killed her.'

I remember the mechanic Steve mentioned. He said he was young, and it was only Steve's assumption that the guy was Amber's drug dealer.

'Like mother like daughter,' Colleen goes on. 'The police are waiting for the forensics report, and I imagine they're hoping there'll be something there that proves it.'

I close my eyes for a second, say a silent prayer of hope, then look back at Colleen. I hate the idea of manipulating her, but in a few hours' time I'll return to the reality of my home – an accusation of murder and a ransom demand – and I need to have done everything possible to help my family. 'And how is Jess coping?' I ask. 'It must be awful for her.'

Colleen drops her head to one side. 'How did you know Amber's sister was called Jess?'

'Oh, sorry,' I say again, an automatic response when I'm on the back foot. 'I live in Chinnor too – that's why I found Amber, it was on my running route. Jess is in my daughter's year at Lord Frederick's.'

'Oh gosh, I didn't realise you knew the girls. And with a teenage daughter of your own, how terrifying that must be, a murder in your village. You won't say anything about …'

I shake my head. 'Of course not.'

Colleen smiles her gratitude, and it causes another jolt of guilt to flare up. She's quick to trust me because I'm a social worker, with similar principles. But I don't deserve it.

'I took on their case as soon as I joined,' she says. 'A couple of months before they moved to Chinnor. There'd been an incident involving a particular boy, a lad with a bit of a reputation, which led to my predecessor resigning. It absolutely wasn't her fault, but she felt responsible, asleep at the wheel, that kind of thing. I was given the task of moving the girls out of harm's way.'

'Out of harm's way? So is there a chance this boy could have killed Amber?'

'I mentioned it to the police,' Colleen says. 'But they weren't that interested, and I can understand why. You see, it was Jess who was thought to be in danger from him, not Amber. To be honest, Amber would probably have described him as a friend; I mentioned her sass, didn't I?'

'What did he have against Jess? My daughter says she's quite shy?'

'She is, yes, has tended to hide in Amber's shadow rather than make her own friends.' Two small lines appear between Colleen's eyebrows. 'What happened is complicated. Let's just say that Jess dug herself a hole that she couldn't – or perhaps wouldn't – get out of. She can be very stubborn about certain things.'

I think about the girl I saw in the Co-op. Her vivid blue eyes and flame red hair. Her angry, defiant expression. Will her stubbornness be Lucy's downfall? 'How do you think Jess will cope without Amber?' I ask.

Colleen sighs. 'She was very reliant on her younger sister, so it's a worry. And she refused to speak at all for two days after Amber's murder. But I think she's emerged stronger actually, almost like she's taken on a bit of her sister's personality. Maybe the trauma has given her a new hunger to survive. No, my real concern now is that she'll run away.'

'Oh?' I lean forward. Leaving home with no support network is incredibly dangerous for a vulnerable teenage girl. But the thought of Jess not being in the village lifts my spirits. I despise myself for it.

'She hates it at her foster home now, which of course I understand. Her dad lives in a small village in the Peak District,' Colleen goes on. 'And I think she has notions about moving in with him.'

'She has a dad?' I ask, surprised.

'Yes, and he was around for a year or so after Jess was born. But he'd served in the military in Afghanistan, and there were both physical and mental health issues. When Jess's mum died, the team contacted him. But there was no way the family court would have given him custody, and he had no interest in requesting it.'

'But you think Jess might go to him anyway?' I press.

'I've seen a photo of him. He's Scottish, and she's the spit of him. I think that makes a difference, doesn't it? Being able to see where you come from in someone's face? That's why I'm going up to Derbyshire tomorrow, to talk to him. I don't mean for him to take her on – that wouldn't be right for either party – but to organise a visit. Because Jesus wept, the girl deserves something good in her life.'

AFTER

Friday 10th May

Rachel

I check my watch for the millionth time. Matt was on the first flight out of Geneva so he should be home by now, but there's no sign of him yet. I'm desperate to tell him about Jess's ransom demand; I couldn't stomach doing it over the phone, without the fortifying effects of physical touch, but we're supposed to be doing the drop tonight, and I still have no clue what to do.

I hear his car pull into the drive and sigh with relief. I should wait, give him a moment to take his shoes off, but I'm too impatient for that. I leap up from my chair and accost him as he walks through the porch. 'Thank God you're back,' I exhale, wrapping my arms around him and burrowing my face into his neck.

'Whoa, it's only been forty-eight hours.' When I don't respond, he slowly returns the hug, and we stand like that, in silence, for a few moments. Lucy went to school today – she said it was her choice, but I suspect Milla encouraged it, her mission for us all to appear normal to the outside world – so there's just the two of us in the house. I suddenly have a crazy urge to go upstairs, to have daytime sex like we did before the girls came along. But that feels like a lifetime ago now, so I pull away.

Matt looks at me. 'So what's happened?' he asks.

I can't tell whether he sounds worried, or annoyed. But I have to remember that either would be fair. Just back from a two-day work trip, no time to relax, an early morning flight. He's been drawn into this nightmare like I have, purely as punishment for loving his family. 'Things have got a hundred times worse,' I admit quietly.

He rests his hand on the side table. 'Why?'

'Lucy did go and meet Amber on Friday night,' I explain. 'They argued. Lucy even lashed out with that broken vodka bottle. And that's when the video ends.'

His eyes widen. 'What video?'

'Jess was up there too, hiding – probably planned that way – and she filmed it.'

'Oh God, poor Lucy,' he moans, his voice cracking. He walks over to the living area and sinks into the sofa.

'Poor Lucy?' My voice rises. 'She lied to us! And she was flinging a makeshift weapon around. Honestly, Matt, I hardly recognised her on that footage. She was so angry.'

He sighs, lowers his head. He stays like that for a while, but just as I'm about to say something – anything to fill the silence – he looks up again. 'What were they arguing about? Could you hear them on the video?'

I sigh. 'Not really. Something about Lucy knowing some truth.'

His head jerks. 'What truth?'

I sigh. 'I've no idea. But I think Amber stealing Bronwen's letter was the main issue.'

'I wonder what it says,' Matt murmurs, sliding the heel of his hand across his forehead. 'For it to matter so much.'

I feel awkward, divulging Lucy and Bronwen's secret, but it's better that Matt knows, so I tell him about the kiss, and the feelings Bronwen admitted to. How Lucy naturally wanted it to stay private between them.

He's quiet for a while, taking it in. 'I wish she'd told us,' he says eventually. I want to ask whether he's talking about Lucy kissing Bronwen, or about Amber finding out about it, but his voice is so heavy with regret that I don't say anything. He's been telling me not to worry since Saturday morning, getting cross that I could suspect my own children. Seeing him like this, the realisation of the predicament we're in, has taken that safety net away and I feel like I'm falling.

'I need to tell you how we got the video,' I murmur.

'Go on.' His expression is calm, clinical now. He's always been better at self-control than me.

'Jess emailed it to Lucy. She wrote that she saw Lucy kill Amber – which Lucy has promised can't be true – but she wants money.'

Matt's eyes narrow. 'Blackmail?'

I nod. Tears are rolling down my face now. 'She wants ten thousand pounds. Dropped in a bin up by Kiln Lakes at midnight tonight. Jesus, just saying that feels surreal, like I'm in an American cop show or something.'

'Ten grand?' He sounds relieved, like Milla did. 'At least that's doable I suppose,' he continues.

'Doable? A girl has been murdered, Matt! Her sister thinks Lucy did it. And Lucy could well have been the last innocent person to see Amber alive. And she's lied to the police about it!'

'Look, I get that things aren't good. But if she was asking for fifty grand, or a hundred, we wouldn't be able to pay it. And then Lucy's future would be entirely in that girl's hands. But ten grand means we have options. We can get it out of the bank this afternoon, do the drop, and at least we'll be in with a chance of the problem going away.' His expression sours. 'Although I do see that we only have Jess's word for it that she won't post the video somewhere anyway. It's not like we can demand the original with everything in the cloud these days.'

As Matt falls silent, I replay Milla's suggestion from Wednesday night, and wonder if I could sink that low, if protecting my family trumps every moral code I've ever lived by.

'Milla had an idea about that,' I start slowly, my voice already cracking. 'She thought we could include a note with the money, a threatening one.'

'You think we can scare her into silence?'

Shame burns my cheeks. Colleen trusted me with the girls' background, and now I'm using their trauma to my advantage. Is this because I love my child so much? Can I hide behind something as honourable as that? Or is this just ruthless determination that my family survives above anyone else? 'Yes,' I admit quietly. 'If we say you'll hurt her if she breaks her promise about the video. Her mum was a victim of domestic violence, so Jess knows what men are capable of.'

'That boy's accusation – the police investigation is dormant, not closed,' Matt reminds me. 'So if the police found out that I've threatened violence against another child.'

'You're right,' I interrupt. 'It's too big a risk, a stupid idea.'

Matt shakes his head. 'No. It's a good idea. I just need to think it through.' He rubs his head again. 'Someone like Jess would be petrified – you're right. And she's shown her opinion of the police by blackmailing us rather than taking the video directly to them. It makes sense that she'd be suspicious of the police too – they didn't save her mum, did they? I think we should do it.'

I walk over to the sofa, drop into it. Matt is right – Jess would see the police as the enemy. But there is another explanation for why she hasn't shown them the video. One I really hope is true. Jess could believe – like the police apparently, hopefully, do – that the boyfriend killed Amber. Maybe she's an opportunist, using the footage of Lucy to her advantage without believing for a second that Lucy's guilty.

Or it could just be that she's desperate. Willing to try anything to get away.

155

I think about my conversation with Colleen. Jess's hope to be reunited with her father. Both Milla and Lucy adore Matt. They weren't around to witness his first bout of depression, but they lived through his second. Matt was not easy company – constantly shouting at us all, complaining about the mess, obsessively tidying – but still, their love for him didn't budge an inch. It's not surprising that Jess dreams of a life with her father – especially with both her mother and only sister taken from her – and it's heartbreaking to think her only remaining family member doesn't want her. Ten thousand pounds in her pocket might change his mind.

There's even the possibility that Jess deserves this money.

'Shall I phone the bank then?' I ask.

Matt nods back. 'Tell them it's for a car, for Milla,' he improvises. 'Then I'll drive into Thame to pick the cash up.'

I head back into the office to make the call. I don't know why. I could get the number from searching on my phone. But I want this to feel like a business transaction – like buying a used car from a bloke I don't quite trust and hoping it doesn't have a dodgy chassis. The woman on the other end of the phone does ask what the money is for, but in a bored tone, like it's on a list that needs ticking, so it's easy to regale the lie Matt suggested, and she accepts it without question. Then she books the cash in for collection. I call to Matt that it's done and then watch him back the car out of the drive a minute later. His expression is resolute, resigned to the fact he'll do anything to protect his daughters. It makes me feel proud.

But also scared how far our love will force us to go.

AFTER

Friday 10th May

Rachel

We stare at the Waitrose bag – sitting in the middle of our kitchen table – like criminals. Not a sturdy bag for life, but one of those flimsy ones that tears on the corner of ham packets.

'It doesn't look that impressive,' Milla observes from her normal place at the table – facing the kitchen, opposite Matt. 'You'd think ten grand would be a chunkier wad than that.'

Matt shrugs. 'I thought the slimmer the better, so when the bank teller asked if fifties was okay, I said it was.' He reaches over and tucks the bag in a bit tighter at the sides. I can see that he's fidgety, looking for any way to expel the adrenalin, and I think about the note inside the bag, typed out and printed.

Your accusation is false, but the money is here.
Stick to your promise and destroy that footage.
If the video appears online, my dad will kill you.

We all fall silent again. Milla and Matt look deep in thought while Lucy's face is unreadable. Frozen. It's not yet five o'clock,

157

the girls only recently back from school, so we've still got seven hours until the drop. I imagine skulking over to the designated bin, checking over both shoulders in the darkness, then dropping the money in. There'd be no point waiting to watch Jess collect it. I already know her identity, and if I thought confronting her would make a difference, I wouldn't have agreed to her demand in the first place. Theoretically, Jess could just knock on our door and ask for the money, so maybe these cloak-and-dagger tactics are a sign that she's scared of us. And that Matt's note might work.

'I'll take the money,' he says grimly. 'I'll park up on Chinnor Hill Road and walk down, so there's no chance my car will be spotted.'

'No, I should go,' Lucy pipes up. 'It's me who's got us into this mess, so I should be the one to take the risk.'

'No!' Matt and I cry out in unison. Then I gesture for him to follow it up. 'You are the last person who should be going up there,' he says sternly.

'Because I can't be trusted, you mean?' she asks, tears catching at the back of her throat. 'Because it's me going out at night that got us into this trouble?'

'Lucy, Jess thinks you killed her sister,' Matt reminds her. 'You can't risk her finding you up there, all alone; we don't know what she might do.'

'But what if you get caught, Dad?' Lucy pleads, not willing to back down. 'Especially with the note, and all that stuff from before.'

'I won't get caught,' Matt says grimly.

'I think I should go,' Milla announces. 'I know the area much better than you do, Dad. There's a short cut from behind the station, where they keep the old carriages. A hole in the wire fencing. Did you know that?'

'No, but …'

'That way I wouldn't have to use the main road at all. No chance of any video doorbells picking me up.'

I think about last Friday night. How furious I was with myself for letting Milla search for Lucy alone. 'No, I'll go,' I say, entering the fray. 'I'll wear my running gear, so if anyone sees me, I can say I went for a run because I couldn't sleep.'

Milla shakes her head, drops her bottom lip. 'No one's going to believe that.' She exhales a deep sigh. 'Look, I know I freaked you out last Friday, but that was different. I'd had a few drinks at Ava's party, and actually I'd smoked half a joint too – don't squeal, it was a one-off – and that's why I got sleepy. Tonight, I'll be one hundred per cent focused. In and out super quick, I promise.'

'Look, I'm taking the money, okay?' Matt says, his voice rising. 'It's my job to protect this family.'

'Oh my God, seriously?' Milla spits out. 'Did I miss our U-turn back to nineteenth-century patriarchy?'

'You're happy to use my physical stature when it's about scaring Jess!'

The doorbell goes, but instead of feeling saved by it, my heart catapults into my mouth. I push my chair back, praying it's just a delivery. I watch Matt slip the bag of money into the drawer of our dresser with fake nonchalance, then go to find out.

'DI Finnemore,' I announce as I pull the door open. The high volume is mainly to warn the rest of my family, but it's also an escape route for the scream surging up from my lungs. 'How can I help?'

His expression is hard to read. 'Could I come in for a moment?'

'Of course,' I say, smiling brightly to distract him from my rising pitch. Then I gesture to the living area – away from the kitchen – and sit down in the sofa opposite him. I don't trust my voice, so I wait silently for him to explain why he's come.

'They're dismantling the crime scene today,' he starts. 'So I went up to take a last look round. Make sure it's ready to be returned to the public. Not that I don't trust my team of course …'

As his voice trails off, I think about the bluebells crushed by a dead body and dozens of heavy black boots. The blood-smeared foliage. I push my lips together and nod.

'And as I was passing,' he continues, 'I thought I would drop in. We found a couple of hairs on Amber's clothing, and I'd like to check if they're yours, for elimination purposes. The hair is broken, which means we can't extract DNA, but I was wondering if I could ask for a sample of yours for visual analysis?'

'Um, yes, that's fine,' I mumble. He's taken me off guard, and as I pull out my scrunchy, my mind careers through what this could mean. *Of course it will be my hair. At my age, I moult like a dog.* I curl a couple of hairs around my finger and feel a sharp sting as I yank them away from my scalp. *Yes, Lucy's hair is similar, but it's not the same as mine; the police will see that.* I wait for the detective to open an evidence bag, then with shaking hands, I drop the few strands inside.

'Thank you,' he says, sealing the bag. But he doesn't move to get up. I wait, every muscle taut. 'I also wondered if Lucy could spare me five minutes,' he goes on.

'Oh?'

'There's just something on her statement that I wanted to clarify; nothing to worry about. Is she in?'

I pause, smile, wonder if my heart is going to gallop right out of my chest. 'Sorry, no. Lucy's at a friend's house for tea. I was with her during her interview though, so perhaps I can help with whatever you need clarifying?'

He stays silent for a moment, nodding gently. 'Lucy told DC Bzowski that she went out last Friday night,' he finally says.

'Yes, that's right,' I whisper. My mind races. Have they cleaned up the CCTV footage DC Bzowski mentioned? Do they now know for certain that it was Lucy on Keens Lane, forty-five minutes earlier than she claimed to be out?

'And I wonder if you could confirm her timings for me again.'

I bite the inside of my cheek, taste blood. Should I admit to this one lie to keep the detective from uncovering any more, or is it like Jenga, with each lie dependent upon the others? I hold my breath for a moment, then slowly exhale. 'She said she left home about ten forty-five,' I whisper.

'She said?' he picks up, lifting the words into a question.

'I was out for supper,' I explain. 'A curry, at the Indian, with some girlfriends. I got back soon after that, and Lucy wasn't in her room. She'd left a note saying she couldn't sleep and had gone for a walk to clear her head. But she'd left her phone at home, so the only option was to go out and look for her. And that also might mean she got her timings a bit out.'

The detective frowns. 'How so?'

'Lucy's phone was out of battery,' I lie. 'That's why she didn't take it with her. But it's also her only source of telling the time. Lucy doesn't wear a watch, you see. So she told DC Bzowski that she went out at ten forty-five, but it could only have been a guess.' DI Finnemore has already told me that he's got teenage children, so I try to give him my 'we're in this together' smile.

'And do you remember what time you found Lucy?' he asks, his tone suggesting my efforts haven't worked.

I think about my frantic journey up Church Road followed by my relieved one back down with my daughter in tow. I stayed on the opposite side of the road to the shops on my way there. Can I risk assuming the cameras didn't pick me up? Or is continuing to lie pointless now? If they can put Lucy on Keens Lane before 10 p.m., then theoretically she'd have time to kill Amber anyway. 'Lucy was in the churchyard,' I say nervously. 'I don't know the exact time I found her, but it was around eleven fifteen, or a bit later. We stayed for a while, chatting, before heading home. It's hard to be certain how long we were there.'

DI Finnemore nods. 'Of course, I understand.' He lifts out of the sofa.

'So that's everything you need?' I ask, mirroring his movement.

'For now, yes. We might need to talk to Lucy again, but it can wait until next week. I'll let you know.' He smiles and I return it.

Surely he wouldn't be this nice if he thought Lucy was a killer?

'How's the investigation going in general?' I ask, trying to sound like I'm just making conversation.

'There's been some progress,' he says sagely. 'I'm doing a press conference in an hour actually, so there'll be an update on the local news this evening.'

'Oh?' I think about Steve's account of the young mechanic getting hauled off by the police, and Colleen mentioning a boyfriend. 'Does that mean you have a suspect?'

He looks at me quizzically, and I worry that I've gone too far. But then his expression softens. 'We have somebody in custody, but it's early days. Now, I must go, otherwise I'll be late for my own TV show.'

'Well, good luck,' I mumble. He nods, then walks through the door and pulls it behind him. I take a long breath.

'They've arrested someone then,' Matt says, appearing from the kitchen. 'That's good news.'

'Yes,' I say in a quiet voice, forcing myself to block out the detective's interest in Lucy and focus on the positive. 'Do you think we should call tonight off? If they've got someone in custody, and are willing to tell the press, they must be pretty confident he did it. And then there would be nothing for Jess to blackmail Lucy over.' I watch Matt consider my question in his usual way, pitting the pros and cons against each other.

'No,' he finally says. 'Let the girl have her money. Then tomorrow it will all be over.'

Email from DI Finnemore (SIO) to DCI Bishop

Subject: Friday 10th May update

Sir,

You must be all conferenced out by now. Hope you enjoy your few days' break in Copenhagen with the missus.

We are building a case against Caden Carter – a 17-year-old trainee mechanic from Towersey with a historical conviction for serious assault (at 14 years old). We believe he was the victim's boyfriend at the time of her murder. We initially picked him up on Tuesday – the kid even had scratch marks on his face – and interviewed him under a caution plus three. He was predictably uncommunicative but did admit to knowing Amber. We got a warrant to search his home, which took place on Wednesday. We found two lip balm tins in his drawer – one with ecstasy pills, and another with hash parcels wrapped in clingfilm. He has no history of either possession or supply, so our working theory is that he stole these from the victim. We also took a number of personal items from his room. I fast-tracked the samples for analysis and the results arrived yesterday.

It gave us all the relevant forensic evidence we needed to arrest him – which took place today – and we're hopeful the CPS will allow us to proceed to charge. Carter's DNA was already on NDNAD from his earlier conviction. Both the saliva around the victim's mouth and the skin cells under her fingernails are a match. Blood found on Carter's jumper is a DNA match for Amber. Fibres from the jumper were also found at the scene. Carter's car was picked up passing the railway station car park CCTV camera driving up Hill Road at 22.20. No more cameras past that point, but it is the obvious route to access the nature reserve car park via Hill Top Lane. His car was then picked up making the return journey at 23.31 – plenty of time to commit murder.

Mud in his trainer treads matched that collected from the scene. As Carter also has a history of violence (and in my opinion was lucky to get off with a youth rehabilitation order for his earlier offence), we believe there's a strong case against him.

BUT forensic report also brought up a few anomalies. Most of the blood on the victim's clothing was her own, but there were two additional samples found, neither of which are a match for Carter. Forensics extracted a full DNA profile from one – no match found on NDNAD – but only a partial from the other. There is a new test that should give us the full profile, but it's pricey. I'd like to proceed (Carter's defence team could have a field day if we can't explain it) – and am attaching the quote for your sign-off. Also, victim's blood found on Carter's clothing was relatively minimal – nowhere close to what we'd expect from major head trauma. Blood spatter team are currently assessing whether this could be explained by him wearing a jacket over (that he later disposed of – although nothing found). Still no sign of the murder weapon. Final pathology report says it's something with an even narrower circumference than a baseball bat – possibly rounders bat, bicycle pump, iron bar, even tree branch – although no wood splinters or metal fragments found.

Duty solicitor present at Carter's interview. He began talking when forensic evidence was presented to him. He admitted to having started seeing Amber in the weeks preceding her death – said he believed her to be 16 but no sign of sexual assault anyway – and (eventually) to being with her at the nature reserve on Friday night. He claimed that she'd ignored him earlier in the evening, but then suddenly messaged asking him to meet her at the scene. He explained to us that he'd tried and failed to gate-crash the 18th birthday party in the village, then tried and failed to get served at The Crown, so had nothing better to do. They made out, then had an argument (during which Amber sliced his cheek with her fingernails) and he left. According to Carter, victim was alive and well at that point (approx. 23.10 according to him, which does fit with CCTV). Usual excuses for not revealing all this in his first interview – not trusting corrupt police, etc. etc.

However, I'm sure you won't be surprised to learn that he's still our number-one suspect. We have him in custody for another day, so will go again tomorrow.

One other development – CCTV picked up Lucy Rose (bullying victim) twice on Friday night. Following some technical wizardry, she's been identified as the girl who walked past the post office eight minutes after the victim was spotted there – at 21.55 – carrying a plastic bag that looks like it contained a bottle of vodka from its shape – plus another object that COULD be the shape of the murder weapon (stretching here though). Then at 23.49 she was seen with her mother outside the parade of shops on Church Road. That's nearly two hours unaccounted for. Also, Lucy initially told Bzowski that she went out around 22.45 for thirty minutes – so why did she lie? And Lucy has very similar hair to the strands we found on the body (although so does her mother, Ms Salter, who found the body – sample currently with CSI).

However, this evening Ms Salter gave me a relatively plausible explanation for the discrepancy in Lucy's timings. And if Carter is to be believed, the victim was alive at the crime scene at 23.10 – and even though it's logistically possible, it's hard to believe that Lucy could have killed her, and be back in Chinnor, walking along with her mum, in less than forty minutes. To be honest, she is so far removed from the profile of a murderer that I just can't see it anyway. But she may know more than she's currently letting on. Am planning to talk to her again next week.

But for now, Carter is our priority.

Simon

THE NIGHT SHE DIES

Friday 3rd May

Jess

Jess eyes the CCTV camera – the back of it, she's not stupid – and wonders how long she should wait at the railway station car park. Jess was sure that Amber would appear from the trail that leads into it, but she hasn't yet, and she's also turned her map function off on Snapchat so Jess can't track her.

The only other routes away from her meeting point with Lucy are back to the village – but that would mean her passing where Jess had been crouching – or heading up towards the Ridgeway, and she can't believe Amber would go up to the woods in the pitch-black on her own. But she's been waiting for over ten minutes now, and has sent like a thousand messages, and there's still no sign.

She frowns. Did Amber definitely get away? It was completely still and silent up there, so Jess had assumed both girls had gone. But it was hard to see in the darkness.

And they had been fighting.

Did Lucy do something bad to Amber? Something bad enough

for her to not be moving or speaking? But that wasn't what she was threatening. She said she was going to tell everyone the truth. Which could mean she knows what Amber and Jess have done.

And on top of all that, there's Sean, his weird, creepy message:

I see you.

Jess checks Snapchat again. But there's no response from Amber, and with her map function switched off, Jess can't tell if she's chatting with Caden or Sean or anyone else.

Then a new thought glides forward. Sean is Amber's friend, not hers. The two of them message all the time. So why has Sean messaged Jess tonight?

Is it because Amber is ghosting him too?

Amber never normally turns her map function off. Jess had assumed it was to do with her meet-up with Lucy, but could it really be about Sean? Is she hiding from him?

And if so, why? What does he know?

A jolt of anger rushes through Jess. Why does Amber always have to push her luck? Without ever considering the consequences? And why does it feel like Jess is the one who always gets burned for it?

She tries WhatsApp.

I'm out. Where are you?

The ticks stay grey.

Jess squints her eyes in concentration. However tough Amber comes across, if she knows Sean's on to her about the money they've been skimming, she'll be scared. Would she turn to Caden for help? Would she suddenly fancy him again if she needed protection from her dealer? Then Jess thinks about her message exchange with her ex, how he changed his mind about meeting up with her, and shudders with anger, grief, stupidity. She can't believe she's risked getting into more trouble with Molly and Bill for this. Shivering in a railway station car park with Sean on her case, and no idea where Amber is.

Her phone buzzes in her hand. And this time, it doesn't stop. She squints at the line of numbers glowing on her screen; not someone in her contacts, but it might be Amber on the dumb phone. She lifts the handset to her ear. 'Hello?'

'Jess?'

Extra saliva forms in her mouth like it does when she's about to be sick. 'Yeah?'

'Where the fuck is Amber?'

'Uh, I dunno.' But she needs more than that, a realistic excuse to calm Sean down. 'I was grounded, so she went out without me.'

'Don't bullshit me! You're by some train station.'

Jess swears silently. Why didn't she follow Amber's lead and turn her Snapchat map off? 'Yeah, okay. I escaped, like twenty minutes a go, but I can't find Amber either.'

Sean clicks his tongue. 'Is she with that Caden guy?'

'I swear, Sean, I don't know.'

'You expect me to believe that? You live in a village in the middle of nowhere. You're hiding her, aren't you,' he accuses, his voice rising. There's drill music in the background; it's loud but scratchy, like the speakers can't deal with the volume setting.

'No, I promise,' Jess says, not even trying to conceal her fear anymore. 'Why would I hide her from you?'

'Because she's been skanking me, the bitch!' His paranoia about privacy even on burner phones has clearly been side-lined by his fury. 'Creaming a fiver off every gram. I can't believe she'd do that to me.' There's a dull thwacking sound, like Sean hitting something inanimate, and Jess wonders where he is. Does he still live in his mum's flat on the Leys estate or have the council kicked him out now? But suddenly there's another background noise, a car horn hooting, and Jess realises he's in his car. A Honda something, black with alloy wheels.

'She never would, Sean,' Jess tries. 'Whoever told you that, they're wrong.' He goes quiet, but Jess finds the silence even more terrifying, so she prompts him. 'Sean?'

He snorts bitter laughter. 'You know, that's what I thought,' he says, the anger now replaced with an icy chill. 'At first. Even when my mates warned me that she couldn't be trusted. So I tested her, the last time we met, and I could tell something wasn't right. She couldn't look me in the eyes when I talked about upping the price – even though it was easy extra p's, she didn't want to know. So when she said she was going to hang around that party house tonight, I got a mate's sister to pretend she was going to it, and buy some gear from Amber. Fucking fifteen quid, that's what she charged.'

'It's only a fiver difference,' Jess whispers, changing tack, but then falls silent. She needs to think of something better to say, find the words to get them out of trouble. But thinking and talking are two things that she's not very good at under pressure.

'It's NOT only a fiver, though, is it?!' Sean shouts, the anger and volume back. 'It's a trust that's been broken. And after I gave her a second chance.'

'To do what?' Jess whispers, her voice warbling, but loyalty giving her just enough courage to speak out. 'She acts like you're some kind of god, and you just use her to sell your drugs.'

Why is she saying this? Winding him up? Would Amber do the same for her?

'You don't know what you're talking about. You're the one who fucked up her life, not me,' he hisses.

Jess's eyes grow hot. Because he's right, she did fail Amber. And whenever she thinks about it, she hates herself for it.

But maybe this is a way to make up for her mistake, to show her sister that she's not chickenshit anymore. 'You get the same amount of money from her deals, so why shouldn't she make a bit more? She's the one taking all the risks.'

'Ha! Are you really that stupid?'

Jess closes her eyes. The energy, her fight, disintegrates. Of course she can't win this. 'I'll get Amber to call you when I see her. But it'll be tomorrow …'

'Jesus, you are that stupid!' he shouts, interrupting her. 'Stop pretending you don't know where she is! I'm on my way to Chinnor now. She's told me about some parkland by a lake. Make sure she's there in thirty minutes or I swear I'll kill the fucking pair of you.'

The call cuts out and Jess's hand shakes as she lowers her phone to her side. Her heart is beating like she's sprinting the hundred metres, but her legs won't move. She warned Amber against stealing from Sean, yes, but with how much force? And how genuinely? The truth is, she liked seeing Amber treat Sean like everyone else – like her – rather than being completely caught up in his spell.

And now they're both going to pay for Amber's deceit.

Except Amber doesn't know Sean's on his way.

Jess thinks again about the different routes Amber could have taken. And how there's only one that really makes sense. Does Amber have the nerve to go up to the Ridgeway, through the woods, alone, in the dark? They both love it there in the daytime, and think of it as their safe place. If Caden's with her, maybe it's exactly where she'd want to be.

And there's only one way to find out.

Jess turns towards the Ridgeway and sets off.

AFTER

Friday 10th May

Rachel

'I still don't think Milla should go,' I say, but in a quiet voice and behind the closed kitchen door, in case she overhears and starts pulling me up on my feminism.

'Me neither,' Matt murmurs back. The room's not warm, but sweat is trickling down his temples. 'But it is true that she knows the off-road route better than either of us. And I trust her.'

'I trust her too,' I counter, hoping I don't sound defensive. 'I just don't like the thought of her being in danger. Christ, her A levels start in a couple of weeks. Most parents would have their kids chained to the desk by now, and we're letting ours do a ransom drop in the middle of the night. How has this happened?' My eyes bubble with tears.

Matt sighs. 'Life throws curveballs, Rachel. And there's no point asking why, because you won't get an answer. Do you know how many times I asked that question when that kid accused me of hitting him? I never worked it out, but I did get through it. Truth and fairness reigned in the end. You could say the same about this situation. It's terrible right now, and tragic for Amber's friends and family. But they've got a suspect in custody. And you never know, without anyone bullying her, Lucy might even start enjoying life again.'

I push my lips together. I still hate thinking that Lucy benefits from Amber dying, even though it's true that she does. 'None of that keeps Milla safe tonight,' I remind him.

'Well, I have an idea about that. I'm going to follow her.'

'What?' My volume rises a bit and Matt puts a finger to his lips.

'After she leaves, I'll go in the car. Park up on Chinnor Hill Road and walk down from there. I'll keep out of sight, of course, but the trees will give me plenty of cover. And I'll be close enough to help if Jess does do anything. Not that she will,' he adds. 'I'm sure she just wants the money. But it's good to cover all eventualities.'

I open the fridge door and pull out a bottle of beer. I shouldn't really drink at a time like this, not when I might need to make some quick decisions, but DI Finnemore's visit has been rapping at my temples for hours now and I need something to relax me. 'Want one?'

'No thanks. Are there any Cokes in there?'

We sit down at the kitchen table and listen to the gentle fizzing as our drinks are exposed to the air. 'Do you really think this will work?' I ask. 'That Jess will take her ten grand and that will be the end of it?'

Matt flicks at the ring pull on his can. 'We're doing what we can to make sure it is,' he says grimly. 'And she's a 15-year-old girl who's just lost the only member of her family. She's not going to be thinking too clearly, is she?'

His incorrect assumption about Jess's family tree makes me think about Colleen, and Jess's father, and my earlier thought that perhaps she'll go to him once she gets the money. God, I hope so. For her sake, and for ours.

The door swings open and I turn to look at Milla. She's dressed all in black. Leggings, hoodie, socks, even her trainers. Her hair is neatly braided in a French plait and she's wearing a serious expression. 'It's eleven forty,' she says. 'I'm leaving in a minute.'

'You'll need gloves,' Matt says.

'I have a pair in my bag.'

'And a torch,' I say, trying not to remember the last time I handled that, the dried rivulets of too-red mud.

'I've got everything I need, Mum,' Milla says, a look of annoyance darkening her face. 'Except the cash. That's what I came for.' Matt stands up and retrieves the Waitrose bag from the dresser drawer. His hands are shaking as he proffers it towards Milla, and it reminds me that tonight is upsetting for him too. He went out on his road bike when he got back from the bank this lunchtime. And then he spent another hour fitting some new kit to it that had been delivered while he was in Geneva. I could tell he was trying to distract himself.

'Thanks,' Milla mumbles. She hesitates for a moment, then sighs. 'And also thanks for trusting me, both of you. I promise I've got this; you really don't have to worry.'

I want to say something, to remind her of the dangers, or plead with her to reconsider. But I stay mute as she pulls her baseball cap on. I follow her out of the kitchen, and then watch her disappear down the drive. Lucy is lying on the sofa watching TV, or at least pretending to – an episode of *Friends* from one of the early seasons – and I don't disturb her. Instead, I return to the kitchen. Matt is getting ready to go out – zipping up an old bomber jacket I'd forgotten he had – and suddenly he's wearing all black too. Would I have thought about camouflage if I'd been doing the drop? Maybe.

'What if Milla sees you?' I ask. 'It's not like she doesn't know what car you drive.'

'She's going via the railway dumping ground,' he reminds me. 'I'll park on the top road. We won't cross each other's paths.' He looks at his watch. 'I guess I should go.' Instead of going out the normal way, he disappears through the French doors at the back, and I realise he doesn't want Lucy to spot him leaving. I'm not sure when our family became so deceitful.

With nothing else to do, I wander into the living room. 'Mind if I join you?' I ask. Lucy doesn't look up, but she shifts her feet off the sofa, and I take that as an invitation. 'How are you doing?' I ask as I lower myself down.

She sighs. 'Can we just watch TV, Mum?'

Her tone is more pained than curt, so I turn towards the screen. She's hardly spoken since the detective left, hasn't asked me why he came, and I'm too tired to push it. It's the episode of *Friends* where Ross and Monica become ultra-competitive at a fun game of baseball, and it makes me think about my own children's sibling relationship. I've always assumed their differences mean they can't be that close. But I was wrong. Because Milla is out there, alone in the dark, risking her safety to protect her sister. She hasn't questioned Lucy's innocence at all – unlike me – or berated her for ignoring her big sister's advice. She's showing more empathy towards Lucy than I thought she was capable of.

I look at my watch: 11.58.

'You could go to bed, you know,' I say to Lucy. 'It's late, and there's no reason for you to stay up.'

'You really think I could fall asleep without knowing that Milla's okay? When she's doing all this for me? Where's Dad, anyway?' she adds tetchily.

I can't tell her the truth. She's bound to tell Milla that Matt went out to spy on her. 'Um, he went to the Co-op,' I lie. 'He's got a headache and we've run out of paracetamol.'

She looks at me suspiciously for a moment, then turns back to the TV. Perhaps it's safest not to talk after all.

I sneak a look at my phone: 00.05. Milla will have done the drop by now. God, I hope she's on her way home. Milla is hard-wired to stand up for herself, so I know her instinct will be to wait for Jess to appear and confront her. But Matt is watching the proceedings, I remind myself. If Milla tries anything like that, he'll intercept her.

The familiar *Friends* theme tune spills out of the TV speakers signifying the end of the episode. But after a few adverts, it strikes up again with a new one. I can't really follow the story – my head is too full of panic – but the sound of canned American laughter manages to worm its way in. I don't check my watch again, but the adverts come and go, and I know Matt and Milla should be back by now.

The theme music again. Black and white outfits. Ross falling into the fountain. Another episode has started. It's 00.49.

I push up off the sofa. I can't just sit here, waiting, hoping that my husband and firstborn are going to reappear. Why the hell did I ever think that being this passive was a good idea?

'Where are you going?' Lucy asks, fear creeping into her voice.

'I think I should go and find them.'

She looks at me. 'Dad followed her, didn't he?' It's more of a statement than a question and I bite my lip. 'He should trust her more.'

Before I can work out how to respond, there's a noise by the porch and we whip our heads around in unison.

'Milla!' I exhale. But my relief disintegrates when I see her expression. Her face is deathly pale – at odds with her normally warm complexion – and her eyes are red-ringed like she's been crying. 'What happened?' I ask. 'Are you okay?'

'I put the money in the bin,' she says quietly. 'Then I came home.'

'But you were gone for ages.'

'I had to …' She pauses, like she doesn't want to tell me. 'I had to hide behind one of the train carriages for a bit. To make sure I wasn't seen. But I'm exhausted now. I'm going to bed.'

'Hide? From who?'

'Please, Mum,' she says, a bit more forcefully. 'I need to sleep.' I watch her walk towards the stairs, then plod up them, her head looking too heavy for her shoulders. I want to go after her, demand that she tells me everything. But I know that's selfish. My interrogation will have to wait until morning.

'You should go too, Lucy,' I finally say. 'Milla's back now. Safe.' She doesn't move straight away, but after ten or so seconds, she pushes off the sofa, clicks the remote to turn the TV off, and wordlessly follows her sister upstairs.

But not everyone is home safely. I press on Matt's name in my call history, and listen to his phone ring and ring. I send him a WhatsApp message and will the ticks to turn blue. But I refuse to worry about him. Matt is a grown man – a physically intimidating one at that – in a reliable car with central locking.

He is not in danger.

AFTER

Saturday 11th May

Rachel

It's raining but I don't care. I always run on a Saturday morning, and I need it more than ever today. An outlet for my pent-up energy. But I'm wearing trainers, not trail runners, because there's no way I'm venturing beyond the solid safety of the pavement.

Matt finally got home at 01.38, nearly an hour after Milla, and looking equally shellshocked. But unlike our eldest daughter, after having a shower to calm himself down, he wanted to talk. Right from the beginning he'd found it difficult, he said, watching his little girl prowl across empty parkland. Not because she seemed fearful, but for how easily she took it in her stride. The drop itself had been uneventful, and with Milla appearing so in control, he'd decided to wait for Jess to turn up. While the place was deserted, he was paranoid that some chancer might wander past, find the bag, and pocket the money. And then it would all be for nothing.

Jess didn't come straight away and, crouching in the damp undergrowth in the shadow of oak trees, Matt had started to wonder whether she would. Getting out of her house after midnight – especially with what happened to her sister – can't have been easy. But after a while, maybe only fifteen minutes, although it felt longer, he'd spotted her. She'd arrived from the far side, by the old cement works, shoved the Waitrose bag in the pouch of her hoodie, and left via the same route Milla had taken. He'd not worried about that because he'd assumed Milla would be safely back home by then, and he'd returned to his car, grateful that it was done.

But emotional and exhausted, and with the road darkened by bowing trees on both sides, he hadn't seen the badger lumber across in front of him. Until he caught its startled zebra face in the car's headlights a second before he smacked into it. It had made such a thud that he irrationally thought he'd hit a person – even though he knew that wasn't the case – and the shock had proved too much. After checking and confirming that the badger had died on impact, he'd got back in his car and burst into tears. And once he'd started, he couldn't stop. He cried for the badger, for Amber, and for the effect her death was having on his family. And then his misery widened, crying for the career that was stolen from him, and the dad he'd never felt he properly grieved for.

He told me all this in bed, lying on his back, staring at the ceiling. But when I crawled my fingers towards his, he took hold of them. And then he apologised. He said that he knew he was hard work at times. That he was grateful for my patience, and sorry for being so fixated on having everything tidy. How he understood his obsessive nature was a crutch, but that he couldn't figure out how to let go. Instinctively I knew not to contribute, that he needed my ear, not my advice, so when he finished, we lay in silence for a while, hand in hand, until I eventually fell asleep. I'm not sure when he drifted off, but he was fast asleep when I crept out of the bedroom this morning.

I don't want to go anywhere near Chinnor Hill – Matt said that he would call the council this morning, but I assume the dead badger is still there at the moment – so I run towards the hamlet of Aston Rowant instead. On the quieter road, I hear the familiar call of a red kite – something between a cat's meow and a child's whistle – and I look up into the sky. It's a beautiful bird. Reddish brown with a deep fork in its tail. It was threatened with extinction in the UK once, but now they're thriving in the Chilterns – a whole species indebted to a few conservationists from the 1980s. It's another reminder that small decisions can have long-lasting consequences, and I run a little faster to deal with the adrenalin spike that thought causes.

If I want to stick to the roads, I have no choice but to turn around when I reach Aston Rowant and run back the same way. I jog past a row of large, detached properties, set back from the road, Range Rovers or Teslas parked in their long drives, and try to imagine living in one of them. But I quickly give up. I know it's weird to shun the idea of space, but I'm wary of it. Much better to have my family cramped together, in each other's pockets, than at a distance with places to hide.

When I get back to the village, my legs are feeling the 10km run, and I'm looking forward to a soak in the bath. The fresh wind has blown away the rain, and the sun is edging its way around the clouds. After Lucy's caginess last night, Milla's pale face, and Matt's distress, a day of sunshine feels like exactly what we need, and I stare upwards, willing it along.

'Whoa, Rachel!'

I stop, stumble backwards. Charlotte has just stepped out of the bakery, and we almost collided with each other. A sweet smell spills out from the paper bag she's holding.

'Gosh, you startled me,' I respond, drawing my palms into my chest to calm my breathing.

'It's good to see you,' she says, her voice softening now the shock has worn off. 'I thought about calling, after what happened, but I didn't want to make a fuss.'

My instant reaction is guilt – for both the real and imagined crimes my family have committed – and I can't help wondering if Annie has told Charlotte about Milla going missing the night before Amber died. But there's no accusation in my friend's face, so I smile my thanks. 'Not making a fuss is perfect, thank you,' I say. 'It was awful, poor girl, but I'm trying to put it behind me.'

'Of course,' she says, nodding her understanding. 'And hopefully the boyfriend being arrested will help with that.'

'Boyfriend?' I ask. I saw the item on the local news last night – DI Finnemore standing outside Aylesbury police station and announcing that they'd arrested a 17-year-old male in connection with Amber's murder. Colleen had suggested he was Amber's boyfriend, but I wonder how Charlotte knows.

'Yes, I saw Bill last night. Their family liaison officer told him and Molly that a lad from Towersey had been arrested, and that he was Amber's boyfriend. Bill had no idea she was even seeing anyone, poor man.' Emotion catches in her throat.

'Have you seen much of them?' I ask. 'Amber's foster carers?'

'A few times. The church community have pulled together to help them. It's one of the things I like best about it. Molly is out of hospital now and seems fine physically – albeit with a load of new pills to take – but she's devastated. Keeps blaming herself, like you would, even though of course it's not her or Bill's fault. I shouldn't say it, but it sounds like that girl was trouble. I doubt they'll foster ever again,' she adds sadly.

'What about Jess?' I ask. 'I suppose they're still fostering her?'

'She wants to leave. Apparently, her social worker tried to persuade her to take a bit more time to figure it all out. But then she started acting up – of course she'd be angry, wouldn't she – and Bill realised that he and Molly wouldn't be able to cope. Not after everything that's happened. So the social worker is trying to sort something out. It might mean a children's home though; sadly there aren't a steady stream of foster carers willing to take on a messed-up teenager in Oxfordshire.'

'Poor kid,' I mumble. And for all Jess has done to my family, I mean it. Oxfordshire is one of the UK's most affluent counties, so it shouldn't be hard to find a spare room in a stable setting, even for someone with as many issues as Jess. But perhaps that's hypocritical. I mentioned the idea to Matt once, of fostering when both girls had left home. His answer was a flat no – that we do enough for vulnerable children already – and I've never felt strongly enough to try and change his mind. 'Let's hope she gets a chance to start over,' I continue.

But Charlotte's gaze has shifted away from me. 'That's him,' she whispers, hardly moving her lips.

'That's who?' I want to turn in the direction of her stare, but the memory of bumping into Jess at the Co-op is still raw.

'Bill Wainwright, just coming out of the post office. He looks so sad; I should go and check on him. Come with me?'

'Well, I should really be getting back …'

'Please?' she asks. She shifts along the pavement, and as we haven't resolved our conversation, I feel compelled to move with her. Bill is walking in our direction too, and I realise I can't escape this. 'Hey, Bill, how are you?' Charlotte asks when we reach him, each word gilded with sympathy.

'Hello, Charlotte,' he says, his voice hoarse. 'Not great.' He turns to look at me, narrows his eyes. 'You're the lady who found our Amber.'

'I am, yes,' I mutter. 'I'm so sorry, such a tragedy,' I force myself to make eye contact and then wish I hadn't. Tears are welling up in his, and before I have chance to look away, he's sobbing, his shoulders spasming.

'Oh, Bill,' Charlotte murmurs, putting an arm around him. 'You poor, poor thing. I can't imagine what you're going through at the moment.'

'It's awful, Charlotte,' he splutters. 'Every minute is like a living hell. You think it can't get any worse, and then it does. And it's all my fault.'

'No, it's not,' Charlotte says sternly. 'You can't wrap them up in cotton wool, Bill. You thought she went to youth club, then

181

came home, like normal. You could never have known her text wasn't true.'

'And what about Jess?' he throws back at her. I hold my breath.

'What do you mean?' Charlotte asks gently.

'She's not in a good way,' he says, his voice cracking. 'I haven't let her out of my sight since she came back from that emergency foster carer on Tuesday. But she must have sneaked out in the middle of the night, or maybe first thing this morning, because she wasn't in her bed when I got up. She's not answering my calls either. I've asked around and no one's seen her.' He drops his head so low that his chin is almost touching his chest. 'I know I need to tell the police, and Colleen, her social worker, that she's missing. But I'm not sure I can bear it. Not after Amber.'

His face creases again, then disappears into his hands. Charlotte and I exchange horrified glances, but she has no idea what's fuelling mine. Have I caused this? Has the money we provided given Jess the means to break this man's heart a second time?

AFTER

Saturday 11th May

Rachel

Milla is sitting at the kitchen table when I get back, eating a Lindt chocolate bunny, leftovers from her Easter stash. I consider pulling her up on her unhealthy breakfast choice, but I just reach for a piece instead, and enjoy a rare moment of pleasure as the milk chocolate disintegrates on my tongue. But its residue reminds me that I'm thirsty after my run, so I pour a large glass of water and gulp half of it down.

'How are you doing?' I ask, once my hydration levels have risen.

Milla shrugs but doesn't look at me. 'Fine.'

'No after-effects from last night?'

'I said I'm fine, Mum,' she reminds me in a stern voice. She breaks off a rabbit's ear, angles it to the side of her mouth, and gnaws with her back teeth. When I first woke up, I was determined to ask her what happened last night. Why she'd been crying. Who she needed to hide from among the disused train carriages. Especially after Matt telling me that Jess left via the same route. But my run has changed that, created some distance between last night and today. And now with Jess probably gone from the village too, maybe it's time to let things lie.

'Have you seen Dad yet?' I ask. He's usually up early, but after his eventful night, it wouldn't surprise me if he was having a lie-in.

'He went out.'

My forehead lifts in surprise. 'For a bike ride?'

'To the garage. Says he hit a badger yesterday afternoon, and it did some damage to the front of the car.'

'Oh. That's right, he did,' I say weakly.

'Badgers don't come out in the daytime, Mum. He followed me last night, didn't he?' She doesn't wait for an answer. 'You know, I'm glad his car is damaged. He deserves it for not trusting me.'

The muscles in my neck tighten. I want to scream at her, to tell her that she's wrong, that it was love, not mistrust, that compelled Matt to follow her. But she'll just brush me off with the conviction of someone who hasn't had an ounce of it knocked out of her yet. So instead, I silently remind myself that Milla's self-confidence is a good thing, and head upstairs for a hot shower.

I'm sitting on my bed twenty minutes later, drying my hair, when a message pops up on my phone. It's from Annie to our mums' group.

Have you seen the post on Nextdoor?

My heart sinks. That website is more popular than you might imagine in a village where gossip is still spread very effectively face to face. This will be about Jess running away. Bill, or one of his friends from church, must have decided to reach out to a wider audience. With my spare hand, I push the phone across the duvet, out of sight. But when it beeps again a few seconds later, I can't help reaching for it.

Yes! Can't believe it.
Do you think she's been hurt?
God, hopefully not a repeat of last Friday night.

The hairdryer slips through my fingers. Hot air blasts my midriff until I find the off button. *Jess has run away*, I remind myself silently. *Because we gave her the means to do so.* Then a message pops up from Charlotte.

Police with Bill and Molly now.
Worst Groundhog Day EVER.

My eyes sting with tears, but I refuse to cry. My friends don't know what I know. If they did, they'd realise that Jess's disappearance makes sense. That she's left – ten grand richer – of her own accord. Devastating for the Wainwrights, yes, but not for her.

But still, I wish I knew this for certain.

I can't contact DI Finnemore – and it's not like he'd tell me what's going on anyway. I could go to the pub, talk to Steve, see if he's heard anything. But that's like relying on Dr Google for a medical diagnosis.

There is someone else who the police would keep updated though: Jess's official guardian. I've only met Colleen once, but I liked her a lot. And she trusted me with Amber's background. I'm sure she'd put my interest in Jess's disappearance down to a mix of my finding her sister's body last Saturday morning and professional curiosity.

I head downstairs and straight into the study where my laptop is still plugged in. I pull up my staff database and pause. What's her surname? I scrunch my eyes in concentration until it comes to me – Colleen Byrne – and then the rest is easy. But as I stare at her list of contact details, I hesitate again, except this time through indecision. An email would be more professional, but a text is bound to elicit faster results. Decision made, I add her number to my contacts and tap out a text. It takes a few aborted attempts before I'm happy with my wording, how I've heard the news from Bill, and feel a sense of responsibility. And then I press send before I change my mind. Her response is almost immediate.

Yes, very worrying. I'm on my way to her foster carers now. Police already there. All hoping she ran away but keeping an open mind.

I read her message again. And again. Then I tap out a reply.

Could she have gone to see her dad? Did you say he lives in Derbyshire?

I'm staring so intently at my screen – willing for it to light up with a response – that I almost drop it when it rings. But I collect myself and press to accept the call.

'I'm in the car now, so easier to talk on my hands-free than text,' Colleen explains in her soft Irish accent. I mumble something incoherent in response. 'You're right about Jess's dad being in Derbyshire,' she goes on. 'I went to see him yesterday. The local police are going over to his flat this morning, but I'm not confident she's going to show up there.'

'I remember you saying that she had ideas about moving in with him,' I start tentatively. 'Wouldn't that be the obvious place for her to go?'

'He's her hero, it's true,' Colleen says. 'But now I've met him, I'm not sure I got that right. His mental health seems very fragile, and Jess is smarter than she lets on. I imagine, deep down, she knows he's not capable of being a proper dad to her. Between you and me, I'm worried that Jess hasn't run away at all. She hasn't taken much of her stuff, if any – Molly and Bill are too upset to know for sure if anything is missing. And if she wanted to start a new life – with her dad or whoever – wouldn't she at least pack a bag?'

My mind whirs. 'Maybe she wasn't thinking straight?' I try. 'Grief making her want to cut all ties?'

'Maybe.' But Colleen doesn't sound convinced. I close my eyes, and then squeeze them more tightly shut.

'But nothing could have happened to her, surely?' I sound like I'm pleading. I cough, level my voice. 'And it's not like Amber's killer could be involved because I heard on the news that he's in custody.'

'If he did it,' she murmurs.

'What?'

'Sorry, ignore me. Listen, Rachel, I have another call coming through, so I better go. Thanks for calling, for caring. I'll keep you updated.'

I nod, but can't speak, and a second later, the line goes dead. I stare at the sleeping laptop screen. Whatever Colleen thinks, the mechanic boyfriend murdered Amber, and Jess ran away. It's the only explanation. Isn't it?

I drum my fingernails against the desk. Matt saw Jess collect the money from the bin at Kiln Lakes at about quarter past midnight, so she was fine then. She left in the direction of the disused carriages. Milla had to hide from someone there. She looked ashen when she eventually got home and Milla never gets scared. Could Jess have come across the same person when she walked through fifteen minutes later? Did they do something to her? Something violent?

Is the boyfriend innocent after all? I was so desperate for Amber's killer to not be either of my daughters, that I leapt on the first suspect who was mentioned. But him being innocent doesn't make Milla or Lucy guilty. It would just mean that it was someone else. And if it was, that person is still out there.

Did Milla come close to being a victim herself?

I move from the study to the kitchen – conflicted in my dual urge to hold my daughter tight, and demand that she tells me who she was hiding from. But I can't do either because the room is empty, just a note on the table – *Gone to library to revise*. I swear under my breath and slump down into my usual chair. I try calling, but her phone is switched off. A few minutes later I hear the porch door open, and Matt walks into the kitchen. He looks exhausted.

'Milla said you took the car to the garage?' I say gently.

'Yeah,' he mutters. 'The paintwork is scuffed and there's a ding from where I hit that badger. I called the council by the way,' he adds, running his hand up and down his opposite arm, the swish of skin on skin. 'They're going to send someone to pick it up this morning.' He shifts his gaze downwards. 'I still feel terrible about it.'

I reach a hand towards him, but he doesn't reciprocate, as though the intimacy of our conversation last night never happened. 'It was an accident,' I remind him, lowering my hand back down. 'Badgers are really hard to see at night. Don't blame yourself.'

'I know. I just need to put last night, in fact the whole of last week, behind me and move on. God, what's all this mess on the table?' He grimaces, then grabs the dishcloth and starts wiping up the tiny brown slivers, what's left of Milla's Easter bunny.

I know this is a sign he's struggling, but I can't deal with the news about Jess by myself. 'She's gone missing,' I tell him. 'Jess. She wasn't in bed this morning, and no one's seen her.'

Matt keeps wiping. Then he pulls the bench out and starts wiping that down too. 'She'll have done a runner. Taken the money and gone. I mean, what's left for her in Chinnor? Two old people and a personal tragedy that people will never stop talking about?'

'You're right,' I say nodding. 'She's got a lot to run away from. But I spoke to her social worker just now – I met her at work on Thursday – and the police think something bad might have happened to Jess. Her disappearing so soon after Amber's murder, and also because she doesn't seem to have taken any stuff with her. Her foster carers didn't know for sure, but wouldn't she have taken all her things if it was planned?'

'Who knows how the mind of a troubled, grieving teenager works,' Matt says, his tone prickly. He straightens up, pushes the bench back. 'Look, I've got to work this morning. My bike ride yesterday afternoon went on longer than planned, and my inbox has piled up.' And before I get a chance to respond, he brushes past me, his gaze averted, and leaves the room. I listen to the study door close behind him.

AFTER

Saturday 11th May

Rachel

'When will you get your car back?' I ask, picking at the Moretti bar mat. It was my idea to come out for a drink this evening. Matt's black mood has continued all day and I thought a change of scene might help. But now I'm here, I feel on edge.

'They couldn't say,' he says tightly. Then he clears his throat, and his voice softens. 'There's not much damage, but the garage is busy next week, so they need to fit it in around their existing schedule.'

'What about work?' I ask.

He shrugs. 'Most of the team are away this week, various school visits, so I'll just work from home.' He falls silent again and then takes another gulp of beer. He scans the room and I wonder if he feels exposed, like I do, or if it's because he doesn't want to look at me.

'You don't seem yourself today,' I try.

'I'm fine.'

'Is it about Jess disappearing?'

He gives me a disappointed glare, then looks away. 'Why would

I be worried about that? She'll have used the money to run away, just like we predicted. Like we hoped for, remember?'

I think back to our stilted conversation as we counted down the hours before the drop last night. Our hope that Jess would take the money and then vanish from our lives. Is Matt right? Should I be celebrating rather than catastrophising? Then I think about the Waitrose bag, the note Milla typed. *My dad will kill you.*

Why the hell can't he even hold eye contact with me?

I take a gulp of my gin and tonic. 'Are you worried about the police then? That detective coming round with more questions for Lucy?'

He closes his eyes, lets out a deep sigh. 'I know what being falsely accused of a crime can do,' he murmurs, his voice stretched by emotion. 'I couldn't bear it if Lucy suffers the same fate as me, and for something much more serious. She's been through enough already.'

'She's got us,' I say. 'She knows we'll always be there for her.'

'And what 15-year-old girl is satisfied with that? Lucy's best – and let's be honest, only proper friend – left her. Whether there's something romantic going on between Lucy and Bronwen or not, those two girls have been practically joined at the hip for a decade. Losing her must have been devastating.' He pauses, his features soften a notch. 'Hey, do you remember them doing that blood-sister ceremony?'

I nod. Smile at the memory of two 8-year-old girls. A solemn ritual of friendship until Milla made them both cry with stories of cross infection and vampire diseases.

'But instead of having time to adapt to life without Bronwen,' Matt continues, his face hardening again. 'Lucy was suddenly being picked on, relentlessly, by two fucking nasty teenage girls for no reason at all. And then manipulated into meeting Amber on the very night the girl's killed.'

It's all my fears echoing back to me. But I can't let them drag me down, otherwise everything we've done so far – all the lies we've told, the ransom demand we've met – will be for nothing. 'It being a more serious crime should work in our favour,' I point out. 'Murder is investigated with much more depth than assault. Even if they find out that Lucy met Amber, it's only circumstantial. They'll need more evidence than that to charge her with murder. Real forensic evidence.' I push away the image of Lucy's jeans; the blood spatters that I did my best to wash away. The missing jumper. The denim jacket she supposedly lost.

Matt's face clears slightly. 'Yes, you're right,' he says, exhaling. 'And I'm sorry.' He reaches for my hand, grazes my fingers with his. 'I'm probably just tired.' Then he shifts backwards, picks up his pint glass and drains the remaining beer. 'Another drink?' he asks, standing up.

I watch him walk to the bar, then make conversation with Steve's wife Jade. He's smiling, nodding, and to anyone else he might seem totally at ease. But I can see the muscles in his jaw tremoring. His fingers drumming against his side.

Is this really fear for Lucy? Or is something else making him stressed?

My dad will kill you.

I think about the badger he hit, the damage to the car, his lost hour crying by the roadside. But that's all it was, I remind myself, a string of unfortunate events. And he's explained why he's acting strangely.

'Here you go,' he says, handing me a fresh gin and tonic. I take the goblet from him – the ice clinking as my hand shakes – and watch him sit down. He eyes the Moretti bar mat I've ruined, then slides it across the table and puts it in his pocket. Needing its scrappy edges out of sight.

He was tidy even when we first met, back when we were two uncool students at one of Oxford's most elite colleges. I remember the cleaner calling him her golden boy because his room would always be spotless. But in those days, I could tease him about it, and he wouldn't mind; he'd just raise his eyebrows and look at me sheepishly. That changed when his dad died, and the carefree side of him has never fully returned. I know if I referenced his discomfort with the bar mat now, he'd snap at me.

'I didn't get a chance to tell you about Milla's journey home last night,' I say instead.

He narrows his eyes. 'I saw Milla this morning, she said everything went smoothly.'

'She was cross with you; she didn't fall for your story about hitting the badger in daylight.'

'Too smart, that one,' he murmurs. 'So what happened on her journey?'

'I don't have the full story,' I admit. 'But she didn't get back until ten to one. And she'd been crying, which is not like her at all. She said that she'd seen someone when she was walking past the derelict carriages and had to hide from them, presumably until they left.'

'Poor kid,' Matt mutters. 'On top of everything else. But she didn't tell you who it was?'

I shake my head. 'She was exhausted last night so I didn't push it. And then she was mad about you following her this morning, so I didn't try. And she'd gone to the library by the time I came back downstairs after my shower. I haven't seen her since.'

He stays quiet for a while, rubs his forehead with the heel of his hand. 'Do you think it could have been Felix?' he asks eventually.

I look up, surprised. Milla hiding from her ex-boyfriend hadn't crossed my mind.

'I've heard that teenage romances, um, blossom in that railway dumping ground,' he goes on. 'If Felix had been there with some other girl, Milla wouldn't have wanted to interrupt that. And I imagine it's one of the few things that she might cry about?'

I sit back in my chair. Could it be something as simple as that? Milla has never explained why her relationship with Felix ended so abruptly, but teenage boys cheating on their girlfriends must be relatively standard behaviour. But if it was Felix who Milla was hiding from, then the threat was personal to her. It wouldn't explain why Jess disappeared.

'If Milla was hiding all that time, she must have seen Jess walk past,' I say.

Matt's expression sours. 'What?'

'Well, if Jess picked the money up about fifteen minutes after Milla dropped it, then she'd have been walking past those carriages less than ten minutes later. As I said, Milla didn't get home until nearer one o'clock, and it's only a ten-minute walk from there, so their paths must have crossed.'

He blinks. It's warm in the pub and beads of sweat are forming on his forehead. Why does he look so uncomfortable?

A weight sinks onto my chest. I take a deep breath. 'That makes sense, doesn't it?'

'Did Milla say she saw Jess?' he asks.

I shuffle backwards on my chair, push my spine against its hard wooden back. 'I told you,' I say carefully. 'I haven't had a chance to talk to her properly.'

'Properly?' He lets out a crack of laughter, then lowers his voice. 'Don't you think it would have been her headline comment if she'd seen the person who's blackmailing us?'

His question suddenly breathes life into the first thought I had when I found out Jess was missing this morning. That Milla wouldn't admit to seeing Jess in that train carriage graveyard if she'd done something to her. Just like she could have done something to Amber during those lost hours on Friday night. I wonder if the police have searched the disused carriages. There must be at least thirty of them in various states of disrepair up there. I wonder how long it would take to look through them all. 'I just can't work out how she could have missed seeing Jess,' I say.

'It's a big place,' Matt counters, his voice stripped of all warmth. 'It was dark. Milla was hiding. If she heard someone moving, she would have assumed it was Felix – or whoever she was hiding from – and kept her head down even more.'

My skin prickles. Matt's explanation makes a lot of sense. Why didn't I think like that? Why did I jump to Milla being violent?

Does that mean I'm being equally unfair about Matt? Being obsessively tidy and unusually quiet isn't a crime. In fact, many wives would love their husbands to be more like him. 'Do you really think Jess just ran away?' I ask.

'One hundred per cent,' Matt says, his voice firm. 'I can see why other people might question why she didn't take all her stuff. But that's because they don't know she's got a fresh ten grand in her pocket. Why bother packing your old clothes when you've got plenty of money to buy new ones?'

This makes sense too, I realise. 'Where do you think she's gone?' I ask quietly. 'She is only 15.'

Matt's eyes shift. 'Who knows,' he says gently. 'But it's not like the system has done her any favours. With some money in her pocket, maybe she'll thrive on her own.'

This is symbolic of the new Matt, his disillusionment with the state who employed him for fifteen years. It goes against everything I believe in, and listening to him be so dismissive of a system that might creak but is filled with people who genuinely want to make a difference, is hard to deal with. But it's easier to let his comments go rather than get into an argument.

'She's got a dad,' I tell him. 'Up in Derbyshire. Her social worker told me she idolises him.'

'Really?' He looks at me, then away. 'Do you think she might have gone there?'

'The police were checking this morning. I suppose she wouldn't have been able to get that far so quickly, even with money for the train fare. But hopefully her dad will keep the police updated.'

'Or hopefully he won't,' Matt murmurs. 'That kid deserves some space. And a chance to make her own decisions. If that translates as her trying to make it work with her dad without social services meddling, then I think she should be allowed to – whether the state thinks he's a fit parent or not. They don't always get it right.'

I look away, tip the ice-cold drink down my throat.

You don't always get it right.
That's what Matt is really saying.
And perhaps he's got a point.

Email from DI Finnemore (SIO) to Det Supt Bishop

Subject: Sunday 12th May update

Sir,

Victim's sister – Jessica Scott – was reported missing yesterday morning by her social worker, Colleen Byrne. She went to bed as normal on Friday night but was not there when her foster carer checked at approx. 08.30. Missing person investigation has been opened by the area team – but we're pooling info and resources as the cases are so closely linked.

Property searched. No sign of forced entry, or of a struggle. No window open in Jessica's bedroom. Assumed she left the property of her own accord. Small rucksack missing. Possibly some clothes as well but foster carers were unable to confirm. Most of her belongings remain. No sign of phone, but records show it hasn't been used since Friday night. All usual checks (hospitals, known acquaintances, etc.) have proved unsuccessful so far. CCTV footage being collected today. Open mind about third party involvement at this stage – but Caden Carter clearly not involved as he was in police custody. Will keep you updated.

Caden Carter was released on police bail with strict conditions yesterday evening. Interviews were going nowhere, and CPS want answers to forensic anomalies before they'll consider charging him so that's our focus for now. Also, between you and me, I am conflicted. He has stuck to his story without any of the usual lying tells. Hard to believe that Amber saw two different people in such a remote location, but not impossible. And the multiple blood samples support that theory. She was

196

an active user of Snapchat so theoretically her location could have been known to all her followers via the map function. Am trying to get more data but you know social media companies and their f**king privacy obsession.

I think I mentioned a lead that Colleen Byrne gave us after Amber's body was found. Raj has been looking into this. About a year ago, Amber was roughed up by an older boy with query gang affiliations while at their last foster home. This is what prompted the girls' move. But the threat was actually aimed at her sister, Jess, and all indications so far are that the girls have completely disengaged from their old life, so this remains a low priority line of inquiry. However, Raj is tracking down the male involved (now 19 years old) to question him.

Also, I was looking through witness statements again last night. There was an eighteenth birthday party in Chinnor the night of the murder, and the mother of the host was interviewed. Two children had taken ecstasy, which we discovered was supplied by the victim and the team understandably focused on that. But I noticed that Mrs Ainsworth (the host's mother) also mentioned that she saw Mr Rose – Lucy's father – in his car when she was taking some bottles to her recycling box at the front of her house at about 00.45. He asked if the party was over, she confirmed that it was, and he drove away. But Mrs Rose told me that her husband was fast asleep when she got home at 22.45.

I have asked DC Williams to check all CCTV during the evening for his car specifically. I'm starting to wonder if that family aren't as sweet and innocent as they look.

Simon

AFTER

Monday 13th May

Rachel

I roll onto my back and open my eyes. The darkness is almost absolute, but I can just make out the shadow of our glass pendant ceiling light above me. Its filament bulbs look like three black eyes, and I stare into them, willing them to bring me some clarity. But there's nothing, so I turn onto my side, away from Matt, and look at my watch on its stand instead: 04.47 in loud fluorescent green.

Of course I wasn't going to sleep well after the Sunday I had. Or Sunday afternoon to be exact, because the day started quite well. Milla offered to come to Waitrose with me, which must be a first, and it gave me a chance to ask her about Friday night. While she didn't exactly shower me with details, after a little encouragement, she did explain what happened.

And it turns out Matt was right. It *was* Felix that Milla was hiding from. And that led to a conversation about why they split up in the first place. Quietly, without making eye contact, Milla told me that Felix had admitted to cheating on her. She didn't know who with, and he promised her that it was over. But she wanted out. And once she got over the initial shock, she found that she liked being single again.

Unlike Felix, who just got more desperate to get her back. Milla was starting to entertain the possibility of a reconciliation when she came across him snogging someone behind one of the derelict carriages on Friday night. In the darkness, Milla couldn't make out who it was, so the girl's identity remains a mystery. But he'd lied, and she almost fell for it; and that hurt a lot. I explained this all to Matt when I got home from the supermarket, how he'd guessed right. I thought he'd be relieved, but he didn't react one way or the other.

I tried to make lunch feel normal. Cooked a roast lamb with new potatoes, spring vegetables and home-made mint sauce. Even convinced Matt to open a bottle of Pinot Noir. Milla did her bit – telling us about the revision schedule she'd devised for her study leave – but Lucy was mute, Matt grim-faced, and my own conversation was stilted as I tried not to mention Amber Walsh, Jess Scott, blackmail, bullying, drugs, dead badgers, violent mechanics or blood-smeared bluebells.

And then Charlotte's message popped up on my phone.

Have you heard the news?
Wainwrights told this morning.
Suspect in custody has been released.

I didn't go back to her. Perhaps I should have done, to keep up the pretence of being a gossip fiend like everyone else in the village. But I didn't have the strength for more bad news, so I turned my phone off completely, and stacked the plates in the dishwasher with so much gusto that one of them smashed. When the landline rang a few hours later, I chose to let it ring out, but I couldn't completely leave my head in the sand because, when I saw the red light flashing, I listened to the voicemail.

It was DC Bzowski. As soon as I heard her voice, the memory

of Lucy's interview sprang into my mind, making my chest tighten. But the message wasn't for me, or Lucy. The detective was asking for Matt to call her. She didn't say anything more, but that didn't stop my mind racing.

My dad will kill you.

Was she calling about the note? Had Jess got it to them somehow before running away? Or maybe she dropped it, and the police have come across it. It was typed rather than hand-written, but with the link to Lucy, maybe it would have been easy for the police to work out which dad the note was referring to.

I couldn't settle after that, or bring myself to tell Matt about the message, so I picked up my car keys, muttered something about going out for fuel, and escaped the house.

I had nowhere to go, but I took the main road out of the village towards Kingston Blount. I kept my eyes focused on the tarmac as I passed Kiln Lakes, but just beyond them, in the open fields, I saw a flash of something in the corner my eye. A sight that made me retch.

There were at least a dozen police officers. Eyes down, walking slowly across the fields beyond the lake. And there could only have been one reason they were there. The police must think Jess has been harmed otherwise why would they be searching in the undergrowth? And so close to where Milla left the ransom money. Matt said Jess came from those fields but left in the other direction, so they're looking in the wrong place. But of course Matt can't explain that to the police.

My dad will kill you.

Just like Lucy can't admit to seeing Amber on the night she died.

I wish she was dead.

My phone moves past 05.00 and I decide that's close enough to morning to get up. I push back the duvet, shuffle out of bed, and creep from the room. As I wait for the kettle to boil, I stare into the garden – dawn sneaking its way over the fir trees – and try to make sense of what's happened over the last ten days. How my family has become so entwined in another family's trauma.

Except it's not ten days, I realise as I pour steaming water into my mug and watch the teabag balloon then settle. It began last autumn when Amber and Jess initiated their bullying campaign. Lucy did nothing to provoke them, not at the start or later. But for over six months they wouldn't leave her alone. If anything, their bullying escalated over the period. All I could think about was stopping it, so I never put any energy into understanding why they did it in the first place.

I lean against the kitchen counter, sip my tea, and realise what I need to do.

It's half past six when I arrive at my office. I washed in the kitchen sink at home, and chose clothes from the laundry pile to avoid going back upstairs, so I look a mess. But luckily the place is deserted. The cleaners have been – they work overnight – and there's a strong smell of furniture polish in the air. I drop into my chair, plug my laptop into the cable curled around my stand, and open up the client database. During the car journey here, I promised myself that I wouldn't pause. That I mustn't give myself an opportunity to change my mind. But as I stare at the search function, my fingers hover over the keyboard.

We only have one database in Children's Services, and of course I have access to it – I'm one of the team's most senior employees. At any point during this whole messy time, I could have logged in, brought up Amber's and Jess's file, and found out everything about them. But I have been doing this job for twenty-five years, and reading the details of cases you're not involved in just isn't done. It goes against the principles that have etched their way into my skin over the last two and a half decades.

But this is exactly what I came to do this morning, so I need to stop pretending that I'm grappling with my conscience and get on with it.

I type *Amber Walsh* and click into her file. It's all there. Her mother being killed by her abusive partner when Amber was 6 years old. The series of short-term foster carers who looked after her while something more permanent was set in place. The move to Littlemore, a neighbourhood south of Oxford's city centre, with her sister Jessica a year later. And then to Chinnor in July 2023 due to "safety concerns" which all fits with what Colleen told me.

But then I notice the secondary school that Amber attended for a year before she moved, and I feel blood drain from my face. I lean back for a moment, close my eyes. I think about the dead badger and wonder whether the council removed it like they promised Matt.

Whether it exists at all.

Then, very slowly, as though there's tonne of pressure against my chest, I lean forward again. I crawl my fingers across the keyboard until Jess's file appears and, with a final push of inner strength, I press open and watch the information expand on my screen.

TWO YEARS, TWO MONTHS BEFORE

Thursday 24th February 2022

Jess

In the year and a half that she's been at Oxford Comprehensive, this is the first time Jess has been in the head teacher's office. Despite her being a foster kid, and related to Amber, the most badly behaved student in Year Seven.

But that's not why she's petrified.

She knows it shows on her face. Even with all her freckles for camouflage, she can't hide her fear.

'You look worried, Jessica,' Mr Pearson says in a voice that's supposed to soothe but does the opposite. 'Listen, don't be. It's brave of you to come forward, and we're grateful. The welfare of our students always comes first, and that means you *and* Sean.' He gives her an encouraging nod. As head teachers go, Mr Pearson could be worse. He's not young, but he's not old either. And he doesn't have anything gross like hairy ears or bad breath. Just a grey suit, grey eyes and, she supposes, a half-decent smile.

'Okay,' Jess mumbles, pulling at the hem of her skirt. 'But can I go now that I've told you? I have geography next period.'

'I'm afraid I need to keep you for just a bit longer.'

'What for?' Jess's right leg starts jiggling all by itself. She pushes down on her thigh, but instead of her leg settling, her arms join in. She's wobbling all over the place now.

'Mrs Davis has informed your tutor,' he explains, misinterpreting her concern (like she's ever cared about geography). 'So you won't get into any trouble for missing your lesson.'

'But I've already told you everything,' Jess whines.

'I know, but I've asked your social worker to come in, Jess. Gail Thompson. And, uh, the police.'

Jess looks up. 'The police?' God, she didn't think this through at all. She assumed that she'd tell Mr Pearson, and that would be it. He'd deal with it from then on. She can't talk to the police. She'll die of a heart attack before doing that.

'Yes, well, they are already involved,' Mr Pearson explains. 'It's a serious allegation, you see, so we informed the police yesterday, when Tuesday afternoon's incident first came to light. And I think they will really want to hear what you have to say first-hand.'

'Can't you tell them,' Jess begs weakly. 'Please.'

Understanding wafts across his face. Of course he'll know about her past, her mum. 'I'm very sorry, but it doesn't work that way. That's why I asked Gail to come along. Someone familiar to support you.'

Jess bites her lip until it hurts. Gail is their official stand-in mother but in reality, she's useless. Lou – their foster mum – is much nicer, but even she isn't great. Jess and Amber have been living with Lou and Justin for four years, so she should feel like a real mum by now. Especially as she's the mumsy type. But there's something so *unreal* about it all. She's too nice; too kind; too try-hard. Most of the time it's easier to take advantage of her good nature and not think too hard about it.

They wait in silence. Jess wants to get her phone out, scroll through Instagram (that cow Gail won't let her have TikTok yet), but she daren't risk it in front of her head teacher. So she tries to think about nothing, but that doesn't work either. Not with the police on their way.

Her memories about the night her mum died start vague. Lying in bed in the darkness, Amber asleep next to her, or at least pretending to be. The TV on loud in the living room, crackling with cheering crowds and shouty sports commentators. At first her mum and Tyler sounded happy; they even sang when the national anthem played. Glass bottles clinked and thudded on the carpet. But then things shifted. Tyler's voice became angry, her mum's grew cagey. There was shouting, a few slaps, wailing. Then a loud smack and thud. A moment later, the front door banged, and it was silent.

That's when Jess got out of bed, even though she'd been told never to do that when her mum and Tyler were fighting. She wanted to check her mum was okay.

Jacqui was lying close to the table. There was blood coming out of her head. It was the worst thing Jess had ever seen in her life but also mesmerising. The stain spreading like spilled Ribena. Jess thinks that's why she froze. Seconds, minutes. In the five and a half years since, she's not been able to work that out. But she hopes it was seconds. That there was nothing she could have done.

It was the noise outside that made her move again. She thought it was Tyler, coming back, so she ran into her room and scrambled into bed. But it wasn't Tyler. The neighbours had called the police, and there they suddenly were, more and more of them, and all of them scary in their black uniforms and clomping boots. In her rush to get into bed, she hadn't shut the door properly and over the years, counsellors and social workers have made a thing of that. She's never once told anyone the truth of it.

Some muffled conversation in the corridor brings Jess back. Someone knocks on the door.

'Come in,' Mr Pearson calls out, not hiding his relief at the arrival of suited backup.

Jess turns to see Gail walk in the room, followed by a man and woman in dull clothing. Detectives. Mr Pearson gestures to some chairs lined up against the back wall and they all dutifully pick one up and place it closer to his desk – as though he's their head teacher. Gail draws her chair closest to Jess and reaches for her hand. But Jess reacts in time, pulling it away and sliding both her hands between her knees. Everyone pretends not to notice, even though everybody does.

'So, Jess,' Mr Pearson starts. 'Obviously you know Gail. And this is DS Sawyer and DC Blake.' He gestures towards the woman, then the man. 'They're investigating the incident. I just want you to tell them everything you've told me this morning.'

Jess tries to pull her face into a smile, but it doesn't work.

'Hi, Jess,' DS Sawyer says, spotting her terror in a nanosecond. She's got red hair too, and a translucent complexion, although no freckles.

'Hi.'

'Thanks for talking to us. Mr Pearson said that you witnessed the assault on Sean Russo on Tuesday afternoon. That must have been shocking.'

The detective's being nice, Jess thinks. Is this because she's a 13-year-old kid or is it standard behaviour for the police? A way to catch people off guard? She sighs and looks down at her lap. God, why did she decide to stay behind for art club on Tuesday? And then spill water on her painting – her *watercolour*, of course – and skulk out because she was too embarrassed to clean it up. More importantly, why did she then go home and tell Amber what had happened? She knows that Amber is basically in love with Sean, even though he's five years older than her. Of course she'd make Jess talk to Mr Pearson.

'Um, yes,' she starts. 'From outside. Through the window.'

'Sorry, Jess, could you hold on a sec,' DC Blake interrupts, unfolding his laptop. 'I'm just going to type up your statement, and then you can sign it at the end, okay?'

Jess has never signed a document before. The thought makes her skin itch, but she gives him a small nod.

'Great. So you saw Mr Rose strike Sean Russo on Wednesday at about 4.45 p.m.?'

'What? Um. I'm not sure what time it was,' Jess says, panic really setting in. 'I just saw the punch, through the window.'

The red-haired detective gives her colleague an annoyed look. 'Sorry, Jess; you tell us in your own words. Let's start with why you were still at school at that time.'

'I'd been at art club,' Jess starts. 'But I was feeling a bit sick, so I decided to leave early. I went to the loo, and then headed for the school gates, which meant walking across the courtyard. I suppose it was about 4.45 p.m.' Jess pauses, but no one says anything, just looks at her expectantly, so she carries on. 'The English classrooms run across the back, and I saw Sean in the middle one. I don't think I knew his surname was Russo.'

'But you do know him, then?' DS Sawyer pushes. It's gentle, but Jess still wonders if the detective thinks she's lying. Which isn't fair. For one, she's not friends with Sean. And for two, she would not put herself through this horror show for the sake of friendship even if they were. This is only about doing the right thing.

'I know *of* him more than know him,' she says, which feels like a good answer, and almost the truth. 'He's way older than me.'

'Jess is in Year Eight,' Mr Pearson pipes up. 'While, as you know, Sean Russo is resitting his maths and English GCSEs, so he's effectively in Year Twelve.'

'Thank you for clarifying.' The detective smiles at the head teacher then turns back to Jess. 'You saw Sean,' she prompts.

'Yeah. He was at the front of the classroom, standing up, by the desk. I couldn't hear anything, but he looked like he was shouting.'

'At Mr Rose?' DC Blake interrupts again, and then looks embarrassed when the woman detective gives him another one of her looks.

'I don't know because I didn't recognise the man with him;

he doesn't take any of my lessons,' Jess explains. She's feeling a bit bolder now. 'I guessed he was a teacher because he was old and wearing a suit. But really, he looked more like a boxer. Although not a very good one because when Sean pushed him in the chest, not even that hard, he stumbled. I couldn't see him then – I guess he fell over – and when he came back, his fist was clenched, his left, I think, and he just swung it at Sean, smashing him in the face.'

'So Sean pushed him,' DS Sawyer repeats. 'And the teacher retaliated by punching Sean in the face. What happened after that?'

Jess squints her eyes in concentration. 'The teacher pulled his arm back again, as though he was going to hit Sean a second time. But Sean ducked down. He had his hands over his eye like this.' Jess cradles her right cheekbone in her cupped palms. 'I think he grabbed a bag from the floor and left. The teacher kind of slumped down and I lost sight of him again.'

DS Sawyer leans back against the plastic chair. 'Thank you, Jess. You've been really helpful.'

Jess gives her a half-smile and then signs a shaky squiggle on DC Blake's screen.

TWO YEARS, TWO MONTHS BEFORE

Thursday 24th February 2022

Jess

Jess watches the boys shoot hoops. Sometimes she wishes she could join them – she's tall enough – but one of them might tell her to fuck off and she couldn't stand the shame. So she turns to Amber leaning against the fence next to her instead. 'Shall we go home?' she asks. 'I'm freezing my tits off in this wind.'

Amber smirks. 'What tits?'

'Ha-ha, very funny,' Jess responds, trying to look like it doesn't bother her that Amber is only 11 and already wears a bigger bra size than her. 'Honestly though, why are we even here? An empty park when it's freezing cold and spitting rain.'

'We'll leave soon,' Amber says, dismissing Jess's request with a flick of her hand. 'But Sean's coming down tonight.'

'You're obsessed with that guy,' Jess grumbles.

'No I'm not,' Amber snaps. 'We're good mates, that's all. You're just jealous.'

Jess looks at her sister like she's crazy for suggesting that, but secretly it's true. She is jealous. Except not in the way Amber thinks. Jess isn't interested in Sean. She just wishes Amber would look up to her like she does to him.

'Anyway, it's you he wants to talk to today,' Amber continues.

Even though it's arctic, a sheen of sweat starts to form on the back of Jess's neck. 'Me? Why?'

'He wants to thank you, for going to see Pearson today. I've told him about Mum, so he knows how hard it was for you.'

Jess nods slowly, unsure how she feels. She doesn't like that Sean knows how their mum died – it's private, and embarrassing. Murdered at home, Jess and Amber there, Tyler still in prison for it. But she likes the idea of being thanked. Sitting in Pearson's office with those detectives this morning was proper peak; she deserves some praise.

Five minutes later, Amber tips her head towards the park's entrance, and they watch Sean walk across the grass with some mates. She forces herself to keep her gaze steady, which is why a small whimper escapes when she sees his face up close. Amber has already shown her a photo, but it's nothing compared to the real-life version. Sean's right eye is swollen closed. The whole eyelid is bruised; mainly deep blue, but with a red lightning strike above his eyebrow where the skin has split. There's more bruising around the eye and it's working its way down his cheek too.

The last time Jess saw injuries like this were on her mum. Her knees feel wobbly, and she wonders if they're going to fold. She shifts her gaze, just over his shoulder, and it's enough to find control of her limbs again. 'Wow, he really slammed you,' she says.

'Yeah, you noticed.' Sean tries to smile but his face is off centre. 'He's out of control, that guy. And now the world's going to know about it, thanks to you.'

'I don't think you needed me to tell anyone,' Jess says, still staring at his injury. 'I think your face does a pretty good job of that by itself.'

'Not with the way the feds around here think. They'd always take a teacher's side over mine. Say I got this in a gang fight or some bullshit like that. But now there's a witness, they can't pull that stunt.'

Jess feels both proud and scared by the responsibility. 'Well, he definitely shouldn't get away with *that*,' she offers, nodding towards Sean's face. She's known Sean for about six months now, but he's always been Amber's friend. This is the first time they've had a proper conversation.

'I heard he's been suspended,' Amber pipes up, edging forwards, perhaps sensing a new threat from her sister. 'Maybe even fired. He hasn't been in school since it happened, they reckon.'

'That piece of shit deserves to be in jail,' Sean says gruffly. 'First the guy makes me stay behind because of fucking backchat, and when I refuse to apologise, he goes mental. I halfway stand up for myself and the psycho does this.'

'Did the police take photographs?' Jess asks. 'Of your injury?'

'Yeah. Yesterday. I went into school like normal, but Pearson saw me in the corridor. He asked what was up with my eye, so I told him. He sent me home, and then the feds turned up about an hour later. I told them everything, and they said they'd look into it. I didn't think shit would happen to be honest, until I heard you'd talked to Pearson today.'

'What did your mum say about it?' Amber asks.

The idea of Sean having a family feels weird to Jess. He's always seemed so old, like an adult, with mates who own cars. But he's still at school, so he must be looked after by someone.

'I haven't told her,' Sean says, his voice a mix of defensive and sad. 'Made sure the feds and school keep their mouths shut too. She only had her operation on Tuesday, so she'll be in the hospital for another week.'

Jess glances at Amber. Her sister doesn't look surprised by Sean's comment, so she must know what he's talking about. Jess knows enough about sick mums not to ask about it, but the damage to his face makes more sense now. Like he went looking for a beating because he was worried about his mum. That doesn't excuse the teacher though. Makes it worse in fact.

'So you're on your own until then?' Amber asks. 'Maybe I should come over – we could watch a movie or something?'

'Thanks, but all I can think about right now is making sure that prick Rose gets his punishment.' He leans back against the fence and kicks it with his heel. 'I just can't believe it's going to take so long.'

Amber takes a side step closer to him, his brush-off already forgiven. 'What do you mean, so long?'

Sean purses his lips, then blasts a shot of air through them. 'The police told me. Apparently assault cases are taking months to get to court, maybe even years. And it's not like the feds would lock Rose up on remand for one punch.'

Jess doesn't know what these phrases mean. On remand. Months to get to court. Don't the police just arrest you and put you in prison? That's what happened to Tyler – she's sure of it.

'So what happens between now and then?' Amber asks – and thank God she does because there's no way Jess was going to risk speaking.

Sean shrugs. 'Nothing. Rose will probably be chucked out of school, but he won't get done properly until the court case. Let's just hope Jess remembers what she put on her statement when it finally comes around.'

Jess's head jerks as she hears her name. 'Me? What do you mean?'

'Well, you'll have to go to court, won't you? Tell the judge what you saw?'

'Court?' Jess's mouth is so dry she can hardly speak.

Sean pulls back his face until it looks somewhere between disapproving and confused. 'What did you think was going to happen?'

'I, I don't know,' Jess mumbles. She feels unsteady on her feet. She wonders if she's going to faint. Then Amber's hand slips discreetly into hers, and the feel of her sister's cold fingers are just enough to settle her.

ONE YEAR BEFORE

Tuesday 16th May 2023

Jess

'Come on, Jess. At least eat the mash.' Lou's voice whines. Pleads. Frustration hovering underneath.

Jess doesn't want to cause another argument, and she's not keen on seeing Lou cry again either, so she dips her fork into the grey-white stodge and scoops up the smallest bit she can. Three little peaks of mashed potato on the fork's prongs goad her. *What are you going to do now, bitch?* She jams her eyes closed – a perverse attempt to shut out the voices – and forces the gunk into her mouth. She almost gags, but somehow manages to control her reflex and it mercifully slides down her throat.

Lou looks relieved. Justin hardly looks at her at all anymore. Not for the last six months at least. She's heard them arguing about it, hissed whispers through the thin bedroom wall when she's supposed to be asleep. Justin admitting that he doesn't understand it. She's already skinny, he says. So if that's why she's doing it, congratulations, Jess, you've got what you want. And then Lou explains – always crossly – that it's nowhere near that simple. That Jess has a serious mental health condition with physical symptoms. And that the effort it takes to put one morsel of food in her mouth is like swimming a mile against the strongest current. Jess doesn't understand why Lou gets it. But it's probably got something to do with her trawling eating disorder websites and reading a load of books.

Except she doesn't *always* get it. Like now. Lou's expression has already changed; the relief gone. She's not thinking about the hellish current Jess is swimming against; she just wants Jess to eat more, and more, until she finishes the whole fucking plateful. A burst of anger fills Jess's chest – why does everyone always want stuff from her? Things she's not capable of giving them? She pushes back her chair, flips open the bin, and deposits the food in one motion.

'Jess!' Lou cries out. 'Why did you do that?!'

'I'm not hungry,' she mutters.

'You can't live on thin air, for God's sake!'

'She ate loads of biscuits after school,' Amber pipes up. 'That's why she can't finish her dinner; that's right, isn't it, Jess?'

'Did you?' Lou asks, and her voice is so dripping in hope that Jess wants to laugh, cry and scream all at the same time. Except she's too tired to do any of them.

'Yeah,' she manages. 'Sorry.'

'Okay, well, I guess biscuits are better than nothing.'

'Can I go now?'

Lou nods, looks away, dejected. Jess closes the kitchen door behind her – she's doesn't even feel like hanging out with Amber right now – and tackles the stairs. She's exhausted, weighed down by fear, and every step takes effort. But eventually she reaches her bedroom and flops down onto her bed.

Justin is wrong, she thinks as she strokes her jawline with two fingers, feeling for the soft hair that she discovered there a couple of days ago (something else that doesn't make sense – the feel of it both comforting and gross). She doesn't give two fucks about being skinny. It's more that she's too full to eat. A supersize serving of dread that's been growing in her gut for more than a year, waiting to explode.

Which it will do in exactly seven days' time.

She's been thinking about nothing but the upcoming trial since last February and yet getting that envelope through the post – and the cold, formal letter inside – sparked a whole new level of terror.

And it wasn't even about the actual trial. The letter says she's got to have a meeting with the Crown Prosecution Service and their advocate – whatever that means – who's going to argue the case in court. The letter called it an opportunity for Jess to familiarise herself with what will happen on the day. A valuable experience to help put her at ease. What the fuck is valuable about talking to a bunch of strangers who use words she doesn't understand? People who've got the power to put her in jail? She's never been inside a court, didn't even know about them when Tyler got done for her mum's murder. But she's seen enough movies since to know how scary they are.

God, she's going to be sick. She rolls onto her side, closes her eyes. Bile collects underneath her tongue, but she waits, and the moment passes. There's a knock at the door, followed immediately by it swinging open. Without looking, Jess knows it's Amber. Lou and Justin would never walk inside until she gave them permission.

'What's going on?' Amber demands, dropping onto the end of Jess's bed. 'Why the fuck have you stopped eating?'

'I haven't,' Jess whispers lamely.

'It will kill you; you do realise that?' Amber throws back. 'And then it will just be me on my own. Dead mum, no dad, dead sister. It's easy to cover for you – Lou is so gullible, it's embarrassing – but that's not a good thing. Not with this anyway.'

'I'm sorry,' Jess whispers, heavy tears now rolling onto the pillow. 'I want to eat,' she tries to explain. 'But when I look at the food, I don't know … It looks disgusting. Like a pile of maggots.'

'That's bullshit talk!' Amber spits back, her eyes ablaze. 'You need to snap out of this crap, all right?' She's so angry she's almost snarling. But Jess knows Amber. And how much meaner she is when real feelings threaten.

'I will, I promise.'

'And soon, yeah? You're a fucking skeleton, Jess. You can't keep doing this.'

'I said I'd eat, okay?'

Amber doesn't respond, but she doesn't move either. She hovers at the end of Jess's bed, staring – her expression both furious and upset. Jess needs her to leave; needs some space outside the glare of her sister's eyes.

'I'm really tired now though,' she says. 'I'll get some sleep and then have some toast when I wake up.'

Amber's face softens very slightly. 'You promise?'

'On my life.' The words hang between them for a moment, then Amber shakes her head, lets out a resigned sigh, and leaves the room.

Jess rolls onto her back. Amber is right. She is slowly killing herself. And she doesn't want to die – at least not always. Sometimes it feels like the easiest way out, in the middle of the night when the house is deathly silent and she can't sleep, but those thoughts never last. She wants to escape her life, her future, not destroy it.

And there is another way.

It's the cowardly thing to do, so she doesn't understand why it's so fucking scary. With just one phone call, the dread would vanish. And hopefully, with it, the tightness in her throat; her chest; her gut. Lou would stop crying; Justin might look at her again. And most importantly, Amber wouldn't have to worry about losing her sister.

She can hardly move she's so tired. But she forces herself to roll over, then sit up. Her phone is still in her school bag. She's even lost interest in that over the last few months. The funny memes that mock her. The inspirational quotes that shame her. But this is her way out. She finds her social worker's contact details with shaking fingers and presses on her number.

'Hello, Gail Thompson.'

'Um, it's Jess,' she starts. Her head is swimming now. She lies back down but keeps the phone by her ear.

'Hi, Jess,' Gail says, her voice slowing. 'Are you okay?'

'I can't do it,' she whispers. Tears bubble in the corners of her eyes.

'Can't do what?' The words are blunt, but Gail's tone is soft enough for Jess to keep going.

'I can't go to court.'

'Oh, okay, I see.' Jess imagines Gail's mind whirring, her hair flaring with the static it causes. 'I could talk to DS Sawyer,' she suggests. 'See if you could give your evidence by video link instead. There are lots of options for child witnesses. Would that be better?'

'I can't do any of it, Gail. Court. Telling everyone what I saw. Answering their questions. It was too long ago; I can't remember anything.'

'You'll have a chance to read your statement—'

'No, Gail. No. I just can't.'

Gail hesitates. She knows about Jess's issues with eating, her query anorexia except without a diagnosis because the waiting list to see a specialist is too long. 'Jess, I'm really sorry,' she says carefully. 'But it's not that easy.'

'What do you mean?'

'Well, you're a witness in a criminal case. You provided a signed statement. The CPS decide whether it goes to court, not you.'

'What? No!' Panic rises in Jess's chest. She pushes up against the headboard. 'So how do I get out of it?'

'You're the only witness,' Gail reminds her quietly. 'Without your testimony, I imagine the CPS wouldn't have a case. I'm sorry, but I don't think you *can* get out of it.'

'But I didn't see anything!' Jess blurts out.

A second lapses as Gail catches up. 'What?'

'Yes, sorry,' Jess babbles. 'I made it all up. I didn't look through that window at all.'

'Why would you do that?' Gail asks. She's trying to sound calm, but her quivering voice gives her away.

'I … I don't know.'

'Did the boy, Sean Russo, force you to?'

'What? No. Nothing like that.' Jess pulls her knees up to her chest; wishes she could fold in on herself so tightly that she disappeared. 'But I didn't see anything, so the CPS won't want me to go to court, will they?'

ONE YEAR BEFORE

Wednesday 17th May 2023

Jess

Jess turns onto her street. She's feeling so much better already; even school was halfway decent today. When she told Gail last night that she hadn't seen anything on the afternoon Sean was assaulted, and Gail had reluctantly offered to talk to the police on her behalf, she'd felt giddy with relief. She still couldn't face normal food, but she'd gone downstairs and asked for some chocolate. Lou had watched on, rapt, as Jess gobbled down a whole Dairy Milk. And Jess had woken up this morning with some energy inside her for the first time in ages.

Lou and Justin's house is nothing special. Paving slabs at the front, a PVC door, a few windows. Pebbledash on the outside, which Lou hates but Justin says they can't afford to remove. But it's home, and Jess feels a sense of peace descend as she slots her key into the lock and turns.

'Jess, is that you?' Lou's voice is tight, stressed, and it stops Jess in her tracks. An image pops up in her mind: a car she didn't recognise parked right outside the house.

She coughs. 'Yeah?'

'Can you come in the kitchen? Gail's here.'

Jess's shoulders drop. Didn't she tell Gail everything she had to say last night? Do they really have to go over it all again face to face?

'And, um, some police officers,' Lou adds.

Jess reaches out for the newel post to steady herself. Gail was supposed to deal with it all; she promised that she would. She could run back outside, Jess thinks. But if she did, would they come after her? Tackle her to the ground in front of the neighbours? With a sense of inevitability, she kicks off her scuffed school shoes, and trudges into the kitchen.

The room is too crowded, and Jess instantly feels like she's suffocating. Their table is supposed to seat four, but it's always a squash, and that's with her and Amber still being kids. Now there's DS Sawyer, DC Blake and Gail all sitting down, plus Lou hovering close to the kettle.

'Hello, Jess,' DS Sawyer says, nodding to the empty chair. 'Do you want to join us?'

No, I want you to leave my house. I want to go to bed and pretend you don't exist. Jess sinks into the chair. To avoid eye contact, she stares at the garden through the window – a small patch of grass and a rusty trampoline.

'So I understand you've changed your story?' DS Sawyer starts. There's an edge to her voice: accusing. She's not pretending to be nice anymore. 'Which, to be honest, was quite a shock to hear,' she goes on. 'A few weeks before the trial is due to start. So which is it, Jess? Are you scared to go to court, or did you really not see the incident take place?'

Jess keeps her eyes fixed on the window. Amber can do backflips on that trampoline, but she's always been too scared to try. 'I didn't see it,' she whispers. 'I'm sorry.'

'You're sorry? Did you know that making a false statement is a crime?' the detective says curtly. 'And your evidence was critical to this case. There's no way we'll get a guilty verdict without your testimony.'

Jess's eyes sting. It's not like her to show her emotions, especially not in front of strangers, but she can't keep them in. She's tired. She planned to eat lunch in the dinner hall today but there was nothing she liked so she made do with an apple and a packet of Skittles from the tuck shop. 'I just want it to stop,' she whispers. She drops her head onto the table. The washing machine is mid-cycle, and she stares at the knickers and T-shirts being flung around the drum.

'Jess has been through a lot,' Lou reminds everyone softly. 'Both a while ago, and more recently. I think the most important thing is to make sure she's okay.'

Gail sits up taller, maybe realising that was her line. 'Lou is right. Jess's wellbeing must come first. If she feels that she made a mistake in her original statement, then we need to accept that.'

'Let's not forget, the defendant has always maintained his innocence,' DC Blake says. 'Very strenuously. If Jess didn't see anything, then perhaps he didn't do it. Maybe our first instinct that Russo picked up his injuries in a street fight – and just blamed Mr Rose because he didn't like him – was correct all along.'

DS Sawyer stares at Jess, as though trying to drill the truth out with her eyes, but eventually she looks away. 'Okay, well, I'll speak to the CPS,' she says with an air of defeat. 'And I guess I'll tell them that I don't think we should charge Jess with anything,' she adds begrudgingly. 'It isn't really in the public interest.' She pauses for a moment. 'But, Jess?'

'Yes?' Jess whispers, her voice trembling.

'Don't ever pull a stunt like that again, okay?' DS Sawyer pushes up to standing, and her colleague follows suit. A chink of light sparkles dimly in Jess's mind, the possibility that this might finally be over.

'Wait,' Lou says, lifting her hands. 'Do we need to talk about Sean Russo?'

'In what context?' DS Sawyer asks, her hands resting on the top of the chair, her mind already onto the next case.

'Well, he's not going to be pleased about this, is he?' Lou goes on. 'The case against the guy who assaulted him – allegedly or whatever – being dropped. He'll see it as Jess's fault, and he's a tough 18-year-old guy. What if he takes his frustration out on her?'

'We have no record of Sean Russo being violent,' DC Blake says. 'He's known to us, but for different offences.'

'And how many assaults actually make it onto the police database?' Lou throws back. Jess doesn't know this Lou, the one who raises her voice. The strangeness of it makes her feel uncomfortable.

DS Sawyer turns to Lou and lifts her hands. 'I understand your concerns, I really do, but we can't help, I'm afraid. A potential crime in the future definitely isn't within our remit.'

'Could you not even give him a warning?' Lou asks. 'Tell him you've got your eye on him?'

'The law doesn't work that way; not anymore anyway. There are options – court injunctions for example – but Sean was the victim of this crime, so I doubt any judge is going to curtail his freedom just because you ask them to. Sorry,' she adds as an afterthought. 'And now, we need to go.'

As Lou shows them out, Jess feels the oxygen levels in the room rise a fraction. But she can't fully relax until Gail has gone too. The social worker twists in her chair to face her. 'What do you think, Jess?' she asks. 'Are you worried how Sean Russo might react?'

Jess pulls at her bottom lip. Lou slips back in. She must have heard Gail's question because she stares expectantly at Jess.

'This whole thing happened ages ago,' Jess starts, trying to sound offhand. 'Maybe he won't care about it anymore.' She's not sure she believes it, especially with the stories going round about Sean. How he's hanging out with a gang now. Selling drugs for them. But she wants to stop Lou worrying.

'Do you think so?' Lou says, breaking into a relieved smile. But it folds into a frown when there's a loud thud in the hallway – the front door flying into the adjacent wall – and thumping footsteps towards the kitchen.

'What the fuck have you done?!' Amber screeches from the doorway. Her hair is sweaty and tangled; her shirt collar ripped.

'Oh my God, Amber! What happened to you?' Lou reaches out, but Amber shrugs her away, irritated by the interruption.

'Is it true?' she demands, narrowing her eyes at Jess. 'Have you pulled your statement?'

'I can't go to court,' Jess whispers. 'It's too much. You told me to sort myself out, remember?'

'I meant your eating!' Amber shouts. 'Not this! Not signing your own fucking death warrant!'

'Oh shit,' Lou moans in the background.

'But Sean might not care anymore,' Jess pleads, clinging to her own version of reality.

'Oh my God, you're fucking delusional!' Amber drops down into the chair next to Jess; grabs both her wrists and pulls her round, forcing her to make eye contact. 'Why do you think I look like this? And how much worse do you think you'd look if it was you he caught instead of me?'

'Did he hurt you?' Jess whispers, her voice trembling.

'He was my friend, Jess!' Amber screeches, squeezing tighter, digging her nails into Jess's soft flesh. 'And now he hates me. How could you do that to me?'

'What if I explain?' Jess whines. 'Tell him that I'm sorry?'

'Are you really that stupid?!'

Jess's bottom lip quivers. She grabs it with her top teeth but that makes her eyes water.

'That's enough, Amber,' Lou says, her assertive voice back. 'Let your sister go.' Then she turns to Gail. 'But we can't ignore it; Jess could be in real danger here.'

'What do you think he'll do to me?' Jess whispers. Her chest is constricting again. Her eyes swimming. Jesus, when is this all going to be over?

'I don't know, Jess,' Amber hisses. 'But you brought this on yourself.'

'I don't like this at all,' Gail says decisively.

'Me neither,' Lou agrees. 'But what options do we have? The detective already said the police can't help.'

'Leave it with me,' Gail says grimly. 'I need to discuss this with the team.'

TEN MONTHS BEFORE

Saturday 22nd July 2023

Jess

Jess looks around the unfamiliar living room and feels an intense urge to reach for her sister's hand. But she's too old for that. And also, Amber is still barely speaking to her.

'Right, we don't stand on ceremony here,' Bill says with the ease of someone who's fostered lots of kids before. 'There are a few rules of course – shoes off at the door, help with the washing-up after dinner, that kind of thing – but mainly we just ask for honesty and some mutual respect. Does that sound okay?'

The words wash over Jess, but she nods, and it seems enough.

'Thank you, Bill. We really appreciate it,' Amber says. She's been slagging off their new Jesus-loving, geriatric foster carers since they were first introduced to Molly and Bill a few weeks ago, but now she and Jess are officially moving in, she's got a job to do – getting their foster carers onside enough to cut her the slack she needs.

'That's nice, Amber,' Molly says, but in a tone that suggests Amber needs to work a bit harder than that.

'Now, do you fancy seeing your bedrooms?' Bill asks. 'You might have to toss a coin for them though. One is a decent size. It's got bunk beds, a desk and plenty of storage. But the other is a bit more of a box room if I'm honest. Come on.'

They traipse up the stairs in a line – Bill at the front, Jess pulling up the rear as usual. Bill was right about the second bedroom being small, but maybe Jess should take it anyway. A peace offering. Amber was so mad when social services said that it wasn't safe for them to stay with Lou and Justin – just three days after Jess withdrew her statement about that teacher hitting Sean – and she couldn't take it out on Gail because it wasn't her who delivered the news. It was a new woman with an Irish accent – Colleen – who explained that Gail had moved to a new job.

Colleen said that their current situation had been deemed unsafe, and Amber and Jess would be moving to a new foster family as soon as they could organise it – probably at the end of the school year. Somewhere far away from Sean Russo. Amber had been furious, and had stormed out of the house as soon as Colleen left. Jess had worried that she might never see her sister again, that Sean would find her and hurt her, but Amber had turned up eventually, drunk and stoned, but alive.

She didn't learn her lesson though. The next day, Saturday, she disappeared again, and was gone all day that time. Lou was proper freaked by the time she got home, around seven o'clock, but luckily that was the last time Amber went AWOL. She never liked that they had to move, but she seemed to accept it after that. She even talked to Colleen about her GCSEs and asked for her preferences to be taken into account when the foster team looked for a new home for them.

She and Amber then spent their remaining weeks living in semi-confinement. Driven to and from school. Not allowed out unless it was to a specific event with a defined guest list. And then finally term finished, and it was time to go.

Saying goodbye to Lou and Justin had been hard. They all cried. Even Amber got a bit teary. But what broke Jess's heart the most was seeing the relief that diluted Lou's sadness.

'What do you think, Jess?'

She snaps back to the conversation. 'Sorry, what?'

'We could share, couldn't we? You take the top bunk; I take the bottom. It'll be more fun if we're together.'

'Really?'

Amber beams at her. Jess doesn't understand what's going on. Is this part of the act? When Colleen picked them up this morning, Amber was still giving her the silent treatment. What could have happened in the last couple of hours to cause such a big shift?

'Of course!' Amber calls out. 'Is that okay, Molly, Bill?'

'I think that's a wonderful idea,' Molly says, breaking into a smile – already starting to fall under Amber's spell (not so savvy after all). 'Our own girls always shared – they're in their late twenties now and still thick as thieves. Now, why don't we let you settle in. Come down when you're ready, no hurry.'

They watch the old couple trundle back down the stairs, then Amber steps inside the bunk bedroom, and Jess follows. It's a good room. Bill and Molly's house isn't any bigger than Lou and Justin's, but there's grass in the front garden rather than paving slabs, and Jess can see three majestic birds circling the sky as she looks through the window.

'Maybe it will be all right here,' she ventures. 'In the countryside.'

'Yeah, maybe.' Amber's response isn't exactly enthusiastic, but it's so much better than the usual '*I'd rather fucking die*' that Jess can't hold back her curiosity any longer.

'Why are you being so nice all of a sudden?'

Amber's expression becomes thoughtful. 'Because maybe I agree that it's not all bad, us moving out here.'

'Do you mean that?' Jess squints in confusion.

Amber pulls her phone out of her back pocket, taps it against her thigh. 'Well Sean thinks so anyway.'

Jess's heart rate ticks up. 'Sean?' she says guardedly. 'We're not supposed to be—'

'Sean was my friend, remember?' Amber cuts in. 'Before you screwed things up.'

'He hurt you. He threatened me.'

'You provoked him.'

Jess wonders if she should leave it, just be grateful that Amber's finally softening towards her. But Sean Russo isn't the boy Amber fell in love with anymore. Since his mum was told that her cancer was terminal, he's been hanging out with proper roadmen on the estate, and he's got into drugs – both taking and selling them. As her older sister, doesn't she have a duty to protect Amber?

'Why are you so desperate to be friends with someone like him anyway?' she asks.

Amber twists to look at Jess, her expression confrontational. 'Because he's exciting. And hot. And he thinks I'm cool – at least he used to.' She turns away again. 'And he's offered me a job. Which means I won't have to live off the shit pocket money we get, and that'll be good for both of us.'

'A job? Doing what?'

Amber shrugs. 'Selling a bit of weed.'

'What?' Jess splutters. 'We're supposed to be cutting ties with our old life. And especially – mainly – him.' Jess's knees suddenly feel weak. She folds down onto the carpet. 'You said he'd kill me if he saw me.'

'Yeah, and that's why I went to see him the night we were told we had to move,' Amber explains, her irritation growing. 'To beg him to forgive you. It wasn't for me. I needed to get him back onside, so that you'd be safe. You don't think us being the other end of the county would stop him tracking you down if he wanted to?'

Jess blinks back tears. 'Does he know where we are now? Did you tell him our address?'

'Stop stressing, sis. And no. He doesn't know where we are exactly.'

'Exactly?' Jess whispers, horrified.

'Just trust me, okay?'

EIGHT MONTHS BEFORE

Tuesday 12th September 2023

Jess

Jess reaches her hand into the packet of Jelly Babies and pulls three out. Two red, and an orange. Overall her eating hasn't improved much since she arrived in Chinnor, but sweets never seem to stick in her throat. She puts one in her mouth and chews.

'So?'

Jess turns towards her sister. She and Amber are sitting on the thick grass, heels up to their bums, the brightly coloured rations placed between them. They found the nature reserve on Chinnor Hill – a small clearing surrounded by tall trees a mile or so up from the village – soon after they moved to Chinnor, and it's become their favourite place to hang out. 'So, what?' she asks, although she knows exactly what her sister is asking.

'She's in your year,' Amber reminds her, already impatient. 'So have you seen her? Do you have any lessons with her?'

Jess pulls at the grass. When Amber confided in her about her big master plan – the one she'd come up with on that Saturday she disappeared, the day after she got wasted with Sean and he'd told her there was only one way she could earn his forgiveness – Jess was so shocked she could hardly breathe. Everything had seemed okay at first, Amber told her. Sean had invited her to his flat, given her wine and a spliff, talked about his mum and all the side effects of her chemo. But then he turned. Bang. Like Tyler used to do. Told Amber that if she didn't find a way to pay for Jess's fuck-up, he'd kill them both. He said that Rose needed to suffer, and if Jess was too chickenshit to go to court, then Amber needed to find a less legal way to make him pay.

And then he gave Amber Mr Rose's home address – she still doesn't know how he got hold of it – and chucked her out of his flat.

Amber can be resourceful when she wants to be, and she got up early the next day, worked out which bus went to Chinnor, and got on it. Finding the house was easy, she said, but she still had no clue how to go about making Rose pay. She was 13 and short for her age. Rose was in his forties and built like a brick wall. But she watched the house, saw the family come and go, and slowly the plan formed.

When Amber first explained it, Jess wondered if the plan started with jealousy – although she didn't dare suggest it to Amber. The perfect family – two daughters with a mum and a dad who loved them. Just like her and Amber in some ways, and completely not like them in others. But Amber said it was the way Rose acted around the younger, skinnier one. Like she was a precious doll that he adored and needed to protect. She realised that *he* might be too difficult for a 13-year-old kid to punish, but his daughter wasn't. And if he loved her like that, wouldn't hurting her hurt him even more?

Amber asked around in the village, worked out that all the kids went to Lord Frederick's in Thame, then looked it up. She found out that it was the only school in Oxfordshire that offered Arabic GCSE, and then told Colleen that she had a burning desire to study the language. Of course the sad fuck social worker loved the idea of Amber having ambition, and began looking for a foster home in the catchment area. That their new foster carers turned out to live in the exact same village as the Roses was just a mad coincidence – or a sign, Amber said, that someone was on their side, looking out for them.

Maybe their mum.

Jess and Amber have been students at Lord Fred's for one week so far. There are a similar number of kids overall to their last school, but the Lord Fred's site is bigger with different blocks dotted all over the place. Jess has spent most of the week getting lost, but she does have good news for her sister. 'Yeah, she's in my Art class. She's called Lucy.'

'That's amazing, sis, well done.' Amber's eyes shine with a mix of excitement and relief. 'Have you spoken to her?'

'Not really.'

Amber nods slowly. 'Okay, don't. Not yet anyway. I'll talk to Sean first, then tell you what to do next.'

Jess is so used to being bossed around by her baby sister that her instruction barely registers as one. 'Do you feel bad at all?' she asks quietly. 'What we're about to do to Rose's daughter? It's not like *she* punched Sean. It doesn't really feel fair.'

Amber gives her a dark look. 'Is it fair that our mum got killed? Or that your dad is too mental to look after you?'

Tears threaten. Jess widens her eyes, prays for the cool air to dry them. 'I guess not,' she whispers.

'Her dad should be in prison, remember. For what he did to Sean. But because he's got a good job, wears a suit, lives in a little cottage with his perfect family, he gets away with it. Yeah, you fucked up, pulling your statement, but the police could have believed Sean anyway, couldn't they? Except they never would, because Rose is a saint in their eyes and Sean is a scumbag. Like us. And that's why we need to stick together. Take matters into our own hands.'

'Maybe,' Jess whispers. What Amber says does make sense, but she was hoping that this new start in Chinnor would mean she didn't have to think about Sean's assault, or her screw-up. That she could start afresh. 'I guess I was hoping I could move on from all that,' she admits quietly.

'But this is the only way that's going to happen. We make Lucy Rose's life a fucking nightmare, or Sean will come for us. It's that simple. Think of it as survival.'

Jess considers that. It's true that Lucy's much luckier than her, that she's never had to deal with rejection or death. Why the hell should she feel sorry for a girl like that? 'Yeah, you're right,' she concedes. 'But we've only been there a week – what if we get in trouble?'

Amber pulls out another Jelly Baby. 'Don't worry about that. I know exactly how to play the foster kid card with that snooty head teacher. And there's after school too.'

'But what if her dad sees us?'

'He never taught either of us; he's got no clue who we are.'

'Pearson might have told Rose that I was the witness,' Jess says, airing the worry that's been rumbling around her head since Amber first explained her plan.

'No way,' Amber says. 'Pearson pretended to be cool, but he loved rules. Especially all that safeguarding stuff. He knew you had a right to anonymity. He wouldn't have broken it.'

'Sounds like we're doing this,' Jess murmurs.

'Yeah.' Amber nods her head slowly. 'Watch out, Lucy Rose, we're coming for you.'

AFTER

Monday 13th May

Rachel

Jess is Witness A. The mystery student who said she saw Matt hit Sean Russo and then changed her mind. Who ruined Matt's career, pushed his mental health to the limit.

And who is now missing.

With Matt the last person to see her.

My dad will kill you.

It can't be a coincidence that Jess and Amber targeted Lucy. Maybe they saw Matt around the village and recognised him, and then attacked his daughter, like predators preying on the weakest of the pack. Or was there more scheming involved than that? If they hated him enough to make up a false claim about him hitting a student, did they also orchestrate a move to his neighbourhood? In a perfect world, perhaps Matt's address would be flagged, a danger zone drawn around it in Colleen's search for new foster carers. But police and council databases don't align like that. And Jess had her anonymity, so protection from Matt wasn't something Colleen needed to factor in.

And it's true that the witness's identity was never revealed during the investigation. But Matt might have become suspicious after Lucy told us about being bullied by two new girls. If he did some digging around the village, he could easily have found out that Amber and Jess had moved from Oxford. His old school – Oxford Comprehensive – isn't the only secondary school in the city by a long stretch, but it's one of the biggest. If he reached out to an ex-colleague, the story could have unravelled from there.

I close down Jess's file. Log out of the database. Turn off my laptop. Slam down the lid. I pause for a moment, then do everything in reverse. I need to print a copy. Of both their files. See the truth in black and white.

I walk over to the printer to grab the warm sheets of paper, then physically jump as I hear a noise. I look wildly for somewhere to hide. This is my office – I'm perfectly entitled to be here – but there's no way I can come into contact with another human being right now – make conversation, pretend to be fine.

All this time I've been questioning my daughters' involvement in Amber's death, but it's Matt who's embroiled in this tragic mess. Jess lied to the police to get him charged with assault. He lost his job – the career he loved – because of it. He's got plenty of reason to hate her. I think back to Friday night. How Matt wanted to deliver the money. And when Milla wouldn't back down about taking it, he decided to follow her. Was it all a lie, his wanting to keep her safe?

Was it really about following Jess in the dead of night?

A series of images flood my mind. His pale, tear-stained face when he returned on Friday night. Our bedroom ceiling as I lay next to him in the near darkness, listening to the story of his traumatic night. The apologies. His black mood on Saturday. His distracting explanation of why Milla didn't see Jess by the old train carriages.

But there's no image of the badger who lost its life.

Because I never saw it; I only have Matt's word.

Bile collects in my mouth, and I dry-heave.

The noise has stopped, and no one has appeared – a false alarm, thank God – but next time it won't be. It's seven o'clock and I know plenty of my colleagues who like to start early. I need to get out of here. I shove my laptop and the printouts into my bag, push my chair under the desk, and scurry back to the car park. I unlock my car door and sink into the fake leather seat. But it only gives me a few seconds' reprieve before I realise that I could still bump into someone I know. I imagine the tap on my window, the small wave as they wait for me to join them. I push my key into the ignition and drive away, my tyres spinning with desperation.

I stir my cup of tea. I don't take sugar so it's a pointless endeavour, but I like watching the liquid swirl in a smooth circular motion. It's calming. But then a drop spills, breaking the flow, and I reluctantly lift my gaze.

Despite the early hour, the small café is half-full. There's a group of four men in dusty clothes and high-vis jackets eating bacon rolls and drinking fancy iced coffees. Another man is alone. Smartly dressed, drinking Lucozade from the bottle, and frowning at his phone. The rest of the clientele look to be students – their final pit stop after a night of partying on their way back to their tatty student houses. People always associate Oxford with its famous university – dreaming spires and cerebral students navigating cobbled streets on old-fashioned bicycles. But the reality is mostly different. Especially around here, where cheaply built post-war housing sits alongside 1960s tower blocks, and all of it is covered in a thin layer of grime from the factories that line the city's ring road.

'Mind if I wipe your table?' A woman's voice wafts into my brain. I look up, nod, then lift my mug as she smears a cloth across the laminate. 'Ta,' she says, then moves on to the next table, oblivious to my problems. Of course she is. That's how the world works.

But I can't deal with this on my own. It's too much. Matt and I have been together since we were 18 years old. We're a team – for better or worse, that's what we said on that sticky August day with our friends and family watching on. Our marriage isn't perfect, Matt isn't perfect, but he's still my soul mate. The only person I confide everything in. In the past, we've always talked through our problems, and I want to do that now. Go home, confront him. But what would I say?

Did you know Lucy was being bullied because of you?

Did you find out the truth about Jess Scott?

Did you follow her on Friday night, then hit her with your car?

Have you hidden her body?

But I know there are even more gruesome questions than that because this didn't start with Jess. Amber was murdered a week before her sister went missing. Matt's case wasn't referenced in her file, but she was Jess's sister, so she must have been close to it. Her file did mention the incident that led to the girls being moved. It was dated as May 2023, which was the same month that Jess pulled her statement. The file didn't give a name, but the boy concerned was five years older than Amber and known to the police. It all points to him being Sean Russo – and the incident being linked to Jess's change of heart.

If Amber was Sean's friend, like Colleen said, Jess being the fake witness makes sense. Sean asks Amber to help him out, and because she's devious and selfish, she gets her biddable sister to take the risk instead.

Except Jess changed her mind.

How would Amber have reacted to that?

Yes, Sean roughed her up. But maybe she cared less about her safety, and more about getting back into his good books. Perhaps she devised the plan to terrorise Lucy, punish Matt the only way she could, so that she could deliver what she'd failed to do when Jess pulled her statement.

And if Matt had come to the same conclusion – and then

watched his own daughter suffer at Amber's hands – would he see the younger girl as the real culprit and want to make her pay? He did seem anxious when he came back from searching for Lucy on that Friday night, and he was later home than I expected. But killing a child?

I push out of the chair, and there's a screech as its metal feet slide across the tiled floor. Conversation halts around me; builders and students turn to stare. God, I can't stay here either. I lunge for the door, and a few seconds later, I stumble onto the pavement.

I breathe in the early morning air and feel instantly calmer.

This is ridiculous. Matt can get angry – when the house is a mess, or if he feels undermined – but he's calm, controlled, never violent. I can't imagine him ever hitting another person. Except …

I blink.

Have I got this wrong from the start?

The police left a message for him yesterday. Maybe it's got nothing to do with them finding the note – if Matt did something to Jess, he'd have destroyed it anyway – but while Amber's file might not mention the court case, Jess's does. Now that she's gone missing, the investigation team will be combing through her history for clues. They might even be at our house now. Pounding on the door. Matt cowering in the kitchen refusing to let them in, making it worse for himself. But would that be because he's guilty, or because he's scared of being wrongly accused for the second time?

I need to find out the truth.

But Jess is missing, not dead, I remind myself. She might well have run away – like Matt said – now that she's ten grand richer. And the boyfriend was arrested for Amber's murder. Yes, the police have let him go for now, but that's probably while they gather more evidence. I'm letting my mind go crazy, just like I did with the girls, blaming someone I love for an appalling crime just because I've found a hair's breadth of a connection. Where's my loyalty?

I need to prove that Matt is innocent. Milla and Lucy too. And that starts with establishing that Jess is fine – spending her new cash, not buried in the woods, or dumped in Kiln Lakes.

Colleen told me that Jess's father had been contacted by the police, but she didn't mention her old foster carers. The girls lived with Lou and Justin Trapnell for years, so they must have been close. Could Jess have gone there? Or at least contacted them? Littlemore is only a fifteen-minute drive from here. I climb into my car, check the printout of Jess's file for the address, and set off.

AFTER

Monday 13th May

Milla

'Milla!' A sound burrows into Milla's consciousness. She bats it away, rolls onto her side, pulls the duvet over her face.

'MILLA!'

She groans. 'What?' she tries to shout, but it comes out as a croak. She fumbles for her phone and checks the time: 07.48. Does her dad not remember that she's on study leave now? She rubs her eyes. But as she slowly wakes, the sinking feeling returns to her gut. Could he not have allowed her this one thing? The escapism of sleep? Being able to sink into oblivion and stay there all night – despite everything – has been the only thing that's got her through the hell of the last ten days.

Her bedroom door flies open and her dad storms inside. 'Your mum isn't here!' He stops, looks around, curls his lip into a grimace. 'God, your room is a pigsty.'

Milla ignores his criticism – they have a deal after all – but she doesn't understand why he's so agitated. Her mum has always been work-obsessed and loves an early start on a Monday morning. 'So?'

'She left before I woke up; didn't say goodbye. And she'd told me she was going to work from home today.'

Milla lengthens her arms, arches her back, and tries to stretch out the tension. It doesn't work. 'So call her then.'

'Don't you think I've tried that?' her dad snaps, running his palm along his forehead.

What the hell is wrong with him?

'Chill, Dad, okay?' Milla pushes up to sitting, then swings her legs out of bed and pulls on the joggers that she'd left on the floor the night before. She grabs a scrunched-up sweatshirt from the bottom of the bed and puts that on too. Her dad is pacing her room and it's giving her a headache. 'I don't understand why you're so stressed about Mum going AWOL for five minutes.'

'There's a message on our answerphone.'

'What, like a human voice coming out of a machine?' Milla can't help mocking him, even though she knows it will incense him more. She loves her dad, deeply, but it can be hard to like him sometimes. Especially when he's like this, feeling out of control and lashing out.

'You know, one day someone's going to take exception to your smartarse tone.'

Milla glares at her dad, but forces herself not to come back at him. Her mum is an open book – so easy to read – but it's different with him. She can't always predict how he'll react. 'Who's the message from?' she asks instead.

'That detective who interviewed Lucy. DC Bzowski.'

'Oh.' Milla's voice lowers.

'Yeah, exactly. She wants me to call her. It must be about Lucy, talking to her again; they'll probably want a DNA sample too.'

'Fuck.'

'But why did they ask for me, not your mum? I know I'm Lucy's dad but …' His voice trails off.

'Maybe they'd already tried her phone?'

'Exactly. You see now why I need to track her down.'

Out of nowhere, Milla feels tears burn the backs of her eyes. She gives them a quick brush with the back of her hand. God, why didn't Lucy listen to her last Friday night? Milla made it so clear. *Stay away from those girls who are making your life hell.* But for once in her life, Lucy decided to ditch her compliant – bordering on submissive – nature. And what a stupid decision that proved to be. 'Does Lucy know?' she asks.

'I haven't told her,' Matt admits, looking towards the window. 'She left for school about ten minutes ago. And she seemed a bit happier, at last. As though she thinks that paying Jess the ransom money has solved all her problems.'

'Well, you can't blame her for that. That is what you keep telling her.'

'I thought it would work out,' Matt whispers, more to himself than Milla. 'That making sure Jess kept her mouth shut would be enough.'

Milla squeezes her eyes shut, then flicks them back open. 'Maybe it will be. If Lucy holds her nerve. She can't have killed Amber, can she, Dad?'

God, why did she say it like that? Like she's asking him to make it true.

'I wish I'd known about that blog,' Matt mutters, frustration seeping out of him. 'It's so threatening, isn't it? What she wrote?' Matt looks towards Milla for assent, but she turns away. It's strange. She feels more loyal to Lucy now than she's ever done before. Now – when her sister might actually have done something terrible.

'Hindsight is a wonderful thing,' she says instead.

'Maybe I should take her away.'

'Huh?'

'I don't have any school visits this week; I could work from anywhere,' Matt explains, speeding up as he warms to the idea. 'And Lucy deserves a break. We could go wild camping in Wales, or maybe Ireland. A chance for Lucy to clear her head.'

'Do you not realise how that would look?' Milla asks, her pitch rising. 'You and Lucy running away when the detective wants to talk to you?'

'It's not running away,' Matt counters. 'A father and daughter spending some quality time together. We could say we missed her message.'

'I don't know, Dad,' Milla stutters. She tries to run the idea through her brain – the risks and the possibilities – but it's sluggish. Like it needs a service due to overuse. 'Wouldn't they come find you?'

'But the alternative feels …' Her dad's words peter out, and as his breathing becomes heavier, the whoosh and whirr of it filling Milla's room, she feels an intense urge to get rid of him.

'Go and call Mum again,' she instructs. 'She was probably in an early meeting. We can work out what to do about that detective later. It will all be fine.'

'You're a tough one,' her dad observes. 'It's a good skill to have.'

It's not a skill, Milla thinks. It's bloody-mindedness. She doesn't ignore the fears in her head. She can't. She wrestles them to the back of her mind and locks them away. And then she suffers the pain of them knocking against her skull as she pretends to the world. 'I'll come down in a bit,' she says abruptly.

Matt scratches his forehead – as though he genuinely doesn't know how to function – then finally twists away from her and leaves the room.

Milla sighs with relief, then pulls down a textbook and flicks to organic chemistry. She needs to revise, act normal. But the words just swim in front of her eyes. She folds at the waist and lets her head rest on the cool pages.

Of course she doesn't know for sure that Lucy killed Amber. She hasn't asked her. But her dad must think so too if he's suggesting hiding out in some remote wilderness. And Milla can't get the phone conversation she had with Lucy on Friday night out of her head. How angry she sounded. Like her elastic band of suffering had been stretching for months – pinging every time Amber did something cruel. It stretched to breaking point when they stole her sports bag Friday lunchtime, and then she discovered that Amber had stolen Bronwen's letter. SNAP. Suddenly Lucy was flying free of it.

But Milla would never have suspected her sister of a violent crime if she hadn't seen her later that night, when Lucy was missing, and she and her mum and dad were searching. It was 23.25; she'd seen the time on her phone. And it was a sight that made her blood run cold. Lucy crouching outside the RSPCA charity shop, heavy breathing like she'd been running, rummaging through a bin bag of donations. Milla had paused, confused, and watched her sister pull out a T-shirt and jumper. Then as she'd stood up, swaying a little, it had suddenly made sense. Her own top was covered in blood, and the front of her jacket too. And not just a few drops. Big smeary patches. Not knowing what else to do, she'd followed Lucy into the churchyard, and watched from a distance as her sister changed into the new clothes, then dropped her own ones into the bin.

Milla didn't know then that Amber was dead. She didn't know who the blood belonged to. But she knew that throwing the bloodstained clothes into the church bin was a very stupid thing to do. That's why she waited until their mum found Lucy, and a while longer to make sure she wouldn't bump into her dad, and then retrieved Lucy's dirty clothes and took them to Kiln Lakes. Once they were stuffed inside scavenged plastic bags, weighed down with heavy rocks, and thrown into its deep centre, she knew they wouldn't rise to the surface any time soon.

But burying the memory – and what it might mean – is proving a lot harder to do.

AFTER

Monday 13th May

Rachel

The door opens a few inches; the chain stretched to its limit. 'Yes?' a woman's voice says. 'Can I help you?'

'Um, hi,' I start, hovering on the paving slab outside the Trapnells' house. I know that my credentials are my ticket inside. 'I work with Colleen in Children's Services. I was hoping …'

'Oh God, hold on,' the woman interrupts. The door slams shut, then opens fully, the newly freed chain swaying against the frame. She looks distraught; doesn't ask for my ID. Of course the police will have already been here, told her that Jess is missing.

'Have you found her?' she asks. 'Please tell me that you have, and that she's safe. I couldn't bear it if, you know, after what happened to Amber.'

'I'm so sorry,' I start. 'We don't have any news yet. But could I possibly come in? Colleen thought it would be a good idea if we had a chat, just talked through any possible places that Jess might have gone to.'

'I've been racking my brains …'

'Please?' I press.

Her head jerks up as she realises that she's being rude, leaving me on the doorstep. 'Yes of course, I'm sorry; I'm not thinking straight.' She takes a step back and I walk inside. It's a small hallway with stairs to one side and a mirror on the other, which I avoid looking into. No sign of any children though. They must have decided to take a break from fostering.

'Come through,' she murmurs. 'Justin had to go into work early this morning, so it's just me.'

She doesn't offer me a drink, and I'm grateful. My hands are shaking too much to lift a glass or mug. I perch on the edge of the sofa that she gestures towards. 'I'm not sure how much Colleen has told you,' I start. 'But we're hopeful that Jess left of her own accord, rather than the alternative.' I'm spinning this narrative to focus Lou on possible destinations, but it also reminds me that it could be true. Matt could still be innocent in all of this.

But Lou's face falls rather than brightens. 'I'm not sure that's good news,' she says, her voice cracking.

I tilt my head. 'How do you mean?'

'When Colleen told me Jess was missing, right before the police turned up, my first thought was that she'd done something terrible to herself. She and Amber were so close, and Jess relied on her sister for everything. Jess was vulnerable too, especially when she was under stress. I suppose you know about the anorexia?'

I nod dumbly as my mind tries to tally the eating disorder with the Jess I saw in the Co-op. Lean yes, but tall and intimidating.

'I knew how much Jess would have been struggling after Amber's murder, especially with their mum dying in a similar way,' Lou continues. 'But Colleen was adamant that Jess wasn't suicidal, that if anything, she'd gone the other way. Angry rather than broken. Like she'd taken on some of Amber's fight.'

That's how Colleen described it to me too. And there's the

message Jess sent to Lucy. The video. The demand for money. 'From what I've seen of Jess since Amber's death, I agree with Colleen,' I say truthfully. 'I really don't think Jess was in the headspace to harm herself.'

Lou's shoulders visibly drop with relief, and she even manages a small smile. 'Thank you.'

'But we still need to find her,' I remind Lou gently. 'Can you think of anyone around here that she might have gone to for help? A good friend from when she was younger maybe? Someone she had regular playdates with?'

'No, nothing like that. Jess was shy. She didn't seem to want – or need – many friends. She just wanted to be with Amber. That's why I've been so worried since Amber's death. I've tried to call Jess. Loads of times. But she never picks up.'

I think about the girl I saw that lunchtime. The range of painful emotions visible on her face. Perhaps it's not surprising that she has avoided the woman who cared for her for five years. 'And was Amber the same?' I ask. 'Was it always just the two of them?'

'Amber was much more outgoing than Jess; you'd never call that girl shy.' She gives me a sad smile then looks away. 'But actually, she didn't really have any close friends either. Both girls were defined by their start in life, sadly. Wary of others who might want to label them as victims – or worse. But while Jess reacted by staying in the shadows, Amber came out fighting – like she was constantly daring people to feel sorry for her. But she'd either fail and hate them for it, or make enemies through her own bad behaviour. So in a different way, she relied on Jess too.'

'What about other family?' I ask, desperate for some bread-crumbs to follow, even though I know the police will have already covered this ground. 'Jess's dad has been contacted, but was she in touch with anyone else? Grandparents? Aunts? Cousins?'

'No, no one,' Lou says, shrugging her shoulders. 'Jacqui – that's the girls' mum – had two brothers. But the whole family disowned her when she was still a teenager, and then when she died, they wanted nothing to do with her daughters – that's why the girls ended up in care in the first place. I'm not sure whether there are relatives on her dad's side, but Jess was barely in touch with him, and she never mentioned anyone else to me.'

'And there's really nowhere else you can think of?' I lean forward, plead with my eyes.

'Well, there is Sean Russo,' Lou murmurs.

'But isn't he the reason the girls left Oxford?'

'I never supported that decision,' she mutters. 'After the initial shock of his threatening behaviour wore off, it felt like a sledge-hammer to crack a nut. Yes, he was angry with Jess, and a risk in the short term, but I'm sure it would have faded over time. He'd started hanging around with a new crowd, not nice people granted, but older. With bigger fish to fry than hassling teenage girls.'

'And you think they'd become friends again?' I ask, trying to work out why she mentioned his name. 'Sean and Jess?'

Lou shakes her head. 'Oh no, that's not what I meant at all. He was only ever Amber's friend even when they lived here. Not that she introduced him to me,' she adds. 'But I was curious to know who they hung out with in the park, so I'd wander past sometimes, by accident on purpose, you know.' She gives me a sheepish half-smile.

I smile back, an approval of her sleuthing, then look at her expectantly, hoping she'll share more detail. It works.

'I was a bit worried, of course,' she continues. 'Seeing Amber talking with an older boy, hanging on his every word, obviously smitten. But I asked around – that's how I found out his name – and people said he was harmless back then. Bark worse than his bite. I'm pretty sure that's changed now, sadly.' She tilts her head. 'Anyway, I knew it wasn't ideal, but as I said, Amber didn't have many friends, and I didn't want to be too narrow-minded about what a good one looked like.' She sighs. 'And then his mum got sick, and soon after that, he got punched by his teacher. Poor kid. I imagine he was difficult to teach, but there's still no excuse.'

I fix on a smile. She says it like it's a fact. 'Didn't Jess admit that she lied about seeing that?' I ask, my voice stilted. 'The case was dropped, I think?'

'It was, yes,' Lou agrees. 'And if you didn't know Jess, you might be suspicious, with her knowing Sean through Amber. But I don't think she was lying about seeing the assault. Jess would have found it incredibly difficult to talk to the head teacher, and then the police. And you can times that by a hundred if her story was also a lie. Even if they were good friends, which they weren't, I can't see her going to those lengths for him.'

I grip the soft velour of the sofa arm and pull in a silent breath. I need to get this conversation back on track. After all, she still hasn't explained why Jess might have gone to Sean's. 'But if it was Amber who was friends with Sean, why do you think Jess might be hiding out there now?'

Her expression becomes embarrassed. 'Look, I'm probably wrong. But Amber idolised Sean. And for whatever reason, he had a lot of time for her too. Jess and Sean have Amber in common, and now she's gone. Suddenly and brutally. It happens, doesn't it? People coming together through shared grief?'

I blink. Jess hiding out with Sean Russo seems crazy – the boy considered so dangerous by Colleen and her team that Amber and Jess were taken away from their home – but Lou's exactly right, it does happen. I find myself hoping that she and Justin do decide to foster again, so that more children can benefit from her thoughtfulness and humanity.

'Do you know where Sean lives?' I ask.

'Blackbird Leys somewhere. At least he did, and I suppose he's still there. I heard his mum died recently. She had cancer, must have only been mid-forties, poor woman. But I don't suppose the council would have thrown Sean out yet. His mum used to work at the girls' school actually, as a cleaner, so they knew her a bit. I remember someone organising a collection when she had her first op.' Lou gives me a sad smile. 'Anyway, I don't know the address, but I suggest you check with your colleagues at the police. I reckon they'll have his details on file.'

THE NIGHT SHE DIES

Friday 3rd May

Jess

She thought she'd be scared. Fuck, she should be scared, alone at this time, on the remote trail up to the Ridgeway. Only the stars and moon for light. But there's another harder emotion rising to the surface.

Is it determination to fight back this time? To find Amber and, together, stand up to Sean?

Or is it anger at her sister?

Because it's Amber's fault that Sean is on his way to Chinnor, wanting their blood. But so far, it's only Jess he's tracked down.

There's also the Lucy factor. She clearly knows something, something big enough to put a scared little mouse like her on the attack. Could it be about Jess being the anonymous witness in her dad's case? And if Lucy does know, how dare Amber keep that information from her?

Except that's Amber all over. Only confiding in Jess when it's good for her. Like sorting their move to Chinnor. Amber came up with this big master plan to punish Mr Rose and get Sean to like her again, and didn't even tell Jess until she needed her help.

And like tonight. She's still only guessing that Amber is at the nature reserve – because she hasn't returned any of Jess's messages.

Jess reaches the Ridgeway and takes a left. It's even darker here, surrounded by trees, and a sharp fingernail of apprehension scratches at her neck. She pauses, flicks the torch on her phone. The path jumps out, but her peripheral vision disappears into total blackness. Instantly she feels watched. There's a broken branch on the pathway, thick and heavy, with its bark completely stripped away, yellowy white under the torch's glare. She reaches for it, curls her fingers around the smooth wood, and pulls it into her chest, grateful for the sense of protection it gives her. Then she takes a breath and turns her phone off again – she doesn't want to announce her arrival too early – and sets off.

She shouldn't really be scared here, she tells herself as she walks deeper into the woods. Scared is walking through Blackbird Leys at night, its dim lights throwing shadows around every corner, knowing that Sean hates her for what she's done – or more accurately, can't do. Chinnor was supposed to be their escape from him, until Amber screwed that up. But Sean is a city boy. Thick woodland and muddy trails feel like the best protection from him.

Ten minutes later, she pauses. Hears voices. She guessed right – Amber is here, and Caden too. Maybe she invited him to protect her from Sean. Or maybe she was only pretending to go off him, to create some drama. Suddenly that feels more likely, and the thought fills Jess with rage. Amber playing with people's feelings purely to relieve her own boredom.

Their voices whisper through the trees. Jess crouches down on the compacted mud to steady her breathing. The volume of their conversation is too low for Jess to make out what they're saying, but there's a general hum of contentment. A giggle wafting over every now and then. The sound pulls at her chest – causes actual physical pain – but she needs to ride it out.

Because she needs to warn Amber about Sean.

Being sisters might mean nothing to Amber, but she refuses to sink that low.

And for all Amber's faults, Jess knows that she still owes her. For refusing to go through with the court case, and everything that came after.

But the problem is, she can't move. Can't push her way through the final few trees and announce her arrival. Can't interrupt the lovebirds. She needs Caden to leave first, because the thought of looking at the two of them, draped over each other, and pretending it doesn't bother her is too much.

Impossible.

When Jess saw Caden by the memorial statue in Thame, her first thought was that Amber had done it on purpose. Snatched the one guy that Jess had been on her way to falling in love with: Caden Carter. The boy she'd met by the lakes when Amber was out with Sean that Sunday. The completely gorgeous almost-man she'd struck up conversation with, and then had dared to believe might become her boyfriend one day – until he broke it off with barely any explanation. But Jess had kept Caden and Amber a secret from each other, so it can't be that Amber stole him. It was just one of those terrible coincidences. A boy who's attracted to damaged goods falling for two samples from the same batch.

But that was before his message this evening. Caden asked to meet up with Jess knowing full well that she was his girlfriend's sister. It doesn't matter that she said yes, or that Caden changed his mind before anything happened. He showed what a cheating prick he is, and Amber deserves to know.

Especially as it's the fastest way to get him out of the way.

Jess creeps a bit closer. She can see them now. Or at least slivers of them through the slim gaps in the trees. They're lying next to each other on something dark – not a blanket, but maybe a jumper. Caden's, probably. Amber's phone is lying close to her fingertips on the grass. She might not be responding to Jess's snaps, but she's clearly reachable. Maybe an old-fashioned text message will grab her attention.

Still sitting on her haunches, Jess scrolls to her photos, and looks at the last one she took. A screen grab of her Snapchat conversation with Caden. She edits it guiltily, making sure Caden's Snapchat tag is visible at the top, but her own messages are cut out, then reads the words. *Was supposed to be at a party tonight but can't face it. Want to meet up?* Without giving herself the chance to change her mind, she taps out a text message to her sister – *he doesn't deserve you* – and launches the photo into cyberspace.

She peers through the trees.

Amber's phone screen lights up, sending an eerie glow across the grass. Jess prays for her sister to pick it up. And it works because a moment later, there's movement. Amber's arm extending, grabbing the device, then her torso curling and rising into a sitting position.

Panic suddenly floods Jess's insides. What has she done? Why is she causing another argument when they already have Sean to worry about, and Lucy too? How can she be so stupid?

Jess watches Amber turn to face Caden, a slow-motion movement, weighed down by shock. Disgust. She dips down onto her hands and knees, creeps forward. Close enough to hear their conversation.

'What the fuck is this?' Amber hisses, her voice low but venomous.

Caden sits up. 'What?' he throws back, instantly aggro.

Jess tilts back onto her feet, curls her hands into fists.

'Did you ask to meet up with my sister tonight?'

'Huh?' A stalling tactic. Fear creeping into his tone.

'How could you?' Amber cries out, the sound echoing off the heavy branches.

Jess sucks in a breath, listens to it judder out of her. Her feelings for Amber are so complicated. She can despise her at times, but she also hates hearing her upset. It always reminds Jess of their mum, her saying sorry to Tyler on a loop as he screamed at her.

'It was a mistake, babe,' Caden says, changing tack again. 'A moment of madness. You were airing me. I got thrown out of that eighteenth party by Ava's Nazi dad, then out of The Crown. I sent Jess a message on some weird impulse, but I straight off regretted it, and told her that.'

'But my sister?' Amber says incredulously.

Caden's response is quieter, so Jess has to strain to hear it. 'Babe, it's not like it's that shocking, is it? You know I was with her first.'

Jess blinks, swallows a whimper, sinks onto her backside.

Amber knew?

'But that was before we got together,' Amber wails. 'How could you even think about going back to her when you have me? I'm much prettier than her. That's what you said.'

Jess bites her lip. Tastes blood. She and Amber only have each other. It's been that way for what feels like a lifetime. Yes, Amber bosses her around, takes the piss out of her, puts her down. But loads of sisters do that.

They don't steal first boyfriends. They're not that fucking cruel.

'All right, chill,' Caden mutters, shuffling away from her. 'I don't think I said that; and you shouldn't either, about your own sister.'

Jess looks up at the black sky. Her mouth pulls at the edges. Is Caden defending her? Is she supposed to be grateful for his scraps?

'Me chill?!' Amber shouts, twisting round onto her knees, no sign of remorse or shame. 'You're chasing my dumb ginger beanpole of a sister, and I'm supposed to be cool about that?'

A moan escapes, Jess can't stop it. But Amber and Caden are too lost in their argument to hear.

'I don't fancy her, not anymore. But you shouldn't talk about her like that.'

'You fucking do, you liar!'

The thwack of a slap rings out. Suddenly Jess is transported

256

back seven years. She sees her mum, the blood pooling on the carpet, her eyes like marbles. She feels sick.

Is Caden going to retaliate? Like Tyler always would?

Does she even care anymore?

'Fuck this,' Caden spits out. 'You're a crazy bitch!' He stands up, turns away.

Amber scrambles to her feet and reaches out to him. As she grabs the neck of his hoodie, she flinches, and Jess remembers her fight with Lucy earlier, the broken bottle, Amber lifting her hands to protect herself, her fingers making contact.

'No, you can't go,' she says, trying but failing to sound tough. 'I don't want to be here by myself. At least drive me back. And you've got my gear in your jacket!'

'Get off me,' Caden growls. 'I don't need to do anything. We're done, Amber. Jesus, it was stupid to begin with. What kind of bitch steals their sister's boyfriend anyway? I should have told you to fuck off when you first messaged me.'

'Don't twist the truth! I just wanted to be friends. To get to know the boy who my sister was keeping a secret from me. You were the one who pushed things. Told me I was beautiful.'

Caden chuckles coldly. 'And one measly compliment was enough for you to betray your only relative. You're just a cheap slag; goodbye, Amber.' He reaches down to pick his jacket off the ground, but she lunges at him.

'Don't say that!' Long fingernails, flashes of electric blue, the sound of skin tearing.

'Shit!' Caden cups his cheek. 'You're fucking mental!'

Jess's phone vibrates in her hand. A new Snapchat message. Habit kicks in and she clicks on it.

I'm here. Be scared.

'How could I not have seen it?!' Caden shouts. 'Why the hell did I find that story about why you moved to Chinnor so funny? When it was the biggest red flag ever!'

Jess can't breathe. She was so focused on finding Amber that she forgot to turn the Snapchat map function off. She's led Sean right to them.

But it's Caden's next words that hollow her out like an exploding bullet.

AFTER

Monday 13th May

Rachel

I swing off Blackbird Leys Road and park outside Evenmarle Tower. I don't want to think about how I got Sean's address, going back into my work database, searching for another case file that's got nothing to do with me. As soon as Lou said that Sean's mum had died of cancer, I suspected we'd have his records. Sean is only 19 now, so it's likely he'd have been a child when his mum was first diagnosed. And a single mum in and out of hospital would always lead to social services involvement, if only to check that no support was required.

And I was proved right, because there it was. Sean Russo, son of Lizzie Russo and Jed Brown. Father absent; mother deceased. Currently residing at 504 Evenmarle Tower.

Work has brought me to this deprived area many times over the years, but I haven't been since my promotion, and it looks like the tower has had a facelift. It used to be a bleak concrete block, but there's a new glass entrance porch now, and deep-blue cladding on the walls. As I walk inside, I wonder if there's a new security system, but both the doors are wide open. I press for the lift, and miraculously it's working.

The closer I get to Sean's flat on the fifth floor, the faster my heart beats. Do I really think Jess has come here? Or am I searching for answers about Matt? As though by seeing Sean Russo in the flesh, I'll be able to decide for myself whether my husband inflicted his injuries over two years ago. I reach his door, and without letting myself question what I'm doing, rap my knuckles against it.

No one comes.

But I can hear movement inside, so I knock again, louder. But still nothing. I push open the letter box. There's no hallway – the door leads straight into a front room – and I can make out the dark outline of a man pacing. 'Sean?' I call out. 'Sean Russo?'

The dark mass freezes for a moment, then grows in size. A moment later, the door edges open six inches or so. Enough for me to see Sean's eyes. Pupils big enough to swallow me whole.

'Who are you? What do you want?' he hisses. There are grazes on his cheeks. Blood on his T-shirt. I've dealt with many agitated teenagers over the years, but it feels different this time. Because it's personal – and more dangerous with it.

'Um, my name is Rachel Salter,' I start, silently thanking my past self for keeping my maiden name. 'I work for Oxford City Council in Children's Services.'

His eyes narrow. He glances down at his clothes, as though suddenly remembering what he looks like, then edges the door closer to the frame, so only half his face is on show. But his hand is still visible, and I can see that his knuckles are missing a few layers of skin.

'I'm not a kid,' he says. 'I'm 18 now, so you don't need to come here.'

'I know,' I say, with a conciliatory smile. Listen. Relate. De-escalate. These are the pillars of my job and I draw on them now. But inside, I'm on high alert. Because it's obvious that he's hit someone. Was it Jess? Is she in his flat now, injured and in need of help?

Is Matt innocent after all?

'I was hoping you could help me,' I continue to explain. 'I'm looking for Jessica Scott and I thought she might have come to see you.'

'I don't know her.' His eyes dare me to contest his lie, and for a moment I wonder if I should let it go, walk away. But I need to get to the truth.

'She was the witness to your assault claim,' I say. 'And I know that you know her.'

'Claim?' he says, his voice rising. 'I was smacked to shit by my teacher and he got away—'

'I was told that you and Jess were friends at the time,' I cut in.

'You're fucking kidding ...' He stops, changes tack. 'She's not here,' he says. 'I haven't seen her.'

It's a double denial. I consider his clothes again, his raw knuckles. How defensive he appears. That he won't open the door. 'But you know that Jess is missing?' I press.

He blows out air, then clicks his tongue. 'Okay, yeah, I heard,' he admits. 'But I haven't seen her, all right? I said that already.'

I'm running out of rope. And I'm no closer to working out whether he's done something to Jess, or it's just my imagination running wild, trying to find a suspect to replace my husband. I take a deep breath, then slide my foot between the door and its frame. 'It looks like you've been in a fight.'

'That's none of your business.'

I gesture towards his hand, still curled around the door. 'That you've hit someone.'

'I reckon you should move your foot. Before my door cripples it.'

'Was it Jess?' My heart is pounding inside my chest, my muscles taut with conflicting urges – to push harder, and to run away.

'You're crazy, you know that?'

'Did she come to you for help? And then you took advantage of her vulnerability?'

'Her vulnerability! Hah! You've no idea what that selfish bitch is capable of!'

His words trigger memories. Jess's fierce blue eyes. Her threats and demand for money. Colleen's belief that Amber's death has toughened her. Have I underestimated Jess in all of this? Is she more than the distraught sister of the victim?

I find my soft social worker voice. 'So tell me then. I'd really like to hear your thoughts on where Jess might have gone.'

But it doesn't work.

'No. You need to leave. You can't force your way in.'

He's right, I don't have that power – legal or otherwise. But Sean Russo is hiding something. Maybe it's to do with the money. If he'd found out Jess had ten grand in her pocket, I bet he'd want it. And I doubt she'd have made it easy for him to take it.

She could be in there now. Lying unconscious on the floor. There's clearly something in there he doesn't want me to see.

I lean forward a few centimetres, shift left. Our faces are close now, I can smell his sour breath, but I keep my eyes away from his, and towards the slim pickings of view beyond the curve of his neck. I can see the shadows of living-room furniture, but the curtains are drawn across the back window, so it's too dark to see much more.

'Fuck me,' he hisses. 'Do I need to call the feds?' Spittle lands on my face, and I instinctively tilt backwards. My foot is stopping him from shutting the door, but it's also tethering me to him. He could reach out and grab my hair in a second, slam my head into the door frame. Suddenly I think of the policeman who first talked to me on Chinnor Hill. The red light on his chest that told me he was recording our conversation. That's what I need, I think. If I film this, Sean won't be able to hurt me. I turned my phone off when I left my office – in case Matt called – but it's in my pocket. I turn it on as I pull it out.

262

But my fingers haven't got full purchase. I fumble, feel the smooth surface of the phone case slide away from my grasp. It lands on the concrete floor, on its back, with a thud. The screen lights up.

Shit. I fling my head up, look at Sean. His eyes widen even more as he stares at my phone, then they narrow.

In an instant, he scoops up the device, then grabs my arm above the wrist and yanks. There's no time to resist his pull, and a second later I'm tumbling inside his flat. The door slams shut behind me. I turn, lunge for the handle, my instinct to find Jess switching instantly to a desire to get away. But he's too quick. There's a second lock, a bolt, and he slides it across before grabbing me again and shoving me away from the door.

I need to remember my training. I've done a two-day workshop on crisis management; I should know how to resolve this, persuade him to let me go, for his own sake. But I can't think straight. I open my mouth to speak, but no words come out, and then it's too late. He pitches forward, pushes one hand over my face, and grabs the back of my head with the other. I gag, but he doesn't release the pressure. My mouth is still partly open; I can taste his sweat, blood.

'Why did you lie to me?'

'I didn't lie,' I try to say, but it comes out as a muffled bray.

'You're his wife!' he spits out. 'Not a social worker. You're married to that fucker who hit me. I saw his face on your phone, with you and those girls. And I know they're his daughters, so don't deny it. Why did you come here? How do you know about Jess? What the fuck do you want with me?'

He's rambling, caught off guard, but what does it matter? He's ten times stronger than me.

Why the hell did I come here? Did I not realise it would be dangerous? I'd never take such a risk if Sean was a client; I'd bring a colleague, maybe even ask for police backup with his record. But the only person who knows I'm here is Lou, and of course no one would think to ask her. How soon will it be before someone notices I'm gone?

'Sit down,' Sean orders, although he doesn't give me any choice, just pushes down on my head, which forces my knees to bend. I drop onto a wooden chair. Suddenly his hand disappears from my mouth, but as soon as my head computes that I'm free, I feel a sting of pain at my temple.

And a second later the room goes black.

AFTER

Monday 13th May

Milla

Milla hears the knock on the front door. She lifts her head, drops her pen onto the still-unread textbook on her desk. A heartbeat later, the sound of a man's voice. It's DI Finnemore, the detective who dropped round on Friday night to talk to her mum. There's someone else with him today, a woman, introducing herself as DC Bzowski. The detective who interviewed Lucy at the station.

Fuck.

Her dad will be petrified. Ever since they arrested him for that fake assault, her dad's lost all trust in the police. And today, he'll be scared for Lucy. Milla is almost certain her dad suspects she might be Amber's killer, just like Milla does. Not intentionally, but reaching breaking point; a flaring of anger with tragic, unintended consequences. Milla pushes her chair away from her desk and stands up. She can't let her dad deal with this alone.

When she gets downstairs, the two detectives are sitting on the sofa underneath the window with her dad opposite them. Milla

265

drops down next to him. 'Hi, I'm Milla,' she says, as breezily as she can manage. 'What's going on?'

'Good morning, Milla,' the woman says pleasantly. 'I'm DC Bzowski and this is my colleague, DI Finnemore. We've stopped by for a chat with your dad.'

'You don't have to be here, Milla,' her dad interjects. 'I'm fine. And you've got lots of studying to do.' He throws Milla a glance – she knows it's conveying a message but can't figure out what it is. Either way, Milla's not going anywhere.

'I could really do with a break to be honest,' she says, smiling brightly at the detectives. 'If it's just a chat, I guess I can join you?'

DC Bzowski looks at her dad. When he turns away from her glance, she shrugs. 'So, Mr Rose,' she says. 'Your wife told us that you returned from Thailand last Friday 3rd May at around 8 p.m.?'

'That's right. I'd been there all week with work.'

'And how did you spend your evening when you got home?'

Milla smiles to hide her discomfort.

'Rachel was out for a curry with some girlfriends,' Matt starts. 'And Milla was at a party.'

'Ava Ainsworth's party?' DC Bzowski asks.

'Yep,' Milla says, then seals her lips back together.

The detective nods and turns back to Matt. 'And Lucy?' she asks.

'Um, she was at home with me,' Matt says. 'We chatted for a while, then she went up to her room around nine. I put a film on, but I think I was asleep in seconds. Jet lag, you know.' He produces a wide smile, but neither of the detectives react.

'And did you wake up at any point?'

'Um, yes.' Matt screws up his face as though trying to remember. Like he hasn't been going over it a zillion times a day since Amber's body was discovered. 'A while later though. Lucy and Rachel were in the kitchen together, having a hot chocolate.'

'They'd been out for a walk I believe?'

'That's right. But I slept right through that.'

'And you didn't go out yourself?'

266

Milla's mind races. She remembers climbing into her dad's car, him rolling it out of the drive quietly, heading towards the railway station to drop her off, then going looking himself. It was late; traffic was sparse. Could a camera have picked up his car as they drove past? 'You came to get me, remember?' she spurts out. She's been focused on Lucy, but she needs to protect her dad too. After all, he's the one with a black mark against him.

'What?'

'From Ava's party. I had a blister, and you took pity on me.' A moment of silence. Milla's heart punches her ribcage.

'Yes, of course,' he finally offers. 'I'd forgotten about that.' He smiles at the detectives.

'And what time was this?' DC Bzowski asks.

'I'm not sure exactly.' Matt tilts his head. 'Maybe twelvish? Or a bit later?'

'And did you see anyone at the party?' the detective asks.

'Yes,' Matt says. 'Ava's mother.'

Milla shifts in her chair. This is news to her, actual human contact, but at least her dad remembered in time to cover himself.

'Milla and I had our wires crossed,' he goes on. 'I thought she was still at the house, but she was waiting for me further up the road.'

'And you didn't go anywhere else? Just to the Ainsworths' house and back?'

'I ... um, yes, that's right ... I took the long way home though, so I did a full loop of the village.'

'Thank you, Mr Rose, for clearing that up,' DI Finnemore says. But her dad doesn't look relieved, and Milla understands why. Those timings relate to when she was missing. He must have remembered speaking to Ava's mum and so prioritised covering up for that. But he was out earlier too, searching for Lucy, so how is he going to explain that if they ask?

'There is another thing we'd like to discuss with you,' the detective goes on.

Milla shuffles against the sofa cushion.

'I believe you're aware that Jessica Scott has gone missing?'

Milla concentrates on her breathing. She's never had a panic attack before, but one feels dangerously close now. Colour is draining from her dad's face too. Can the detectives see it?

'Yes,' her dad whispers. 'I heard that she's run away.'

'Maybe.' DC Bzowski purses her lips. 'How well do you know her?'

'I don't know her at all. Well, not personally. She was bullying Lucy with her sister, so I know *of* her.'

'Are you aware that Jessica was a student at Oxford Comprehensive before moving to Chinnor?'

Matt doesn't answer. He's so still, Milla isn't even sure he's breathing. She wonders if she should nudge him.

'No, I didn't know,' he finally says. He rubs his bare head with the heel of his hand.

'Or that she has links to the victim of the assault you were charged with?'

'No,' Matt repeats, his eyelids flitting like butterfly wings. 'What links?'

'We can't disclose that,' DC Bzowski says quietly.

Milla's mind whirs. Why can't they disclose that? If Jess was friends with Sean Russo, surely they'd just say so? And anyway, it would be weird if they were friends. Sean was nearly 17 when he accused her dad, and Jess is only 15 now, so there's a big age gap. But how else could she be linked to him? They can't be family. There's no way it's anything wholesome like church or scouts.

Milla's mouth suddenly fills with saliva, as though she's going to be sick, and she swallows hard. Her dad was first summoned to the headmaster's office when Sean Russo turned up at school with a black eye and then made his false claim. But it was only when a witness came forward that things got really bad for him. He was suspended straight away, but Mr Pearson kept in touch for a while, and it was during one of their phone conversations that he let slip that the witness was female. But her dad never knew who she was.

At least that's what Milla had thought.

Could Jess Scott be the mystery witness? Is that her link with Sean Russo?

Whoever it was, they pulled their statement fifteen months later, a year ago now. Milla never questioned why the witness changed her mind – no one in her family did, they were too busy celebrating – but should she have? If it was Jess, could her dad have got to her somehow?

But that doesn't make sense because Jess and Amber moved to Chinnor after the case was dropped, not before.

Milla lurches forward in her chair with a sudden adrenalin spike, then shifts back slowly as both detectives turn to stare at her. She gives them a relaxed smile, but inside she's reeling. Did the girls come here on purpose? Wangle a move to Chinnor somehow? Christ, Amber might just have the smarts to do it. But why would they do that unless they wanted to make trouble for her dad?

Did Jess pull her statement so they could inflict their own style of justice? Punish her dad by making his daughter's life hell instead? Anger throbs in her chest at the thought. Two fucked-up social care kids and a roadman – of course they wouldn't trust the police, the courts, to defend them. And yeah, maybe they've got a point. But taking it out on Lucy? That is too fucking low.

Milla tries to keep her expression clear, calm, in front of the detectives, but damn, it's hard. Her dad followed her on Friday night, so he was the last person to see Jess. And she might well be the person who ruined his career, and almost his life, before doing the same to his daughter to twist the knife even more.

His favourite daughter. Milla has always known that.

She thinks about the note. *My dad will kill you.* She chose the words and typed them.

But could it be possible that he carried them out?

AFTER

Monday 13th May

Rachel

My eyes are open, but the room is so dark I can barely see anything. There's tape across my mouth, sticking to the dry skin on my lips, so I can only breathe through my nose. I know the most important thing is to not panic – that clamouring for oxygen will have the opposite effect – so I close my eyes and try to imagine I'm somewhere else. Lying in my bed at home, Matt snoring beside me; the kids asleep in their respective rooms.

But it's hard to pretend because my hands are tied together behind my back, and my upper arms are straining in their unnatural position. My legs are clamped together too, at both the knees and the ankles. I'm lying on my side, staring at a thin line of dim light slipping under the door.

When Sean hit me, I rode the pain, but then the bag was over my head a second later. I should have either engaged him in conversation, or tried to kick and punch my way out, but I did neither. I was too disorientated. And then he dragged me into this room, heavy curtains shut tight, and flung me on the bed. My urge to fight finally kicked in at that point, but I was no match for his strength. Despite my flailing arms and legs, he had me tied up in minutes. The bag came off, but he pasted tape across my mouth. He stared right through me for what felt like ages, then twisted around, flicked the light switch, and left the room.

It was a relief then, but that was almost an hour ago. My muscles are sore, and I'm desperate to pee. I also need to know why I'm here. Yes, Sean saw the wallpaper on my phone and worked out who my husband is. But is that really enough for him to tie me up like this? Kidnap me? The incident happened over two years ago, and it's not like I was directly involved.

Perhaps it's because this kind of violence is normal for him. He's high. He's already been in a fight today. And he seemed paranoid when he came to the door. Is this about Jess? Has he hurt her too, or done something worse?

And if he's capable of this, could he have been involved in Amber's murder as well?

The door swings open. I gasp, but the tape across my mouth means it's more of a chest heave. His shadow appears. I body pop away from him. There's a click and the room fills with light. I close my eyes against the sudden glare, then gradually peel them back open. There's wallpaper on the walls, a soft lilac, and the bedspread is pale green. Tranquil. In different circumstances. It must be his mum's bedroom. I feel a jolt of compassion, him still keeping it nice after she died. But then I zoom in on his sallow face, and the feeling evaporates. His fists are clenched, like before, but now one of them is holding something. A knife. It's small, like a Kitchen Devil, but it's still a weapon.

He rips the tape away from my mouth, holds the knife up at his shoulder, like he's going to jab me with it. 'What do you want?' he demands. 'Why did you come here?'

I force myself to take a long, controlled breath. 'Not to hurt you,' I say. 'Not to blame you for anything. And I wasn't lying about being a social worker.'

'You said I'd hurt Jess.' He lowers the knife, then lifts it again, as though remembering I'm his enemy. 'I haven't touched that stupid bitch, okay?'

'I'm sorry,' I lie. 'I shouldn't have said that. I actually thought she might come to you for help.'

'Why would I help her?' he asks incredulously. 'She could have killed Amber for all I know.'

'What?' I shake my head in confusion.

'She was there. In those woods. I saw her location on Snapchat. I thought it was that prick Caden who killed Amber at first; I even walked past the fucker. But nah, he's too pathetic.'

'But you can't think Jess killed her own sister?' I can't process what he's saying. Was he really there that night? Is he throwing out a list of suspects to cover up his own guilt? Or are the drugs making him talk nonsense?

'Unless your old man did it,' he suddenly growls. 'Is that why you're here? To brag about what he did?'

My head spins. Sean's thoughts are so chaotic, it's hard to keep up. I try to move my hands, but they're tightly wedged together, like my legs. I'm stuck here until either he lets me go or someone comes to rescue me. But who? Everyone thinks I'm at work. I don't know what Sean's done with my phone, but even if Matt or the girls can check my location, this is my area so they won't think anything of me being here. No one will miss me for hours.

'It's so fucking obvious,' Sean continues, nodding as he warms to his theme. 'Because I know what a cold-blooded psycho he is. He must have worked out who she was. Then killed her. Maybe I should tell the feds. Then he'd be banged up like he should have been two years ago.'

A wave of nausea passes through me, like seasickness, as though I'm in a boat's hull instead of a dead woman's bedroom on the fifth floor of a tower block. But Matt can't have known who Amber was, because he would have told me.

And why would I believe the words of a drugged-up thug over

my husband? And one who has accused three different people of Amber's murder in the space of a few minutes.

Maybe it's all too obvious. Lou called Sean Amber's friend, but what kind of friend could he have been? The girls were forced to leave their whole life behind because of the threat he posed. And right now, he's off his head, standing over me with a knife. Someone was supplying Amber with the drugs she sold in the village. And if it wasn't the boyfriend, it must have been Sean. If they'd had a falling-out over drugs, anything could have happened.

'But then again,' Sean continues, 'telling the feds did nothing for me last time, did it?' He starts pacing the small room but doesn't break eye contact with me. 'Especially after Amber's stupid sister went rogue.' He clicks his tongue. 'And Amber was repaying that debt too, by fucking with his daughter.'

My daughter. My kind, innocent Lucy.

'And then the little bitch screwed me!' He lifts the knife again, his hand shaking.

'So you killed her,' I hiss, not caring about the danger. 'Not Matt. Or Lucy. Or Milla!' I twist around on the bed. It won't help me, but I need to expel some energy. 'It was you!'

He lunges forward. His free hand lands on my mouth, pushes hard. He's half lying on me now, his breath acrid, his forehead dripping in sweat. My chest sinks under his weight. He pushes the knife against my neck; I feel a sharp sting as the tip digs into my flesh. But I won't show him I'm scared.

'You wish it was me,' he hisses. 'Because you can't stand to admit the truth. That your old man killed her.'

'He didn't.' I close my eyes, but Matt's image appears behind my eyelids. His disapproving stare. The quiet anger that can radiate off him if he feels out of control. I've always envied his self-discipline. But a deep, buried part of me has wondered what would happen if he ever snapped.

My dad will kill you.

'I've seen it for myself, don't forget,' Sean goes on. 'Him losing his shit. I bet he did Amber. And then gave Jess the same treatment. You might think you're some kind, caring social worker, but you're still married to a murderer.'

AFTER

Monday 13th May

DI Simon Finnemore

Jodie Bzowski got highly commended on the advanced driving course, so there's never a discussion when they travel together. Simon opens the passenger door, sinks into the seat, and thinks about the conversation they've just had with Matthew Rose. His explanation about why he was out on the night Amber Walsh died stacks up in part – picking his daughter up from a party. But it doesn't explain why his car was seen idling in the railway station car park over an hour before.

And there is also the Jessica Scott connection. Rose shouldn't know that she was the key witness in his case – her identity was supposed to be protected – but these things have a way of getting out. And the guy acted very cagily when he asked about her. If Rose had suspected that the sisters were bullying his youngest daughter to get to him, especially with the way it escalated last Friday, that might cause him to lose his temper with one – or both – of them. But would he really follow Amber into the woods in the middle of the night? And how would he know she was there? Plus, his

DNA is on NDNAD from his previous arrest, and there are no forensics linking him to the crime scene. Not yet at least – they still haven't had the results of that partial blood sample.

Then there's Lucy Rose to consider too. There is plenty of CCTV evidence that disproves her account, and she had a well-documented reason to hate the girl. But murder? He thinks about his own daughters, similar in age to the Roses, their attention wholly taken up by TikTok and American TV shows. He just can't make the mental leap to treat Lucy as a suspect, but is that profiling gone wrong? He drums his fingers against the hard plastic of the seatbelt buckle. He needs to be more objective. Use the hard graft of proper policework to shape his opinions. He'll get one of the team to look at Lucy Rose's digital footprint.

Simon pulls out his phone to call the incident room, but before he gets a chance to dial, it buzzes in his hand. 'Finnemore.'

'Raj here, sir. Glad I caught you; there's been a bit of a development.'

Simon leans forward in his seat, ignores the quizzical eyebrow raise Jodie gives him. 'Oh?'

'Caden Carter's been assaulted. Not far from his house. It sounds like someone jumped him when he left for work this morning. Area team have given it to us for obvious reasons.'

Simon narrows his eyes. This was supposed to be a shocking and sad, but also clear-cut, murder investigation – a drugs-related killing and a dispiriting social care statistic – but now the sister of the victim is missing, and Raj is telling him that the prime suspect has been attacked. It's getting harder to piece together by the minute. 'How badly is he injured?' Simon asks.

'Broken nose. Two broken ribs. Hairline fracture in his jaw, sir. Otherwise just cuts and bruises. He'll live of course, but he took quite a beating.'

'Is he talking?'

'There are two uniforms at Stoke Mandeville hospital with him at the moment,' Raj explains. 'And if you mean can he enunciate his words, then apparently no, not brilliantly. They reckon he sounds like a cross between an elephant and a pisshead. But if you mean talking in the sense of honour among thieves' discretion, we don't know yet. Uniforms know of his involvement in our murder case, so they're leaving it well alone.'

'Fair enough,' Simon murmurs. 'We'll head over there now. ETA twenty minutes. Can you let the hospital know?'

'Yeah, will do. Oh, and we've got some CCTV,' Raj goes on.

'Already?' Simon is impressed.

'Well, the idiot who attacked him started the assault on a residential road. He dragged Caden down the alleyway pretty quickly, but not before a couple of video doorbells picked him up.'

'And can you identify the assailant?'

'Nothing yet, sir. But the digital guys are blowing up some images. Hopefully we'll get something soon.'

'It sounds like this crime might be one we'll actually solve,' Simon murmurs, before ending the call.

'How are you feeling, Caden?' Jodie asks as they walk up to his hospital bed. There's no sign of sympathy in her voice, even though his face is a mess. The nurse explained when they first arrived that his jaw doesn't require surgery, but it's heavily swollen and he'll need to be on a liquid diet for the next few weeks. His nose is split at the bridge, and there are bruises forming around both his eyes.

He shrugs and makes a sound somewhere between a grunt and a moan.

Simon pulls up a chair – its metal legs screeching as he drags it across the floor – and lowers into it. 'Do you know who did this to you, Caden?'

'Yeah,' Caden mumbles, his voice thick with soft tissue damage. 'Fucking nutter.'

'I need a bit more detail than that.'

'He's called Sean,' Caden lisps. 'Dunno his last name.'

'Any idea why this Sean assaulted you?' Jodie asks.

'Same reason he killed Amber I guess,' Caden murmurs. His words are quiet, but his eyes show that he's aware of the bombshell he's just dropped.

'What did you say?' Jodie asks, her voice rising.

'He was ranting,' Caden says. 'As he did me. Saying he saw me up there. Passed me on his way to teach Amber a lesson about trust, he said. I know I didn't kill her, so it must have been him.'

'Hang on,' Simon says, raising his hand in some pointless attempt to restore order. 'Let's take a step back. Who is Sean?'

'Amber knew him. Called him a friend from her old life in Oxford. But I reckon he was her dealer.'

'What makes you say that?'

'I dunno,' Caden mutters. 'Because he looks and acts like one.'

Simon rolls his eyes, but privately he logs it. Making quick-fire judgments about people might be frowned upon in some circles, but not the police force. It's been helpful too many times to ignore its value.

'And you say he confessed all this while he assaulted you,' Jodie says, hands on her hips, disbelief leaking out of every word. 'That's very convenient. The guy who beats you up, suddenly announcing that he was at the scene of the murder that you're in the frame for. And had an issue with the victim. I suppose there weren't any witnesses to this admission?'

'It's not my fault he dragged me down an alleyway.'

'If he killed her, why would he come after you?'

'I dunno. You're the feds. You work it out.'

Simon feels a buzzing in his pocket and fishes his phone out of his jacket pocket. He looks at the screen, then walks out into the corridor. 'Yes?'

'We've ID'ed the suspect from the CCTV, sir,' Raj says. 'His name is Sean Russo. I'll send you his address.'

'Thanks, Raj, that's good work.'

'There's more, sir.'

'Oh?' Simon says, lifting his nose. An embarrassing habit he's picked up on the job.

'Do you remember the social worker telling us about that incident with Amber's sister when they lived in Oxford?'

'Yeah.'

'That's him, Sean Russo.'

'What?' Simon's pulse quickens.

'Yeah, he's the kid who threatened Jess. Why they had to move.'

'So he came after them,' Simon whispers.

'Looks that way, sir.'

Simon breaks into a broad smile. Yes, it means the suspect was on their radar from day one, but that's policework – finding a needle in a pile of shiny needles. He wonders if Caden was right about the rest of it: Sean supplying Amber with drugs, and how that played its part. And with Jess missing, he must be in the frame for that too.

'Jodie and I will head over their now,' he says. 'Get a response team to meet us there. And send CSI too.'

'Will do. And talking of CSI, they've compared the sample of Ms Salter's hair with those found on the victim and believe it's a match, so no breakthrough there. But the results of that partial from the victim's clothes are back from that swanky lab, so that might give us something. I'm heading over there now.'

'Keep me updated. And let's keep our fingers crossed that it belongs to Sean Russo.'

AFTER

Monday 13th May

Sean

Sean slams his mum's bedroom door closed. What has he done? What the hell would his mum think about him tying up a social worker in her bedroom?

It's the coke he took when he got back from Towersey. He shouldn't have touched it; he was wound up enough. But the baggie was sitting there, on the work surface, calling to him, just like it was last Friday night when Amber went dark on him, blocking him on all her socials. Without his mum around to hide stuff from, it's too easy. He'd cut a couple of lines this morning, and instantly felt better for it, so cut a couple more. But then Rose's wife turned up, screaming his name through the letter box. And then everything went south.

At least he remembered to put the piece of tape back over her mouth. It had lost some of its stickiness, but he pushed hard – hard enough, he hopes, to keep her quiet.

Sean drops onto the sofa and instinctively reaches for his pipe. He pulls a few buds out of a Tesco carrier bag, packs them into the bowl, and reaches for his lighter. As the thin curls of weed catch alight, he drags on the pipe, and feels the pleasure of sweet smoke entering his lungs. This is what he needs. Something to calm his nerves. He leans back against the soft cushion, closes his eyes, and pretends there isn't a middle-aged woman tied up in his mum's bedroom.

Not that she could tell him off for it anymore.

The memory of finding out his mum was properly ill is like a horror movie imprinted on his brain. And however much weed he smokes, it doesn't fade. He'd been back at school for a couple of weeks and was hating every minute of it. Just him and a few other dumb kids from his year resitting their maths and English GCSEs. He'd already decided that he couldn't stick it, that no exams were worth the shame of being associated with those thick twats, when she messaged him.

Which was a shock. His mum worked at the school, as a cleaner, and when she first started, she'd say hello to him when they passed each other in the corridor. She even asked him about his tea once; jeez the embarrassment. But he'd always fully blank her, so it didn't take her long to work out what the deal was, and she kept her head down after that. So when she messaged asking him to meet her by the ground-floor fire exit that afternoon, he knew it was bad.

She'd been sick, she told him, when he found her leaning against the heavy door. A few times. She'd done it outside the fire exit, and was sure no one saw her. And it was a watery sick, she said, so she knew it would soak into the grass. But she was scared. Not of the nausea, or whatever was causing her to be so ill in the first place, but that she would vomit somewhere in the school. Make a mess in the place that she was paid to keep clean.

Sean never liked to show his violent side in front of his mum – a trait he reckoned he'd inherited from his dad if the rumours about the badass Jed Brown were true – but he was angry that day. The truth is, the image of his mum being sick grossed him out, along with the chance any one of his mates might have seen her doing it. But it was her fucked-up priorities that really got to him. His mum had been trodden on all of her adult life – first by her dad when her own mum got sick with cancer, then by Jed, who'd pretended to be her saviour until Sean came along and ruined the vibe. And then by a long line of employers as she took anything going to keep on top of the bills.

Lizzie the cleaner. Making everyone's life better, but still treated like scum.

Sean was about to remind his mum that she owed the school nothing, when Mr Rose walked past. Sean's new English teacher and a patronising dickhead. His mum tried to smile at the guy, even though she clearly felt terrible, her insides all messed up from the bowel cancer she didn't yet know she had. But he didn't smile back. He asked her why she was chatting to a student when the library was a mess, and the staff loo had run out of toilet paper. Sean started to tell him why not, but his mum interrupted – even apologised, for fuck's sake – and explained that she wasn't feeling great but that she'd pass his message on to the after-school cleaning team.

It should have ended there. His mum had been working at that school for nearly four years by then, and Rose should have trusted her. But instead, he told her that she couldn't just leave on a whim. That she needed to clear it with her manager. Then he wanted the name of her manager, so he could check she followed his instruction. But his mum was confused by then, dehydrated, exhausted, and the name wouldn't come to her. And that bastard looked all triumphant, like his superior brainpower had exposed Sean's mum as a lazy, lying scam artist.

And then she was sick on the floor.

Rose looked horrified, not sympathetic. Lizzie looked ashamed, not redeemed.

And Sean had the strongest urge to kill them both.

He settled on Rose. Got up in his face, told him what he thought of him. Ignored his mum when she begged him not to use those kinds of words. Then that prick of a teacher got a handkerchief out of his pocket and wiped his cheek. As though Sean had been spitting on him, and he didn't want to be infected by scum.

Sean knew he couldn't control himself after that, so he took off. It was the right decision, but when he finally got home, their neighbour told him that Lizzie had taken herself off to the hospital. And she didn't come home for another three weeks. And when she did, it was with a bunch of pills and a terminal cancer diagnosis.

Rose was his sworn enemy after that. And as it's turned out since, the teacher seems to have a surprising capacity for hate himself.

And now his wife is tied up in Sean's flat.

He knows what his mum would think of that, how she'd bawl him out, but what about the other dead female in his life?

Amber would love it of course. He can almost see her eyes lighting up with the drama of it. He smiles at the image.

Is he sad that she's dead? It's hard to say.

There was a time when he liked her hanging around him. When things were difficult at home, his mum getting skinnier by the day, nurses and carers all expecting him to do his bit, when he didn't have a clue how. And him trying to impress the right people, to find ways to make money without being shafted like his mum had been. It was good to be someone's hero. But she let him down big time last summer – or at least her sister did – and then just two months after his mum died, the greedy bitch stole from him.

The pipe is empty now and Sean is properly wasted.

His mum's gone. Caden's probably in hospital snitching on Sean as soon as his jaw's fixed. He can't even remember what he said to him, but he knows he was rambling about Amber. Maybe Jess too. So the feds will come after him.

But he's not run out of road yet. Business has been good lately, so he's got cash. Plus, he knows people now who'll be able to get him off the feds' radar.

And Rose's wife is tied up in the next room. Maybe she's a final gift from Amber.

He'll sort her, and then he'll be gone.

AFTER

Monday 13th May

Milla

Milla makes eye contact with the school receptionist. She needs to find a balance between friendly and assertive if she's going to get what she wants. It worked with Felix – convincing him to lend her his ancient Fiesta – but she had more collateral with him. Like bringing up his snogging session with Ava behind the old railway carriages. Fucking Ava, for Christ's sake.

'It's a family emergency,' she explains to the older woman with pencilled eyebrows and an electric blue streak in her hair. 'Mum asked me to pick Lucy up. Can you get a message to her?' She squeezes out a tear. 'Please?'

As soon as the detectives left, Milla announced that she needed some fresh air, and escaped the house without having to make eye contact with her dad. She phoned her mum from a few metres down the road, but her mobile went straight through to voicemail, and her office said she hadn't been in. So now Milla is trying the other person who might know the truth. The girl who's been suffering the most from all of this.

'From the timetable it looks like Lucy is in a biology lesson. I'll pop down to the science block and get her; you wait here.'

A few minutes later, the receptionist reappears with Lucy trailing behind. Her face is ashen white, and Milla feels a pang of regret for the family emergency line that she ran with. 'Hey, Luce, I've got Felix's car, come on.' She turns her back before Lucy has the chance to ask her anything, but she can sense her sister following so doesn't slow her pace. She parked in the leisure centre car park next door, so it's an awkward five minutes as they cross the school grounds to reach it.

'What's going on?' Lucy asks as they sink into the threadbare seats.

Milla swallows, prepares herself for the question she needs to ask. The truth that she needs to know for anything – everything – else to make sense. 'Did you kill Amber, Luce?'

'What? You can't actually think I'm capable of murder?' There's a mix of shock and hurt in Lucy's voice.

'It wasn't murder though, was it? Just one hit that led to her dying. And I wouldn't blame you, not with all the fucking shit she put you through.'

'But when have you ever seen me do anything violent? Even once?'

'Well, in that video for starters.'

'That wasn't a fight … hang on, what do you mean "for starters"?'

Milla pushes the heel of her hands against the steering wheel, stretches out her fingers. 'When I got back from the party, and Mum said you were missing, I knew you'd gone to meet Amber,' she starts, the rest of the explanation feeling sticky on her tongue. 'I didn't tell Mum and Dad about it, but I went straight to the railway line where she'd asked you to meet her. There was no one there – not surprising because it was past eleven by then – but I saw two sets of footprints heading up towards the Ridgeway.'

'Amber went up that way, but I didn't,' Lucy whispers. 'There can only have been one set.'

Milla knows what she saw; and she had her dad's torch with her, so the two sets of fresh footprints were high-definition clear. 'Maybe,' she murmurs. 'But then I did see you. A little while later.'

'Saw me where?' Lucy asks. 'Why didn't you talk to me?'

'Because you were covered in blood.' Milla says it quietly, but the sound bounces around the constricted space. 'And out of breath. You were rummaging through a black bin liner outside the charity shop. I saw you take a T-shirt out, and a jumper, then go to the churchyard and change into it.'

'You followed me there too?' Lucy's voice is vague now, almost dreamy.

'I watched you get changed, then throw your top and jacket away,' Milla goes on. 'Afterwards, when Mum had found you and taken you home, I took them out of the bin. They were so bloodstained. And the church bin was a properly shit hiding place,' she adds, 'so I took them up to Kiln Lakes. Chucked them in with some rocks. I got blood on my own jacket too, so that had to go in with them.'

'You thought my clothes were covered in Amber's blood?' Lucy asks. 'That I'd hurt her that badly?' Her voice softens. 'But you got rid of them anyway,' she reflects. 'To protect me.'

'You're my sister,' Milla says simply.

'And later, after we knew Amber was dead, you figured I must have killed her,' Lucy says quietly. 'That's why you wanted Mum and Dad to pay Jess, and why you didn't want me to talk to the police.'

'I know how bad you are at lying.'

'It was my blood, Milla,' Lucy says. 'Not Amber's. Yeah, I pretended to be dangerous, poking the vodka bottle at her. But she grabbed it off me. Then she cut *me*. My hands first; then she sliced my stomach. It wasn't too deep, but it was long, all the way across, and God, it hurt so much. I collapsed on the mud, and she ran away. Completely fine except for a few cuts on her fingers.'

'*Your* blood?' Milla repeats, getting her head around it.

'Yeah, what a warrior I turned out to be. Do you know, I took the rolling pin with me, as sort of a defence weapon. But that never made it out of the plastic bag. I lay on the ground for ages after she left. I think I was in shock, or just exhausted. But eventually I found the energy to get myself up.'

'But if Amber attacked you, why didn't you just tell us what she'd done?'

Lucy looks away, out of the car window, but pulls her school shirt out of her skirt, and opens the bottom few buttons. The material slips apart and Milla stares at the long thin scab splitting Lucy's midriff in two. 'It was a warning,' Lucy explains, still not making eye contact. 'I knew something about Amber, and Jess. Something Bronwen had found out and told me in her letter. I was trying to figure out what to do about it, but then Amber stole the letter. She threatened me. Said that if I told anyone else what I'd learned, my family, the school, then she'd kill me.'

'But Amber's dead,' Milla murmurs. 'She can't hurt you anymore.'

Lucy turns back to face Milla. 'I know. But I couldn't have predicted that when I was bleeding everywhere and trying to work out what the hell I was going to say to Mum, could I? And then afterwards, I suppose it felt easier to keep it to myself. I'd cleaned up by then; found a dressing. Realised that the wound wasn't too bad. And I didn't want anyone to know I even saw Amber that night, let alone fought with her. Plus, there was always the chance that Jess would act on Amber's threat if I did say something. It was easier to stay quiet.'

Milla thinks for a moment. 'I get that in the beginning,' she starts. 'But what about later, when everything came out, and Jess was accusing you of killing Amber? Surely you could tell that Mum was suspicious of you then? Didn't you want to explain?'

Lucy bites her lip, looks towards the window again. 'I wasn't thinking straight.'

Milla studies her sister in profile. Her pale skin and dainty nose. Long, light eyelashes. We judge people on their appearance, she thinks, however hard we try not to. And Lucy looks like she needs protecting. But is that really true? Or is she stronger than that? 'I don't believe you,' she says.

Lucy turns to face her.

'It's because you thought I killed her, isn't it?' Milla presses. 'That's why you kept quiet. Because when I was busy covering your tracks, you thought I was hunting Amber.'

'I was more grateful than horrified,' Lucy whispers. 'I didn't think about you being a killer, just an incredible sister. That's bad, isn't it?'

'I didn't kill her, Luce.'

'I know that now. Hopefully I always knew it, and that's why it was easy to accept, because it was only ever a story I made up.'

'But someone did.' Milla pauses for a few seconds, but she needs to say this. 'This thing you'd found out about Amber, what was it?'

Tears glisten in Lucy's eyes. 'Bronwen couldn't believe anyone could hate me enough to bully me like that,' she says, looking straight ahead. 'So she tried to find out more about Amber and Jess, what had happened to make them such bitches, and why they were picking on me specifically. It took her a few months, but Amber eventually accepted a follow request from one of the Instagram accounts she set up.'

'Did she find out that Amber and Jess went to Dad's old school?' Milla asks. 'And that Jess was probably the anonymous witness in the case against him?'

Lucy's head whips round. 'How did you know about that?'

'The police know,' Milla says. 'They came to the house.'

'Shit.' Lucy's brow creases.

'That's why I came to get you. Why I had to ask if you killed Amber.'

'Because you think …' Lucy starts, but can't finish.

'Dad was the last person to see Jess before she went missing, wasn't he?' Milla says. 'And he was out, in the car, on the night Amber was killed. We all were. But maybe he found Amber instead of you.'

'But he didn't know who she was. At least, I hadn't told him …' Her voice trails off, perhaps realising that if Bronwen could find out the truth, so could their dad.

'How was he when he got back that night?' Milla asks.

'Well, he didn't come back straight away,' Lucy admits quietly. 'And when he did, he seemed distracted. But that was understandable; he was exhausted from his trip, and he'd thought something bad had happened to me. He went for a shower, and I went to bed, so I didn't see him again that night.'

'Luce,' Milla says, taking a breath. 'Do you think he could have killed her?' She forces herself to look at her sister, sees the tears, now snaking down her cheeks. But Lucy doesn't answer her question.

'Where's Mum?' she says.

'I … I don't know,' Milla stutters. 'I tried calling but she didn't pick up.'

'Try again,' Lucy begs. 'Please.' Milla does as she's asked and switches to speaker mode, but it goes straight through to voicemail again. She frowns. She's left a couple of messages now, and her dad must have left dozens. She phoned her mum's work too, and they said she wasn't in the office.

So where is she?

Milla opens Find My iPhone, but her frown deepens at the *No location found* written underneath her mum's contact. 'That's weird,' she murmurs. 'She never turns her phone off.'

'Dad said she left before he woke up,' Lucy whispers. 'You don't think she's left him, do you?' Her eyes widen. 'Do you think he confessed to killing Amber and she ran?'

'Don't be stupid!' Milla throws back. 'She'd never leave us.' Not *Dad would never kill Amber*, she realises with a stab of guilt.

'Well where is she then?' Lucy whines.

Milla thinks. This is 2024. There must be some way of finding her. Not Snapchat – her mum's never been near it – but some way. She feels the cold metal of Felix's car key in her hands. 'Fuck, I know!' she calls out, then checks if the app from that impulsive Christmas present is still active on her phone.

A car key tracker.

AFTER

Monday 13th May

Rachel

He's back. He looks different now. Calmer. I should be relieved, but I'm scared. There's an intent in his expression that wasn't there before.

When he pushed the piece of tape back over my mouth, I thought he was going to smother me to death. And even when his hand lifted, I struggled to breathe; my nose filled with snot. But then he left the room, and gradually I found some rhythm again. That's when I realised that the tape had lost some of its glue, and I've been moving my face ever since, like a cow chewing grass, to try and loosen it further. But even if I do dislodge it, I'm not sure what I want to use my voice for. To scream for help, or to persuade him to let me go?

'Your old man's a fucking prick,' he murmurs. 'He thinks he's better than people like me. That he can do what he wants to us, because we don't really matter.'

I move my mouth, but the tape holds.

'But you matter to him, like his precious little girl matters.'

He leans forward, his face hovering close to mine. I push my head against the pillow to gain as much distance as I can, but it only gives me millimetres.

'He treated my mum like filth,' Sean growls, the knife appearing in his hand again. 'When she was clearing up his mess, and fighting cancer at the same time. And he never once said sorry, not even when she told the school about her diagnosis.'

I can smell his breath, feel his spittle on my skin. The blade grazes the exposed part of my shoulder. I don't know what he's talking about, but my throat is too constricted to ask.

'And then you turn up at my flat,' he goes on. 'Shouting your mouth off. It's like you're asking to pay for what he's done.'

I want to ram my eyes shut, make Sean disappear, but they widen in fear.

Bang, bang, bang.

It takes a moment for my brain to register that someone is thumping on the front door. Sean rears back. A look of fear passes across his face, then it hardens as he realises my mouth isn't covered up and moves forward again. He drops down on top of me. One hand clamps my mouth, the other holds the knife against the dip of my neck. 'Don't speak,' he mouths. His body is heavy. I feel like I'm suffocating.

'Sean Russo!' The words catapult through the letter box. My chest explodes with an adrenalin surge. It's DI Finnemore. This is my chance.

What will they do when no one comes to the door? Do the police know Sean has kidnapped me? Or is this about Jess? Or Amber? Either way, they can't break in without a warrant. If Sean is a suspect in a murder investigation, or that of a missing child, the courts would issue one without question. But if this is just a routine inquiry, Finnemore wouldn't have even applied for one.

Am I really going to lie here passively and wait to find out?

I whip my head to the right, then switch left, and again, hurling it side to side. My lips slide against his fingers. The traction loosens his grip, just enough for my mouth to open a fraction. I grab his middle finger between my teeth, clamp down.

'Ah, fuck!' he hisses. But as he tries to pull that hand away, the other pushes forward. I feel a sudden, searing pain as the knife cuts through my skin below my collarbone. But instead of stalling me, it has the opposite effect. Fight. I fling my head forward, it slams into his. He's dazed for a moment, and I use the chance to twist and squirm underneath him. I can't get away, but it's enough to make him feel unbalanced. He puts his free hand on the mattress to steady us both.

And I scream.

The hand is back over my mouth in an instant, pushing hard. The knife slides deeper into my shoulder. It's agony. My vision blurs.

I force myself to pull back, focus on the noise.

Banging, rustling, thudding, shouting.

The door flies open. The pressure on my mouth, the knife, disappears. I gasp for breath. Sean is dragged off me. I hear the crack of a Taser, watch his body stiffen, then collapse inwards.

Sean Russo, I'm arresting you on suspicion of kidnap and false imprisonment, grievous bodily harm with intent, and also for the murder of Amber Walsh …

Sean murdered Amber. He's the criminal, not my husband. I always knew that.

… And for the grievous bodily harm of Caden Carter. You do not have to say anything but …

Who is Caden Carter?

I see someone I recognise, a woman who's been my adversary for the last week but is now my rescuer. I try a smile, but her eyes are on the knife jutting out of me, it's handle butted up against my collarbone. Bzowski pulls out her phone and calls for an ambulance. As the adrenalin ebbs away, I feel spent. Like I could drift into unconsciousness and sleep forever.

'Stay alert, Rachel,' Bzowski says quietly. 'The paramedics are on their way.' I try to focus on her face, her concerned eyes. 'And lie absolutely still. From the blood loss, it doesn't seem like the blade has hit any major blood vessels, which is good, but it's important not to move.'

I blink to tell her I understand, that I'm grateful. Then I hear his voice. Sean shouting at DI Finnemore. 'I didn't kill Amber, you fucking moron!'

But Finnemore cuts him off. 'I've just had confirmation that your blood was found on her body, and we have a witness who places you at the crime scene, so I suggest you keep the insults to a minimum.'

'I … I saw her afterwards, all right!' Sean stutters. 'After she died. And I cut my hand on a bramble when I was walking there! I freaked when I saw her, did a runner. I'm not gonna trust the feds, am I?'

'That's the most rubbish story I've ever heard,' Finnemore mutters. Then he shoves Sean, still arguing, out of the bedroom and it's just Bzowski and me.

'Sean killed Amber then,' I whisper, wanting to hear her say it too, like a child seeking more reassurance.

'It looks that way.'

'And Jess?' I ask, my heart rate ticking up despite the pain as I think about the Waitrose bag of cash. The badger. The car in the garage.

'He'll be asked about her in his interview,' she explains quietly. Then she sits up straighter as a noise filters through the thin walls. 'That must be the paramedics,' she says.

I say a silent prayer of thanks for the imminent pain relief and turn towards the door. But the sight is better than anything paracetamol could do.

'Mum!' two voices screech in unison, then my daughters come tumbling into the room.

AFTER

Monday 13th May

Rachel

'Girls? What are you doing here?'

'Oh my God, Mum! What's happened?' Lucy lurches towards me, but Bzowski reaches out, stops her from getting any closer.

'Sorry, Lucy,' she says. 'The ambulance will be here any minute, but for now, we need to give your mum some space.'

'What the hell's going on, Mum?' Milla asks, her voice crosser than her sister's. A coping mechanism she's inherited from me. Then she gives Bzowski a sideways glance. 'Never mind, I'm just glad you're okay.'

'How did you find me?' I whisper. 'Is Dad here too?'

The girls exchange a look, then shift their eyes back to me. 'Felix lent me his car,' Milla starts. 'I got Lucy from school and then tracked you via that GPS key ring I got you for Christmas. It said your car keys were somewhere in this block. We were trying to figure out which flat you might be in when a police response van arrived, and we just followed them in.'

'But … but why were you even looking for me?' I stutter. Lucy opens her mouth to speak, but Milla jumps in.

'You weren't answering your phone. And no one at work knew where you were. I knew I had to find you. Call it a daughter's instinct.'

My eyes fill with tears. It's all too easy to dwell on what you lose when your child becomes an adult; it's good to be reminded what you gain. I want to tell them everything. Tell Lucy that none of this is her fault, that she was only bullied because of who her father was. And that the boy who made their dad's life hell two years ago was behind it all. That he was friends with Amber, but that it must have been a toxic kind of friendship because the police think he killed her. And maybe he's behind Jess's disappearance too.

But I can't say any of this in front of Bzowski so we fall into an awkward silence. Milla's expression is closed, Lucy's wide-eyed, and Bzowski's curious. But suddenly there's a buzzing sound. Bzowski's phone is ringing, and I say a silent prayer of thanks. She looks at it for a moment, then back at me. 'I'll just be a minute. Remember, no movement.' Then she puts the phone to her ear and slips out of the room.

'This is Sean Russo's flat,' I admit quietly once she's gone.

Lucy darts a look at her sister. 'The guy who accused Dad? Why did you come here?'

'I was looking for Jess. I felt responsible I suppose, with Dad being the last person to see her before she went missing.'

'That's crazy,' Milla mumbles, but it sounds false. I give her a questioning look, but she shifts her gaze away from me.

'I knew Jess would have her own file at work,' I continue. 'I shouldn't have looked, it was very unprofessional, but I thought if I found out a bit more about her, I might be able to figure out where she'd gone.'

Lucy's head jerks up. 'Did her file say why she moved away from Oxford?'

'Yes,' I say cautiously. 'Why?'

'Did it talk about her being the mystery witness in Dad's case?'

I inhale. 'How did you know?'

'Bronwen worked it out, at least that's what she thought based on what she'd found out. It was all in her letter,' Lucy explains. 'That's why I snapped on the night Amber died. Not only was she making my life hell, she was involved in ruining Dad's. Bronwen thought she'd found a way to solve my problem. She was so happy for me, but then Amber stole the letter and threatened to kill me if I told anyone.'

'I found out this morning,' Milla jumps in. 'Well, guessed really. When the police spoke to Dad. They asked him if he knew who Jess really was.'

As I look at their faces – the mix of fear and anger in their expressions – I realise that they're suspicious of Matt too. 'Yes, but that doesn't mean …'

'Mum, what if Dad didn't hit a badger on Friday night?' Milla asks quietly. 'What if he actually hit Jess, then got rid of her body somehow? He's been acting weird since then. Fuck, he could even have killed Amber when he was supposedly out looking for Lucy. Don't say you haven't thought it too.'

God, my shoulder is hurting. 'Sean killed Amber,' I tell my daughter through gritted teeth. 'DI Finnemore has just arrested him for it.'

'Like they arrested that other guy, do you mean?' she throws back. 'Before letting him go?'

'Jesus, Milla!' I hiss as quietly as I can. 'Your dad isn't a killer.'

'You thought I killed her though, didn't you?' Lucy says, her voice small. 'When you found out about the blog, and then me meeting up with her. You thought I was capable of it.'

'And me,' Milla whispers. 'When you talked about the torch being dirty. That was because you thought I might have whacked her with it.'

'No,' I say, tears welling up in my eyes. Then: 'I'm sorry.' Because they're right; I did suspect them, if only fleetingly. How could I possibly have thought that of either of my children? And the truth is, I suspected my husband too. Do I still? Sean has been arrested for Amber's murder, but even as the police dragged him away, he was still shouting that he was innocent. And Jess is out there, her disappearance unexplained.

I look at my daughters again. I brought these two young women into the world. Please God, don't let me have burdened them with a father who kills teenage girls.

The door opens and two paramedics stride in. 'Sorry to keep you waiting,' the first one says, her ponytail bobbing as she delivers her apology. 'Manic shift already. I'm Hema, and this is Jon.'

'Hi,' I murmur. 'It's fine.' I listen to the thwack, thwack of them pulling their gloves on, then feel a tourniquet tighten around my arm. As I wait for the sharp scratch of the needle – and the longed-for pain relief – Bzowski walks back in.

'Good news,' she says, a grin spreading across her face. 'Jessica Scott has been found. Alive.'

A warm feeling floods through me. A heady mix of pain relief and knowing Jess is safe.

'Wow.' Milla exhales. 'Where is she?'

'Scotland,' Bzowski says. 'Apparently, there's a distant relative of her dad's living up there. He mentioned her – a godmother called Mary Turner – in one of his phone calls with Jess, and she remembered. Turned up on Mrs Turner's doorstep yesterday, but only admitted to being a runaway this morning. God knows how she got all the way up there on her own steam without being caught; I can't imagine she had the money to pay for the train ticket.'

I daren't look at Lucy or Milla – especially in my newly drugged state – but I smile at the ceiling. Sean has been arrested for Amber's murder. And Jess has just run away after all, just like Matt said, and to a fairy godmother. My husband isn't a killer.

'The analgesia should be working now,' Hema says. 'We need

to transfer you onto a stretcher to move you to the ambulance, but I promise the worst of it is over.'

I smile, steal one more glance at my daughters, then let my eyelids fall closed.

The worst of it is over.

AFTER

Wednesday 24th July

Jess

If the village hadn't been called Hopeman, she doubts she would have remembered it. But when her dad told her about his godmother, his mum's best friend from college, Aunty Mary, and how she'd sent him a birthday present out of the blue, he'd said she lived in Hopeman, and they'd joked about how maybe they should move there one day. At least, he'd joked.

Jess had kept the conversation in her head. Daydreamed about it coming true one day. Her dad and her; Aunty Mary; hope, man.

And now she's here.

'You warm enough, love?' Mary says, pulling at the zip on her fleece, even though it's the middle of summer. Jess has seen photos of Mary when she was younger. She's shrunk a bit since then, but she still projects the same aura of strength. Security.

'Yeah, I'm fine,' she says, nudging her butt cheeks further into the soft sand and looking out to sea. Hopeman is in the Highlands, on the Moray Firth coast. There's always a cold North Sea wind whipping against the shore, but Jess likes the feel of it on her cheeks. Just as she likes the fresh, salty air and the houses with no stairs (they're called bungalows apparently). She also likes the slower pace of life, the friendly locals, and how people seem to accept her without question.

Hopeman is in a whole different country, five hundred miles from Oxford, but it's still where Jess feels most at home.

When she picked the Waitrose bag out of that bin up by the lakes, she didn't know that she would end up here. At first, she was scared that Mr Rose would ambush her. When that didn't happen, she expected the police to appear. But the park stayed quiet, and she walked to the fence where the old carriages are kept. Hidden by bushes, she stopped to open the bag.

My dad will kill you.

Reading the note inside the bag made her dizzy. Caused dozens of bad memories to flood in. That terrible year at Lou and Justin's, barely able to eat, counting down the days to the court case. And further back. Her mum. Glassy eyes, and a carpet changing colour. But she forced herself to think straight, and realised that the Roses' anger was justified. Jess knew that Lucy didn't kill Amber, so accusing her, threatening to post that video, was a shitty thing to do. And they had given her the money, a chance for her to start over.

She snuck through the hole in the fence and walked past the dead railway carriages, where the only people she came across were a couple snogging, and they didn't take any notice of her. Then she made it onto the high street, and the euphoria finally set in. The freedom of having ten grand in her pocket. After being the unluckiest person in the world for fifteen years, something had finally gone her way. She'd not planned to keep on walking, but equally she hadn't wanted to stop. She threw her phone into the bushes beside Thame Road – she still had the dumb phone that she'd been hiding from the police since finding out Amber had died – and two hours later arrived at Haddenham & Thame Parkway. That's where she'd thrown away the Decathlon bag, still with a dozen grams of weed inside, that she'd also kept secret. Then when the first train left for London in the morning, she was on it.

It took four trains, two Tubes and a bus to get to Hopeman. And when she arrived on Saturday evening – exhausted, freezing cold in the clothes she'd chosen for temperatures ten degrees warmer – she realised she had no clue where Mary Turner lived. She thought about calling her dad and asking for Mary's full address, but she guessed that people would be looking for her by then – Bill and Molly, Colleen – and she didn't want to risk him ratting on her. Plus, he probably didn't have Mary's address. Life admin had never been his thing.

So she found a pub and tested out whether she looked old enough to book a room by ordering a whisky (she'd never tried the drink before, but she knew it was Scottish). The girl behind the bar didn't ask for ID, the advantage of being tall maybe, and a minute later Jess was trying to swallow the disgusting liquid while the girl pointed out a B&B a few doors down.

'Want some tea?' Mary asks, pulling a flask out of her Paisley rucksack, because some Scottish clichés really are true. Jess nods, and watches the older woman pour some of the steaming liquid into a small plastic cup, her hand perfectly steady. It's not age that makes you shake, Jess thinks, it's secrets, and Mary doesn't have any. Maybe she never did, or perhaps living somewhere like Hopeman means they get carried away with the wind, out into the North Sea. Gone forever.

Jess hopes so.

The couple who ran the B&B knew where Mary lived. It turns out Hopeman is that kind of place. So Jess walked to her house on Sunday morning and knocked on the door. No one answered, but an hour or so later, Mary came back from church to a real charity case sitting on her doorstep.

Jess sips at her tea. Without really noticing it, she has shuffled closer to Mary – for warmth, or reassurance, or both, who knows

– and she drops her head onto the older woman's shoulder. Why does Mary already feel more like a mum than Lou, or Molly, or maybe even Jacqui ever did? Jess isn't a psychologist, but she's not stupid either. It's because Amber isn't here. Jess always thought that Amber was the strong one between them. But she's realised lately that her sister was weak. Because Amber only survived by putting other people down. And Jess was damaged, but loyal, so was always her prime target. There's no way Amber would risk losing that, so she made sure Jess didn't get close to anyone else.

God, she was angry with Amber that night. She thought that she couldn't feel any more heartbroken after finding out that Amber had stolen Caden from her. But then Caden started talking, and she realised she was wrong. There was plenty more damage that Amber could do.

Amber was the only person in the world who knew the truth about what Jess had done that terrible night. That she'd sneaked out of their bedroom, watched their mum bleed to death, then lied about it to the police. Because she was too scared to admit, to them and herself, that maybe her mum was dead because of her. Amber knew that Jess would be petrified about lying to the police again, pretending she'd witnessed Mr Rose punch Sean when she hadn't. But Amber convinced her to do it anyway. Convinced her that Sean's injury was so bad, he deserved justice.

But the real story, as Jess found out that night, was very different. Mr Rose was innocent. Sean had a vendetta against him – Jess never found out why – so he got into a street fight on purpose and then blamed it on Rose. And then Amber lied to her face.

Caden was so mad with Amber that he threw the story back at her, detail by devastating detail, at a volume that meant Jess heard every word. And the urge to punish her sister had been painful in its intensity. Jess had listened to them argue until Caden walked away in disgust, and the night had fallen quiet. Her sister all alone.

'That empty, love?' Mary asks, nodding to Jess's cup. Without waiting for a response, Mary reaches for it, flicks the residue onto the sand – three dots and a line, like Morse code – and screws it back onto the flask. 'Ach, my old bones can't sit on this sand for long.' She pushes up to standing, and for all her words, Jess thinks how quickly she does it. Mary might be in her sixties, but she's fit and healthy. She's not going anywhere soon.

Jess pushes up too, and the pair of them walk away from the sea, towards the road that will take them back home.

Home.

On that Sunday two months ago, when Mary put a plate of cottage pie in front of her, and Jess was so hungry that she ate it without worrying about the wriggly meat or the mashed potato getting stuck in her throat, things hadn't been so certain. It wasn't that Mary wasn't pleased to see her – her godson's only daughter – but they were strangers. Jess was a runaway. A troubled teenager with a dead mum and a dead sister. And it didn't help when Jess offered Mary a load of cash to put her up either. But Mary offered her one night's stay. And in the morning, Jess returned the favour by giving her Colleen's number. Her whereabouts became common knowledge, and gradually things moved from there, to where they are now. Official. Settled.

Mary slides the key in and pushes open the front door of her two-bedroom bungalow, five streets and ten minutes back from the coastal path. Jess follows her inside, and they both head into the living room where Milo and George are stretched out in front of the window. Jess rakes her fingers through their thick tortoiseshell fur and listens to their synchronised purring.

'You going to write that letter now?' Mary says gently, and when Jess doesn't answer, she adds, 'I think it's time to tell the truth.'

Jess looks out of the window. Is Mary right? It's easy to feel safe up here, so far away from the first fifteen years of her life, all the mistakes she's made. But she knows how easily things can come crashing down.

'It will be okay, you know,' Mary says, reading her thoughts. 'And I promise you'll feel better for it.'

Jess hesitates a moment longer, then walks over to the table and picks up the pen and notepad that's been waiting for her all morning.

AFTER

Saturday 27th July

Rachel

My heart is racing so fast I think it might space-hop right out of my chest, but I don't slow down. This isn't about my fitness. It's adrenalin, and memories, and regrets, and irrational fear, all bundled together like a home-made bomb and the only way I can defuse it is to run faster, all the way to the Chinnor Hill nature reserve and then through to the other side.

This is my first trail run since I found Amber's body. I couldn't run anywhere for a while – as the stab wound in my shoulder healed – but my physio signed me off two weeks ago and I've been dithering ever since. It was getting Jess's letter yesterday that spurred me on. Her raw words of apology and the bravery I knew it would have taken for her to confess.

First, she apologised for accusing Lucy of killing her sister when she knew that Amber had left their argument alive and well – in fact, in a much better state than Lucy did, as I discovered from my hospital bed when Milla forced Lucy to lift her blouse.

But it was Jess's second apology that meant the most to me.

She had lied about seeing Matt punch Sean Russo. And more than that, she found out on the night Amber died that Matt didn't even do it. Sean had set the whole thing up, with Amber's help, to punish Matt. Jess didn't know what he'd done to become Sean's target, but from Sean's rambling accusations when I was tied up in his mum's bedroom, I could guess. *That prick treated my mum like scum.* Matt isn't a killer, but he's got faults. Sean's mum was a cleaner at the school. With his tidiness obsession, I can imagine Matt giving her a hard time, not realising how his criticism will have sounded. Especially with her so poorly. But none of us are perfect. And at least Matt has agreed to see a therapist now, and be assessed for OCD. Hopefully that will prove to be a catalyst for change.

In Jess's letter, she explained that she felt betrayed by her sister. And that there were reasons why Amber's behaviour was especially hurtful. She even said that she wanted to kill Amber when she found out, but only for a split second. Amber looked like her mum apparently. And she could never inflict injuries on that face. So she'd walked away, assuming that Amber wouldn't be far behind her.

But she never fully thought about what the lies did to Mr Rose, or Lucy, until she got to Scotland, where the fresh air, and Aunty Mary, had made her think more clearly.

There was more than a letter in the package Jess sent too. I counted nine thousand, four hundred and twenty pounds, still wrapped in the same Waitrose bag.

I reach the edge of the nature reserve. This is it. I slow for a moment, then speed up, and pound through the long grass. I don't look at the place I found Amber's body, but otherwise I let myself take in the luscious trees – now in full summer bloom – and view of my village below. The run is hard but not impossible. It a sign I've survived this.

And Jess's letter has played a big part, dispelling a fear I've been living with since Sean was charged with Amber's murder. There is a stack of evidence against him – his blood at the scene, her blood on clothes found in his flat, his car picked up on CCTV, and its tyre treads matched with those found in the car park. Plus the circumstantial evidence: the drugs in his flat, phones without SIM cards, Caden's statement, Amber and Sean's turbulent history including the time he roughed her up. And having me tied up for hours, sticking a knife in my shoulder.

And yet I couldn't quite wipe the memory of his words. And how, even though he was high, or stoned, the whole time, he kept accusing other people of killing Amber: Jess, Caden, and Matt. Mostly Matt.

On top of that, there was the admission that Milla gave, quietly, just to me, before her first A-level exam – the need to clear her mind, I think. That she had seen two sets of fresh footprints heading up to the Ridgeway from the railway crossing where Lucy met Amber. The police didn't know about either of them because the overnight rain had washed them away, but both Caden and Sean had parked on the top road, and Jess had taken the route from the railway station, so who did the second pair belong to? And the mystery of what happened to Bronwen's letter has never been solved either.

But none of it matters. Not after reading Jess's letter – that Matt isn't violent, and Sean is an accomplished liar.

I make it through the nature reserve, then gradually drop down onto the bridleway and head back towards Chinnor. As I run past the fenced area that stores the derelict railway carriages, my mind wanders to Felix. I was shocked when Milla told us it was Ava he'd been with the night Jess disappeared, but Matt wasn't. He then admitted that he'd seen them together a couple of weeks before while out on a bike ride, climbing through the hole in the fence, their body language furtive. That's why he'd guessed correctly in the pub. But he'd chosen not to tell Milla about her best friend and boyfriend. It wasn't a choice I would have made, but who knows which one of us is right. Or even if there is a right and wrong in these situations.

When I get to the parade of shops, I slow down. As I laced my trainers this morning, Matt suggested that he come and meet me after my run, and that we go to The Crown for breakfast together – Steve and Jade's new initiative to make the most of their beer garden in the summer. Milla is in Corfu – her A-level exams already a distant memory – and Lucy is otherwise engaged too. Now that the school holidays have started, Bronwen is visiting from Wales, staying with her grandparents for a week.

'Ah, Rachel!'

I turn around, shield my eyes from the sunshine, laugh silently at the coincidence. Bronwen's grandfather is walking out of the bakery. 'Hello, Michael,' I say, smiling at the older man. Even though the late July heat is already strong, he's wearing a long-sleeved, button-down shirt and beige slacks.

'I hear we've got Lucy coming over again today?'

'Yes, thanks for having her. And an advance apology, because I think she might end up basically moving in with you this week. She's been so excited about seeing Bronwen. She's missed her a lot this year.'

'It's lovely to see them getting on still,' Bronwen's grandfather says, nodding. 'I thought, after her last visit, that Bronwen might have cut her ties with her life here, moved on. But it seems not, which is a good thing, obviously,' he adds, suddenly worried that he's offending me. But I'm too intrigued by his words.

'Her last visit?' I ask. As far as I knew, this was Bronwen's first time back since the family moved away last August. I know they didn't come for Christmas because Michael and Jean went to Wales, and Lucy hasn't seen her this year.

Michael's eyes tilt downwards. 'They came for a weekend in the spring,' he explains. 'The traffic was bad – usual bank holiday exodus – so they arrived later than planned on the Friday evening. It was all a bit chaotic to be honest – a couple of Jean's bridge cronies had dropped by and we couldn't get rid of them once

Thomas and Liv arrived – so I didn't think much of it when Bronwen snuck off to the garden room early.'

'Garden room?'

'Oh, we've had one of those glorified sheds installed at the bottom of the garden so that she can have her own space when they visit. I think she slept in there okay, at least she didn't complain, but she wasn't herself all weekend. Quiet. Withdrawn. Like she really didn't want to be here. And every time one of us suggested she get in touch with Lucy, she bit our heads off. Anyway, they left early, on the Sunday, in the end.'

'You said bank holiday weekend. Which one was it?'

He sighs. 'Jean said it was probably for the best, Bronwen not turning up on your doorstep asking to see Lucy. It was the weekend that poor girl died, you see. And I know you were the one to find her body. I imagine you were reeling.'

I lift the corners of my mouth into a smile, but it's like dragging sticks through cement. 'Yes, I was reeling,' I repeat, anxious to get away, to have some space to process what he's telling me. Bronwen was in Chinnor when Amber died. She was sleeping in a room in the garden by herself. She stayed away from Lucy all weekend.

'Hey, Rachel!' I tether myself to Matt's familiar voice, turn towards it. 'Oh, hi, Michael,' he continues as he gets closer. I watch Matt reach out his hand; Michael clasp it; the rhythm of their connected limbs moving up and down. 'Thanks for having Lucy again today.'

'We should go,' I say. It's too abrupt, but I can't take it back now, so I smile again, the cement getting denser.

'Someone's hungry,' Matt says, plastering over the crack in my social skills. 'See you around, Michael.' He lifts his hand in a small wave, then drops it onto the small of my back and ushers me towards the pavement. 'Is everything okay?' he asks when we're out of earshot.

I don't answer straight away. I think about what Bronwen knew,

311

the weight she carried on her shoulders, a burden that should have been mine. It was Bronwen who read Lucy's blogposts, her sole follower; not me. It was Bronwen who Lucy confided in too, daily, probably hourly, as I resisted, too caught up with the idea that Lucy should give the troubled sisters a chance. It was Bronwen who never believed that Lucy could be rude to another girl, and cared enough to dig up the real reason Amber and Jess were bullying her best friend.

Did Bronwen know about Lucy's meet-up with Amber that night? And how Amber had stolen her letter? Of course she would have done. She was Lucy's first choice of confidante.

Did that second pair of footprints belong to her?

Amber's death wasn't planned. It was a dark, messy end to a spontaneous lashing out.

It was tragic, yes. Like her life. But Amber never tried to change, never took responsibility for the suffering she caused – to Lucy, or to her sister. How many other lives would she have damaged if she was still here?

No one deserves to die, but who deserves to be punished more? Bronwen for protecting her innocent friend? Or Sean, a drug dealer who stabbed me, and tried to make Matt pay for a crime he didn't commit?

It's not a hard question.

I tilt my head and lean in for a kiss. 'I think we're all good.'

Epilogue

I look at Amber.

Why isn't she moving? Why do her eyes look like that? Rolled back, like marbles, the moonlight bouncing off them. The bluebells are wilting around her head, drowning in something dark and globular.

Why is she so completely still?

Oh God, what have I done?

My hand is still in the air, I realise, Grandpa's torch from his shed still clenched between my fingers. It starts to shake. I think it's the effort, the burden of fighting gravity, but it doesn't stop when I lower it. My other arm starts to shake too, then my legs; my chest goes into spasm.

Is she dead?

Should I check?

It's dark, I can't see. But that's stupid. I'm holding a torch. It takes five attempts to press the small rubbery button, but eventually I do it.

Light.

The bluebells are covered in blood. Amber's eyes are glassy, unseeing. I stare at her chest. Will it to rise and fall.

It doesn't.

I replay it in my head. Lifting the torch, swinging it at her head, hearing the thud, watching her fall.

But she deserved it, I remind myself. Mocking Lucy, bullying her for months, slashing her with that broken bottle. Stealing our letter.

On the day I left Chinnor, I kissed you. You kissed me back
… The truth is
(wow, if you could see me blushing right now) it felt totally right for me.
That we can be best friends and something more – without it being an either/or.

But the blood coming out of the back of her head; I didn't do that.

That was an accident.

Except the police won't see it that way. I've seen enough true crime programmes to know that.

Except nobody knows I'm here. I didn't tell Lucy I was visiting for the weekend because I wanted to surprise her. But then she snapped me about her meeting with Amber while we were on the motorway. When she said it was at 10 p.m., I thought I could join her. Two against one. But then the traffic got bad, and we were late arriving, so I didn't make it in time. I raced to the railway track as quickly as I could, but Amber and Lucy were already there, arguing, fighting, so I hid in the bushes. Then Amber lunged at Lucy with that broken bottle, and Lucy folded so fast it was like she disappeared. I didn't know what to do. I wanted to help Lucy, but I was angry. Too angry. So I followed Amber up to the Ridgeway. I thought I could message Lucy, check on her, but she didn't open my snap. It scared me, her not responding, but now I'm glad. Because it means I can delete it, and she won't find out where I am.

I heard the man's voice before anyone saw me, so I had the chance to hide. Him asking why Amber had ignored his messages, her appeasing him, saying how cool it was for them to hang out

314

off grid together. Then the sister turned up, hiding too, and things got wild. But I waited, and eventually got Amber to myself.

It was my chance to teach her a lesson. Show her that Lucy has friends too.

But Amber wasn't sorry, or scared. She kept mocking our kiss, calling us freaks. Laughing at my detective work. Telling me that Lucy was too scared, too worried about her dad, to ever use the information I'd given her.

And now this.

There's a flash of light in the distance. A torch? Has someone seen me, called the police? I need to get away.

A noise in the trees. Was that human? Or animal?

But there's something I need to do before I can leave. I lower the torch, away from Amber's face, down to her jeans.

'Amber, I fucking know you're here!' A different man's voice, angry, close. 'And I know what you've been doing to me!'

I need to hurry up.

I pull the sleeve of my sweater over my hand, slide my fingers into Amber's jean pocket. There it is. The letter; crumpled but whole. A love letter. A motive.

On my third fake profile on Instagram, Amber finally dropped her guard and accepted my follow request … A picture of Jess in a school uniform that wasn't Lord Fred's … I zoomed in on the crest … another photo on her grid – of an older boy holding his palm up to the lens … #sean #russ0 in the comments … and the hashtag #cutarose

I pull the letter out, scrunch it between my fingers, and run.

A Letter from Sarah Clarke

Dear Reader,

Thank you for reading *The Night She Dies*. I really hope you enjoyed it. Before you carry on reading this letter, I want to warn you that there are spoilers.

The Night She Dies was in part inspired by my own daughter becoming an adult, and a realisation that every stage of parenting brings its own set of questions and challenges. I wanted to build this uncertainty into Rachel's character.

How do you rate Rachel as a parent? And as a social worker? She was conflicted initially due to her job, but later pushed her principles aside to protect her family. Do you think she was right to make those choices? Or did she cross a line and lose your sympathy? She also protected her family while suspecting them of a terrible crime. Should she have been more loyal, or was it natural for her to suspect them under the circumstances? Do you think Matt's previous charge of assault influenced her behaviour?

Amber and Jess suffered enormously as children, but responded to their trauma in different ways. Did you feel any sympathy for Amber before she died? And do you think the impact of her death on Jess's life would be positive or negative? Sean exploited Amber, falsely accused Matt, and assaulted Caden and Rachel, but did you feel any sympathy for him?

I'd love to know what you think about all these questions. You can reach me by email at sarah@sarahclarkeauthor.com or via social media. I am on Twitter as @SCWwriter, and on Facebook and Instagram as @sarahclarkewriter. And if you enjoyed *The Night She Dies*, I would be very grateful if you could leave a review. It really makes such a difference.

If you like short stories, I have written one called *The Morning After* which you can download for free by joining my mailing list. You can also follow my publisher @HQstories for lots of book news and great giveaways.

Happy reading,
Sarah

Acknowledgements

I grew up in a village near Thame and went to a school called 'Lord Bill's', so it feels apt that my first thank you is to my sixth-form English teacher, Mr Foulkes (sadly no longer with us). He was a great man with a contagious love of literature, who was less surprised by my top grade than I was. Chinnor is a real village in the Chilterns and most of the descriptions I write are accurate, but I did give myself a little creative licence. There is no way of sneaking into the storage area for disused train carriages (that I know of), and I made up a few additional off-road routes between locations. I'm sure there are other inaccuracies too (like girls being murdered on the Ridgeway, for one) and I apologise for those. Chinnor is a lovely, thriving village – and I'm sure not nearly as gossipy as I make out! A big thank you to my mum for chauffeuring me around the area as I plotted routes and scenes – at least I didn't ask you to join my muddy hike on the misty Ridgeway.

A lot of my initial research focused on the foster care system and social work in general. A big thank you to Elaine Knight who has worked in foster care for many years, and gave me invaluable advice in the early stages of planning *The Night She Dies*. Thank you also to Hugh Constant, another experienced social worker, for all your help in building a credible career for Rachel. In the interests of story-telling, I have stretched the truth in both areas, but I hope not enough to make either of you wince. Thank you to the now former Inspector Simon Stone for sitting with me for hours to answer my many, many questions on police procedure – at least we did it with a beer in hand. I am very lucky to have a police expert on speed dial, and I appreciate all the effort you put in to making sure your answers are accurate. Any mistakes are mine.

The Night She Dies covers some sensitive topics, and I hope I do them justice. For two years during the pandemic, I worked as a Digital Volunteer for the eating disorder charity Beat (beateating-disorders.org.uk). I learned a lot from talking online with sufferers and carers, and I hope this is reflected in the book. As a mother of teenagers, I am aware of the different challenges teenagers face. I wanted to shine a light on some of these, without judging or purporting to have the answers. I hope I have achieved this, and I apologise if any elements don't quite hit the mark.

Thank you also to everyone at HQ. To Becci and Caroline for your PR and marketing support. To Seema for answering my many queries, to Helena Newton for your eagle eye, and to my lovely editor Cicely Aspinall. This is the fourth book we've worked on together, and I feel very lucky to have you in my corner – both for your frankly magical editing skills, and your calm and enduring positivity. Thank you also to Sophie Hicks for the part you've played in bringing *The Night She Dies* to life.

I wrote this book while launching *The Ski Trip*. I had a new level of support for this book, from authors, festivals, book bloggers and reading groups and I am so grateful to everyone who took the time to read, review, and shout about the book. A particular thanks to Adele Parks for including *The Ski Trip* as a Book Club pick in *Platinum* magazine, to Bookscape Books for choosing it for their book club, and to Bob McDevitt at Bloody Scotland for inviting me to talk about it.

Support from fellow authors is one of the best things about

this job. A special thank you to Diane Jeffrey for reading an early copy of *The Night She Dies* – your suggestions were invaluable. And thank you to all the authors who are at the other end of a WhatsApp message, or plea to meet for coffee, especially Catherine Cooper, Lucy Martin, Jac Sutherland, Alex Chaudhuri, Katy Brent, Joy Kluver, and Sophie Flynn. Thank you to all my friends and family for heroing my books – and for coming to my first book launch, possibly lured there by toffee vodka! A special thanks to my dad, always my first reader, and to Hannah for being all-round awesome.

I still get such a huge buzz from knowing that strangers are picking up my books and investing their time in my characters and story. It is an honour to be an author, and it is readers who make the job possible, so thank you to everyone who has bought or borrowed my books, and a particular thank you to those who have taken the time to write a review, and to recommend my books to others.

And finally, my family. Thank you, Finn, for your Snapchat expertise, and Chris, for keeping me functioning. And thank you, Scarlett. My now 19-year-old who is venturing out into the world. So far, so good.

Dear Reader,

We hope you enjoyed reading this book. If you did, we'd be so appreciative if you left a review. It really helps us and the author to bring more books like this to you.

Here at HQ Digital we are dedicated to publishing fiction that will keep you turning the pages into the early hours. Don't want to miss a thing? To find out more about our books, promotions, discover exclusive content and enter competitions you can keep in touch in the following ways:

JOIN OUR COMMUNITY:

Sign up to our new email newsletter:
http://smarturl.it/SignUpHQ

Read our new blog www.hqstories.co.uk

X https://twitter.com/HQStories

f www.facebook.com/HQStories

BUDDING WRITER?

We're also looking for authors to join the HQ Digital family!
Find out more here:

https://www.hqstories.co.uk/want-to-write-for-us/

Thanks for reading, from the HQ Digital team